GREATER LOVE
A COVENANT COLLECTION CHRISTIAN NOVEL — BOOK 1

ELIZABETH TOMME

"*An enthralling, adventurous, heart-stopping, climax!* Toward the end my heart was broken, then up-lifted again. A joyful, wonderful story that draws the reader to God's heart and demonstrates the meaning of Greater Love. So well written and woven together, my heart was captivated by the picturesque beauty and charm of Greece. The character's life changing experiences evoke such delight and longing to be a part of her journey.
Richly blessed by this endearing, spiritually-uplifting story."
—Julie Newbold

"*A must read!* The overarching theme is our LORD's intimate involvement in the lives of His beloved children. I was drawn into the people and culture with its rich history, sprinkled with beauty and romance which made it sparkle. The intensity was so great that I had to stop and catch my breath. *I didn't want it to end!* As any good book will affect the reader deeply, *Greater Love* did so for me. Hurry up and write the next one!"
—Linda Fellows

"Elizabeth Tomme has so expertly penned her thoughts that this reader longs to taste and see Greece and the islands of the Aegean. In reading *Greater Love* I found myself bound to the main characters, in sync with their hearts, *reluctant to put this book down* until the mysteries were solved. What a wonderful surprise ending! Most of all, she has woven the LORD

throughout her manuscript bringing us a fresh look at relationship with Him. *Glorious!*"
—P. K. Wedel

Copyright © 2024 by Elizabeth Tomme. All rights reserved.

Written by Elizabeth Tomme

Miette Publishing

Edited by Karen Steinmann, Majestic Edits

Scripture quotations marked ESV are from the ESV® Bible (The Holy Bible, English Standard Version®), © 2001 by Crossway, a publishing ministry of Good News Publishers. Used by permission. All rights reserved.

Scriptures marked KJV are taken from the King James Version of the Bible. Public domain.

Scripture quotations taken from The Holy Bible, New International Version® NIV® Copyright © 1973, 1978, 1984, 2011 by Biblica, Inc. Used with permission. All rights reserved worldwide.

Scripture quotations marked (NLT) are taken from the Holy Bible, New Living Translation, copyright ©1996, 2004, 2015 by Tyndale House Foundation. Used by permission of Tyndale House Publishers, Carol Stream, Illinois 60188. All rights reserved.

Scripture quotations marked MSG are taken from The Message, copyright © 1993, 2002, 2018 by Eugene H. Peterson. Used by permission of NavPress. All rights reserved. Represented by Tyndale House Publishers.

Scripture quotations marked TPT are from The Passion Translation®. Copyright © 2017, 2018, 2020 by Passion & Fire Ministries, Inc. Used by permission. All rights reserved. ThePassionTranslation.com.

Scripture quotations marked TPT are from The Passion Translation®, Isaiah: The Vision. Copyright © 2018 by Passion & Fire Ministries, Inc. Used by permission. All rights reserved. ThePassionTranslation.com.

This novel is a work of fiction. Any references to historical events, real people, or real locations are used fictitiously. Other names, characters, places, and incidents are the product of the author's imagination, and resemblance to actual events or locations or persons, living or dead, is coincidental. All rights to reproduction of this work are reserved. No part of this publication may be reproduced, stored in or introduced into a retrieval system, or transmitted, in any form, or by any means (electronic, mechanical, photocopying, recording, or otherwise without prior written permission from the owner. Thank you for respecting the copyright. For permission, other rights, or other information, contact the author, et@elizabethtomme.com, or Miette Publishing, PO Box 784, Westcliffe, CO 81252.

eBook ISBN: 979-8-89316-582-1

Paperback ISBN: 979-8-89316-583-8

Hardcover ISBN: 979-8-89316-584-5

 Created with Vellum

CONTENTS

Author's Note — ix

Chapter 1	1
Chapter 2	3
Chapter 3	11
Chapter 4	16
Chapter 5	22
Chapter 6	32
Chapter 7	37
Chapter 8	43
Chapter 9	51
Chapter 10	57
Chapter 11	63
Chapter 12	69
Chapter 13	73
Chapter 14	80
Chapter 15	88
Chapter 16	95
Chapter 17	100
Chapter 18	106
Chapter 19	111
Chapter 20	118
Chapter 21	125
Chapter 22	131
Chapter 23	138
Chapter 24	145
Chapter 25	150
Chapter 26	158
Chapter 27	163
Chapter 28	171
Chapter 29	177
Chapter 30	186
Chapter 31	192
Chapter 32	198
Chapter 33	206

Chapter 34	213
Chapter 35	221
Chapter 36	228
Chapter 37	234
Chapter 38	242
Chapter 39	250
Chapter 40	259
Chapter 41	265
Chapter 42	274
Chapter 43	282
Chapter 44	289
Chapter 45	294
Chapter 46	303
Chapter 47	309
Chapter 48	315
Chapter 49	321
Chapter 50	325
Chapter 51	331
Chapter 52	340
Chapter 53	345
Chapter 54	354
Chapter 55	359
Chapter 56	368
Aaronic Blessing	377
Part One Characters	379
Part Two Characters	383
Lisa's Notes-to-Self	387
Study Guide	389
Note to Readers	407
Acknowledgments	409
About the Author	413
MORE TO COME...	415

AUTHOR'S NOTE

I am a believer in, and follower of Jesus Christ, the Son of the Living God. Jesus is my Redeemer, and *Friend*.

In John 15:12-13, Jesus commanded: "Love each other deeply, as much as I have loved you. For the greatest love of all is a love that sacrifices all. And this great love is demonstrated when a person sacrifices his life for his friends." (TPT)

This story is written from the perspective of my relationship, my *friendship* with Jesus. I pray this book immerses you in His immeasurable love, and deepens your friendship with Him.

Parts of this story may seem too good to be true, other parts will take your breath away, or bring you to tears. I find that's how life truly is with Jesus—because of His greater love in all our lives.

You are *the one* this story is meant for. You are *the one sheep* Jesus left the ninety-nine to rescue. With guidance from Jesus, Father God, and the Holy Spirit, this book was sent Special Delivery to rescue your heart and kindle your faith in Jesus' greater love for you.

Like the characters in this book, your story is unique. Every moment is lived within a larger story, a tapestry, interwoven with God and others. Whether your story is blessed or broken, it is God who perfects you by His nature, transforming your joys and brokenness into something beautiful, whole, and redeemed. You are His sea glass, polished by His nature . . . His jewel . . . His love.

In celebration of God's goodness,
Elizabeth

P.S. I've included a Study Guide at the back of the book to prompt self-reflection, group discussion, prayer, and quiet moments with your Great, Covenant-Keeping God.

*To My Beloved God: Father, Jesus, and Holy Spirit,
whose steadfast love never ceases.*

*For Curtis, my brave and handsome husband,
my one true love and soulmate.
You gave me the most precious gift—yourself
and your solemn vow.
You forever lay down your life for me
in Greater Love.
I adore you.*

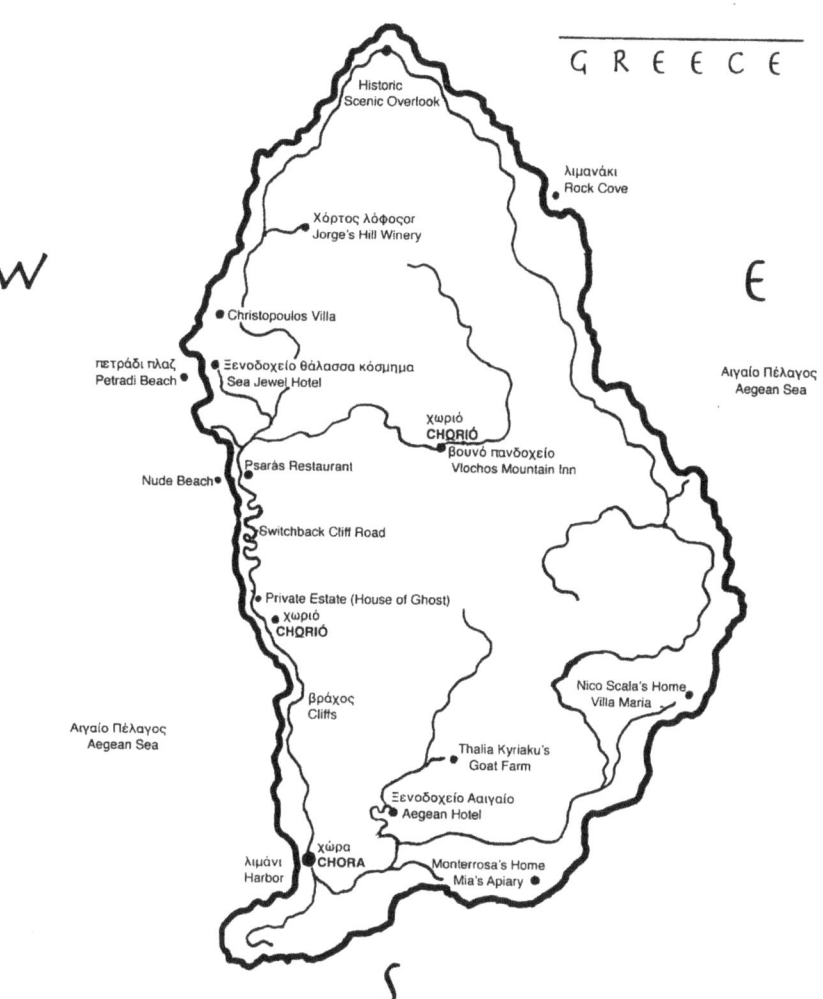

Greater Love hath no man than this,
that a man lay down his life
for his friends.
—John 15:13 (KJV)

PART ONE

The Sojourner
Ο Πουχούρνερ

. . . You know every step I will take
before my journey even begins.
You've gone into my future to prepare the way,
and in kindness you follow behind me
to spare me from the harm of my past.
With your hand of love upon my life,
you impart a blessing to me.
—Psalm 139:4–5 (TPT)

CHAPTER 1

Commit everything you do to the LORD.
Trust him, and he will help you.
—Psalm 37:5 (NLT)

Lisa's Story
June 2016, Athens, Greece

One-way ticket clinched between her teeth for lack of a third hand, Lisa Abbott edged sideways through the aisle, tote in one hand, coffee and pastry bag in the other. Her number one travel rule: keep all essentials within grasp. The checked suitcase could go missing-in-action for all she cared. A wayward bag meant shopping, a new wardrobe, *and* a vacation. Win-win-win.

Navigating the crowd of milling passengers, Lisa inched forward toward her row on the third deck, starboard side of the Athenian Waterways high-speed ferry. She wished her final destination were as certain as the location of her assigned seat. The open-ended journey reflected her personal status—absolute uncertainty. Her life, upended three weeks before, was in flux.

Like most significant detours in life, Lisa was caught unaware—blindsided in a carefree moment. In the blink of an eye, a new reality replaced the old, familiar one. Her cozy life took a jagged turn, pitching her off a cliff. All foregone conclusions she'd made about her mother's life evaporated into thin air, like the ground under her feet.

Lisa would wish for a do-over of that moment, except her curiosity had now gotten the best of her. Finding the unexplained trinkets among her mother's prized possessions literally sent her packing. The tangible evidence of the traumatic event was secured in her tote. In a matter of twenty-one days, Lisa dropped everything and flew halfway around the world in search of answers.

Now en route to a tiny Greek island somewhere in the Aegean Sea, Lisa questioned her own sanity. What pushed her so far? Was boredom with her daily routine to blame, or her insatiable curiosity?

After three weeks of intense research, the items in her tote remained a mystery. Were these trinkets mysterious enough to justify the sudden departure from her over-planned life? She was unsure, especially with the wedding just months away.

To cap it off, Lisa wrestled with one huge question: had her mother hoped she would find these things and search for answers, or desperately prayed they would remain hidden forever?

CHAPTER 2

For where your treasure is,
there will your heart be also.
—Matthew 6:21 (KJV)

Three Weeks Before
Alpine Lake, Colorado

"Mom?"

"Um-hm?"

Brushing streusel crumbs from her lap, Lisa leaned closer to better hear Cate. The din of coffeehouse chatter and background music eclipsed her daughter's soft voice. It was early Friday morning, and every seat was filled. Caffeine and conversation buzzed off the walls, reverberating with loud, nervous energy.

Cate leaned closer, too, and said, "So, umm, you know, I haven't found my wedding dress yet."

With an exhaustive string of bridal shops peppering her memory of recent months, Lisa suppressed the urge to spaz-out and remind

Cate time was running short. Instead, she smiled, nodded her encouragement, and sipped her coffee.

Cate's eyes sparkled. "I've had an idea. I mean, something *totally different.*"

"Wow . . . okay. Sounds interesting." Appreciating that Cate was a creative genius who, for the most part, had some amazing ideas, Lisa felt a twinge of excitement. "Spring it on me."

Cate made the pitch, "What if I went retro?"

Surprised and intrigued, Lisa leaned in even closer. "Retro? How do you mean?"

"What if I wore Grandmother's wedding dress?"

Lisa's eyes widened in surprise. She clapped her hands at the possibility and let out a happy squeak. "*Yes! Ooh, yay!*" With ties to only one set of grandparents, this meant her precious daughter wanted to wear her maternal grandmother's dress. Giddy, Lisa bobbed, head-dancing in her seat and said, "Ooh, yeah . . . You can bet Grandma Cynthia and the angels are dancing in heaven, thrilled with your idea."

Cate giggled, "So, you really like the idea?"

"Noooo, I *love* the idea," Lisa jumped up and hugged Cate. "You're brilliant." Lisa rocked a series of dance moves. After watching Cate try on a hundred dresses, Lisa was ecstatic. Eyebrows raised in question, the ladies at the next table stared at her.

Without apology, Lisa pointed to herself and said, "*Happy dance goin' on here. My little girl has just said 'yes' to a wedding dress!*"

Cate, the blushing bride, beamed and flashed her engagement ring in their direction. Caught up in the girly moment, too, the ladies cheered.

Lisa sat and dabbed the tears from her eyes. "Oh, honey, it's a gorgeous dress. You'll look beautiful in it. I never even thought of the possibility. When did you make up your mind?"

"I was looking at Grandma's wedding portrait the other day. I *love* that dress. Always have. For days I looked all over the Internet for one like it. Then I realized," she smacked her forehead as if realizing she could've had a V-8, "I could wear *hers.*" Cate gushed on, "Do you think it'll fit me? Looks like she was tiny. I'm sad I don't remember her. And, you don't think she would mind if I wear her dress?"

Where to start? "Oh, baby, you were only three years old when she died; I wouldn't expect you to remember her. She loved you so much. She'd be thrilled for you to wear her dress, and, I'm sure it will fit you. I think you're even more petite than she was."

Mind racing, Lisa sipped her coffee. "It's a knee-length dress. You're okay with that?"

Cate's eyes danced. "Absolutely. Since it's a small, private wedding, I think it's perfect. I think a big dress would be too much."

"Good point."

"Oh, and, we changed our minds about the time of the ceremony."

Used to the frequent changes in their wedding plans, Lisa nodded, curious to hear the latest wrinkle.

"Derek and I want a morning wedding. Wouldn't that be sweet? Say, eleven o'clock, followed by lunch at Mon Cher Henri, with champagne and lots of wedding cake piled high with frosting. I wish every piece could be a corner piece with a rose on top. Oh . . . maybe we should do cupcakes . . . or petit fours."

Lisa suggested, "Better yet, forget the cake, just serve frosting." With a shared love for frosting, Lisa and Cate high-fived over the idea.

Lisa said, "I'm all for a morning wedding. They're lovely. Everything feels so bright and joyful with each new day."

Cate batted her thick, dark eyelashes. A pale blush colored her fair cheeks. "And, we can schedule an earlier flight—leave sooner on our honeymoon."

"Sweetheart, your ideas just keep getting better and better." Lisa dug to the bottom of her purse and raised a set of keys in triumph. "I can get us into Grandma's cabin. Wanna go try on your dress?"

"Oh, yes." Cate vocalized the no-brainer. "Oh, wait—it's a workday."

"It's okay. I know the boss. Let's go."

Snapping the lids over their half-finished coffees, they rushed for the door. Lisa sped along the rural route, airborne dust in their wake. Ten miles from town, she parked in front of her parents' cabin on Shadow Ridge Road. She and Cate climbed the steps to the front porch, then turned and admired the grand view of the snowcapped mountain range hemmed in by grassy wildflower meadows. The last of the snow was almost melted, revealing rugged, craggy boulders beneath.

"Oh, Mom, what an adventure you had growing up in this house."

"It was. Did I ever tell you about the time we took our sleds—"

"To the old mine shaft?"

Lisa rolled her eyes. "Of course, I did. Sorry. Anyway, I still miss making forts in the woods and splashing in the creek. Even though I'm grown, I'd still like to do that again." But for Cate trying on the wedding dress, Lisa would kick off her shoes that moment—and grab onto Cate's hand to join her.

"Me, too. We should spend more weekends here. Why did we ever stop?"

Lisa clicked her tongue. "We got too busy and forgot what was important."

She did not admit how it saddened her to revisit here. Her mom, dad, and husband, Cate's father, had all passed, leaving hollow echoes from the past inside these walls.

"You know, you and Derek should make your own memories here. Begin your own family history at the cabin. Sometimes on special occasions I could join you."

"Let's have Thanksgiving and Christmas here this year."

Lisa unlocked the door. They entered, and Cate switched on lamps. Lisa pushed back plaid, woolen curtains, revealing the view of the mountains. Shaking off the memories, she said, "Let's do this."

They climbed the split log stairs to the third-floor attic. Cate surveyed the jumble of trunks, boxes, and old furniture piled about the musty space. She opened the closet door and eyed the stack of boxes. "Any idea where it is?"

"Umm, I'm pretty sure the dress box is in the top of one of these trunks over here."

Lisa opened one trunk, rummaged through the contents and closed it. She took her bearings once again and opened another trunk near the dressing table. Cate took a pillbox hat from a hat-stand, set it on her head and coaxed the netting over her eyes. Making pouty lips, she eyed herself in the mirror.

Lisa announced, "Found it."

Cate abandoned the hat, nudged a stack of boxes out of the way with her hip, and peered over her mom's shoulder. Lisa folded back the tissue paper revealing the vintage dress.

Cate crooned, "Oh, it's more beautiful than in the photos."

Pulling the dress from the box, Lisa shook it out, and handed it to Cate. She turned toward the full-length mirror and held the dress against her shoulders, "It's the one!"

"Let's see how it fits you."

Cate slid out of her clothes and stepped into the dress. Lisa raised the zipper and fastened the line of loops over the tiny satin buttons in the back. She let her hands rest on Cate's hips as the young bride admired herself in the mirror. The white satin, empire waist dress fit almost perfectly.

"Gorgeous. It only needs a bit of alteration at the sides."

The sheer bodice and three-quarter length sleeves were covered in lace and silk-ribbon embroidery and rosettes. It was edged in a rolled satin collar that swept widely over the shoulders and plunged to an open-backed V that met the buttons mid-back.

Their eyes met in the mirror. Together they said, "It's perfect."

Seeing her daughter in *the* dress, Lisa dabbed the tears from her eyes. "You're a beautiful bride. I wish your grandmother could see you. She'd love that you chose to wear her wedding dress."

"It's elegant, classy, and timeless. Do you know what kind of bouquet she carried? —Mom?"

Lisa reached back into the dress box and rummaged through the tissue paper.

"Mom? What is it?"

"There's something else in here." Lisa picked up a purple velvet drawstring bag. Together they stared.

"What is that?"

"I have no idea. I've never seen it before."

"Why is it in the box with Grandmother's wedding dress?"

Lisa sat at the dressing table, and laid the velvet bag on the embroidered dresser scarf. Cate balanced nearby on a rickety piano stool.

Lisa illuminated a shadeless lamp, loosened the braided gold drawstring, and opened the bag. She withdrew the treasures it held. The first object, a crystal bottle with a wine cork for a stopper. The bottle was filled by two-thirds with pale, pebbly sand. As she turned the bottle in her hand the grains of sand and tiny pebbles tumbled over one another racing toward the flat edges of the glass. A few grains glistened in the ambient light, but overall, it was unremarkable.

Sealed in the bottle amidst the sand were little rocks in frosty hues of blue, green, and white.

Cate asked, "Are those jewels?"

Lisa handed the bottle to Cate. "I don't know. If so, they are natural, uncut."

Lisa retrieved the next item, a wooden cross. "This looks hand-carved from some kind of exotic wood, doesn't it?"

"Look, Mom, there's something carved on the back."

Lisa looked closer. "Mmmm...two letters, maybe from the Greek alphabet, and a date...1967." She handed the cross to Cate. "You were in sorority, you know the Greek alphabet, don't you?"

"That inverted-looking V is Lambda—L, and of course, the A is the Alpha. So, LA, probably the initials of the artist who carved it in 1967."

Lisa placed her hand inside the bag once more, withdrawing an envelope with an insignia printed on the unsealed flap.

Curious, Cate said, "That insignia also has Greek lettering, but I can't read it. I only know the Greek alphabet. Is there anything inside?"

"A folded sheet of paper. It has the same stamp at the top. It looks like stationery. Something's written on it in your grandmother's handwriting."

Lisa read,
Like the surge of the ocean, the roll of the waves,
So is My love for you ... relentless.
My love is like the sand on the shore,
Multi-faceted and plenty.
You are My sea glass,
Polished by My nature ... My jewel ... My love.

"How sweet. A love note from Grandpa Wells?"

"I don't think so. He was not one to write love notes, and it's in

Mom's handwriting, not his."

"Oh, yeah. So, then, she wrote about someone being *her* sea glass, polished by her nature? Maybe it's about you. It's not warm and fuzzy, but was sea glass her pet name for you?"

"No." Lisa laughed at the thought. "Nor did she call me the apple of her eye, though I know I was."

Cate frowned. "What is sea glass anyway?"

"I have no idea. We'll have to look it up."

"Along with the Greek words." Cate paused. "I don't remember you telling me about Grandma going to Greece."

"I didn't—she didn't. She never mentioned Greece. This is odd. Why would this be in the box with her wedding dress?"

"And, why the Greek lettering? There's no date on anything except the wooden cross. How old was Grandma in 1967?"

"Twenty, no—twenty-one."

"Maybe she had friends in Greece."

"I suppose it's possible. She never mentioned them, either."

Turning back to the box, Cate rustled through the tissue paper looking for more clues. The satin gown with the tulle underskirt swished as she moved. The old, yellowed box surrendered no clues of the secrets it held. "I thought there might be a note explaining why those things were in the box. Nothing."

Lisa stared at the objects on the dressing table. "Why would Mom have a bottle of sand?"

Cate said, "Look, there's writing on the cork. What does it say?"

Lisa examined the cork. "It's written in Greek-ish looking letters.'"

"Another Greek clue? This can't be coincidental."

Lisa shook her head. "What is it they say, 'how many coincidences before something becomes mathematically improbable?'" Lisa stared at the items. "Your Grandmother was a fun-loving, free-spirit, but, she was intentional about what was important to her."

Cate smoothed the satin skirt. "Like carefully packing away her wedding dress—and, the velvet bag with her treasures."

Lisa nodded, deep in thought. "Mom would never put meaningless trinkets in the box with her wedding dress."

"So, you mean these are a treasure of equal or greater value?"

"Exactly."

"Why would grandma treasure a bottle of sand, a wooden cross, and a love note as much, or more than her wedding dress? And, why did she never tell you about it?"

Lisa's eyes met Cate's. With a look of determination shadowed by apprehension, Lisa said, "I cannot imagine, but I plan to find out. I have a feeling this could change everything."

CHAPTER 3

Receiving a gift
is like getting a rare gemstone;
any way you look at it,
you see beauty refracted.
—Proverbs 17:8 (MSG)

Unexplained treasure. Lisa's own words echoed in her mind. *This could change everything.* The return to the cabin triggered an avalanche of thought and emotion. The pull of nostalgia coupled with the mystery of the velvet bag trespassed upon her awareness and haunted her every thought. They sparked an untimely curiosity, inspired fresh conviction, altered her trajectory.

With Cate and Derek's wedding four months away, she would limit her research to only what she could squeeze in around work and wedding plans. She would keep it to herself and investigate under the cloak of darkness. Her top priority was Cate and Derek.

The morning after their discovery Lisa reported to her study, retrieved her leather binder, and organized a research notebook. She created fact sheets to catalogue and cross-reference each item.

Headers included Carved Wooden Cross, Crystal Bottle, Wine Cork, Sand, Frosty Rocks, Envelope and Letterhead, and Love Letter.

At the credenza behind her desk, Lisa poked mechanical pencils into binder loops, added section dividers, clear page sleeves, and a zipper pouch for sundries. She felt like a kid organizing school supplies for the first day of a new term.

"Mom?"

Lisa jumped out of her skin and performed a supersonic one-eighty swivel in her office chair.

"*Oh, my gosh!* Where did you come from?"

"Through the front door. It was unlocked. Do you also hold flashlights for burglars?"

"Not funny. Speaking of burglars, you're a burglar. Intruder alert!" Lisa narrowed her eyes. "Maybe I should make a citizen's arrest."

"Hardly," Cate smiled. "Your case would never hold up in court. I'm not even an unannounced visitor. I called and texted to say I was coming over, I knocked on your door, I rang the doorbell, *and* I called out to you as I came down the hall. Didn't you hear me?"

Lisa pursed her lips. She did not want to admit to Cate she had been totally absorbed in a clandestine project.

Cate remained in the doorway where she stood against the frame, hands behind her back as she peered into her mother's study. "So, what are you up to?"

"Oh, nothing much. Just organizing some papers and stuff." Lisa put her hands on her hips to eclipse the view of evidence in the background.

"Oh, yeah . . . *stuff.*" Cate nodded her head. "Stuff is *really* important. I'm glad you're getting some stuff done."

Cate's gaze settled on the purple velvet bag on the desk in front of her. *Uh-oh.*

"Ah-ha!" Cate said.

"You don't have to look so smug."

"You've started the research, haven't you?"

Lisa swiveled her chair in guilty semi-circles. She wondered when their roles reversed.

Cate persisted, "Have you organized your old leather notebook with tabs and pouches yet?"

Lisa loosened the collar of her shirt venting the heat that rose from her neck to her face. Considering her options, she gave up, and raised her hands, "Okay, busted. I give up. I'm guilty. I did it. But I promise, my total focus is on your wedding."

Cate smiled affectionately. "Mom, I love your tenacious spirit and curiosity. You get all happy and sparkly when you have a new project. You look happy as a dog with a new bone when you're joyously focused in relentless pursuit. You don't give up until you find it out, dig it up, research it to death, pick it clean, buy it, sell it, explore it, read it, write it, explain it, kill it, dissect it, revive it, bury it, or whatever it takes. You're a 'to the ends of the earth,' 'until my last breath,' 'faithful to the end,' and 'over my dead body' kind of woman. You know what I *really* love about you? I mean, not in general, but today, right now, this minute."

"Ummm—"

"I love that you're a steadfast old soul, curious, kind and loving, and tough as nails when you need to be. It's good to see that side of you come alive again."

"Oh, Cate, that's sweet, but I—"

"Mom, let me finish. Without a doubt, if I ever need a mystery solved, I'd pick you as the investigator."

"I'd pick you, too, baby girl, you've always got what it takes to get the job done."

"Speaking of which," Cate raised an eyebrow, "I'm a woman on a mission." She extended an arm into the room. At the end of it, clutched in her hand was a shopping bag dangling in mid-air. "I brought you a present." Cate placed the shopping bag on Lisa's desk. "Ta-da!"

"What is this?" Wary, Lisa eyed the bag, "what are you up to?"

"Open it. No arguments. Just open it."

Lisa smiled and shook her head. Her beautiful, endearing, bubbly, and loving daughter never ceased to amaze. Cate always thought of others and her love language was "gift giving."

Lisa pulled at the fuchsia and orange curly ribbon tied about the handles of the large shopping bag. Before she could look inside, Cate ran around the desk, sat on top of it, reached in, and pulled out the present. She gained so much joy from gift giving she could never wait for the person to open it on their own. Impatient, she finished the job for them and thrust the gift under their nose.

"Oh, wow. It's *gorgeous.*"

"Do you love it?" Cate beamed as Lisa beheld the designer leather, robin egg blue tote.

"Yes, I love it. I absolutely love it, but—"

"No buts. Looky, looky." Cate jumped off the desk, grabbed the notebook from the credenza, and slid it inside. "See? And the velvet bag fits perfectly in the zipped side pouch. It won't fall out when you take it places."

"I'm taking it places?"

"Yes." Cate continued the orientation. "Here are pockets for your phone, keys, and lipstick. It's the perfect project bag for your research, and—" Lisa put a hand on her daughter's arm.

"The bag is beautiful, honey, but you shouldn't have. It looks so expensive. I'm afraid you're getting ahead of yourself. I'll feel so silly if I look into this and don't find anything."

"Mom, keep the tote. It's a love gift. It doesn't mean you *have* to do the research or find anything. But I hope you do, because I think a project would be good for you. It's been too long since you've plunged into something *you* wanted to do."

Lisa nodded. Her tears fell. In truth, she deferred her own needs with John's diagnosis. His death shattered her world.

"Yesterday you said finding Grandma's hidden treasures could change everything. I hope it does. I want to see you catch another spark, one that will ignite your passion for life again. It's time for you to try."

Lisa snatched a tissue for herself and handed one to Cate for her tears.

"If you don't find anything. . .so what? You've always said you enjoy the research process as much or more than you do the findings. If you figure out Grandma got these things at some garage sale, we'll have a good laugh. But neither one of us believe that for a second. Why else would you get your notebook ready? I bet you've already made tabs.

"Anyway Mom, the wedding is months away. Everything is

planned. All we have to do now is show up. Which leads me to my next point."

"Your next point? Do you also have a power point presentation and handouts?"

"Mom, if you would only let us, Derek and I will run the business while you take some time off. How long has it been since you took time off? Don't answer that. It's a rhetorical question. I know the answer; I'm making a point. Never. You never take any time off."

Lisa sighed.

"When Dad died, you buried him in the ground and buried yourself in the business. I know you were grieving and had to keep things afloat, but you stopped living your life. You've gotten us all to safety. Let me and Derek carry *you* a while. *Go!* Have some fun. Grandma left you a puzzle to solve. I've given you a designer bag so you can tote it all around. So, *please . . . go tote it somewhere!*"

Lisa sat in silence, aware Cate was watching her. Lisa took a deep breath and let it out slowly. She looked from Cate to the bag in her lap. She grabbed the tote bag with both hands, pondering. Lost in thought, she traced the gold designer logo with her finger. She loved the bag. It *felt* right.

"Cate, you're a game changer. If you hadn't wanted to wear your grandmother's dress, and if you were not such a remarkable person, we would not be having this conversation."

Cate jumped to her feet and squealed. Lisa picked up her laptop . . . and tucked it into her beautiful new bag.

"Thank you, my precious, precious, baby girl. Your heart is beautiful. I love the gift. Come here, you." Lisa hugged Cate tightly and kissed her on the head. "I love you."

"I love you, too, Mom."

Lisa finally pulled away and made for the door. "I'm headed to the coffeehouse to sit, plan, and organize my *stuff!* Rob the refrigerator or pantry of anything you want, but I am not holding the flashlight for you. You'll find fresh homemade cookies in the jar. Get some for you and take some to Derek. And please, don't forget to lock the door on your way out."

CHAPTER 4

Ask, and it shall be given you;
seek, and ye shall find;
knock, and it shall be opened unto you.
—Matthew 7:7 (KJV)

After Lisa fled the scene of the burglary with her new loot, she huddled up in a quiet corner at The Board Room coffeehouse. She pulled her laptop from her handsome new tote, powered it up, and outlined her thoughts. In rapid fire succession, she tapped out an email to Cate and Derek. "Meeting Notice: Business Transition Plan, 9A, Monday." Send.

"Wow, you sound like Machine Gun Annie on that thing. You're a woman who speaks her mind. Would I want to be on the receiving end of that email?"

"Hi, Silvie." Lisa pulled off her magnifiers and pushed the laptop aside. "You bet you would. Power meeting with the next generation. I'm relinquishing most of the keys to the kingdom."

Silvie raised her eyebrows. "Hmph. This your idea or theirs?"

"All of us, in our own ways. We're ready to take the next step. Cate grew up in the business and has her master's degree now, and John trained Derek and brought him along for such a time as this. Honestly, he's already carried the lion's share of the business these past two years. He's ready."

"You're too young to retire."

"I said *most of the keys*, not *all* the keys. And, I'm chairman of the board and retain enough shares. I've got the deciding vote. I'll keep my hand in things."

"Good girl. I expected something like this after the wedding. Why now?"

"Cate gave me a present this morning. So, I decided to take some time off and step back."

"What?"

"Long story. Anyway, Cate and Derek are a compatible, high-energy couple. And, they're in love. They already run the business as well as John and I did, perhaps better. I'm thankful, relieved, and excited."

"Well, I'm glad to see you do this. I can't think when you last took a day off or did something for yourself. You've pushed relentlessly since John's death . . . and before."

"It's time to re-establish balance in my life."

"Mmm-hmm. Once you figure it out, I need the cheat-sheet on that one."

"I'll start with prayer. Ask for guidance from the One who knows me better than I know myself."

"Amen to that." Silvie's pen hovered over the pad. "You're looking hungry, so don't tell me you just want coffee."

"I'm starving. I'd love a cranberry orange muffin, please."

"Extra orange glaze on that?"

"Lots, and some butter on the side, too."

"And your brew?"

Lisa swayed as Frank Sinatra crooned "Summer Wind" from a speaker somewhere overhead. "A carafe of your Bold and Smooth Frank Sumatra Blend, 'My Way.'"

"Comin' right up. By the way, that is some gorgeous tote bag you've got there. Mmm-mmm. I'm lovin' that color. What do they call it?"

"Robin egg blue. It's my new project bag. I may take up space here for awhile. Are you charging rent today?"

"Honey, this is your booth. Stay as long as you like."

Pencil in hand, Lisa opened her research binder and shifted gears. Clearly, it was time for an important meeting between one "Chairman of the Board" and another. They had a mystery to solve.

Lisa downloaded a Greek to English translation application on all her devices. She entered the characters printed on the stationery. ξενοδοχείο Μάκαρι. An array of options appeared on the screen. Eager to make it come alive, she clicked on the pronunciation tab. The emotionless, dismembered computer voice uttered, "Xenodocheio Mákari." Lisa mimicked the sound and clicked the tab again.

She tapped the translation tab, and the English version appeared, Hotel Mákari. She texted Cate, "The stationery is from the Hotel Mákari!"

"Wow! Where? BTW, D and I r at Rothwell & Sons ordering his new suit for the wedding. He's going retro too."

Not sure what it meant for the groom to go retro. Lisa hoped it meant suave, not gangster. She texted, "Sounds great. Enjoy ur special day together."

Lisa searched the Internet for the Hotel Mákari, *0 found*. She tried every combination of words and ideas for Mákari, hotels in Greece, and 1967. She repeated the query on several search engines and found no Hotel Mákari anywhere in the world, past or present. Dead end number one.

Lisa poured the last drips from the carafe and moved on to the wine cork. Dead end number two, only worse. She found no Greek letters that matched those on the cork. She could not even type them in. Dead end number three was having no clue why her mother had the stationery in the first place. She pursed her lips, and with stubborn, nervous energy, tapped her pencil hard on the table.

Coffee pot in hand, Silvie paused at her table, "Honey, what did that pencil ever do to you? I think you better switch to decaf now. Want another pot?"

Lisa nodded and dropped the pencil. "If I were the Hotel Mákari, where would I be?"

"Not on the menu here, that's for sure. I think you're snacking on brain cells, now. You need to eat again. Just baked some of those individual quiches. I'll bring you one with a salad, and fruit cup on the side. The usual vinaigrette?"

After quiche, Lisa read and reread the words on the Hotel Mákari stationery. *You are My sea glass, polished by My nature... My jewel... My love.*

My sea glass. Lisa rubbed her chin. Sea glass. Time to look up sea glass. She flipped to the corresponding tab in her notebook, then typed "sea glass" into the search engine. A series of colorful images populated the screen. Lisa stared in disbelief. Bingo. The images were identical to the blue, green, and white rocks in her mother's bottle of sand.

"Mom, why did you have sea glass? When did you get it? Where did you get it? Why did you write about it on Greek stationery? Why did you keep it in a crystal bottle? And why was it in your wedding dress box?"

For the next hour Lisa read about sea glass. It was indeed rare. Sea glass resulted from glass items that somehow ended up in the ocean. Some came from shipwrecks. Much of it was glass dumped in the ocean as trash. The collectible nuggets were formed from the broken pieces. The chemical properties of saltwater and relentless tumbling on the ocean floor or in the sand and surf smoothed and polished the shards—and gave them their frosty appearance. It took as long as thirty to fifty years, or longer, for sea glass to acquire its beautiful, jewel-like qualities.

Hmmm. Out of something ordinary and broken, something beautiful. Oh . . . Oh, my. Realization dawned. Lisa read the hotel stationery once again. *Surge of the ocean . . . roll of the waves . . . you are My sea glass, polished by My nature . . . My jewel . . . My love.*

Lisa felt certain the love letter was a parable. It likened the rough-and-tumble making of sea glass to the metamorphosis of a person's life. Every M was capitalized . . . *click!* Her mother capitalized words referring to God. So, it was the metamorphosis of one loved relentlessly by God . . . and perfected over the years by *His* nature.

Fueled with fresh excitement, Lisa scrolled and read everything possible about sea glass. It was highly collectable and sought by beachcombers worldwide. *Worldwide?*

Okay. Let's narrow the field. She entered a more focused search: "best beaches to find sea glass." Lisa stared at the results: "northeast and northwest United States, Mexico, Hawaii, Scotland, Bermuda, Nova Scotia, and Spain," to name a few. So, worldwide meant worldwide.

Mom never went to any of those places. At least not that I know of.

Lisa shook it off and read more. There were sea glass enthusiasts, sea glass color classification charts, sea glass collections, sea glass jewelry, sea glass societies, sea glass newsletters, even sea glass associations, and sea glass conventions.

Who knew? Well, obviously Mom knew. Mom had sea glass. Wonder why she never told me the facts of life about sea glass?

Lisa dumped the sugar packets from the bowl on the table and poured the sand and sea glass from the crystal bottle. She picked out a few pieces of sea glass and examined them closely under the beam of the flashlight on her cell phone. It softly illuminated their muted, luminescent color.

She took a pinch of sand in her fingers and drizzled it back into the bowl, certain the sand and the sea glass came from the same beach. If she could find one, she would probably find the other.

Perhaps she could contact a sea glass association—maybe they could help? She wondered if there was a local chapter. Probably not since they were land-locked. She pulled up the sea glass color classification chart. The pieces her mother had were the most common types. Lisa pulled off her reading glasses, pinched her nose, and rubbed her eyes.

Silvie approached the booth. "For someone on vacation, you sure are working hard."

"I'll take a break if you will."

"Now you're talkin' some sense." Silvie slipped into the other side of the booth. "What's this in my sugar bowl? Is this your new project? If you tell me what you're working on, I'll know exactly what to pray for."

Lisa closed the laptop and told her friend, prayer partner, and favorite coffeeshop owner everything.

Silvie's eyes sparkled with wonder. "So, Cynthia had all this tucked away with her wedding dress? My, my. What a wonderful opportunity to learn something special about your sweet mama."

"So, you think she meant for me to find this and look into it?"

"I think she was countin' on it."

When Lisa climbed into bed that night, Silvie's words echoed in her ears. *Your mama was countin' on it.* She closed her eyes for sleep, and exotic images of the Hotel Mákari quickened her imagination. She prayed she could find the hotel. She hoped it sat proudly on a Greek shore, with a lovely sandy beach—and sea glass. She hoped to find everything her mother counted on her to find.

Lisa prayed, *Father God, tell me the story of how Cynthia was polished by Your nature to become Your precious sea glass, Your jewel, Your love.*

As sleep grew near, God's presence grew nearer and comforted her wondering soul.

Beloved Daughter, I am in all and through all, and I know your story from beginning to end. I will answer your every question and bring you full circle, for I Am a Covenant-Keeping God.

CHAPTER 5

Maintain your ability to perch.
Assume nothing, see the obvious.
Be willing to travel a little . . . bit . . . farther.

Lisa prayed for answers and surfed the Internet for two weeks. Breakthrough came in the form of a 400-mile drive to meet Dr. Soso Diákos, Greek scholar and university professor. Lisa's heels clacked in steady rhythm as she walked the hallowed halls of academia in search of his office.

She rapped on the solid wooden door. The sound reverberated in the cavernous passageway. She squirmed at an intrusive memory from her college days: the meeting with the proud professor who announced her failure of his horrid mathematics class. Why had he taken such pride in a student failure? A diminished part of her feared asking questions of professors ever since. Lisa broke into a sweat and fought the urge to flee the scene.

"In."

Come on, Lisa, put your big girl pants on, and go in.

A second bark. "In!"

Lisa jerked her hand from the doorknob. Desperation for answers outweighed her panic. The door hinge squeaked as she pulled it open. At his desk, Dr. Diákos sat with his back to the door.

"I'm Lisa Abbott. I have an eleven o'clock appointment."

"If it's about your test grade, I suggest you study more."

"No, Sir. I called yesterday about—"

"Oh, yes, your mother's Greek artifacts."

"They're things my mother had . . . not necessarily artifacts—"

"Oh? I understood you had noteworthy Greek *artifacts*."

Lisa's cheeks flushed red. Ready to bolt, she edged toward the door. *Big girl pants, Lisa, hold your ground.*

Professor Diákos turned to face her. He sized her up over the rim of his glasses, and chuckled. "Took you back to your old college days, didn't I?"

Seething, Lisa scolded, "Bad professor, *bad professor*."

"Please forgive me. My wife tells me to stop already with the kidding."

"You should listen to your wife. She sounds like a considerate lady."

Professor Diákos smiled. "Yes, Mrs. Diákos is lovely. You would like her. Don't mind me. I have a cantankerous streak. I have to keep my bluff in on the students. It's harder and harder to do. Eh, students, nowadays. Please have a seat."

Lisa looked at the one meager seating option, a hard wooden chair filled with a stack of papers. "You have artifacts of your own, I see. Is this chair early twentieth century?"

"Paleozoic era. Petrified wood," Dr. Diákos chuckled.

"Aha. Looks about right."

"The two-foot stack of papers is from the Iflunkedtheclass era, of the twenty-first century. No place else to stack them, I'm afraid. My students usually perch on the edge of the chair. You're still young enough to perch, aren't you?"

Lisa lowered herself to the edge of the chair and angled her legs outward for tripod stability.

"This office and I have shared this space for over forty years. A marriage of sorts, no disrespect to Mrs. Diákos. In here, I am the neat one. The office on the other hand, she is the messy one. She collects everything that comes through the door. Every artifact, paper, book—it is erethistikós . . . irritating. She will not part with a thing. So . . . you see, the fact you have no place to sit, the office is to blame, not me."

"I'll manage. Thank you for seeing me."

"I am a nice man, and a curious man. I ask myself, 'Why would this woman drive so far to ask me questions?'"

"Two weeks ago I found these items my mother tucked away in her attic, in the box with her wedding dress. All the clues I came up with point to Greece. I think they point to something meaningful in her life."

Dr. Diákos offered, "Let's take a look."

Lisa clutched the tote. "I've been obsessed with this. Now that I've interrupted your day. . . I feel silly. Sorry to waste your time."

"Please. Show me these treasures."

Lisa placed the crystal bottle of sand and sea glass stoppered with the wine cork, the cross, and the envelope before him on the desk blotter. She held onto the velvet bag. Nervous, she fretted with the gold drawstring.

"I downloaded a translation app. The print on the stationery and letterhead is Hotel Mákari."

Dr. Diákos stared at the objects. He extended his hand.

"Please also allow me to see the velvet bag you fidget with."

"This? It's not one of the treasures. I believe she just used it for a purse to keep the other things together."

"Please, surrender the velvet purse. I must see."

"Oh."

Lisa divided her attention between Dr. Diákos' artifact examination and the wonders of his small office. Dusty shelves laden with books and periodicals threatened imminent collapse.

A smattering of Greek travel posters layered with postcards papered the wall behind his desk. Seven mini-Parthenon replicas doubled as decorations and bookends.

A glass case held crumbles of broken pottery, pestles, Grecian urns, small armless statuettes, and a laurel crowned bust of a Greek man with blank eyes. Lisa wondered why these artists carved with such detail, yet the eyes were always left blank.

"I see you have *actual* Greek artifacts. I believe I'm outclassed."

"Hmmm. Perhaps not. All those Parthenons are not real."

Very funny.

Dr. Diákos swapped his eyeglasses for a pair of magnified spectacles.

"Xenodochéio Makári. You are correct. The printing on the stationery is Greek for the Hotel Mákari."

Eager, Lisa asked, "Do you know of it?"

"I do not."

"It's strange there is no address on this letterhead."

"There is good reason. It appears the insignia was transferred to the paper with a wooden hand stamp. Small characters like address numbers and letters would be too intricate to carve in the wood. It was probably a challenge just to produce the insignia. Here, look with the magnifying glass."

He repositioned the hinged swing-arm of the mid-century fluorescent metal desk lamp, and pointed to the edges of the insignia with a letter opener. "See the traces of ink. It bled around the edge, and the color is uneven. This is typical of a wooden hand stamp. Now hold the paper up to the light."

Lisa smacked herself mentally. She never thought to check for this. "Oh, a watermark. What does it say?"

"Sifnos Márko."

"Isn't Sifnos a Greek island? Is Márko the name of a town on Sifnos? Perhaps where the Hotel Mákari is located?"

"No. But don't look so discouraged. You'll walk out of here knowing more than when you came in. Sifnos Márko simply means, Sifnos Mark . . . Sifnos *watermark*. So now you know this paper and," he held the counterpart toward the light, "the envelope were made on the Greek island, Sifnos. Congratulations. You have a Greek location."

"Sifnos! Sounds exotic."

"Yes. I have been there many times. Let's do a quick search on Sifnos Márko."

He typed, hit enter, and pointed to the computer screen. "The Sagonas family were artisans who produced specialty papers on Sifnos until 1969. Their registered watermark was SifnosMárko."

"Can you print that for me?"

"Sure. Pick it up from the office next door before you leave. Now, this cross is made of olive wood. It is a typical product of Greece. This artist had the good manners to leave their mark, the initials Lambda and the Alpha, and the year made, 1967." He clicked his tongue. "It was forty-nine years ago. To find this particular wood carver is a long-shot, but perhaps not impossible if it is a multi-generational business."

"So far in my online search, I have not been able to find any Greek wood carvers with those initials."

"Well," he shrugged, "Not everyone is on the Internet. Now, let's examine the velvet bag, bottle, cork, sand, and sea glass."

He examined the velvet, then raised the pouch to his nose, closed his eyes, and breathed in. "Thymíama."

"Excuse me?"

"Thymíama. It is the Greek word for incense. Here, smell."

Lisa closed her eyes, sniffing the velvet. "Oh . . . earthy, woody, sweet. The scent is heavenly."

Diákos emptied the sand and sea glass from the crystal bottle onto a sheet of paper. He examined the empty bottle. The light glinted off the design cut into the sleek rectangular crystal. He ran his finger along one flat side, "At one time, a label was affixed here. Sadly, it was lost at some point, along with the original stopper. Have you examined the bottom of the bottle?"

"Yes. In the center, I found the letter A in a square, surrounded by glass manufacturing press marks."

"Very good. Except in this case, we shall refer to it as the Alpha, the Greek letter A."

"Another Greek clue."

"Oh, yes. Now, look closer with the magnifying glass. Those are not glass manufacturing press marks, rather a special embossed Greek laurel wreath pattern. This is the insignia for Árgyros brand incense. Now, behold." Dr. Diákos slid the bottle into the velvet bag and tightened the drawstring. "The bottle and the bag were made for each other. The other objects just happened to be in the same bag with them . . . not the other way around as you imagined.

"Árgyros Thymíama . . . incense was made of frankincense. It was expensive and came exquisitely packaged. This was an extravagant, highly valued possession your mother had."

"I'm stunned. Where did this Árgyros come from? Sifnos?"

"The island of Crete. It was produced from the time before Jesus Christ until sometime in the 1970s when, sadly, the business closed. The items you hold are now quite rare."

"I'm stunned and overwhelmed. Are you sure another one of my biggest clues is out of business?"

"Yes. So, consider this. Up until now, you've been playing a short game, looking for quick answers. You must play a long game—a marathon, not a sprint. Look at the big picture to gain the perspective of the small details."

Lisa pursed her lips. "You're right. I've just been too eager and emotional to figure this out."

"Actually, you are closer than you know. Now, take this wine cork. What did your research reveal?"

"I feel certain it is not the original bottle stopper."

"Correct. The original would have been decorative crystal, on par with the exquisite bottle. Sadly, that is gone, and you have this in its place. But that is not necessarily a bad thing. It gives you another clue. Did you research wineries?"

"I tried, but I could not even enter the letters from the cork into my translation app. They did not look anything like the letters and symbols on the keyboard."

"That is because they are written in Classical Greek, not the modern, common Koine Greek. Also, it does not bear the winery name. Rather, the winemaker's philosophy. Roughly, it translates, 'Wine sings a love song to the soul.'"

"Oh, I would agree with that. Do you know of this vintner?"

"Ah . . . yes. And, I know this location pictured on the cork."

"The location is pictured on the cork? It's a small, abstract drawing."

Dr. Diákos took the cork from Lisa's grasp, turned it right side up, and handed it back.

"Oops. Well, now I'm totally embarrassed. I've looked at the writing and the image wrong for two weeks, which means I entered the text into the translation app upside down *and* backwards. Now that you mention it I can make out the drawing of a hill with boxy, Greek-looking buildings on it."

"Precisely. Do not be too hard on yourself. I see it clearly because I understand what I see. Here, this will help your research." Professor Diákos wrote six words on a note paper, handed it to Lisa, and sequentially pointed to them. "Your wine cork comes from the winery 'Γιώργος λόφοςor.' In Greek they say, 'Giórgos Iófos.' In English we say, 'George's Hill.' I know this winery and this hill." He swiveled his chair, rolled to a bookshelf, ran a finger across the book spines, and pulled the one he wanted.

"Here," he thumped a page, "have a look at this."

"The drawing on the cork is the exact silhouette of the hill and buildings in this photograph. What does this Greek caption say?"

"It explains Giórgos Hill Winery is located at this iconic location on the Greek island of Míos, M–i–o–s, pronounced, *Mē-ōhs*."

"*Míos?*"

"Geórgious—George, or possessive, George's—*Giórgos* is a male given-name that means one who works or tills the earth. In this case, it is a generational name handed down to the males who tend this vineyard. Many good bottles of wine come from this vineyard. In my opinion—the finest vineyard in Greece."

The professor read the results of another online search. "In 1970, Giórgos Hill Vineyard changed the writing on their corks from Classical Greek to modern Greek. That pinpoints your cork as no newer than 1970, roughly the same time period as all your other artifacts."

"Is the vineyard still in operation?"

"It was last summer when I visited Greece."

Lisa's thoughts raced with excitement.

Dr. Diákos studied the pile of sand. "But I can't address the sand or sea glass. I've lived on the Greece mainland and Greek islands. Every beach is different. One beach, rocks, another boulders, another fine sand, another pebbles, all on the same island. I've seen sea glass on some Greek beaches, but also on other beaches in the world. However, two compelling clues tells us this sand and sea glass came from Greece. They're in a Greek bottle, and the text written on the Greek stationery refers to sand and sea glass. Do you know the handwriting?"

"It's my mother's."

"Do you believe she composed this?"

"No. Honestly, I believe the words were given her by God. He spoke them to her . . . or into her awareness, and she wrote them down."

"I see . . ." He read the text again. "Well, I will not argue. You know your mother perhaps better than anyone. It is a reasonable assumption. I, too, am a believer in God. I hear His voice, feel impressions of His presence, and often journal it. It is a remarkable relationship to have with one's Creator."

Lisa released a long, slow breath.

"Miss Abbott, thank you for trusting me to evaluate your mother's treasures. Because of my experience, I am able to interpret these subtle clues and translate for you. You are holding twice as many clues as you thought, and they all point to Greece. Clearly, you unearthed a time capsule from the late 1960s. The one specific date you have is 1967 on the wooden cross. Do you know of anything special in your mother's life from the year 1967?"

"It's the year I was born. Selfishly, I'd like to think I was the most special thing that happened to my mother that year."

Professor Diákos smiled and scratched his chin. "How old was your mother in 1967?"

"Twenty-one."

"Your mother never said anything to you about a wooden cross from Greece dated 1967?"

"No. Maybe it was a gift from someone."

"She never told you about any of these other things?"

"Never."

"Ms. Abbott, these things your mother treasured are not random. They all point to the same small corner of the world, three Greek islands in the Aegean Sea."

Lisa loosened her neck scarf and fanned herself.

Dr. Diákos faced her and made full eye contact. "I risk upsetting you and your comfortable view of your mother, but I will tell you honestly what I think. You are afraid to face the truth. Your mother never spoke of these things so you want to think she hid them from you. It is the opposite. There is only one important question to ask yourself: why did your mother *want* you to find these Greek treasures from the 1960s that she 'hid in plain sight'?"

"But . . . my mother never went to Greece."

Professor Diákos rested his elbows on the arms of his chair, hands tented. "How do you know?"

"My mother never talked about Greece."

"Ms. Abbott, how many things have you done in your life that no one else knows about? I've been all over the world, had many experiences, yet many of my close friends, even immediate family, have no idea where I've been, when I was there, why I went, or what I did there. We all carry secrets."

"But . . ."

Dr. Diákos raised an eyebrow amongst his kind features. "What do you actually *know* about your mother's early years before you were born? Let me put it this way, can you prove she was *not* in Greece?"

Lisa stared at the seven mini-Parthenons.

"Your mother hoped you would find her Greek treasures. If I were you, and I loved my mother enough to wonder why, I'd buy a ticket."

"A ticket? To where, exactly?"

"The Greek Island of Míos."

"Not Crete, not Sifnos?"

"No, Míos. Míos is centrally located between the islands of Sifnos and Crete, and it's the exact location of Giórgos Hill Winery." He let his hands drop and leaned forward. "Look, at most you find out something interesting about your mother. At worst, you find out nothing, but you have a sunny vacation on a lovely Greek island."

"I can't just fly off to Míos, or however you get there."

A class bell shrilled. "You fly to Athens, then take a ferry."

Soso Diákos cinched his short, wide, threadbare necktie into place and picked up a pile of books.

"Ms. Abbott, you've traveled this far looking for answers, so . . . now, *if* you have enough courage, you do something you've probably never done before. You ask the hard questions . . . you color outside the lines . . . you wander out of your comfort zone with reckless abandon. You travel a *little . . . bit . . . farther!*"

"But—"

Ten paces into the hallway Professor Diákos turned and said, "Hey . . . when you get to Míos, sit on Giórgos Hill, and the wine sings a love song to your soul, please, drink a toast to me."

CHAPTER 6

&

> . . . we are also compassed about
> with so great a cloud of witnesses,
> let us lay aside every weight
> . . .and let us run with patience
> the race set before us.
> —Hebrews 12:1 (KJV)

June 2016, Aegean Sea, Greece

Within hours of meeting Dr. Diákos, Lisa followed his advice and bought one-way tickets to travel *a little bit farther*. Forty-eight hours later she packed her bag and flew to Athens, Greece. Now that she was onboard the high-speed ferry bound for Míos, she questioned her own sanity. On the other hand, in one serendipitous moment, intrigue and adventure had knocked on her door, and for once, thank heaven, she opened it.

Afraid to miss the boat, Lisa was among the first to board. As the boat filled, she sat quietly, lost in thought. Face pressed to the window, she strained to see the dockside activities. The early morning darkness, coupled with the interior cabin lights, turned the plate glass passenger window into a mirror. Lisa's focus shifted from far to near, and she caught sight of her reflection.

She critiqued her appearance and tucked a wayward strand of thick, dark hair behind her ear. Her eye was drawn to the golden glint of the antique locket that hung around her neck and rested just above the cleavage of her breasts. The diamonds and rubies set amid the intricate embossed floral design on the face of the locket winked at her. She placed a hand over the beloved locket.

Lisa shifted her focus back dockside where gangplanks were retracted. As the pre-dawn darkness yielded to first light, the ferry maneuvered from the dock and propelled seaward. Adrenaline surged through her veins. Like horses out of the starting gate, a half-dozen high-speed ferries simultaneously raced from their moors at the industrial harbor. With over a thousand islands strewn across the Aegean, their task was to divide and conquer many ports of call.

The ferries fanned out and jetted toward open water. Lisa watched as they left the Port of Piraeus and city of Athens behind in a mirage of quivering heatwaves. The misaligned heap of ancient and modern buildings melted and dripped into the sea.

The bow of the ferry sliced through the liquid surface of the deep as the enormous ferry sped forward. The water was so blue and beckoning, it pulled her heart toward Míos as surely as the moon draws the tides to the shore.

The engines droned as the ferry surged over the expanse of swells. Lulled by the gentle motion, Lisa scanned the brilliant seascape, eager to memorize every detail of her journey. They were at sea for almost an hour when she spotted brown clumps in the distance. Islands. The ferry closed the distance, and the islands rose above the shimmery surface, materializing into habitable land masses.

Clusters of boxy, white houses and blue-domed churches dotted the barren hillsides. Lisa moved to the edge of her seat at the sight of the foreign, arid land. It called to the empty niches of her spirit like a desert oasis for the soul. She longed to disembark and explore. The ferry throttled on, and the sprinkling of islands sunk into the sea behind them.

Lisa turned to share her excitement with John, a difficult habit to break after twenty-seven years. The companion seat beside her, painfully empty, yet John felt so close. A fresh stab to the heart. Hand pressed to her chest, she blinked back tears. She longed to feel John's hand in hers, feel his tangible presence and companionship.

Lisa closed her eyes and felt him in heart and spirit, ever a part of her, perhaps the strongest part. In life, he protected her and taught her self-sufficiency.

Did you know, John, that one day I must go on without you? I hear your voice in my head, the things you said, your commentary on life, your encouragement to put one foot in front of the other. I hear the echo of your voices, too, Mom and Dad. Your words of love and instruction were not lost on me. Lisa smiled. *You are all among the great cloud of heavenly witnesses who look over my shoulder and cheer me on.*

Gratitude overflowed her heart and spilled from her lips, for the love she had known in her life—and for the journey to Míos. She retrieved pen and paper from her tote and journaled, *My God and steadfast companion, I promise to listen for Your voice and open my heart to the answers You provide. I trust You to lead me safely back home with a renewed heart. In Jesus' Name, Amen.*

Lisa relaxed into her seat, yawned, and stretched her legs. Every moment hurtled her closer to Míos and the reality of what she might discover there. Savory aromas wafted through the cabin. Her olfactory senses were on them like a bloodhound on a trail. Her early morning coffee and pastry had worn off. Her stomach grumbled with complaint as raw hunger set in with a vengeance.

As Lisa rose and eyed the elderly couple in the aisle seat and second seat, she calculated the acrobatics required to venture out and return.

"Excuse me."

Without notice of her, the man and woman stared, weary gazes fixed on the seat in front of them. Wordless, they endured the trip, unyielding to their row mate. Murmuring her excuses Lisa climbed over them, dreading the return trip with food and beverage.

In the aisle, Lisa gained her bearing. The ferry was configured like a jumbo jetliner. Two aisles stretched fore to aft, crisscrossed port to starboard by aisles at midway points.

Aft, a brightly lit gift shop displayed over-priced, shiny tourist fare. Indigenous shot glasses and mini-Parthenons lined glass shelves, amid sun hats, breath mints, magazine racks, and a circular postcard frame. Lisa wondered how many of Dr. Diákos' students purchased mini-Parthenons for him as an afterthought on the ferry home.

In the queue for the snack bar, Lisa squinted at the posted menu. It was in Greek with no English subtitles or pictures. Undaunted, she trusted her stomach to decide for her. The hot bar and bakery case did not disappoint. She pointed at what she wanted and reminded herself not to exaggerate her speech or raise her voice as so many tourists did to breach the language barrier. She splayed paper money and coins on the counter. The cashier took what he needed. Scooping up the remainder, she scuttled it into her pocket and moved on.

Lisa brunched on coffee and a golden triangle of warm spanakopita, a flaky pastry filled with spinach, cheese, scallion, and egg. Dessert was phyllo with cinnamon and almonds, covered with sweet, sticky syrup. Lisa wished for a dozen more of each.

During her feast, the ferry made landfall at two ports of call. A handful of passengers and parcels were exchanged at these small islands. Another long stretch of open water with no island sightings occupied the next hour.

Lisa checked her watch and reconfirmed the arrival time on her ticket. The four-hour crossing of the Aegean was nearing completion. She scanned the horizon. A group of three islands appeared in the distance.

She overheard the man in the row behind. "Míos."

Their row of passengers stirred. Before she could stop herself, Lisa turned, knelt in her seat, and peered over the headrest. "Míos? Is that Míos?"

The man pointed out the window. "Míos. Naí, Míos."

Whirling around, Lisa captured her first glimpses of Míos with her cell phone camera. Anxious to disembark, she shouldered her tote preparing to jump over the couple into the aisle.

In a frothy display of churning whitewater, the ferry slowed, reversed engines, and maneuvered a U-turn toward the dock.

Lisa scanned the Míos shoreline and busy harbor. Her pulse quickened at the sight of it. The sun-washed Greek island was exotic. Idyllic. More alluring than anticipated.

Míos, the place that was a tiny speck on the world map, lured her in. Spoke to her in a foreign language her heart somehow understood. Míos beckoned her to walk its shores, immerse in its blue waters, behold its vibrant red-orange sunsets, and fall in love with its people and culture. Míos welcomed her heart and soul. It assured her she was no interloper, but rather a sojourner who could call this island *home*.

CHAPTER 7

Spévdo!
A.K.A., Move it or lose it!

A recorded announcement in Greek, then English filtered through cabin speakers instructing passengers to take the stairwells to the lower level to disembark. The recorded announcement reminded Lisa of the announcement played in airport terminals. Lisa knew them by heart, "Parking is prohibited in loading and unloading zones in front of the terminal. All unattended vehicles will be towed."

Lisa's personal favorite was the, "You are now approaching the security checkpoint . . ." message that had once blazed from an overhead speaker just as she entered a ladies restroom stall. Startled out of her wits, she looked around for TSA and cameras. *"Really? Here?"*

Lisa hoped she could ride this wonderful ferry enough to learn and recite this recorded message in English *and* in Greek. Passenger traffic in the stairwell moved at an impatient pace toward the cargo hold.

At the lowest level, Lisa shuffled with the crowd into the belly of the beast. Choking on automobile exhaust, she struggled to get her bearings amidst the noisy confusion and chaos.

A dispatch of no nonsense porters blew whistles and motioned the passengers toward the exit ramp. They yelled, "Katevaíno . . . Get off! Spévdo . . . Spévdo . . . *Spévdo!* Hurry. Hurry. *Hurry!*"

In a panic, Lisa approached a porter. "Luggage? Where do I get my luggage?" She made hand motions she hoped telegraphed the idea of a roller bag. He blew the whistle even louder. *Oh, good, now that you've blown your whistle louder, I know what to do.*

Frantic, she repeated the hand motions. He pointed to one side of the cargo hold. Lisa moved in that direction and saw other passengers grabbing bags. She joined in the scramble, desperate to find her suitcase among the dozens of lookalikes in the racks of metal cages.

Once located, Lisa grabbed the handle and tugged. The obstinate suitcase tumbled forth leaving a black smear down her white skirt. She dragged her suitcase, stumbled toward the exit, and queued up among the pedestrian traffic that waited in a cloud of exhaust between the lanes of vehicles.

Cars, trucks, and motorcycles revved their engines, ready to surge toward the enormous exit ramp that spanned the back of the ferry. The moment the ramp was on the dock, the porters yelled and whistled with renewed vigor. It was like "lights out" at a Formula One Grand Prix.

Regardless of the pedestrians, vehicles sprinted forward, brakes screeched, and horns honked. They raced out into the daylight and burned rubber on the dock.

The porters herded the foot traffic. "Spévdo, *Spévdo.* Hurry. Katevaíno . . . come off. *Off!* Go, go!" They pointed furiously at the ramp. Lisa remained at the back of the pack following the others. Dodging between cars and hustling toward the ramp, Lisa vowed never to run with the bulls in Spain.

An alarm blared in her ears, and overhead traffic lights flashed red. *Yikes, what's next, nuclear meltdown?*

"Spévdo. Go. Ramp close!"

The last of the foot passengers frantically busted it down the metal gangplank for dry land. Halfway down, Lisa's suitcase jerked to an abrupt halt. Her grip was so tight, it almost jerked her arm from the socket. One of the wheels on her roller bag was stuck in a divot on the ramp.

Lisa pushed and pulled on the stubborn bag with all her might. It did not budge. She felt movement on the ramp. *Is it going up?* Heart palpitations racked her chest and robbed the air from her lungs. Had she not forgotten her MIA suitcase strategy of shopping and new clothes, she would have abandoned it and run ashore. She tugged at the suitcase. Frantic and helpless, she pleaded, "Jesus help. *Jesus help!*"

A porter noticed and ran toward her. He yanked the bag free, minus the wheel still stuck on the ramp, and shouted at her, "Spévdo! Run, ramp go up!"

Heart pounding out of her chest, Lisa drug the bag and ran for all she was worth. She stumbled over the edge of the ramp and spilled onto the dock as it lifted up. Everything about the high-speed ferry had, indeed, been—high speed.

Incredulous, Lisa laughed and cried simultaneously. "Thank you, Jesus. Thank you."

Lisa arrived on Míos, albeit like a modern-day Jonah, thrown up on the dock from the belly of the boat. She looked back. The punctual ferry, already seaward was but a memory.

In the wake of her near-death experience, Lisa drug the wonky suitcase along and wondered why she had not left it behind in order to safely reach her destination with less stress. She was struck by the irony. *How many times have I drug around cumbersome and dysfunctional emotional baggage that has held me back and robbed me of my potential and peace of mind?* With new resolve, she vowed to lighten the load on both counts.

Lisa stopped in her tracks, took in a deep breath, and reveled in the joy of her arrival in Míos. With fresh determination, she made her way to the first taverna she came upon. It was located dockside in a group of small shops.

She parked herself at an umbrella-topped table, with her quasi-rolling luggage and emotional baggage far off to the side and a catch of fresh octopus hanging on the line above.

"Chaírete. Pós boró na se voithíso?"

"Mílas Angliká?"

"Yes. Hello. How can I help you?" He provided a menu. It was

ELIZABETH TOMME

printed in Greek, with corresponding color photos of dining options. "I am Adonis."

Well, hello, handsome Adonis. You are the most appropriately named human being I ever met.

"I can make suggestions for you, if you wish."

Spellbound, Lisa basked in his beautiful accent for a moment. "Uh. . .yes. . .thank you. I am Lisa. I would love a salad." She returned the menu to Adonis.

"I suggest, Choriátiki Saláta, eh . . . Village Salad. Fresh tomatoes, cucumber, onion, rigani. . .eh, oregano, black olives, feta cheese, olive oil, vinegar, salt and pepper."

Lisa's mouth watered. "Yes, please."

"Choice to drink? May I suggest lefkó krasí, a chilled white wine?"

"Sounds perfect. Just a glass, though."

Adonis returned promptly and uncorked a fresh bottle at her table. He filled her glass and set it before her along with the bottle and the cork.

Lisa began to protest. "Just one glass—"

"No worry," Adonis assured her. "Very casual. If only want one glass, only drink one glass. If want more, drink more." Adonis looked toward the pier where the ferries docked. "You have suitcase. Is this first travel on ferry?"

"Yes."

"You get scary landing?"

Wide-eyed, Lisa nodded.

"Amán! Eh. . .oh, no! I leave the bottle. Welcome to Míos."

"Thank you. Adonis, you are my first friend on Míos."

"And, you are my first new friend today."

Lisa's attention drifted to the table. She frowned.

"What is wrong? Did I offend?"

"Oh . . . no, no, sorry. It's this wine cork. It looks similar to a cork I have seen before. The drawing of the hill, the buildings. Is this from a local vineyard?"

"It is Giórgos Iófos."

"Oh, *Giórgos Hill?*"

"Is there a problem, Miss? You want another kind of wine?"

Lisa smiled. "Everything is perfect. I am thrilled my first taste of wine on Míos is from Giórgos Hill. This is meaningful to me. Adonis, do you believe in God?"

"I . . . am not sure, Miss."

"Why is that?"

He shrugged. "Not enough evidence?"

Lisa held up the wine cork and smiled. "This wine cork alone is more evidence than I need for a lifetime of belief. It proves to me God is in all and through all."

"Hmmm. The joy on your face alone is almost enough evidence to convince me. You may keep the cork. A present from your first friend on Míos. I bring your food now."

Adonis returned filling the table with food.

Lisa prayed. "Thank you for the safe trip to Míos. I am grateful for this beautiful meal, and my new friend, Adonis. Open his eyes to see the evidence that surrounds him. Forgive me, as I forgive the frenzied porters who threw me off the boat. In Jesus' Name, Amen."

Lisa sipped the glass of Giórgos Hill, lefkó krasí. It was light and crisp with refreshing nuances of citrus and quince.

The Village Salad was a Greek party in a bowl, served with a side of french fries, a rustic loaf of crusty bread, and a rich pool of olive oil for dipping.

Once Lisa chewed on the last crispy french fry and pushed her plate aside. Adonis appeared and cleared the dishes away.

"For your dessert, Bakládes."

The aromas of warm cinnamon, cloves, almonds, and honey filled Lisa's olfactory senses.

"Thank you. Oh, I *love* Greece!"

"Please, stay as long as you like."

"At this table, or on Míos?"

"Both. Maybe you decide to stay forever."

Full and happy, Lisa relaxed. She pulled her feet from her sandals, wiggled her toes, and luxuriated in the warmth from the pavers beneath her feet. Face turned sunward, she bathed in its warmth.

The blue sky, unencumbered with clouds, soared unrestrained. She released her mind to do the same as the sea breeze tousled her hair and tickled her skin.

The arrival of another ferry interrupted Lisa's daydream. She watched the harried tourists scurry off the boat. In her mind's eye she pictured a twenty-one-year-old Cynthia Carter Brenner make her way down the ramp, young, healthy, smartly dressed, and ready for adventure on Míos.

Lisa craved a good mother-daughter talk. Among the many questions she would ask, "*If* you were here. . .*why, oh, why* were you here?"

CHAPTER 8

Never judge a Fiat by its hood ornament.

*L*isa left the pavement dragging her suitcase across the dirt lot toward a dilapidated shack. Despite the reservation number on her itinerary, one glance among the weeds and stacks of used tires informed Lisa the car rental choices were limited to nonexistent. Stepping around a heap of rusty bicycles leaning against the structure Lisa approached the customer window.

The attendant in the booth took a long drag on his cigarette and stubbed out the last quarter-inch as he sized Lisa up.

Hopeful, Lisa asked, "Mílas Angliká?"

"Eh, lígo . . . a little."

Lisa pointed to herself. "Mílas lígo Greek. I am Lisa Abbott. Is this the car rental business?"

"Naí . . . yes." Pulling himself off the stool he pointed to his chest. "Iosíf. You have reservation?"

"Yes, a compact car." Lisa placed the reservation paper on the window ledge.

Iosíf waved it away as if it were a pesky fly. "No need. You take scooter."

Lisa bit her lip and looked over the lot. She was almost tempted, for adventure's sake. And, Cate would think it hilarious. Remembering her age and suitcase she snapped back to reality and shook her head.

As if reading her mind, Iosíf said, "I deliver suitcase to you."

"Thank you, no. I reserved a car. I need a car, please." Iosíf scratched his beard. Lisa prayed.

"Okay. Maybe I get you car." He started across the lot. Unsure whether to follow, Lisa waited there with her gimpy bag. Iosíf walked to the house next door and banged on the door.

A man in an undershirt answered. Iosíf gestured toward Lisa, shrugged, and pointed at the car in the driveway. A dialogue punctuated with gesturing and shrugging ensued. Iosíf secured a key, got in the car, and pulled it around.

He announced, "Compact car. Same as reservation. You take." Iosíf manhandled Lisa's suitcase into the trunk and slammed the lid down until it latched.

Lisa made a signing motion on her paperwork. "Where do I sign for it?"

He waved the pesky notion away. "Eh, not sign, you pay now."

"How much do you charge per day? I don't know how long—"

"Pay flat fee. 300 Euro cash, turn in whenever."

Filled with trepidation, Lisa looked at the car. *What do I do? Am I being taken? If it only runs for a day, I'm out the cash. Maybe I should just take a scooter. But then I'd have to trust him with my suitcase. Father God, please give me wisdom.*

Iosíf scratched the back of his head. "It is fair price."

"What if your neighbor needs his car back before I—?"

"You no want scooter, so I give *him* scooter and cash. He do this for you. He trust you with his car."

Wisdom received. Trust is a two-way street, and blessings come in all shapes, sizes, and hood ornaments.

Iosíf held the car door open for Lisa as if it were a limousine. Humbled, Lisa paid the cash plus some extra and got behind the wheel.

The tiny, red, two-door, standard shift convertible clunker was of unknown lineage and year model, despite the "Fiat" emblem tacked sideways onto the front hood with a rusty screw.

The dirty, sunbaked vinyl seats were cracked, and Lisa could see the ground through a hole in the floorboard. The interior reeked of cigarette smoke and garlic. The right side mirror was missing, and the broken metal mount was rusted out. At any rate, it growled to life when she turned the key, and she was thankful for it.

Lisa drove off the lot with a wave out the window and beep of the horn. It had been years since she drove a standard shift, but she quickly got a feel for the clutch and its rhythm. It was a fun little car to drive.

Thankful the owner trusted her not to fowl up the gears, Lisa motored past the harbor and out the opposite side of town in search of her hotel. She only stalled out once at an intersection on a steep hill.

Lisa arrived at the remote Xenodocheío Aigaío, Aegean Hotel, by way of a steep, dirt switchback that snaked its way amid the rocks. Once parked, Lisa climbed out, unfolded herself, and got her bearings. She followed the arrow on a placard that pointed to the office. A jangling brass bell announced her arrival.

"Chaírete. Kalosorízo. Hello, and welcome to the Aegean Hotel."

"Hello."

"You must be Lisa. I am Gianna Gataki. Did you have any trouble finding us?"

"Not at all. This is a glorious location. The scenery is breathtaking. And, I love that it is so private and quiet."

"Then this will be a perfect match for you. If you thrive on night life and clubs, I would recommend you stay in the Chora."

"This is perfect."

"Then let's get you checked in. Still an open-ended stay?"

"That's right."

"I have booked you into our most secluded suite. You will have as much privacy as you want, yet we are available for your needs. Please complete this form."

Lisa put her magnifiers on and completed the simple form.

The bell on the door jangled. "Ah, good timing. Lisa, this is my strong and handsome husband, Skender." Gianna squeezed Skender's left bicep and stood on tiptoe, kissing him on the cheek. "Give him your key, and he will get your luggage."

"Thank you. Just one bag in the trunk. And, I'm afraid one of the wheels is missing—"

"Another victim of the ferry ramp?"

"How did you guess? Here's the key."

"This is my other job. I fix suitcases. Casualties of the ferry. Leave it outside your door tonight. New wheel by morning."

Gianna led the way. "Come, my new friend . . . let's settle you into your new home."

The jumble of guest houses were connected to one another like a higgledy-piggledy row of townhomes, stacked on the side of the terraced hill. In the Greek afternoon sun, they shone as a jewel on brown velvet.

The intimately positioned complex shared a common terrace, luscious pool, stick-roofed loggia, and a sweeping view of the port, Aegean Sea, southern end of Míos, and neighboring islands. A labyrinth of rock pathways and quirky uneven steps webbed from door to door and to the common areas. Fuchsia bougainvillea spilled from rooftops, over blue doorways, and shaded outdoor living spaces.

"Oh, this is beautiful."

Gianna beamed. "It is all by God's grace and mercy." She led Lisa up a rise of steps, crossed the shaded terrace, and opened the door. "Your living room, kitchen, and powder room are on this level. The bedroom and en suite are up one level, topped by a private roof terrace with a comfortable outdoor living room, table, and chairs. The view is phenomenal up there, night or day. And, the stargazing is amazing. Use the pool anytime you wish."

Lisa loved her quarters. It was cool inside the thick, whitewashed walls. The wide windows were cranked open. Gauzy white curtains lifted lazily on the breeze. The space was fresh and new, and quintessentially Greek, with an earthy, country feel.

In contrast with the white palette, Gianna added splashes of color by way of throw pillows, rugs, pottery, and paintings. The weathered wood floors and rough-hewn overhead beams lent a rustic feel. The rooms were comfortable and inviting.

Lamps and pendant lights were shaded with woven baskets. In the kitchen area, a ceramic crock bursting with sunflowers topped a red wooden table and chairs for two.

"Your key is on the peg by the door. Are you tired from your trip?"

"Yes. I arrived in Athens yesterday afternoon, then was up again at four o'clock this morning to catch the ferry. I think I'll stay in tonight."

"I stocked the kitchen so you can eat in—if you prefer not to go to a restaurant or join us by the pool. We grow a lot of our own food, and share from our garden, chickens, and cow. There's a plate of sliced lamb in the refrigerator, and lots of nibbles in the kitchen. Let me know if I can pick up anything for you at the market."

Lisa toured the kitchen. A platter of fresh fruit and cheeses rested under a glass dome on the counter, plus an assortment of breads in one basket and tomatoes piled in another. A wire basket of eggs, a crock of butter, and a jar of thyme honey sat on the shelf.

Artisan pottery and glassware occupied the shelves. An array of Giórgos Hill reds and whites occupied a wooden wine rack. Blue and white linen curtains were pushed to either side of the window over the aproned country sink.

"Everything looks delicious, and your hotel is amazing. You are a talented and a gracious hostess. Tell me about yourself and Skender, and your hotel."

"Skender and I grew up in Athens. We met at university. We both did international studies in the United States, so our English is good. We returned to Athens, married, lived in the city, had corporate jobs, big salaries, and big stress. Two years ago, we woke up one day and decided there was more to life.

We quit our jobs, sold everything, and came to Míos. With our money and inheritance, we bought this old, run-down farm, started renovations, added buildings, and made the hotel. We only have four suites like this and our living quarters. Skender and I live in the old farmhouse next to the office. Not fancy, but more than enough."

"It's wonderful. Thank you for opening your home and your hearts to me. I can't wait to get to know you."

"Me, too. Is this your first time on Míos?"

"Yes. I have already fallen in love with it."

"Let me know if I can help you with information, directions, or reservations while you're here. Are you on holiday?"

Lisa explained how she arrived on Míos and what she hoped to accomplish.

"This is so exciting. Stay with us as long as you want. I hope you will let me help with your search. I'm crazy about intrigue and solving puzzles."

Lisa unpacked, napped, showered, and dressed in a cool cotton shift. Refreshed and hungry, she padded to the kitchen. She carried a tray of nibbles and wine to the roof terrace. The last sliver of golden sun melted into the Aegean. A mantle of soft pink haze settled in its place. Gradients of ever-deepening color seeped into the inky, star-sprinkled welkin above.

The darkening heavens drew nearer and nearer until Lisa felt buoyant among the stars, dancing among the constellations. She reached heavenward tracing the Summer Triangle with her finger. The three bright stars, Altair, Deneb, and Vega winked at her.

Lisa raised her arms in praise quoting one of her favorite Psalms, "Oh LORD, our LORD, how majestic is your name in all the earth! You have set your glory above the heavens. When I look at your heavens, the work of your fingers, the moon and the stars, which you have set in place, what is man that you are mindful of him . . . ?"(ESV)

You are my beloved daughter...

"Oh, wow!" Lisa clasped her hands over her heart, "And, You, are my *beloved Father.*"

* * *

THE NEXT MORNING Lisa woke to warm sunshine pouring through her bedroom window. The gauzy curtains flew on the breeze. Their shadows flapped at the splashes of light slanting across the floor. The cerulean sky promised another cloudless day. At the sound of clanking bells she stretched and peered out the window. A small herd of goats roamed the sparse hillside in search of vegetation.

Ravenous, Lisa took her cue from the goats and foraged for breakfast. In her nightgown, she brewed coffee, scrambled eggs, and piled her plate with cheese, fresh fruit, and toasted bread slathered with butter and honey. Tanked up, she poured another coffee and planned her day. It was time to explore Míos.

Dressed in a colorful cotton T-shirt dress and white Stan Smith's, she scurried to the car slinging the robin egg blue tote onto the passenger seat. With a wave to Gianna in the garden, she nosed the Fiat toward town.

Lisa puttered past the harbor and parked curbside under the meager canopy of an olive tree. Along the street, a line of customers queued up for sodas, ice cream, and crepes at a stand. Just beyond, arrowed signs pointed to the center of town on the hill.

The rock-paved pathway wound past shops, tavernas, and residences toward the domed church at the top of the hill. Bougainvillea framed rooftops and doorways. Laundry hung on lines between the canyons of buildings.

Underfoot, rounded stone pavers outlined in neat circles of white paint tempted Lisa to hopscotch her way along. A church bell tolled, and the ferry blasted its horn at port.

Lisa popped in and out of shops. They were a pleasing mixture of touristy arcades, designer clothing boutiques, art studios, cafes, bakeries, bars, and night clubs. She emerged from one shop with a turquoise sun hat and contrasting scarf, which she knotted around the strap of her tote. She felt glamorous as it trailed behind her like the colorful tail of a kite.

Lisa entered the tourist bureau and collected a handful of glossy brochures and maps depicting the local attractions.

"Pós boró na se voithíso?"

Lisa turned and smiled at the associate behind the counter. "Mílas Angliká?"

"Oh, sorry, I thought you were Greek. How can I help you?"

"Can you direct me to an olive wood carver?"

"Many shops sell olive wood products. Some shops carry a variety of items including olive wood carvings, olive oil, and olive oil soaps." She pointed toward the street. "There is a shop on the left corner that has some things."

"Thank you. I stopped in there. I am actually looking for a wood carver, perhaps an artist's gallery where they sell their carvings. I would like to speak to the artist."

"You want to meet an olive wood carver?"

"I do. Especially one that has been in business for many years. Would you have any information on local artists?"

The tourist associate straightened the blue neckerchief knotted at the neck of her white blouse. It matched her bureau vest with a Greek flag patch on the pocket. "I'll take a look."

She tugged on an old metal file drawer and coaxed it from the overburdened cabinet. She walked her fingers through the files. She pulled a few files, flipped through them, and crammed them back in.

"I have the artist's initials if that would help," Lisa called out.

The associate dug deeper and pushed the cranky drawer closed. "This is the only thing I have. It's a list of local artisans; some might be woodworkers. It hasn't been updated in years, but I could make a photocopy for you."

Over lunch at a taverna, Lisa studied the meager list. Written in Greek, it contained only a few addresses and phone numbers. It would take some research to determine whether it led to LA in 1967.

CHAPTER 9

> Set up road signs; put up guideposts.
> Mark well the path by which you came.
> —Jeremiah 31:21a (NLT)

Lisa spread the glossy brochures and maps across the sofa, and plotted her course for more island exploration the next day. With so many clues to investigate, she deliberated on a starting point.

Since it was the weekend, she decided to drive the coast road around the island and visit beaches in search of sand and sea glass. She planned records research for weekdays.

A knock came at the door. "It's Gianna."

"Hello . . . come in."

Gianna popped in with a basket on her arm. "I brought you some fresh eggs, vegetables, a cruet of olive oil, and an invitation."

Lisa helped Gianna settle the basket on the table. They exchanged a kiss on the cheek.

"Your vegetables are *gorgeous*. You've inspired me to start a garden."

"It's all Mediterranean diet, so it's healthy for you."

"So fresh and flavorful. Thanks for sharing your bounty. I ate on the roof terrace last night, and the lamb was amazing. Ah . . . and the stars were glorious."

Gianna beamed, "God blesses us, so we pass the blessings on to others." She unpacked the basket and replenished the kitchen. "Skender is grilling fresh fish over the fire tonight. He will deliver a portion to your door for your supper tonight. Did you have a good adventure today?"

"I explored Chora today. So picturesque. I shopped and visited the tourist bureau. Made it all the way to the church at the top, but I could not go in. It was locked."

"It is sad. So many beautiful church buildings here, but they are rarely open. Worshippers only have opportunity to attend those churches a few times a year."

"Why is that?"

"There are no priests in residence on Míos. So, the people must wait for them to come here and make the circuit."

Lisa frowned. "Hmmm."

"Now, the invitation. Please come to a gathering tomorrow night and meet our friends."

"Oh, Gianna, I don't know. I couldn't."

"You have other plans?"

"No—"

"Good!" Gianna clapped her hands. "Then you can come to our party."

"I don't want to intrude."

"Don't be silly. Just a casual evening around the pool with good Greek food, and lots of laughter. A perfect chance for you to make Greek friends and learn Greek culture. I promise you are welcome in this group. We are like family. Please say yes."

"Alright. Yes. What can I bring?"

"You bring *you*. Dress cool and comfy. Come to the pool at sunset. I promise, it is a special experience. Who knows? Maybe your life will never be the same again. Skender will deliver grilled fish in a little while." Gianna scampered away and joined Skender by the pool.

Lisa watched the sweet, young couple chatting by the grill and pondered the invitation. Already in major life flux, she resisted the notion that her life would never be the same again after a Saturday night party. Then she had another thought, a better thought: perhaps I should welcome this opportunity for change in my life. It's time to blow out the cobwebs. If I could consider riding a scooter around an island, maybe I could consider a lot of new adventures.

The next morning brought a ten-minute argument with the Fiat's rickety convertible frame. But after Lisa coaxed the top of the car into submission she set out, limbs slathered in sunscreen, sun hat tied on, and an island map spread across the passenger seat. The large, unruly map was in Greek but provided good visuals on roads and the lay of the land.

In town, locals and tourists clustered around the shops and ambled amid stalls at the Saturday farmers market by the docks. Lisa puttered past the hubbub, then turned east to circumnavigate the landmass counterclockwise. The two-lane road mirrored the coastline. Mountains rose sharply on her left. On her right, it clung perilously close to the edge of the cliff. To put one tire wrong meant a hundred-foot plunge to the brilliant blue sea. The scenery proved stunning.

The further north she drove, the road roller-coastered from cliffs to sea level and skimmed along the water's edge. With little traffic, Lisa took her time absorbing the sparkling waters and magnificent views.

Halfway around the east side of the island, Lisa pulled into a scenic overlook. The cloudless sky blended seamlessly with the Aegean. Neighboring islands dotted the horizon. They begged a visit.

Focused in her quest, Lisa snapped photos, continued driving north, and declined the roads with beach access. Obviously rocky rather than sandy, the shore seemed a "no brainer, Mom," as Cate might say. She'd need to look elsewhere for sand and sea glass.

The elevation crescendoed at the north end of the island. Lisa pulled over and hiked a narrow path to a lofty overlook. Her breath caught in her throat at the sight of the impressive 360-degree view. Sunlight shimmered on the water hundreds of feet below. Seabirds soared the thermal updrafts, suspended between heaven and earth. Tears spilled down her cheeks at their oneness with their Creator. She longed to join their carefree flight and soar without fear of falling . . . or failure.

Perched atop the jagged promontory, the Greek version of historical markers stood shaded under an olive branch arbor, the significance of the spot chiseled into the granite tablets. The left marker in Greek, the right in English. The English version read,

"Most north poin
t of Island Míos wh
ere ancient his
tory was happe
ned"

Lisa frowned and re-read it. She burst out laughing. The lettering ran from edge to edge on the skinny space. The marker in Greek was filled with inscription. Lisa decided it must actually detail the "ancient his tory was happe ned" there.

She said, "Fair enough. It gets the point across. I can look it up."

Lisa turned to head to the car. "Wow."

From this "most north poin t" observation site, she beheld much of the east and west coast of Míos laid out before her.

"I'm at the top of the world. Perfect place for a picnic."

She unshouldered her tote and lunched on bread, cheese, olives, fruit, and cold roasted lamb.

She savored the flavors. *Delicious! Why does food taste so marvelous al fresco?* Lisa realized life was too short to hurry through every meal in front of the television. She purposed to recalibrate her life, savor more meals al fresco, and celebrate the flavors and the beauty around her.

Lisa checked her watch and counted the time spent on the road. With a promise to return to this spot, she packed up and hiked to the Fiat. Half an island still to be explored, and a life-changing dinner date lay ahead.

Lisa found the western coast of Míos as impressive, and with its own unique terrain. Sun on her face and wind in her hair, she explored every hairpin curve of the road. Salt air filling her lungs, her spirit soared like the seabirds.

Lisa passed roads that led toward the sea, beach accesses perhaps, and occasional roads that led inward and climbed the barren hillsides. Lisa longed to explore every single path and learn its purpose and point of view.

She roared around a corner and happened upon the entrance to Giórgos Hill Winery. Heart in her throat, she careened into the turn-in and sped past the vineyard toward the collection of structures at the crest of Giórgos Hill.

Lisa gunned the Fiat toward the car park. It was full. She parked on the outer edge, grabbed her tote, and hurried toward the entrance. Her heartbeat quickened at the thought the little cork made it back around the world, finally returning home. She rehearsed questions to ask the owners and imagined their surprise at seeing the fifty-year-old cork.

As she neared the gate, her heart sank. Ahead of her, a wedding party and a crowd of guests moved through the gates into a courtyard. Unwilling to intrude, Lisa held back. Once they entered, Lisa approached the hostess.

"Hello . . . Chaírete."

"Chaírete. Me to gamílio párti?"

"Mílas Angliká?"

"Ah, sure, you with wedding party?"

"No. I hoped to talk to the owner of the winery."

"Very sorry. Today private party only. You come back?"

"Yes, of course. When?"

"Anytime we are open, except private party."

Lisa's shoulders dropped. A lump tightened in her throat, and she fought back tears. The cork was not on her agenda for that day, and caught up in the serendipitous moment of finding Giórgos Hill, she realized how important answers to Cynthia's mystery had become.

Back on the coast road, Lisa picked her spirits up and drove with new inspiration and determination. The road descended from Giórgos Hill to the south and curved along clinging to the shore.

She sighted a village ahead and passed the entrance to an impressive villa on a hilltop. Rock walls flanked the massive wooden gates. Drawn to it, Lisa would've turned in to explore it had the gates been open.

A few miles farther she entered the small village. The road led her within feet of a smattering of residences. A cat sat in one doorway watching her pass. In another, a man sat with a can of beer. He was trousered, barefoot, and wearing a torn undershirt and suspenders.

He read the newspaper, a half-spent cigarette hanging in the corner of his mouth. Lisa heard children's voices coming from within as dishes clattered in the kitchen.

Multi-level shops and a taverna lined the other side of the street. Saturday afternoon shoppers wandered in and out. A young woman, arms full with brown paper parcels, emerged from a market. Lisa parked and joined the flow of window shoppers. She passed a potter, a bread shop, an olive oil shop, a soap shop, and an olive wood shop.

Lisa pulled on the door of the olive wood shop. It was locked. She cupped her hands around her face, pressing her nose to the glass she peered inside. She spied a variety of olive wood bowls, trays, salt and pepper shakers, and sundry wood carvings, but no crosses.

She checked the sign on the door and checked her watch. A young boy on a bicycle pulled up next to her.

"To katástima eínai kleistó. Pigaínoun sto gámo."

"Mílas Angliká?"

"The store is closed. They go to wedding."

"Giórgos Iófos?"

"How you know?"

Lisa smiled at him. "I tried to go there, too."

He smiled back. "You come back on Monday. Tell them Vanko send you."

Lisa pulled a little money from her pocket. "Here. This is for your help."

"Thank you, Miss American lady." Vanko peddled away.

"Hey, what's the name of this village?"

He called over his shoulder, "Chorio"

Out of time for any further exploration, Lisa promised herself a return visit to Chorio and the olive wood shop and the sidewalk taverna. Her list of promises to herself grew ever longer.

CHAPTER 10

> For where two or three are
> gathered together in my name,
> there I am in the midst of them.
> —Matthew 18:20 (KJV)

*L*isa brushed the tangles out of her windblown hair, showered, and dressed for the dinner party by the pool. She pulled her shampooed hair into a sleek chignon and secured it with a tortoise shell comb at the nape of her neck. She slipped on a pale pink sundress, slid her feet into strappy, kitten-heel sandals, and draped a floral scarf about her shoulders.

Music drifted from the terrace, punctuated with the sound of conversation and laughter. Lisa checked her appearance in the mirror, poked a tissue and lip gloss into her pocket, and stepped outside.

Jazzy Greek tunes played on the stereo. Table lanterns flickered in the gathering darkness, and votives shimmered adrift the surface of the turquoise pool. Party lights strung about the terrace mimicked starlight. The jasmine and bougainvillea framed the arbor, their light fragrance sailing on the wind and mingling with savory aromas from the grill.

Lisa approached the gathering, keen to meet her new friends. She scanned the crowd for Gianna and Skender. She spotted Gianna, the accomplished hostess, setting a platter of food on the table. Gianna rushed to collect Lisa and draw her into the dynamic, intimate clique of four women gathered by the pool.

"Ladies, this is Lisa Abbott. Lisa, these are my sisters: Peri, Thalia, Mia, and Sophia."

"Hello, everyone. Wow, are you all *really* sisters?"

Everyone nodded enthusiastically. "Sisters in God's family," Gianna explained.

"Oh, I love it."

Gianna said, "Lisa's staying at the hotel. She's on Míos for a Greek adventure."

The ladies jumped in making introductions. "Hi, I'm Thalia Kyriáku. I'm happy you're brave enough to come to party."

"You'll love Thalia," Gianna smiled. "Her courage is amazing. Her spirit is strong, and she inspires us to be strong, too."

Thalia placed a hand over her heart. "God is my strength."

Thalia embraced Lisa, then looked into her eyes measuring her courage.

"Ah, you strong, too. *Steadfast.* I say you will conquer your adventure."

Lisa marveled at this jewel of a woman brimming with fiery zeal.

Thalia motioned toward the ladies. "We are *real* friends, so, I tell you about real me. I am forty-two. Divorce. Born on Míos to old goat farmer up that hill. I inherit goat farm. You hear goat bells? Those is my goat."

Gianna said, "Thalia turned her father's goat farm into a thriving business. It's not just goat milk anymore. She makes goat cheese, soaps, lotions, has an herb farm, and herbed olive oils. Those are Thalia's products in your kitchen and bath."

"They're fabulous. I plan to take home a suitcase filled with your products."

Gianna introduced the next woman. "This is Sophia Adamos, our angel, so pure in heart." Wavy blonde tresses encircled Sophia's head in a halo.

Sophia said, "I'm twenty-eight. Happy to be Hali's wife. He is youngest man over there. No babies yet, but God will give us baby. Hali and I are Greek, from Mios. Hali is carpenter and stone worker. He works with Skender. I have Glykó Amýgdalo. In English, Sweet Almond. It is bakery and coffee shop near port."

Gianna said, "Sophia's as sweet as her famous Sweet Almond Cakes. Sophia's bread is in your kitchen."

"Oh, wow, I've had some with every meal. I can't wait to visit your bakery and try your cake."

Gianna fondly grasped the hand of the most mature woman in the group. "This is Peri Rossi. She is a mother and grandmother to our God-gathered family. She is wise, fun-loving, and always surprising us with her crazy ideas. She reminds us to use our heads, but not get too serious."

Peri's blue eyes sparkled. "I am seventy-eight years young. I am seamstress, make dress for boutique. Have husband, five children, fourteen grandchildren, two great-grandchildren."

Lisa said, "Your nest was full. What a blessing."

"My nest was full and busy. *Whew!*" Peri said, "I give wisdom to you: remember, you can't do it all." She took Lisa's hand. "Most important thing—joy. God say be joyful, but people say 'no, I want busy, serious, and worry.' Why people not want God's joy? So, I teach these young women to stop busy and have joy and laughter."

Mesmerized by Peri's luminous countenance, Lisa vowed to heed Peri's wisdom.

Peri pointed. "See that old Greek man there? Telling the stories? That is Demetrios. I call him *My Demetri*. My husband for sixty years. *Sixty years!*"

Lisa looked past Peri and saw the men gathered around Demetri. Listening intently, they suddenly roared with laughter, snorted, and spewed drinks.

"That's My Demetri. We," she looked around at all the ladies for confirmation, and as they nodded, "we call him the 'ring leader.' He is retired fisherman, he tells fish stories. Don't start him on that. The young ones have adventures with Demetri."

ELIZABETH TOMME

Gianna said, "It is good for them. We encourage the guys to go have good times together. Let the men be men. Hali still tells stories about their last fishing trip."

Peri's eyes twinkled. "I have sixty years of adventure with My Demetri. Good thing I can laugh."

Lisa decided to find joy in her adventure on Míos, no matter where it led. "I hope I can have an adventure with you and Demetri."

Smiling, Peri nodded. "We take you."

Gianna said, "And, last introduction, this is Mia Monterrosa." Lisa smiled at the woman with the glorious mane of brown hair flowing over her shoulders and down her back. She exuded serenity.

"If you ever need calming, get with Mia. You'll immediately feel her quiet, patient, benevolent spirit. She is settled in her soul. She's taught us how to wait on the Lord, and on each other."

Mia drew Lisa into a warm embrace, then introduced herself. "I'm forty-six, wife to Javier—Javi—and mother to three teenage daughters. I homeschool them. My favorite pastime is research. I'm from Greece; Javi's from Spain and also works in construction with Skender and Hali."

With pride, Gianna announced, "Mia is an apiculturist. The jar of thyme honey in your kitchen is from Mia and her bees."

Lisa pictured this patient woman moving among the bees, harvesting their prized honey.

Mia asked, "Lisa—do you know you have been given a meaningful Greek name?"

"—No. I had no idea."

"It means, My God Is a Vow."

"Really?" Surprised and delighted, Lisa asked, "Like, God is making a vow to me?"

Mia considered this before responding, "I believe by naming you this, the namer proclaimed their belief that God was a faithful Covenant-Keeper with His people. Is it possible your mother and father chose your name to seal a Covenant they made with God?

"Ummm, not that I know of."

"They never told you your name held special meaning for them, or if they made a Covenant with God?"

"No . . . I just assumed they liked the name Lisa."

"Perhaps. Unless they were Greek scholars, in which case, I expect they named you with purpose."

Lisa's thoughts drifted to the Greek items her mother treasured.

Gianna said, "So, Lisa with the special name, tell us about yourself."

"Well, I am forty-nine years old. Widowed two years ago. Mother of one daughter, Cate. She is twenty-four and engaged to be married in a few months. I live in Colorado and run a family business. This is my first trip to Greece, and I have fallen in love with it. I wish I could stay forever. Now that I've met you all, tell me what spiritual gifts you see in Gianna."

Sophia responded immediately. "She has constant faith that endures all things."

"Mmmm. Yes, I see that in her, too. And she is nourishing and giving. She replenishes me in some way, every day." Lisa pointed to the group of men. "There are two more men over there. Who are they?"

Gianna explained. "The middle-aged, tall man is Fred Jackson—but call him Jack; he hates the name Fred. He's an American photographer and multi-media artist. He lives on Míos when he's not on location somewhere else." Gianna winked at Thalia. "We think Jack hopes to find love with Thalia."

Thalia blushed. The other ladies agreed with Gianna.

"And, there is Nicholas—Nico Scala." Gianna pointed to the oldest gentleman in the group. "He is eighty-five. He lost his wife, Maria, last year. He is brave and keeps going, but very lonely. We make sure he is with us as much as we can."

Peri said, "So, now you know who everyone is. Over time, God gathered us together into a family." Peri put a motherly arm around Lisa. "And now, you are part of our God-gathered family. You came here by yourself, but you are not alone on Míos, you have family here."

Inspired by meeting these new friends by their spiritual descriptions, Lisa purposed to look for the spiritual attributes of every person who came into her life. To see them first through Jesus' eyes rather than her own.

Skender and Javi pulled the meat from the grill. Skender called out, "It's ready, come eat."

They gathered around the table as the heat of day ebbed and the edges of everything disappeared into the shadows. Peri and Demetri seated Lisa between them like a new baby chick under their wing. In the joining of hands for prayer, Lisa felt the rough callouses from years of salt sea fishing on Demetri's large, strong hand. In contrast, Peri's smooth, delicate hand cradled hers. From each, she felt the warmth, strength, and peaceful assurance of one who has walked with God and lived a good life. Tears spilled from her eyes as she looked from one bowed head to another, overwhelmed by the love, joy, peace, patience, kindness, goodness, gentleness, and strength of Spirit so alive in these vibrant souls.

Gianna promised Lisa her life would never be the same after this evening. Indeed, it would not. How could she meet these precious people, behold the Godliness in their lives, and not be changed forever? With the exception of her parents, she never so fully witnessed the love of God in human form.

As they prayed, Lisa reflected on her name, "My God Is a Vow." She thought of her parents and how they loved her, and she them. Her life flashed before her eyes, and she was keenly aware of the goodness of God that followed her all the days of her life. Lisa prayed, "Father God, please reveal to me the story of my name and any Covenant my parents made with You. In Jesus Name, *Amen.*"

CHAPTER 11

*And all that believed were together,
and had all things in common;
And they, continuing daily with one accord
in the temple, and breaking bread
from house to house,
. . . with gladness and singleness of heart.*
—Acts 2:44, 46 (KJV)

Demetri refilled Lisa's wine glass. "Peri say to me you come to Míos for adventure. I *live* for adventure. Tell me what you going to do."

Mia yelled out, "We *all* want to hear."

Conversation at the table grew quiet. Lisa felt all attention fall to her. Across the table, Gianna raised her eyebrows in playful challenge.

Sophia reminded, "You are among friends."

"And *family*," Peri chimed in.

Lisa drew a deep breath and put it all on the line, praying they would not decide she was a silly American. Surprisingly, everyone listened with rapt attention. Silence hung over the table when she finished. Lisa looked from face to face and found they were deep in thought.

Hali broke the silence first. "Please, I would like to see the wooden cross. I know a family of woodworkers in the chorio."

"I would like to touch the sand," Demetri said, "As fisherman, I know the beaches—the sand. I must see the sand."

Peri reached across Lisa and squeezed Demetri's hand. "You are good man. You *know* sand." Peri looked at Lisa. "My Demetri, he *knows* sand! He help solve your mystery."

Thalia and Mia exchanged eager glances. "We, Mia and I, will help with the velvet bag and bottle. We work with fragrance, sometimes incense in our products—infusions in the soaps, honey, and olive oils. You let us help you, yes?"

Stunned by their responses, Lisa wiped away tears. "*Yes.*"

Gianna jumped in next. "I will help with hotel research. We belong to a hotel owners society. Maybe there is some history or record of old hotels. I will need to make a copy of the hotel stationery."

Jack chimed in. "I can go to the winery with you. I love winery research and it's a magnificent venue to photograph."

"Hang on, that's a group activity!" Skender said.

Several others jumped onboard. "Group activity. Group activity!" The excitement about the winery gained momentum.

Sophia chimed in, "I will give you Sweet Almond Cakes, pastries, and coffee for your adventure. Come to bakery anytime. My treat."

The landscape of Lisa's life changed so dramatically Saturday night, the excitement robbed her of sleep. As if remembering a wonderful movie, she replayed the scenes over in her mind.

Lisa intended to hit the ground running Sunday morning. Hearing of her plan, Mia, the patient, calm one, persuaded Lisa to put her research plans on hold until Monday, and offered an enticing proposal.

"Come join us tomorrow for house church. We all meet together on Sundays for worship and a meal. Javi and I host this week at our house."

"I'd love to. Gianna told me the church buildings on the island rarely hold services, and I hate to miss."

"The church buildings are beautiful to look at, but they are empty on the inside. All of us here, in our separate lives, we knew something was missing. We wanted more than empty building. We met each other here and there, and over time, God brought us together. Followers of Jesus. We began to study and pray together. One day we realize, *church* is not empty building. It lives in the heart of living, breathing people."

Sunday morning Lisa rode with the Gatakis to Javi and Mia's. Located on the southern coast of Míos, the Monterrosa home was a long, flat-roofed, meandering house that backed up to a mountainside and sprawled along the edge of a cliff. Set amid rocky, arid soil, a temperate sea breeze, and plentiful wild thyme shrubs, it was home to Mia's apiary.

The backside of the house faced the ocean, with walls made of sliding glass panels that opened onto a wide, paved terrace overlooking the sea. Mia said they spent most of their time in the outdoor living spaces.

Everyone gathered on the terrace. Lisa's heart overflowed with a renewed sense of joy as she joined them in worship. She, too, realized something was missing from her life. She longed for more, as well. The church she attended seemed more like the empty buildings Mia described.

Now that she joined her own heart with the hearts of living, breathing people, she did not think she could go back. Lisa thought of the Psalm, "Taste and see that the LORD is good." (NLT) She had tasted and seen that the LORD was truly good, and was ready to jump in, fully trusting.

During the meal, Lisa sat across from Nico Scala. Realizing Nico was staring at her, she smiled back.

"Oh, I stare at you. Please forgive," he pointed at Lisa. "I noticed your gold locket. Please, may I look at it?"

Lisa put her hand to her chest and fingered the antique locket. "This? You want to see my necklace?"

Nico shrugged, "I was jewelry maker many years on Míos. It was my trade."

"Yes, of course." Lisa unclasped the chain and handed it to him.

To Lisa's surprise, Nico pulled a jeweler's loupe from his breast pocket. He peered at length, examining every aspect of the piece of jewelry. Satisfied, he lowered the loupe from his eye. "It is quite unique and beautifully made." Nico handed the locket to Lisa.

"It's my favorite necklace. I wear it often. My mother gave it to me for my sixteenth birthday."

"Eh—so, this is *very* expensive Greek jewelry. You know this?" His eyebrows arched in question.

Stunned and unsure she heard correctly, Lisa shook her head, brow furrowed. "No . . . no . . . I . . . *what?* Did you say it is *Greek* jewelry?"

Nico said, *"Expensive* Greek jewelry." Lisa stared at the locket in her hand. Nico repeated, "Yes, I am sure. I *know* Greek jewelry."

By this time, Peri and Thalia picked up on the conversation. Peri reached for the locket. Thalia hovered. Peri held it by the chain. "This is beautiful. Look everyone. Nico just say Lisa has Greek jewelry."

The men, at the opposite end of the table, stopped talking for a half-moment and looked at the necklace dangling from Peri's hand. Without missing a beat, they returned to their conversation on sports. The women leaned in close and each, in turn, held the locket.

Gianna asked, "Did you buy this here on Míos?" She'd missed the first part of the conversation.

"No, my mother gave it to me on my sixteenth birthday."

Gianna said, "Quite a gift! Especially for a sixteen-year-old. Did you know you were wearing another one of your mother's clues around your neck?"

"I had no idea." This shocked Lisa as much as the other items she found. Lisa bit her lip. "Nico, please show me how you know this is Greek."

Gianna, who now held the necklace, handed it back to Nico. Lisa sat next to Nico. He handed her the loupe. The ladies leaned in as he explained the tell-tale signs.

"This piece was handmade by a jewelry maker; most likely one of a kind. Made of high-quality gold. The design on the face of locket, intricate, three-dimensional floral filigree overlay studded with precious stones." Nico pointed with the tip of his pen. "Each flower, tiny recreation of flora indigenous to Greece. The flowers, with rubies in center, represent the Greek Paeonía Parnassica, eh, the peony. Why ruby? The red peony grows high on Mount Parnassus above ancient Delphi. Flower is named after Paean, Greek mythological healer."

Lisa studied the intricate details through the loupe.

"Now . . . next flora on locket. Achillea Ambrosiaca, eh, called Olympus Yarrow." Nico pointed. "See these leaves here . . . here . . . here . . . and all these clusters of flowers?" Lisa looked through the loupe again.

"Each flower cluster embellished with diamonds to represent white flower."

"Those are really diamonds and rubies on the locket?"

"*Oh, yes.*"

Precious gold, rubies, diamonds—Lisa's head swam. "Please, tell me about the Yarrow."

Nico corrected her. "Olympus Yarrow. Yarrow flower is found all over world, but *Olympus Yarrow* only on Mount Olympus, most important mountain to Greek mythology. Again, like the Paeonia, this flower thrives high on Greek mountain."

Peri put her arm around Lisa and squeezed her shoulder.

"Two more things," Nico said.

"There's more?"

"Look at border around design."

"That scroll pattern?"

"Greek key, eh—Greek fret pattern from ancient Greece. See? Small section of it looks like key. It is symbol of infinity, forever—eternal." Nico looked about at his surroundings, certain he would see the highly used Greek symbol on something. "There. Look at tiles around swimming pool."

Lisa recognized the same repeating geometric pattern above the waterline.

"Oh," Lisa said, turning her attention back to the locket and the scroll design around the edge.

"Now, last and most important Greek symbol on locket." Nico pointed to the front, bottom edge of the oval locket. "There. Greek cross of Jesus!"

"*Oh, my.*" Lisa placed a hand over her heart, then eagerly brought the loupe to her eye.

"Maker or recipient was Greek, *and* believer in Jesus! Everything on locket has special meaning."

Lisa looked through the loupe and, for the first time, beheld the square Greek cross expertly crafted amongst the intricate floral pattern. Without the loupe, it appeared to be part of the leaf design. However, once seen, with or without the loupe, she could not unsee it.

The locket was like God's love and presence in her life. An extravagant gift, given unconditionally to a much-loved daughter, it was always with her. It was beautiful on the surface, but its deeper beauty must be sought. Lavishly fashioned, it was undeserved and given in love at a great price.

"A treasure," Nico said. "Necklace and locket is absolute Greek treasure. I am thankful for opportunity to experience such artistry."

Silence hung in the air. Still holding the locket, Nico opened it with all the ladies watching. "Do you know? Did this ever have photographs inside?"

Lisa sighed. "No. No, my mother put no photos in it when she gave it to me. She probably thought I'd want to put in pictures of my boyfriends. I always meant to put in photos of my parents since they gave it to me . . . somehow, I never got around to it. I wish I had so they would've known how much they meant to me."

Peri said firmly, "They knew. Not need picture to know this."

The locket and loupe were passed from woman to woman.

"Nico, how can I thank you? I would have never known if not for you. Can you help me find the jeweler who made it?"

Nico shrugged his skepticism. "Many years have passed. It could be impossible. But for you, I try."

CHAPTER 12

Dear Lisa . . .

Lisa stared at the ceiling as if the answers to all her questions were written there. Only a shaft of pale moonlight beamed across the ceiling and angled down the wall. She rolled to her side and checked her watch. Two a.m. She pulled the sheet over her head. Repetitious thoughts threatened to short-circuit her brain. She remembered little else since Nico examined her locket.

She made pleasant conversation with everyone, but her mind reeled at the thought her favorite locket was expensive Greek jewelry, given by her mother for her sixteenth birthday. She didn't remember the ride home with Skender and Gianna.

"Ugh!" Lisa said, rubbing her eyes. "Maybe I'm in some kind of shock. I'm talking to myself, but that's not unusual. I wonder how you treat yourself for shock? Should I elevate my feet? My head? Ummm . . . no, nothing's swollen or bleeding."

Lisa threw the covers aside, sitting up in the bed. "Drink water. Lots of water."

It helped her thirst, but did nothing for her racing thoughts.

Greece. Greece. Greece. Greek Hotel Stationery. Greek cork. Greek incense. Greek olive wood. Greek locket—expensive Greek locket. Nothing in my life was ever about Greece. Now, everything is Greece. Greece. Greece. Why?

"Okay, I'll talk it out. That always helps. Let's do the math. Mom died of breast cancer at fifty. I was twenty-eight, four years older than Cate is now. Yikes, I was young when I lost her. Certainly not ready for it. But old enough to be trusted with secrets. I think I could have handled it. So why didn't she tell me?"

Lisa pulled on a robe and paced. Standing over the kitchen sink, she ate a slice of bread with butter and honey. She licked the honey dripping from her fingers.

"Mmmm, yum. Oh, I wish I had some chocolate . . . that always helps in a crisis. Note to self: Find a Greek chocolate shop tomorrow. Buy lots of it."

Lisa poured a glass of cold milk and stared out the window into the darkness.

"So, no reason to think anyone but Mom put the velvet bag in the wedding dress box. Obviously, she had to do it before her death, no later than 1996. That means it's been there unnoticed, at least 20 years. When did I last look in that box? I dunno. I think in the mid '80s, as a teenager?"

Greece. Greek cork. Greek hotel stationery. Greek locket . . .

"Take your thoughts captive, Lisa. Process . . . talk it out." Lisa sighed and refocused. "Okay, two theories: She meant it to stay hidden. She meant it to be found. Professor Diákos, Cate, and Silvie believe she meant me to find it. So . . . why hide it there? Why not her underwear drawer? We would have found it there upon her death. Why leave it to chance for me to *maybe* open the dress box one day?

No, not chance. She *knew* I'd eventually open that box again. Either out of nostalgia or necessity, like for Cate to wear it or cleaning out the attic if the cabin were sold. She knew that no matter what, I would preserve her wedding dress. Okay. . .so, she definitely meant for it to be found."

Lisa relaxed a little. At least her thoughts were more productive now instead of just churning. Something clicked. Lisa's own words echoed in her head. She had told Cate, *"Your Grandmother was intentional about what was important to her."*

Lisa put her hands to her head and massaged her temples. "Ughhh! She did not want Dad or me to find it upon her death." Click. "*Dad!* She did not want *Dad* to find it. That's why she put it in a place she knew he would not look, but *I* would. Dad never went to the attic. The Greek items went unnoticed for at least 20 years. . . Dad lived another fourteen years after her death."

Lisa opened the door and sat in the cool night air on the terrace. Lights on fishing boats trolling beyond the harbor bobbed and winked. Lisa watched their steady progress. Tomorrow there would be fresh octopus hanging on the line at the markets.

So, the intentional Cynthia Brenner meant for her daughter, not her husband, to find her Greek treasures later, rather than sooner.

"Why not go ahead and leave a note of explanation in the velvet bag? A simple letter outlining the details would have done nicely."

Lisa wrote the letter out loud,

"Dear Lisa,

When the doctor told me not to buy any more green bananas, I went through my things and tied up all the loose ends. I know you enjoy a good laugh, but don't bother looking, I've already burned all the embarrassing pictures of myself . . . except for the one of me wearing the flying pig suit and the Groucho Marx glasses, nose and mustache. I could not bring myself to torch that one. Hopefully, it will make you smile. You can find that photo in the top of the old chest of drawers by the west dormer window in the attic.

So, down to the business at hand. You have just found other things I could not part with, my Greek treasures. The summer after my high school graduation, my boyfriend spent the summer in Greece.

He brought these little mementos back to me. They're not valuable to anyone but me, but he was my first true love, and I simply could not throw them away.

On the off chance your father found them, I did not want him to misunderstand or be hurt. So, I hid them here in a place I was certain he would never look. He was not one for rummaging through the attic. And, if he does, he'll also find this note of explanation . . . so I suppose I've covered all the bases.

By the time you find this, my heart will have been captivated by much greater treasures in heaven. So . . . keep 'em or pitch 'em, whatever you want.

Love, Mom."

Lisa sighed. It sounded just like her mother. Then, thinking of her father, she giggled. If Cynthia wanted to put her treasures in a place her husband would not find them, she could have hidden them in plain sight.

She could have left them on the bathroom counter by his toothbrush or in the dishwasher. Her dad was forever looking for his toothbrush and never put a dish in the dishwasher.

As long as Cynthia had not tied them to the television remote, her secret would have been safe . . . forever. Lisa remembered one more thing and added,

"P.S. Don't pitch the locket I gave you for your sixteenth birthday! It is very expensive Greek jewelry."

Lisa laughed, and the tension in her body dissipated. At the sound of her mother's voice in her head, she cried. The tension built up over the past weeks finally broke. She sobbed. Tears spilled onto her cheeks.

"I really miss you, Mom," she said. Her voice all stuffy from crying sounded more like, "I reedy biss you, Bomb."

She laughed again. It was just the kind of moment her mom would have laughed at, too. Lisa pulled a tissue from her pocket and blew her nose. The cry felt good.

A part of her heart ached since she realized there was something important to her mother she did not know or understand. They had always been close. No secrets—until now. In some ways Cynthia had been more like a friend than a mother, especially once Lisa reached her young adult years.

Her thoughts reverted back to the discovery of the locket. She did more math in her head. *Forty-nine minus sixteen.* She stood abruptly and paced.

"Oh . . . my . . . gosh! Thirty-three years." Utter disbelief swept over her. "For thirty-three years I've worn this locket with absolutely no idea about *any* of this."

Lisa's head tilted back, and she rolled her eyes. "And, we were together for twenty-eight years, Mom, and not one word about Greece. Really, Mom? Really?"

Lisa shook her head. If her mom had trusted her with the necklace, why not also trust her with her other secrets?

CHAPTER 13

※

> Jesus said ... Give generously
> and generous gifts will be given back to you ...
> Abundant gifts will pour out upon you
> with such an overflowing measure ...
> —Luke 6:38 (TPT)

At two o'clock Monday afternoon, Hali and Sophia picked Lisa up from the hotel. Tote bag in hand, Lisa climbed up into the cab of Hali's work truck.

Sophia sat next to Hali. Lisa's feet straddled the toolbox on the passenger floorboard. Building plans, levels, and tape measures lined the dashboard against the windshield. It reminded Lisa of John's work truck, always filled with the tools of his trade. For years she rode next to him, in his mobile office.

The three of them chatted as Hali drove past the harbor toward the western side of the island. Lisa recognized landmarks from her trip around the island on Saturday.

"Are we going to Chorio?"

"Which one?" Sophia asked.

"The little village called Chorio. I stopped there the other day."

"I think you are confused by our Greek language."

"Umm . . . I'm sure you're right. Saturday I was told the village was called Chorio."

Hali and Sophia shared a look. Hali said, "It is called chorio, but that not its name. That is what it is. Chorio is Greek word for village; it is not name of village."

"Oh. Huh. Is there more than one chorio on the island."

"There are two chorio on Míos."

Lisa rubbed her brow. "Is the other one called chorio, too?"

"Yep," Hali explained, "and chora is not the name of the town by the harbor. Chora means town. The villages and town on Míos actually do not have names."

"Got it. How do you distinguish between one chorio and another chorio?"

"Easy," Hali said. "This chorio where you saw the olive wood shop, it have stores, fish market . . . it is by the sea, on the west. The other chorio is in middle of island on high mountain. So, seaside chorio, and mountain chorio."

Skeptical of the system, Lisa chose to find it wonderfully Greek.

Sophia narrated interesting facts about the countryside and landmarks.

"If you stop at that overlook, watch out. There is donkey there. If you have hat, donkey come behind and steal from your head. Stole Hali's hat and chew it up."

Sophia pointed out an unlikely building by the water's edge. "That is Psarás. It has been there many years. It is fisherman's taverna. Fresh octopus, so delicious. You can go there by land or sea. There is marina where boats come in and dock."

Lisa pictured squiggly arms covered in suction cups. She was feeling adventurous, but not sure she could eat octopus.

At the seaside chorio, Hali parked on the street near the olive wood shop Lisa found on Saturday. They bailed out of the truck. Lisa started toward the shop. Yet Hali took Sophia by the hand and started off in another direction. Lisa watched for a moment, and hurried to catch up.

"I thought we were going to that olive wood shop."

Hali led them away from the main street and called back over his shoulder, "Not that one. We see my friend first. Go there if this does not work."

Hali turned down a narrow passage that led between two buildings, ascended a steep climb of stone steps, and took them across a sun-drenched courtyard and through an arched passageway. He knocked on the fourth door on the left. Machinery whirred on the other side of the door. Hali knocked again. The machinery stopped. The door creaked as it opened inward.

"Hali!" A stout young man covered in sawdust gathered Hali in a bear hug. Neither cared that he deposited saw dust on Hali's clean T-shirt and jeans.

"Luca!"

They slapped each other on the arm and traded fake punches.

"Hey, man. It's about time you called me. How long has it been? Come in, come in. Hey, Sophia." He opened his arms for a hug.

Sophia laughed and raised her hands in protest. "Hali is a mess now. I love you from here."

Luca pulled a clump of sawdust from his apron and poofed it in Sophia's direction.

Hali motioned toward Lisa. "Luca, this is our friend, Lisa. Lisa, meet Luca Adino, III. He is third generation for this wood shop. We all grew up together."

Surprised, Lisa looked from Hali to Luca. "Luca Adino, III. Hali—you found *LA, 1967?*"

"I think so."

Luca shook Lisa's hand, motioning for them to come into the shop. The space was filled with workbenches, saws, and lathes. An array of carving tools, angles, and levels hung on the walls. Masses of wood curls piled up on all surfaces.

Floor to ceiling wood-paned windows along the back wall admitted natural light to the artist's carving studio. The dusty glass yielded a generous view of the Aegean framed by red bougainvillea that spilled down the corners of the building from the rooftop above. It was an inspiring space, scented with wood, tongue oil, wax, and stain.

Carved bowls, trays, cutting boards, trivets, spoons, spice boxes, mortars, pestles, wall art, statues, nativities, and crucifixes lined the shelves. Filled with peace and inspiration, Lisa wished to examine every creation.

Rolls of yellowed drafting paper filled shelves, and half-spent pencils, clamps, and cheesecloth overflowed their bins. The dusty shop was steeped in purpose and laden with what was, and what would be. Awed, Lisa welcomed the mantle of generational history that filled the space and settled into her awareness.

Luca interrupted her thoughts. "Hali tells me you have a carved wooden cross he thinks came from our shop."

"Yes!" Lisa smiled back.

"I get my papa, Luca Adino, Jr." He went into the back room, and after a brief exchange of dialogue, returned with his father. Luca, Jr., embraced Hali and Sophia.

"Ta paidiá megálosan."

Sophia translated for Lisa. "He says, 'The children grew up.'"

Hali introduced Lisa. Luca, Jr., welcomed her with a quiet, gentle smile.

"Please—" He motioned Lisa to a workbench.

Lisa withdrew the olive wood cross from the purple velvet bag and extended it toward Luca, Jr. Unmoving, he stared at it. Lisa placed it in his hand. He ran his fingers over the surface and nodded. Lisa watched closely as a serene expression filled his countenance. Finally, he exchanged a knowing look with Hali, "Nai, nai."

Sophia put a hand on Lisa's arm. "He says, 'Yes, yes!' He knows this piece."

Filled with excited unbelief, Lisa waited as Luca, Jr., examined it further under an illuminated magnifying glass.

He stared at the initials and date carved into the wood. At last, he touched his fingertips to his lips, kissed them, gently laid them over the initials, then crossed himself.

Luca, Jr., snapped off the light and pushed it aside. He put the cross to his chest, savored the moment, and handed the cross back to Lisa.

"Thank you for me to see and hold."

Lisa nodded.

Luca, Jr., wiped tears from his eyes, speaking in Greek. Hali translated, "I know this carving—Ágios Stavrós tou Sotíra mas—this

Holy Cross of our Savior. I watched my papa, Luca Adino, Sr., make it."

As these words penetrated her understanding, Lisa gasped. Sophia grabbed her arm with excitement.

Luca, Jr., motioned around the room, spoke, and Hali translated. "As a young boy, I played here in my papa's wood shop. He taught me to carve woods. Then, together, we teach my son to carve woods." Luca became more animated as he relayed his story. "Then one day, his friend told him about Jesus, and he believed and was baptized. The next day he carve this cross you hold in your hands. This was *first* cross my papa *ever* carved."

Lisa could not imagine how her mother came to have this very special cross.

"That same day, the man who baptize him came to buy a present for someone special. He asked papa if he can buy olive wood cross. My papa make that cross for himself, but he gave it to his friend. I ask papa why he give that man his baptism cross, and he say to me, 'Jesus say to give your coat if he asks for it,' so I give him this cross.'"

Lisa stopped Hali, desperate for him to translate something for her to Luca, Jr. "Tell him I give this cross back to him. It belongs to his papa."

Hearing the translation, Luca, Jr., stepped toward Lisa. He gently closed her fingers around the cross and urged it back toward her. Hali translated his words. "Efcharistó—Thank you, you are meant to have it." Luca Jr., smiled at Lisa. "Wait, I show you something."

He went to the other room and returned with an identical olive wood cross. He passed it around for them to see.

Hali translated. "That night, my papa make another cross for himself, just like first cross. Papa kept it here in the shop all his days." He crossed himself, "My papa passed to heaven last month."

Lisa bowed her head, "Luca, I am so sorry."

His grief fresh, Luca, Jr., covered his eyes with his hands and wept. He sniffed, straightened, and watched with pride as Hali, Sophia, and Lisa took turns holding the two crosses.

Luca, Jr., explained, "My papa honor God with the special beauty of these first two crosses he carved. Only two of a kind. I was six years old when this happen. Papa taught me the lesson, love others freely like Jesus love them. Papa love Jesus so much he make many more crosses of Jesus, but with different carving. In this shop, we *never* sell cross of Jesus. Papa give them all away."

Lisa held Cynthia's cross tightly against her breast and wept. Sophia wrapped her arms around Lisa and wept with her. Luca, Jr., wept again.

Luca, Jr., motioned with the second cross in his hand and spoke in English. "Your mother's cross came full-circle."

Luca, Jr., spoke in Greek. Hali said, "He is happy you have it. He wonders how you got it."

Lisa wiped away her tears and sniffed. "My mother passed to heaven twenty years ago. I just found it in my mother's treasures. I do not know where she got it. Can you tell me the name of the man who received this cross from your papa?"

Luca, Jr., shook his head, "He never came to see papa again."

Lisa nodded. Lisa asked Hali, "Please tell him I am thankful to meet him. I am honored to know the son and grandson of such a Godly man."

Hali said, "He says it is honor to meet daughter of the woman who kept this cross. He says come back when he is not crying. He say you have the cross for special reason. He is sure God will show you why. He say he love you freely with love of Jesus."

As with the locket, Lisa was shocked by all she learned about Cynthia's wooden cross. She was awed to think God had lodged her at a hotel whose owners knew the man who knew the man who carved the cross in 1967.

Hand in hand, Hali and Sophia led Lisa back to the street. Lost in thought, Lisa fell behind, stopped, and stared out to sea.

Sophia asked, "Lisa? —Lisa? Are you okay?"

"Sorry. It's all so much. A month ago, I did not know any of this. Now, I find my mom had all these things from Greece. And, it's all significant. But I don't know *why* she had them."

"Luca, Jr., is right. *You* have the cross now for a special reason. God will show you why. Just keep trusting Him."

"Just think, if I found my mother's things sooner, I could have met Luca's papa. He could have told me about the man who led him to

Jesus. The man he gave the cross to. Maybe he knew why my mother ended up with it."

"Luca Jr., said the man came to buy a present for someone special. Maybe the someone special was—"

"My mother." Lisa's chest tightened and it became difficult to breathe.

Lisa turned to Sophia. "Is there a chocolate shop in this chorio?"

CHAPTER 14

⁕

> She is clothed with strength and dignity,
> and she laughs without fear of the future.
> She carefully watches everything
> in her household
> and suffers nothing from laziness.
> —Proverbs 31:25, 27 (NLT)

*L*isa paced and fidgeted with the Fiat keys. Itchy to make progress on the investigation, she deliberated between Hotel Mákari research and Giórgos Hill Winery research.

Everyone was eager to help Lisa put the pieces of the puzzle together. Nico busied himself researching jewelry-makers, and Demetri the sand and sea glass. They reported no findings yet.

Gianna and Lisa researched Greek hotel databases the day after she visited the Adino wood shop. So far, nothing on the Hotel Mákari. Lisa hoped to hear something soon from Thalia and Mia on the Árgyros Thymíama.

The findings on Lisa's gold locket and the origins of the olive wood cross exceeded everyone's imaginations and fanned their obsession to figure out more.

Lisa checked her watch. Eight-thirty a.m. She decided to visit Sophia's bakery. She grabbed her tote and stepped out the door in search of Gianna. She found her in the gardener's shed, just as she hung her spade on the wall and pulled off her gardening gloves.

"Hi!"

"Kaliméra . . . good morning!" Gianna picked up a basket laden with produce. "Would you like some fresh veggies?"

"Yes, thank you." Lisa jingled her car keys. "Want to go to town with me?"

"That sounds fun. Where are you going?"

"Glykó Amýgdalo."

"Yum." Gianna checked her watch and tapped the dial with indecision.

Lisa tempted her. "Sweet Almond Cakes . . ."

"I can't say no to that. I would love to see Sophia, and I *need* coffee. Strong coffee." Gianna yawned and pulled the gardening apron over her head. "We better take two cars. I must be back by noon for guest check-ins. You're going to have neighbors."

Lisa followed Gianna to the bakery, and they double-parked in the owner's spot in the back. It was a busy Wednesday morning at the harbor. Vendor trucks were making deliveries, and the ferry had just burped a new gaggle of tourists onto the gangplank at the dock.

Together they entered the hive of activity inside the sunny corner shop. The aroma of coffee and pastries drew them to queue up at the counter. Lisa ignored the decorated menu boards and feasted her eyes on the glass pastry cases. She already knew her order.

Lisa's eyes wandered around Sophia's charming place of business. Pendant lights accented with colorful blown glass shades dangled artfully from the beamed wood ceiling. It was spacious and airy with tall white walls and lots of windows.

Comfy chairs, sofas, and coffee tables clustered around sisal mats in the center of the space. Tables and chairs banked the windowed corners, and quiet reading nooks snuggled between library shelving at the far wall.

The hum of casual conversation and Greek folk music gave the place a laid-back vibe. Beyond the windows, life happened at a steady pace, and the Aegean sparkled in the midmorning sun as the ferries skimmed to and fro.

Lisa said, "Sophia has done well. Everything about her shop is perfect."

"I *knew* you'd love it."

"What does that say?" Lisa pointed to the Greek writing painted on the wall above the coffee bar.

"I will sing unto the LORD as long as I live: I will sing praise to my God while I have my being. My meditation of him shall be sweet: I will be glad in the LORD. —Psalm 104:33–34 (KJV). Sophia says it is her life verse."

"It is so like Sophia. She *lives* that."

Gianna beamed, "She continually inspires me to fall in love with God over and over again."

"She truly glorifies God in everything she does."

Gianna said, "Most business owners are afraid to openly praise God, afraid to offend people and hurt their business. Not Sophia. She *dedicated* her business to God. If someone does not like it, she says to them, 'Let me *tell you* about Jesus. When you know about Jesus, you will love him, too!'"

Lisa reflected on the opportunities she'd squandered. Too often she held back, afraid to offend others rather than speak of her faith. Humbled and convicted, she decided to become a living testimony, to inspire others as Sophia did.

Sophia saw them and rushed around the counter for hugs.

"I am so happy. You came in."

"I love your shop. We want some of everything. And I'm paying," Lisa said bursting with expectation.

Sophia shook her head. "You are *my* guests."

Sophia gave instructions to the barista and motioned for Lisa and Gianna to follow her to a table in the corner. Within moments, a tray arrived with an assortment of sweet and savory pastries and a carafe of coffee. Over the next hour, they visited and feasted on the sweet manna that soothed their hearts and inspired conversation, bonding them even tighter as sisters in Christ.

At the sound of a ringtone, everyone including guests at

surrounding tables checked pockets and purses to identify the recipient. Lisa waved her phone in the air. "It's me."

Everyone resumed eating. "It's Thalia," Lisa mouthed to Sophia and Gianna upon answering. "Uh-huh. Oh . . . uh-huh. Wow. I'm with Sophia and Gianna now at the bakery. Uh-huh . . . okay. Sure." Lisa looked up. Sophia and Gianna stared with curiosity. "Uh-huh. Yes. We'll be right there. Bye." Turning to her two companions, Lisa said, "Thalia and Mia found something. Mia's on her way to Thalia's now. They want us to come."

Gianna checked her watch. "Oh, no. I've got to get back to the hotel."

"I'll call her back and arrange another time."

"No. Go without me. Sophia?"

"I'm in." Sophia took off her apron. She ran out the door with Lisa and piled into the somewhat rickety, yet so far trustworthy convertible.

The little Fiat struggled to climb the rocky track to Thalia's goat farm. Lisa kept one foot on the accelerator, the other ready at the clutch. Sophia navigated.

"Turn in that gate on the right. The road will lead to the house."

They trundled along a quarter mile driveway past large olive, fig, and eucalyptus trees that encircled a collection of rustic, red-tile-roof rock buildings.

Lisa said, "Thanks for coming. Not sure I'd find this place on my own."

Sophia pointed. "Park over there in the goats, by the house."

"Will they move?"

"If not, Thalia will make a delicious goat stew for us."

"Is that supposed to be funny?"

"Not to the goat."

The goats parted like the Red Sea. Once parked, the curious herd mobbed the Fiat. Blank-eyed, they chewed their cud. Sophia reached over honking the horn, letting Thalia know they arrived.

"She's probably in the barn up to her elbows in goat milk."

Wedging car doors open, they got out, nudging their way through the Bovidae welcoming party. Thalia emerged from the farthest barn, smiled, and waved. She wiped her hands on her apron and lifted her forearm to push a wayward strand of hair away from her eyes. She trudged toward them in red galoshes.

Thalia called across the barnyard. "Geia!"

Sophia translated. "She says, hi."

"Geia!" Lisa called out.

Lisa and Sophia turned at the sound of another vehicle. Mia's car flew through the gate in a cloud of dust. She nudged her way through the goatherd and parked next to the Fiat.

They exchanged kisses and hugs. Happy for the company, Thalia spoke in a mix of Greek and English. Her hair was piled up on her head. Her jeans worn, her sleeveless T-shirt exposed muscular, tan arms. She was glowing and looked marvelous. Lisa made a note to self: find a way to look as glamorous as Thalia the next time I work in the yard.

Thalia led them to the two-story farmhouse. At the kitchen door, she shed her mucking boots and led them in.

"You are backdoor friends."

The pale honey-colored structure was rock-walled inside and out. The kitchen was cool, open and airy. Brightly hued pottery lined the open, wooden shelves, and copper pots hung from a rack over the stove.

A book lay open on the worn wooden table, surrounded by mismatched chairs. In the center, a crazed milk pitcher was filled to overflowing with an unruly array of anemone and iris. No doubt, the vibrant magenta, sunny yellow, broody indigo, and playful pink blossoms came from Thalia's garden.

Upside-down bundles of herbs, spices, and flora bound with twine hung from wooden pegs along the wall. Woven baskets lined the shelves of the cool, dark scullery, which was also safe harbor to crockery and a wine collection.

Obviously for Thalia, life was beauty, and beauty was life. In her love for the land and its yield, every little thing was celebrated.

The savory scent of meals past hung in the air. In the windowed back wall, French doors opened to the terrace overlooking the Aegean Sea. They entered the main room. Set at a right angle to the kitchen, its bank of French doors also opened onto the terrace. The house seemed to breathe and sigh lazily with the gentle breeze filling each room.

On one wall, narrow stone stairs led to the second floor. On another wall, a fireplace stood, with firewood stacked neatly in a niche. A basket of gnarly branches sat close by for kindling. Comfortable furniture was centered in the room on a thread-worn, Turkish rug. The bespoken character of the house evolved from a mixture of old and new over the past century. Thalia, bound to this farmhouse for a lifetime, wisely chose which bits of inheritance to keep and which to replace.

They wandered out to the terrace while Thalia freshened up. Scrubbed and lavender-scented Thalia returned in fresh clothes and barefoot. Her damp, shampooed hair was brushed back from her forehead and held by a ribbon.

Thalia served a pitcher of iced water with cucumber slices and mint sprigs. Helping, Sophia carried a platter of sliced tomatoes, olives, figs, and goat cheese; a crock of butter; a loaf of bread; and a jar of thyme honey. Lisa decided Martha Stewart had no idea who her competition was.

Lisa patted her middle. "After pastries at Sophia's, I shouldn't eat another thing, but I'm starving. This spread looks amazing."

Thalia passed plates around the table. "Dig in."

"How do Greek women eat so much beautiful food and stay so thin?"

Mia said, "We eat Mediterranean foods. Good for you! And, Thalia grows all of this."

"Thank you for calling us to come over. It's so rugged and so beautiful here. How old is the farm?"

Thalia smiled proudly. "This goat farm has been in my family many generations . . . over a hundred years. I was born in this house."

Lisa remembered Thalia was in her early forties, only a few years younger than herself. She considered the dynamic of living an entire lifetime in one place. There were pros and cons.

"I have six brothers and sisters. Our mother died when we were young. We were very poor, but God always provide."

Lisa thought of all the "but God" statements she could make about her own life.

"We lived off the land, the goat, fish from the sea . . . traded for what we did not have. Never went hungry. The house was too small for seven kids. We took turns sleeping in the barns and outside under the stars. Every meal, we came together at the kitchen table . . . gave thanks to God for this good life He give to us."

Lisa's thoughts went deep inside herself. Growing up at the cabin was an earthy, carefree season of life. Adulting had established a complicated and stressful season. With a sudden pang, she felt hemmed in, perhaps remorseful. Thank goodness Cate urged her to hit the reset button. She added another note to self: Unplug. Turn off the cell phone. Buy real food from local farmers markets . . . and sleep under the stars.

"My two older brothers and sister helped our patéras, our father, until they grow up and go to see the world. It make patéras sad and proud. He say, 'My children make life into something, more than goats.'" Thalia shrugged, tore off some bread, and added figs and cheese to her plate.

"When they go, it was my turn to be mitera . . . mama, to the three younger children. They leave home, too, when grown. Sometimes I want to be the one to leave . . . to be more than goats, but my heart could not leave. I could not leave patéras alone. So . . . I stayed."

Thalia refilled their glasses and continued her story. "I married. But, my husband, he *hate* the goats. He say, he *hate the old goat the worst* . . . he mean my patéras."

Thalia's countenance fell. She was silent for a moment.

"I understand he not like patéras . . . he was hard man to like. But God say to honor patéras. God also say leave father and mother and cling to husband. What do I do?

"I cling to husband *and* take care of patéras. Husband show no Godly honor to patéras or me. He hate old goat so much he cursed him and left. When patéras died two years ago I followed my dreams and expanded business." Her eyes twinkled. "Not just goats anymore."

Lisa remembered when she met Thalia at the dinner that changed her life. Gianna described Thalia's father as a fussy, old widower. No doubt it had been a difficult challenge for Thalia, duty bound to a fussy, old father, married to a disagreeable husband, and raising three younger siblings.

Lisa said, "You are amazing, Thalia. You have inspired me beyond measure."

Sophia said, "Now, Thalia, we just have to find a way to get you and Jack together."

Thalia said, "That is not necessary."

Sophia persisted. "I'm sure Jack is interested—"

Thalia smiled. "I already have a date with Jack tonight."

They cheered. Mia said, "Well . . . it's about time."

"So, Lisa, it's time to change the subject. Mia and I researched the Árgyros Thymíama . . . the incense, the bottle, and bag you have. You won't believe what we found for you."

CHAPTER 15

&

> Let my prayer be set forth
> before thee as incense;
> and the lifting up of my hands
> as the evening sacrifice.
> —Psalm 141:2 (KJV)

*L*isa pulled the incense bottle from the purple velvet bag and set it on the table. Mia, Sophia, and Thalia leaned in to get another look at Cynthia's treasure.

"Mia, you go first. Tell her your findings."

"I researched and verified everything your Professor Diákos told you about production of Árgyros Thymíama, except..."

"Except?"

"Except there is lot more to the story. Árgyros Thymíama was sold by family Marinákis on Island of Crete until 1972. I say 'sold' because they did not grow or harvest incense. They bought it from a source, packaged it, and sold it."

"Incense is *grown*?" Lisa's brow furrowed. She realized she knew nothing about incense. Her only experience was one stinky package of sticks she purchased with a bamboo holder at the Sunflower Bazaar. She lit one, it filled the room with musty smoke, and it deposited ash on her coffee table. After taking up space for a year in a drawer, she booted the offensive stuff into the trash bin.

"Mia, I'm incense illiterate. Can you give me the whole nine?"

"The *what?*"

"The whole nine yards . . ."

The look on Mia's face was priceless. "Nine yards of what?"

Everyone looked puzzled and then burst out laughing at the absurd words.

"Forgive me. Language barrier. Please tell me *everything* about incense. I don't know anything about it."

"This is like me and Javi. He is from Spain; I am from Greece. Our whole marriage is a language barrier. Happy part, gives us a lot of laugh, and funny story to tell.

"Okay, I start at beginning. Stop me for questions, okay? There are many kind of incense. There are over 500 *species* of tree that make incense, but only *four* kind of tree make Frankincense incense, and this on only *two* continents in the world: Africa and Asia. I will only tell you one very rare kind of Frankincense because that is what was in your Árgyros bottle."

Mia was in her element. Lisa, Sophia, and Thalia listened, captivated by the fascinating information Mia dug up.

"There is rare tree called the *Boswellia Sacra* tree or *Frankincense tree*. This tree is *only* found in Dhofar valley of Oman, Arabian Peninsula. See how *rare*?

"This tree is ugly and unbehave . . . have many trunks, grow in rocky, dry ground and . . .only where *they* want to grow. You cannot make a business to grow Boswellia Sacra tree in dendrókipos . . . umm . . . orchard. Cannot just plant this tree and make to grow. You have to work for it. You find them only where they want to grow. This tree so stubborn they can grow out of a rock!

"When this tree is about ten years old, maybe eight, they make cuts in the bark and harvest resin that drips out. Called 'stripping' the tree. Trees can only be stripped maybe two, three times a year, but that exhausts the tree. Then tree needs to rest five or six years, store up again before you can cut it again.

"When resin drips come out of tree and meets air, the resin thicken on outside of tree . . . called resin *tears*. Sound to me like tree is *weeping* . . . perhaps because it knows it is giving rare and beautiful gift of itself.

"After few weeks, these tears are dry and hard . . . like little rocks or crystals. They take them off the tree and take them to the market. Some resin stay as crystals. Some become powder on sticks. Some made into oils."

Lisa was blown away by the depth of Mia's findings. "How do you know that the incense in my bottle came from the Domar valley?"

"*Dhofar* valley," Mia gently corrected her. "Because . . . and, this is very special part of story, the Marinákis business only purchase Frankincense tears from Dhofar valley. Let me back up and give you more history."

"Sure . . . sorry!"

"So, the Boswellia Sacra tree, which *only* grow in Dhofar valley on Arabian Peninsula, is the only tree that produces the highest quality of resin in the world, called *Silver* and *Horaji*. According to records, it has been harvested there since at least 1000 B.C. Brought great wealth to traders in incense trade business.

"In ancient times, they moved these silver resin tears from the Dhofar valley on commerce trade route called Incense Trade Route or Incense Road. This trade route ran from the Arabian Peninsula coast along the Arabian Sea northward, parallel to Red Sea, all the way to Gaza coast on the . . . *Mediterranean Sea*."

Mia said the last two words very slowly and paused to let the implications of the trade route sink in.

Lisa gasped. "Oh, my! That's kind of in the neighborhood here, isn't it?"

Mia smiled, nodding her head.

"So . . . back to your Professor Diákos. He told you that he knew Árgyros was sold on the island of Crete by a family business from centuries before Jesus Christ until sometime in 1970s."

It was Lisa's turn to smile and nod, "Yes."

"The Marinákis business *only* purchased Silver and Horaji Frankincense tears from the Sacra Frankincense tree in the Dhofar valley. Lisa . . . The Greek word for silver is . . ."

Thalia and Sophia jumped in and said the word along with Mia. "Árgyros!"

"Oooh. Árgyros . . . Silver Thymíama." Once again, Lisa was shocked at the significance of the finding. "So, the incense that was in my mother's bottle was extremely rare."

Mia picked up the Árgyros bottle. It glinted in the sunlight.

"The contents were rare. This bottle is rare. It is one of the last bottles produced by Árgyros before the centuries old business died. It is a collector's item. Worth lot of money. If you find the original crystal stopper, worth even more."

Lisa raised her eyebrows. She had no intention of selling the bottle, but was impressed at the thought of its rarity. She uttered a silent prayer of thanks for Cate, who gifted her a tote with a zippered safety pouch. She would now also be twice as careful not to drop or break the bottle.

Mia prompted, "Thalia, now tell your part."

Thalia rose from the table, disappeared into the house, and returned to the table with a booklet.

Excited, Mia came to the edge of her seat. "Thalia, show Lisa what you find."

"Sunday, when I saw your bottle, I think I have seen it before somewhere. I came home to look. I look and look. Found this catalogue buried in patéras' library shelf. He always keep everything. It is from local merchants advertising specialty products. I looked at these catalogues when I was little girl. That's why I remember it." Thalia held the catalogue up and pointed to the front.

"This is date, 1966 . . . so, year before date on Cynthia's olive wood cross." Thalia opened the catalogue at the bookmark. She placed the open catalogue in Lisa's hands.

Lisa stared at the pages. The advertisement was in Greek. It was a glamorous still-life color photograph of a bottle of Árgyros silver resin crystals. The signature velvet bag with gold tasseled drawstrings was arranged beside it.

Tears filled Lisa's eyes. Sophia huddled in for a look.

"See the price? I looked this up. In 1966, the U.S. money equivalent for this rare Arabian treasure was $500.00!"

Stunned, Lisa stared at the amount. "I can't believe how precious, how valuable!"

Thalia placed her hand over Lisa's on top of the closed catalogue. "I want you to keep this catalogue." Lisa started to protest, but Thalia shook her head. "This belongs with you and your Árgyros Thymíama."

"Thank you both for your time and research. You've given me an amazing gift." Mia and Thalia beamed. "I have another question about incense. The only incense I've seen was on sticks. How are resin tears —these crystals—used? I know some hippies used incense, and sometimes churches use incense, but why would someone buy an expensive bottle of incense like Árgyros? Why is it advertised like perfume?"

Mia giggled, and with a frown repeated a word that sounded like "key peas." Puzzled she asked, "What is *key peas?*"

Lisa bit her lip. "Key peas? . . . Oh, hippies. Sorry. I'll explain that later."

Again, the tag team of Mia and Thalia exchanged glances. Thalia nodded and returned inside the house.

Mia explained. "In ancient times incense had many uses. It was used to cover odors. Some believe it ward off demons and evil spirit. Some use during meditation to bring peace, focus. Bible tells us about incense in sacrifice to God, and church ceremonies and worship. Remember, Bible says our prayers rise to heaven like incense that is pleasing to God.

"In modern times still same reasons, but also special to use at celebration time like family celebration, wedding or childbirth. A very precious and valuable gift to give someone you love. The person you give it to burns it, smells it, thinks of you."

Thalia returned with an old looking decorative brass bowl with a perforated dome lid. She placed it in the center of the table and removed the dome. The bowl had a recessed center containing a lump of charcoal. In her other hand, she held a small glass bottle, which she handed to Lisa. It contained incense resin crystals.

"This is not expensive incense, but it will allow you to experience it. Place one resin crystal on the charcoal. Now light this match and touch it to the incense."

The incense crackled and ignited, and a gossamer plume of smoke spiraled heavenward. Thalia replaced the dome over the bowl, and the smoke diffused through the vents. The sweet, earthy fragrance settled around them.

Sophia hummed a little and then said, "Lets sing praises to our Father, let them rise like incense." She sang and raised her hands. She looked from face to face, smiling at her beloved friends. Her clear, sweet voice led them in an impromptu melody from her heart.

"Our God, we love you . . . with all our hearts . . . with all our souls . . . with all our strength . . . with all our might. We love Your presence . . . here with us . . . we lift our love on wings of song . . . like fragrant incense . . . before Your throne."

Sophia's melody of praise was simple and easy to follow. She repeated the song. Mia, Lisa, and Thalia joined her oohing and humming along. With each repetition, they began to echo the heartfelt words and harmonize. It built and built until they all raised their hands and lifted their song of worship.

Tears filled Lisa's eyes and ran unchecked down her face. In the moment of praise, she rose above all her worldly cares and worshiped God with pure, unfettered love overflowing from her heart. Nothing in the moment mattered except offering praise to a good and gracious God.

* * *

So moved was Lisa by the events of the day, she knew, once again, her life was forever changed, and nothing about it would ever be the same. That evening as the sun set over the Aegean amidst a hazy, pink glow, the earth became quiet and still before the Lord God.

Upon return to the hotel, Lisa tread softly through the deepening shadows and took the back path to her suite. She closed her door and shut behind it the hum of conversation and clinking of glasses and dishes from the gathering at poolside.

The new hotel guests celebrated their first night at the Aegean Hotel with a Greek dinner courtesy of Gianna's culinary skills. Lisa hoped to meet all of them later, but for now, she wished to continue her companionable communion with God. Her soul remained intimately married to the other-worldly experience of the pure worship they ushered in at Thalia's.

That night Lisa lit candles in lieu of electric lights. She turned off her cell phone and banished it to the bottom of her suitcase. She forbade any intrusion on her quieted mind.

She took a lantern, bread, and wine to the roof terrace. She partook of the Lord's Supper, communed with God, spoke Scriptures, and prayed. Sophia's new song of praise fell sweetly from her lips.

Lisa celebrated her relationship with God and His unfailing answers to her prayers. She realized with new depth how God not only provided more than she could ask or think, but He even answered the unspoken desires of her heart. He surprised her with answers to the things for which she lacked the wisdom to ask. He knew her well. He was the, "One God and Father of all, who is above all, and through all, and in you all." (KJV)

With renewed trust, Lisa placed the desire for answers to all her mother's treasures at the foot of the cross. She consecrated her journey to God. She added one more biggie to her growing list of questions. *How, and when, and why, and where had her mother come into possession of the Greek Árgyros Thymíama?*

In the past few days, Lisa learned her locket was expensive Greek jewelry. She learned the olive wood cross was carved by Luca Adino, Jr., inspired by Jesus Christ, and given as a special gift. She learned about the rare and expensive Arabian treasure, Árgyros Thymíama . . . yet she still knew so little.

As the surprising day came to a close, one last prayer danced through Lisa's mind. *Father, Thank you for my mother, her life, her love for me, and this amazing Greek journey of discovery on which she sent me. It only took me twenty years . . . but thank You that I finally found her treasures! I celebrate her life, and I ask for the grace to celebrate however You choose to answer all these questions. In Jesus' Name, Amen.*

Thick, restful sleep gently settled on Lisa as she, like the young Thalia, lay outdoors atop a humble pallet on a Greek summer night, under a canopy of a zillion twinkling stars.

CHAPTER 16

❧

The path of lazy people
is overgrown with briers:
the diligent walk down a smooth road.
—Proverbs 15:19 (MSG)

"Guess what I did last night?"

"Oh, tell me. What?" Sophia's eyes were wide.

"Slept outside on the roof terrace under the stars. Thalia's childhood story inspired me."

"Mmmm. I love to sleep under stars. I haven't slept outside for long time. Why did I stop?"

Lisa said, "Me, too. I get too busy and forget to make time for what's important. Oh, and I turned off my cell phone, too. For hours, I watched the rotation and scintillation of the stars, and talked to Father God. It was magnificent."

"What is scintillation?"

Lisa winked, "Scientific word for twinkling."

"Oh. Well, you and Thalia inspire me to do it, too. Hali and I will sleep outside under stars tonight."

"That sounds fun and romantic." Mia joined the conversation as she took a seat at the table. "Maybe Javi, the girls, and I will sleep outside tonight, too. Why you decide to do that?"

In unison Lisa and Sophia said, "Thalia."

Mia said, "Oh, yes. Her story. She tell about goat farm. She inspires me to do wonderful things. Will Thalia and Gianna join us for coffee?"

"Gianna will . . . here she is now." Lisa waved at Gianna, "Over here."

"Thalia is birthing goats," Sophia said as she served the Sweet Almond Cake. Mia poured the coffee.

"Awww, I want to go see the baby goats," Lisa's mind danced.

"So, I hear yesterday was amazing," Gianna said. She settled into the remaining chair. "Extraordinary finding. Lisa showed me the Árgyros Thymíama advertisement. Exquisite."

"I am stunned by Mia and Thalia's findings, and the significance of Mom's treasures. To think she held these precious things for so many years without a word about their value or importance."

Sophia asked, "What will you investigate next, and who gets to help?"

"After we enjoy your delicious cake and coffee, Mia and I are going to the Government Records Office to search for Hotel Mákari paperwork. Mia offered to translate for me. Everyone is welcome to come. We could turn it into a party."

Gianna said, "I was jealous to miss out on everything at Thalia's yesterday. I'm not jealous today. I have to get back to the hotel."

Sophia said, "I have to stay at bakery. I would have make you double espresso if I know you read records today. Records office is one street over. Come back if you need buzz."

Gianna promised, "If you don't make it back to the hotel tonight, I'll come look for you behind a stack of papers. It's good that Mia's going with you. She knows the system."

"The system?" Lisa looked wary.

Sophia cut a slice of cake. "More cake anyone?"

Uh-oh. Lisa sensed certain avoidance by everyone. Records research should be interesting.

Lisa and Mia entered the Míos Government Records Office. One look inside the dreary, windowless building and Lisa stopped and raised her eyebrows. Unfiled papers rose like skyscrapers from every flat surface in the room.

"This place is not for the faint of heart, is it? Is it too late to go back for that espresso?"

Mia cautioned, "This place needs 'avalanche warning' posted. Ready? Follow me."

Without a word to the clerk, Mia strode past the front desk. She picked her way between canyons of paperwork to the back of the room. With confidence, Lisa strode in her wake. They claimed a small table along the rear wall. Mia muscled stacks of paper aside, creating a workspace. They each took a seat.

"Okay, tell me about *the system*."

"The records clerk at the desk . . . his name is Deacon. He will allow unlimited free access to every record if we do all the work ourselves and don't ask any questions. If you ask him for assistance, it will cost you weeks of time and a lot of money."

"I wondered why we bypassed the desk. Well, if there is a charge for official records requests, I can pay it. I don't want to defraud the government."

"No. Official records requests are free. But if you ask Deacon for records, it will take weeks to get it and cost you money."

"Why would it cost if it's free?" It sunk in. "Ooh."

"So, we hideout back here and do our own research. That's the system."

"Got it. There's file cabinets everywhere. What are all these stacks of paper?"

"Oh . . . that's another part of the system. Do-it-yourself filing. File cabinets filled up years ago. So, people got creative."

"That sounds problematic."

"Well, that's the system."

". . . okay."

"Permits for hotel, building, inspection, registration, and license to operate may be filed under Greek letter for any of those words, or maybe under letter for name of hotel, name of owner, name of builder. And, if cabinet was full, it got put in a stack of these papers."

"Has anything been computerized?"

"No."

"How long has Deacon been the records clerk?"

"Thirty years."

"And, all these records are in Greek?"

Mia looked calm about the task ahead. "I did research here last year for Javi's business. So, I have a feel for the system. I will look for sections in files or stacks that relate to our topic. Then, we both study it. I make a plan for us. I make cheat sheet for you with Greek alphabet, Greek words, and document titles so you can look for those words on forms. See?"

Lisa reviewed the spreadsheet. "Mia, you're a genius. We can do this."

"We'll check file cabinets first. If not find anything, we start through stacks. It will be tedious. If you find any paper with these words, pass them to me and I'll check them."

"Yes, ma'am. I'm all in."

For two days, Lisa and Mia kept their heads down, nudged through files, and asked no questions of Deacon. As with all good government offices, the records office was closed for the weekend. Now on their third day of research, they sat, backs aching, hunched over a corner of the desk in the back recesses of the records office. Lisa finished a stack of papers, stretched, and pushed it away.

"Mia?"

"Mmm . . . hmm?"

"I've decided Deacon is a self-starter with initiative."

Mia raised her head from a stack of papers and stared at Lisa. "Excuse me?"

"Each morning, he starts the coffee pot and smokes a pack of cigarettes. He requires no supervision or prompting to complete these tasks. . . self-starter."

"Me dulévis . . . .are you kidding me? Oh, brother. And, his initiative?"

"He initiated an 'act like you are retired while working program,' and a 'literacy program.'" Lisa motioned air quotes.

Mia shook her head. "And the literacy program?"

"He sits behind the counter and reads all day. And, let's not forget, he also initiated the do-it-yourself filing and piling system. If that's not initiative, what is?"

Mia snorted. "And, he is appropriately named."

"Deacon?"

"Deacon, in Greek, means a helper or servant."

At that, Lisa snorted, too, and they both giggled.

At the end of their sixth day in the records office Mia and Lisa had sifted through virtually every file cabinet and most piles of haphazard, musty, yellowed paperwork. It was slow going and totally non-productive. They read until their eyeballs fell from their sockets, with not one shred of paper to attest to the fact that the Hotel Mákari ever existed on Míos. The best thing Lisa and Mia found at the records office was an enduring friendship and a like-minded sense of humor.

With a salute to Deacon and the records office, Mia and Lisa knocked off early the last day and huddled up poolside to unwind and celebrate over a glass of wine with Gianna.

Soaking up the warm afternoon sun and fresh air, they clinked their glasses and sipped.

Gianna was incredulous. "So, you did not find one single thing on the Hotel Mákari?"

Weary of being cooped up in the cramped quarters and cigarette smoke, Mia closed her eyes and turned her face to the sun. "Nothing, zip, zero, nada, típota."

Lisa formed a circle with her hand. "A big fat goose egg. We're here to celebrate the fresh air and the wine, but not the find. Thanks to Sophia, her pastries and espresso, and to Mia and her eyeballs, we survived, and we can scratch the records research off the list."

Gianna said, "So, now what's next on the list?"

"I will physically scour the island looking for clues. I'll visit all the hotels and ask questions."

CHAPTER 17

~~~

I will lift up mine eyes unto the hills,
from whence cometh my help.
My help cometh from the LORD
which made heaven and earth.
—Psalm 121:1-2 (KJV)

Trundling along on the coast road, Lisa popped the clutch, shifted into fourth gear, floored the accelerator, and prayed for speed. Summiting the mountain required nothing less than flooring the pedal. Lisa prayed she would not punch her foot through the worn-out floorboard. She did not want to pull a "Wilma Flintstone" in the Greek countryside.

"Good car," Lisa patted the dashboard as the car crept onward. The narrow road clung precariously close to the edge of the cliff.

Gianna smiled widely. "I love this road. It's breathtaking."

"That's for sure. You're wearing your seatbelt, right?"

"Nah. It's only a 200-foot drop to the water below. I'm a good swimmer."

Armed with a list of hotels, Lisa and Gianna visited two hotels by the beach in the chora that morning before they headed toward the chorio on the mountain in the middle of the island.

"The next hotel is the oldest on Míos. If it was not previously the Hotel Mákari, I'm hoping they remember it or know something of it."

"Thanks for visiting hotels with me."

"Are you kidding? I would not miss it. I want to be with you when you find the Hotel Mákari."

Gianna pointed ahead. "Take the road on the right."

Ten minutes later, they entered the laid-back little village.

"Park over there, and we'll explore on foot."

"Wow! This location is amazing. We're at the top of the world, surrounded by the Aegean, as far as the eye can see."

"I think this is the most picturesque village in the world. We considered locating our hotel here, but chorio is too small for two hotels."

Together they walked the quiet streets that undulated with the land and led through the labyrinth of white block buildings, toward a large structure on a bluff at the northern edge.

"There it is, up there at the oval sign. The βουνό πανδοχείο . . . the Mountain Inn."

"It's beautiful."

They climbed toward the impressive structure and entered the lobby through wood framed glass doors. The well-established generational hotel was welcoming and stylish.

Gianna admired the surroundings. "This is boutique hotel perfection."

Lisa and Gianna crossed the stone floor and approached the sleek, polished concierge desk.

The attractive young associate greeted them. "Kaló apógevma. Kalos irthes. Pós boró na se voithíso?"

"Naí," Gianna nodded, then gestured toward Lisa. "Mílas Angliká?"

"Oh, yes."

"Good afternoon. Welcome. How can I help you?"

"I am Gianna Gataki. This is my good friend, Lisa Abbott. She is from the United States, conducting research on a personal matter. Would you have a moment to talk with us?"

"Certainly." The associate was bright-eyed and engaging. "I am

Lyra Vlochos. My father, Evandir Vlochos, is owner of this Mountain Inn. I am the manager."

Lisa shook hands with Lyra. "Thank you for your time. I am looking for a hotel, the Hotel Mákari. I believe it was located on Míos in the late 1960s. I've found no information online. Since yours is the oldest remaining hotel on Míos, I thought you might know some island hotel history . . . perhaps know of the Hotel Mákari."

"The Hotel Mákari. Sounds exotic." Lyra's eyes widened with curiosity. She quickly came around the desk. "My father live at this hotel his whole life. Inherited hotel *forty years ago*. He knows much history of Míos. I will ask him to see you. Excuse me."

Lyra disappeared into the back office and reappeared with her father close behind.

"Miss Abbott, Miss Gataki, welcome to our Mountain Inn."

He kissed them on both cheeks. "My daughter tells me you are American lady who visit Míos to find answers. You come to right place. Míos always have answers, even when you do not know question . . . you get answer. Please, come sit."

Evandir gestured to Lyra. "Ah . . . Mikrí Mélissa, eh . . . perhaps we drink a little wine with our new friends, yes?"

"Yes, Ángelos. I'll get it."

Evandir clasped his hands over his heart. "Lyra is the baby daughter of my old age. When my other five children were grown, my wife and I decide, we need *one more baby!* So . . . we have Lyra. So, Lyra . . . Greek word for lyre, which is a harp. She is the sweet music, the last verse of our marriage song. I also call Lyra my *Mikrí Mélissa*. This means little bee." He waved his hand around. "She is *mikrokamoméni* . . . how to say . . . little . . . busy . . . buzzing around . . . put her nose into this . . . that . . . just like little bee with flowers."

Lyra returned with a tray of chilled wine, fresh fruit, and cheese.

"And he is my Ángelos, my angel. Always there watching over me. He makes sure his little bee is safe and loved."

Lyra served the wine. Evandir raised his glass. "Stin ygeiá sas! Cheers! To your health!"

Everyone toasted. "Cheers! To your health!"

"Miss Gataki, I know your name. Aegean Hotel, yes?"

"Yes. The newest hotel on the island. It is an honor to visit the oldest hotel on the island."

"I give you a tour of hotel if you like. You and your husband must come to have meal with us. We join together, help each other, yes?"

"Absolutely."

"Miss Lisa, tell us about your reason for coming to Míos."

Lisa explained finding her mother's treasures, her meeting with Dr. Soso Diákos, and her impromptu trip to Greece.

Evandir's eyebrows shot up with interest. Lyra moved to the edge of her seat with mounting interest.

"So, the name on the hotel stationery?"

"The Hotel Mákari. Do you know of it?"

Evandir was now at the edge of his seat. "You have this hotel stationery with you, yes?"

Lisa nodded and pulled Cynthia's treasures from her tote and laid them on the table. As they drank their wine and nibbled fruit, Lisa and Gianna filled them in on findings on Míos with Luca Adino, Jr., and the wooden cross, the Árgyros Thymíama, and the addition of the locket as another clue.

Evandir listened carefully and studied the items with rapt attention. He pulled on his beard as he considered each element.

"Fascinating." He motioned at the hotel stationery, "May I?"

"Of course!"

Evandir raised the letterhead to the light, squinted, found the watermark, and slowly nodded his head. He studied the inked insignia at the top and carefully ran his fingers over it. "Hotel Mákari," he uttered as he stared at it, deep in concentration.

At last he shook his head. "I do not know of this Hotel Mákari."

Lisa forgot to breathe. If the hotel was not on Míos, she was unsure where to look next.

"But . . . let us consider this together. I have this hotel for forty years. I inherit from my father and mother, Evandros and Kyveli Vlochos, in 1987. I was forty-one years old. I am now seventy years old."

Lisa said, "My mother would be seventy-seven if she were alive. Were you at home in Míos in 1967? That's when my mother might have been here."

"No. I left island for many years to see the world in this time you say your mother and Hotel Mákari might be here. I will think if there is someone to ask about hotels during those years."

Lyra scribbled copious notes and made sketches of the Árgyros Thymíama bottle and olive wood cross on her notepad. "What was your mother's name?"

"Cynthia Carter. Cynthia Brenner after she married."

Lyra made another note and drew a box around it and drew an arrow leading to a question mark. "Papa, do you have any records, tourist books, phone books . . . anything with list of hotels in 1967?"

"We throw out most old papers . . . we computerize." He rolled his eyes.

Lyra accepted the challenge. "I will take a look around in the cellar for old things. Maybe I find something."

Evandir smiled at his daughter, then at Lisa, "Of course." He looked confident and proud as if the entire mystery was already solved. "We look . . . we *find*. Can you show us photograph of Cynthia Carter from 1967?"

Lisa pulled an 8 x 10, black-and-white glossy from her notebook. "This is my mom at age twenty-one."

Lyra said, "She is so beautiful!"

Evandir picked up the photograph and studied it, and then Lisa. He opened his mouth to speak, then did not.

Lyra said, "I make a copy of this photograph, yes? Permission from you to speak her name? Perhaps we ask some people who might remember her."

"Yes, of course. Would you like to copy the Hotel Mákari stationery, too?"

Gianna said, "Yes. and let's all exchange contact information. We can let each other know if we find something."

Evandir said, "Do you know you have Greek name with special Greek meaning?" Lisa and Gianna exchanged glances. "It means, My God Is a Vow."

Tears welled in her eyes. "Our friend Mia believes my mother and father chose it to seal a Covenant made with God."

Evandir nodded. "My God Is a Vow. And . . . do you know the meaning of the Greek word *Mákari*?"

Lisa shook her head.

"Mákari means I Wish."

"I Wish?" Lisa repeated, brow furrowed, thinking the literal translation an odd name for a hotel. She moved to the edge of her seat. "Why would a hotel have such a name? I mean, all the other hotels on the island have names like Mountain Inn or Aegean Hotel, or with a family name like Hotel Giannopoulos. 'I Wish' seems odd."

Evandir shook his head. "Not odd. It is another clue."

"Do you think so?"

"Yes. Every Greek word have *meaning*, have *purpose*." Evandir gestured with a strong fist for emphasis. "This name, it have important meaning . . . just like Lyra . . . Lyre; Mikrí Mélissa . . . Little Bee; Ángelos . . . Guardian Angel; Lisa . . . *My God Is a Vow*; Mákari . . . *I Wish*. Yes, I am sure this is part of the story. Someone make wish and someone believe God will keep His vow, and will do what this person wish for."

Lisa was stunned to think her name and the name of the hotel were connected.

Evandir said, "You ask questions. Míos give answer. God give answer." With compassion, he looked into Lisa's eyes. "You look to see if your mother was here. You pray for answer?"

Lisa nodded.

"So . . . Our God is faithful. God provide. If someone say to God they *wish* for something, and declare, *My God is a vow* . . . if you, Lisa, are *tied* to that wish and that vow, and you pray for answers, God *will* give you the answers."

"Amen."

"There is something more important than to just find this Hotel Mákari. You must find the people who named the hotel. Find the people who make this wish and vow with God."

Confused, Lisa sighed. She doubted that when Cynthia and Wells named her that they knew the Greek meaning of her name, and she was certain they had never been to Greece or named a hotel. She wanted to believe the charismatic Evandir, but she was filled afresh with overwhelming skepticism.

CHAPTER 18

> . . . Now go out to the street corners
> and invite everyone you see.
> So the servants brought in everyone
> they could find, good and bad alike,
> and the banquet hall was filled with guests.
> —Matthew 22:9–10 (NLT)

Lisa and Gianna arrived at the Aegean Hotel late evening just before sundown. Anxious to hear of their expedition, Skender welcomed them poolside with the meal he prepared. The savory aroma of grilled meat kindled their appetites.

Lisa and Gianna filled him in on their visit with the Angel and the Little Bee at the Mountain Inn, and Evandir's invitation for dinner and a hotel tour.

Gianna said, "The hotel is impressive, and they are so embracing. We could reciprocate and invite them for dinner and a tour. We could collaborate on hotel issues. They are followers of God. Perhaps they would like to join our God-gathered family sometime."

Skender filled their glasses and served plates of food. "I look forward to meeting them. So, no new findings in the investigation?"

Lisa fielded the question. "They never heard of the Hotel Mákari, but Evandir told me Mákari means 'I Wish.' He is certain the meaning of my name and the hotel name are tied together."

"But you are not convinced?"

"I struggle to believe it. My parents weren't exactly Greek language scholars. And I'm certain they never named a hotel. Plus, if my name were special, why didn't they tell me about it? I don't know . . ."

Gianna said, "I think you spent too many hours this week with Deacon at the Records office. You have been on Míos for two weeks now. How many times have you gone swimming?"

"None."

"How many times have you walked on the beach?"

"None."

"How many times have you laid out by the pool and read a book?"

"None."

"Sweet friend, take the weekend off. Put your mother's treasures on hold and act like a tourist. God will provide all the answers in His timing."

Ah, yes . . . busted. A feeling of conviction and then relief spread throughout Lisa's heart as she let out a long, slow breath. Once again she managed to over-complicate her life. There was only one way to respond to Gianna. "Thank you."

"You are welcome."

"I've got to get better at relaxing. Maybe I should add that to my checklist."

Gianna rolled her eyes. "You're in Greece. Forget the checklists. You've got to get better at being *Greek*."

Skender said, "We're having a casual party tomorrow night for the new arrivals from England. Cook out, Greek food. Drop in if you want."

Gianna said, "We'll invite them to go with us to Nico Scala's Villa for church on Sunday. You never know, perhaps they'll come."

* * *

Sunday afternoon Lisa rode with Skender and Gianna to Nico's. Following them on a flock of rented scooters were two of the four couples from the UK. They decided to give the church gathering a try.

The informal motorcade skirted around the southern horn of the island and drove northward along the eastern coast. About a third the way up the coast toward "The most north poin t of Island Míos" they departed the main road and drove toward the seashore. After a half-mile of rocky dirt road, they entered the impressive gate to Nico's seaside home, Villa Maria, named after his beloved wife.

Skender parked the SUV on the landing below the house and terrace. The scooter gang were all present and accounted for. Kickstands down, they dismounted and dusted off.

The two young ladies finger-brushed and fluffed their helmet hair. The two guys pulled off their T-shirts, ran for the water, and dived headfirst into the waves. In the few short days since their arrival, they had easily adapted to the island vibe. The warmth, sand, and surf seemed to agree with them.

Lisa envied their casual, new drip-dry lifestyle, and made another mental note to self: ditch the hairdo, swim in the surf, and drip dry in the sunshine. Exhilarated at the thought, she instinctively knew it would do as much to restore her soul as sleeping under the stars.

Lisa helped Skender and Gianna carry platters of food to the broad, stone-paved main terrace that spanned the width of Nico's expansive multi-level house. In true Greek style, flowering bougainvillea spilled from every arbor and framed the crisp blue and white canvas-cushioned visit nooks. Gentle hills rose in semicircles behind the house, echoing the contour of the coast. Waves splashed on the beach just below, and a red wooden rowboat bobbed on tethers to one side. Nico's place was everything Greek at a glance. Lisa breathed it all in.

The doors to Nico's house were open to the terrace. Everyone drifted in and out like a leisurely breeze. Peri and Mia chatted as they prepared to serve the food. Like a mother hen with two new chicks in tow, Gianna made the rounds introducing the two British young ladies, Maisie and Chloe.

Nico greeted Lisa with a kiss to each cheek and a warm embrace. "Welcome to Villa Maria."

GREATER LOVE

"Nico, this is amazing! The location of your home is stunning. Thank you for hosting the gathering."

"It is easy to open the doors for everyone to come. Maria and I always loved to throw the parties. She would love this." Nico motioned toward the men at the grill and the ladies preparing the food. "To serve the food is no worry . . . *I know people.*"

Jack and Thalia entered the terrace together, holding hands. They made a handsome couple. Lisa was filled with joy for them.

Nico's terrace was filled with people. It was a larger gathering than usual. Mia and Javi's girls were among a group of teenagers huddled together away from the adults. Younger children played tag on the terrace and explored the rocks at the water's edge. Their squeals and laughter provided a delightful soundtrack for the evening.

Thalia joined Lisa at the edge of the overlook by the sea. They embraced.

Thalia said, "How was your weekend?"

"Glorious. I swam, read, and rested all day yesterday. Last night I joined the pool party for the UK guests. And yours?"

"Fine. Jack and I went to dinner and dancing last night."

"You two look happy together."

"Yes . . . we are."

"I'm happy for you." Lisa regarded the crowd on the terrace. "This is a great group. Lots of new faces."

"Yes, it's wonderful, really. Nico loves a good party. He goes out and gathers them in from the highways and the byways."

"Really? So . . . do you know all these people?"

"No. Isn't it great? For Nico, it comes naturally to do the things the rest of us only think about doing, but never get around to."

"It just shows that sometimes people are just waiting to be asked."

The thought galvanized something in Lisa. She realized how selfish and untrusting of God she was. She was careless and left things to chance.

"I have passed up too many opportunities. I wish to be more like Nico."

Thalia agreed. "The world needs more Nicos."

"I look at this gathering tonight, and I think surely this is what it will be like in heaven. Praising God, a marvelous party, a jubilant feast . . . and a joyous reunion of loving hearts."

"Mmmm. I think so."

After their jubilant feast, they gathered in for worship, prayer, and the sharing of scriptures. Nico closed the evening with a blessing.

"May we grow closer and closer together as family and to our Great Father. May we know His unlimited love and be filled with the Holy Spirit. May we always give Christ a home in our hearts. May we grow in trust and be strong in God's love. In Jesus' Name, Amen."

After the blessing, Peri approached Lisa.

"Are you ready to find the beach with your mother's sand? Demetri think he know where to take you."

CHAPTER 19

⁂

> . . . O God, your desires toward me are more
> than the grains of sand on every shore!
> —Psalm 139:17-18 (TPT)

*E*arly Monday morning, Lisa, Demetri, and Peri piled into Demetri's ancient Land Rover on a quest for sand. During the past two weeks, Demetri worked to match sand on a beach with the small sample entrusted him from Cynthia's Árgyros Thymíama bottle.

Demetri drove north along the west coast road. Peri looked on proudly as Demetri pointed out interesting facts and features about the geography of Míos' coastline.

"First, we no go to east side of island. Good scenery, but we no look for scenery. We look for *sand*. East beaches, only rocks. Why? Because eroding cliffs produce rocks. No gravel. No sand."

Lisa remembered the look of Nico's beach the day before, which had medium and small smooth rocks that resembled river stones versus sand.

"Here on southwest coast, the ocean topography and the strong currents smash rocks into sand."

The beaches were changing as they headed north. Lisa observed less rock and more gravelly terrain between the land and the water's edge.

Demetri navigated through the seaside chorio, past the cluster of buildings and Luca Adino's olive wood shop. As they pulled free from town, they passed the impressive driveway flanked by tall rock walls on each side. As when she passed it each time before, the heavy wooden gates were tightly closed against the outside world and secured by a large iron hasp and padlock.

Lisa turned in her seat to catch one last glimpse of the property entrance before it disappeared behind a bend in the road. "Who lives there?"

Demetri and Peri exchanged a subtle glance, and Peri turned to Lisa in the back seat.

"That was villa of family that live on Míos many years ago."

"Do they still live there? What is their name?"

Peri answered simply, "All these things . . . it is hard to say."

"Hard . . . why?"

"It is mystery. Who knows what is rumor, what is truth?"

"Did you know them?"

"No. Same island, two worlds. They rich, we poor."

"Does anyone live there now?"

Peri shrugged. She looked ominous. "It is . . . how you say, *house of ghost?*"

"Haunted house?"

Peri nodded. Her eyes were wide for effect, but she was smiling. She clearly enjoyed telling tales of the local intrigue. "Sometimes villagers see lights there at night. Never see person. Never see gates open or close. The village kids go to nearby cemetery at night, watch for lights at house, tell scary stories."

"I suppose every town has a haunted house and a ghost story. When I was a teenager, we drove out in the country to a creepy old cemetery. If you knelt down behind this one tombstone at midnight, you could see lights drifting around in the distance. The ghost story was that it was a murdered, beheaded woman carrying a lantern and looking for her head."

Peri and Demetri both looked back at her, brows furrowed with a look of horror and confusion.

"I know, I know . . . it doesn't make sense. She couldn't look for her head if she did not have one. I mean, her eyes would have been in the head she was looking for. Anyway, it turned out the occasional floating lights were cars on the highway miles away. But I did not know that, and I would sleep with the light on for nights afterward."

They all laughed.

After a series of hairpin curves, Demetri turned off the main road. He navigated an obscure, overgrown beach access. Lisa was thankful for Demetri and his Land Rover. She could never have dared this in the Fiat.

Demetri set the parking brake and shut off the engine. Together they traversed a series of scrubby berms toward the gravely sand. Lisa clutched Cynthia's incense bottle in her hand.

Demetri pulled his own sample of sand from his pocket. A safe distance from the waves washing onto the shore, he knelt down and placed his bottle next to the wet sand.

Lisa gasped. "Demetri, you did it! The sand looks the same."

Demetri nodded, but removed his cap and scratched his head thinking. "Eh, this sand look like, but *not like*. See? Some grains too big. It is not a match."

Lisa knelt down next to Demetri, heedless of the wet sand sticking to her knees and moistening the hem of her beach cover-up. Peri bent at the waist, leaned down, and performed her own inspection. She shook her head and sadly clicked her tongue.

Despite her excitement, Lisa had to admit that the sand was not quite a match.

Demetri shrugged, "So . . . we not find yet, but, I think, we *close*."

Enthused beyond measure, Peri said, "No worry, Demetri. You *know* sand. Where we look now, Demetri?"

"Perhaps a little south, perhaps north." Demetri looked up and down the beach studying the lay of the land, watching the pattern of the waves, and contemplating.

Lisa held her breath.

"We go north. Yes." Demetri pointed up the shore. "We go north."

Together they piled into the Land Rover and reversed course back to the main road. Demetri crept along the coastline for a mile, then pulled to the side of the road and stared out to sea.

"Many years, we fish this waters, this is *spílaio me ammódi pythména* . . . this place in sea where there is cave offshore, and sandy bottom that comes to shore."

Peri glanced back at Lisa, and her look was confident and proud.

Demetri re-entered the road and turned onto the next road. Again, they jostled down another scant, overgrown track, meandering around scrubby berms and rocky outcroppings. It led away from the main road, northward and parallel to the shore. Still clutching Cynthia's bottle in her hand, Lisa strained against her seatbelt and looked for a sandy beach.

After a half mile, the road curved toward the sea and crested a steep hill. A breathtaking vista opened before them. Hidden from the main road, a secluded cove spanned the seaward side of the surrounding crescent-shaped hill. On the south and north ends, the sandy beach was walled off by steep, rocky vertical ridges that extended into the sea.

At the north end of the cove, a long, flat roofed building sprawled across a ledge above the beach. Bougainvillea vines crowned arbors the length of the structure and framed doorways and outdoor living areas.

Stone steps descended from the terrace rendering access to a lower terrace, the beach, and a walkway that meandered northward some fifty yards to another small cluster of buildings sheltered by the hill at the end of the cove. There appeared to be a bait shop, an outdoor taverna, a dock, and harbor occupied by a few small boats. Fresh octopus hung on the line at table side.

Demetri parked the Land Rover. Again, sand samples at the ready, they piled out and scrambled down the stone steps to the beach below. Reaching the water's edge, Lisa knelt down, set Cynthia's bottle beside her, and gathered up handfuls of wet, glistening sand. To her eye, it was a perfect match of color, size, and texture.

Lisa looked to Demetri for confirmation. He and Peri knelt in the sand beside Lisa. She asked hopefully, "Yes?"

"Yes!" Demetri removed his hat and rubbed his head, "I think we find your sand . . . Yes! Of course," he shrugged, "it still possible it come from beach on west side of another island . . . but . . . this is a match. If not here, then someplace in Aegean Sea that make sand just like this."

Lisa, Peri, and Demetri walked the length of the cove inspecting the sand. Lisa collected a bucketful of the matching sand and secured it in the passenger floorboard of the Land Rover. She considered sending in samples for lab analysis and confirmation.

In celebration of their find, they lunched together at the little restaurant by the dock. Upon greeting them, their server placed an opened bottle of wine, three glasses, and an appetizer on the table. Demetri, Peri, and the server conversed briefly in Greek. Suspicious, Lisa eyed the octopus on the line and hoped for a menu.

Peri explained to Lisa, "Here we eat what they serve us. They cook what is fresh caught today. It is all good." Peri motioned to the plate on the table. "This is marídes tiganités . . . small fry . . . called whitebait."

The whitebait looked like breaded and fried minnows, with crispy eyes, crispy tails, and crispy scales. Lisa did not want to eat anything called "bait." A shiver shimmied down her spine at the thought of all the little fried fish parts. Little fried brains, fried innards, fried spines, and fried gills. She wondered if fish had lips. If so, they were fried crispy, too. Did they have little teeth? She expected those would be noticeably crunchy.

Lisa was ready with knife and fork to cut off the creepy little heads and tails and brave the main morsel of meat. Without hesitation Peri and Demetri eagerly picked up the little fish with their fingers and ate them like french fries. Lisa set the utensils aside and gathered her courage. Mind over matter, she went for it. To her surprise the whitebait was actually good, except for the crunchy little tail fin.

Aware of the fresh octopus on the line overhead, Lisa realized the whitebait was the warm up for the main act. What came next was actually one delicious dish after another leading up to the main entree.

The server brought crusty bread and fréskia saláta tría chrómata, a colorful salad of shredded green cabbage, red cabbage, and carrot dressed with olive oil, lemon juice, and salt and pepper. This was followed by a plate of french fries and finally a tureen filled with htapódi stifádo, octopus stew.

The dish looked and smelled delicious, despite all the little suction cups slathered in red wine tomato sauce and sautéed onion. Lisa served a healthy portion onto her plate and discovered the stew was delicious, seasoned to perfection.

Once the tureen was cleared from the table, a plate of dessert and bríki of heavy Greek coffee was set before them. Peri explained that the crispy fried sweets were called loukoumádes, honey puffs, drizzled with honey and sprinkled with cinnamon. They were yummy.

Thankfully, the aroma of the strong black coffee signaled a promise to deliver caffeine that would mysteriously cancel the calories, or at least give Lisa the energy to walk another lap on the beach to work it all off.

The server brought three shot glasses and a bottle of liqueur. Demetri gestured proudly at the tray and announced, "I order this special. We *celebrate!*" Demetri and Peri shared a meaningful glance, and Peri nodded with pride.

Demetri explained, "This is most sacred time of celebration meal together! This is the likér apó víssino, called morello liqueur. We drink this only on rare occasion. We share this as friends. We celebrate love of God with you. We celebrate we find your mother's sand."

Demetri pulled the cork from the bottle and filled each shot glass. He raised his glass, "To our Lord Jesus Christ, to you, and to your lovely mother and her sand!"

They clinked glasses and sipped.

"Mmmm. It's delicious."

"It is cherry liqueur," Peri said. "You put the fresh cherry in a jar with sugar and put out in sun for a month. Add brandy, cinnamon, the clove, again sunshine for twenty days. Then you drink."

Lulled into contentment at the restaurant by the sea in Greece where she found her mother's sand, Lisa sipped the morello and thought how lovely it all was. The water gently lapped against the side of the dock. Lazy shafts of sunlight filtered through the rows of sun-dried branches that made a roof for the arbor. The vague patterns of light cast sketchy shadows across their table, and the salty breeze tousled her hair.

Lisa's eyes rested on the beach. Mesmerized, she watched the waves roll onto the shore. Lost in thought, she wondered how it was her mother came to treasure the handful of sand from this remote and remarkable place in the world.

Lisa's gaze drifted to the rambling building on the ledge, facing the surf. After a few long, distracted moments, her brain registered what her eyes witnessed.

A young couple emerged from one of the doors, tossed their baggage in the trunk of a sporty convertible, and drove off.

The server cleared the dishes. Lisa pointed and said, "Please, can you tell me? What is that building?"

She responded in Greek, "Thálassio Kósmima Xenodochéio."

Lisa did not understand the meaning. Wide-eyed, Peri translated for her, "She says it's the Sea Jewel Hotel."

CHAPTER 20

*The heartfelt counsel of a friend
is as sweet as perfume and incense.
—Proverbs 27:9 (NLT)*

"I've considered every angle and see no other option. I've got to intensify the focus of my investigation."

"I agree, Mom. I know you'll miss Gianna and Skender, but it's time to relocate. Otherwise, you'll spend all your time driving to the west side of the island."

"I'm curious about this Sea Jewel Hotel. Apparently, they don't take just anybody. Gianna called the owner and somehow got me in."

"Oh, I like her more and more."

"She's amazing. And she and the other ladies promised to drive over and continue helping me with the investigation. Plus, I'll see them all each weekend at the church gatherings."

Despite their pact to make it a casual parting, Lisa and Gianna hugged and cried as Skender heaved Lisa's suitcase into the trunk.

Gianna wiped tears away and sniffed. "We all pitched in and packed some provisions for you so you can snack in your room or picnic on the beach. Of course, Sophia sent a Sweet Almond Cake to support your investigation efforts."

The back seat of the Fiat was full of baskets brimming with local fare. Lisa said, "You all are the greatest. I miss you already. I give God glory with great thanks for you." They hugged again. "Okay . . . so, I'll see everyone on Sunday at Thalia's."

Heart full and overflowing, Lisa pointed the Fiat toward the harbor. The dockside Tuesday market stalls buzzed with shoppers, and a frazzled batch of tourists freshly burped dockside from the ferry.

On a whim, Lisa claimed a smidgen of pavement and parked amidst the hubbub. She dashed across the busy road and snagged a table at the sidewalk taverna. In homage to her first meal on Míos she ordered a glass of the Giórgos Hill lefkó krasí, and the choriátiki saláta. She regarded the fresh caught octopus on the line, remembered her delicious lunch with Peri and Demetri, and was actually tempted.

After lunch, Lisa managed to coax the convertible top into a downward position, and continued the drive north on the west side of the island. A new excitement dawned in her spirit as she sped along with the sun on her face and a salty wind filling her lungs. With confidence she motored through the seaside chorio with a glance at her favorite landmarks.

The chorio diminished in the rearview mirror. Lisa whizzed past the massive private gates at the "house of ghost." She slowed her speed and wound her way through the tight series of hairpin curves along the coast. After several miles she passed the first beach access and watched for the second unmarked, overgrown track that led to the well-hidden Sea Jewel Hotel.

With a pang of anticipation, she made the turn and prayed the tiny car could negotiate the primitive road. Successfully past the scrubby berms and rocky outcroppings she ambled toward the shore, crested the steep hill, and arrived at the private hotel.

Lisa parked in the shade of an olive tree and followed the path in search of the hotel office. The grounds were immaculate. In Greek fashion, the paver stones were outlined in precise squares of white paint. The whitewashed buildings stood bright against the cloudless, blue sky. Fuchsia bougainvillea overflowed arbor-framed, blue doorways. The outdoor living areas appeared cool with their white canvas cushions and umbrellas, a promised respite from the afternoon sun.

The bell at the door jangled as Lisa entered the elegant office and approached the desk. The woman behind the desk removed a pair of glamorous, red-rimmed spectacles, her matching red lips broadening into a bright smile. "Chaírete . . . hello." She breezed around the desk, a colorful caftan billowing about her slender frame. "You are *Lee-zah*, yes? Gianna Gataki call me. You are here on mystery from your mother."

She kissed Lisa on each cheek. And, with that, any misgivings Lisa felt about changing hotels flew off on a gauzy breeze in the wake of this charismatic hotelier's caftan.

"I am Zenda Roussos. I welcome you and your mother's mystery to my Sea Jewel Hotel. I help you with mystery, but not today. Today, you arrive. You rest. You get to know Zenda's hotel—you get acquainted to hotel, yes?" Lisa realized it was a rhetorical question, and nodded her agreement.

Zenda's eyes twinkled with a hint of drama, accentuating the laugh lines on her otherwise flawless complexion. "I must tell you," she said, "my hotel, very private. Special guest *only*. I allow other visitors to walk the beach and eat at taverna if my chef is willing. But," she shrugged with a broad smile, "only special guest *stay* at my special hotel."

With flamboyance, Zenda held Lee-zah at arm's length, narrowed her eyes, and scrutinized her from head to toe. "Hmmm . . ." she pursed her lips and nodded her head.

"Yes. I decide you are beautiful Greek goddess, just like Gianna Gataki say to me. I see you, I decide for sure. You are special guest. You can stay."

"Oh . . . good," Lisa laughed, relieved to pass the unexpected inspection. "Thank you for accepting my reservation on short notice." Lisa resisted the urge to explain herself further. She decided less was more at the moment. She fought the temptation to dash out and hide the so-called Fiat behind a bush somewhere, lest Zenda revoke her special guest status.

"Lee-zah, I book you into excellent suite. I tell you . . . you like it very much. I *already* know this." Zenda floated toward the door and waved her arm in Lisa's direction, motioning for her to follow.

"Come. I take you to room now."

Lisa followed.

Zenda pulled a key from her pocket and unlocked the third door from the office. "This is your accommodation. Marvelous view of Aegean Sea and the beach."

Zenda was right. She did like it very much.

"You have three magnificent rooms, open concept. The sitting room, the kitchen, the bedroom and en suite."

The sitting room was furnished with a modern slimline sofa flanked by two matching chairs and a black iron and glass coffee table centered on an exotic animal skin rug. A sleek, black, metal-shaded pendant lamp hung from the ceiling at one end of the sofa.

An expansive arched wall created definition of the kitchen space and framed a black wooden table and four chairs, illuminated by another black metal pendant. In the space beyond, a window was centered in the stone wall, over a basin sink. Goblets and a few dishes lined a live-edge wooden shelf. The lower cabinet housed a micro-refrigerator.

The bedroom with en suite was directly opposite the sitting area. As with the kitchen, an arched opening defined the space. A chic, black iron bed was made with luxurious white linens and an array of plump pillows. The bed rested on a sisal rug, sided by two iron and glass tables and black metal wall sconces.

"This is your en suite—pure luxury. Beautiful oval, freestanding tub, glass shower, marble vanity, and exquisite lighting."

Zenda presented a display of spa products and candles arranged on a mirrored tray. "Pamper yourself. You should also have a massage. I will send my masseuse to you late this afternoon, yes?"

"Please." Lisa reveled in the thought of the blissful extravagance. Oh, the joys of vacation.

Full-glass French doors and large windows lined the front wall of the bedroom and living room and opened onto the private outdoor living spaces and bistro table. The open windows assured the space breathed peacefully with the exchange of sea air. The painting over the sofa, a vase of flowers on the table, and a bed scarf, all in vibrant hues, lent splashes of color to the stunning, modern Greek space.

Lisa pronounced her impression. "It's perfection."

Zenda extended a well-manicured hand. The polished nails matched the shade of her lips and glasses. "If I may have car key, Agapitos will deliver your things."

Lisa proffered the key. Zenda leaned in. "Mwah-mwah, darling."

Zenda breezed out with the same dramatic flair as brought her breezing in.

As promised, Agapitos promptly delivered her luggage. Once unpacked, Lisa called Cate.

"All settled? How is this hotel? Not rundown, I hope."

"Au contraire, ma petite fille. I am situated in a lovely boutique hotel. The vibe is different than the Gataki's countryside hotel, and the Vlochos' historic Mountain Inn."

"Oh . . . wow. So now you've seen three amazing hotels on this one little island. Which one do you like the best?"

"All of them, for different reasons. It will be nice to have a beach so close. I can't wait to explore the area. This hotel appears to serve a rather exclusive clientele. I've either fallen in with the Greek mafia, or I'm at a celebrity hotel for the rich and famous. I cannot imagine the reason I was allowed in . . . but God."

Cate gave a low, appreciative whistle.

"Zenda, the owner, said meals are provided at the dockside taverna, where I ate with Peri and Demetri yesterday, or Chef will deliver to my suite."

"Chef? You have your own chef? I'm tempted to hop a flight and join you."

"Seriously, Catie? That would be wonderful. You could be here in twenty-four hours-ish."

"I wish. I have meetings scheduled all week. And, I don't want to leave Derek. But, maybe we should consider honeymooning there."

"I highly recommend it. I'll talk you up to the owner. Maybe I can get you in."

"So, what is Zenda like?"

"She's marvelous. The quintessential boutique hotelier. Engaging, mysterious, glamorous, extravagant. She has a signature style and is an absolute doll. I'll approach her tomorrow about researching hotel records. For today, I have my instructions. I am to pamper myself. Later this afternoon, she is sending a masseuse."

Cate laughed, "Oh, Derek-Smerek, and cancel the meetings. I'm on my way."

After a refreshing shower and massage, Lisa poured a glass of wine and relaxed in a lounger on the terrace to watch another Greek sunset. The lazy, golden orb melted into the Aegean, and the first star flickered in a pale lavender heaven. The warmth of the day emanated from the stone terrace. Strands of white lights strung over the dock glowed in the fading light. Delicious aromas wafted from the taverna.

Perhaps I could ask Chef to deliver dinner in.

Lisa closed her eyes and pictured Gianna and Skender grilling at poolside. She had grown used to visiting with them in the evenings. She yearned for the distant sound of Thalia's goat bells clanking on the hillsides. And, Sophia, she longed for a chat with her and Mia. She smiled at the memory of lunch with Peri and Demetri on the dock.

Traveling alone, Lisa expected a solitary experience in this remote, foreign land. On the contrary, she felt at home. In a few short weeks, this beautiful community of believers became Lisa's God-gathered family on Míos.

Gianna was right. Lisa spent one evening with them, and her life was changed forever. Their life stories were now inextricably woven together. Inseparable now, no matter what time or distance imposed on them.

And now, the fabulous Zenda entered her life. Lisa's mind danced at the thought of a surprising new friendship on the horizon. It was certain to be remarkable.

A breeze brushed across her skin. *No . . . I am not alone. I am peaceful. Content. Vibrant of heart and mind. Calm and quiet in my soul. Settled. Finally unplugged and unwound.*

Lisa put a hand over the locket that lay against her chest. It was there as always, a reassuring reminder of her mother's love. Here, alone in the quiet, she could think and dream, and wait.

She would walk the sand on the beach. Her mother's sand. And with an open heart she would listen for the voices from the past. She would somehow coax them to speak to her and reveal their long-kept secrets.

CHAPTER 21

Serendipity
... beautiful, glorious, surprising, serendipity.

Next morning, the lyrical chirping of birds lured Lisa from thick, dreamy sleep. Her first conscious thoughts slowly rose to the surface amid the those of the nether dreamworld. Her first desire was to resist and return to her dream, for in it, she was with John.

The chirping continued, and though she grasped at the dream, it eluded her and melted away with the light of day. Lisa sighed. "John."

She blinked back tears, happy at the chance to be with John in her dreams. She did not know if it were so but believed God allowed him to visit her in dreams, especially at times when she really needed him.

Lisa fell asleep the night before, windows open, gazing at the starry heavens. Without a care she drifted into sleep, windows wide open to the world. The pair of brightly colored Bee-Eaters on her window sill cocked their heads, chirped, and flittered away.

After a cup of coffee and a pastry on the terrace outside her room, Lisa headed to the beach. Near the water's edge she slithered from her cover-up and let it drop to the sand. She walked into the water and, with a gasp as it reached her ribs, she drew a breath and submerged.

Carefree, she swam, splashed, and floated in the early morning surf. The water was clear, and she could see her pink-polished toes on the golden sandy bottom. The water, soothing and reviving. She made a silent agreement with herself to go for a morning swim every day.

Finally emerging from the salty spa of an ocean, she pushed her long, dark hair away from her face and wrung the water from it. Having brought no towel with her, she walked along the beach, allowing the wind and sun to dry her skin before she shrugged back into the cover-up.

Lisa made her way across the wet sand near the water's edge toward the south end of the beach. She waded through splashy waves that washed over her feet before they were drawn back seaward. Broken shell fragments, sand, and pebbles caught in their liquid momentum tumbled backward as the pull of the sea reclaimed them, only to be washed up and tumbled again and again.

Mesmerized, Lisa watched this exhilarating dance of nature. Between waves, the sun glinted on the water's shallow surface as the sea rendered its treasure. Among the relentless brokenness of sandy rubble, a jade-colored piece of sea glass was left behind on the sand.

Lisa bent and picked it up. Staring at this precious jewel from the sea resting in her palm, her excitement soared as she realized its meaning. *Sea glass.* She traveled around the world in search of sand and sea glass, and she found them. Her joy soared.

Holding this first piece of sea glass securely in her hand, she quickly looked about, scanning the beach for more. Several minutes passed, and Lisa found another small piece, then another. Obsessed, she searched for more, with her senses so focused she almost forgot to blink. After an hour she had the first larger, jade-colored piece, and eight smaller pieces ranging from white to jade to pale blue. They were identical in shape, color, and size to the sea glass treasured by her mother.

The late morning sun began to sizzle on her skin, and Lisa realized that in her obsession of finding just one more piece, she lost track of time. Reluctant to leave the beach, she returned to her starting point, collected her flip-flops, and padded back to her suite.

Mounting the terrace, Lisa noticed the parking lot had filled with cars. Selfishly she hoped they were lunch customers for the taverna, not the hotel filling with guests. Zenda, in the caftan du jour, breezed along the path, a man in tow. They entered the suite two doors down from Lisa's.

Lisa arrived at her door, dusted the sand from her feet, and entered the cool retreat of her rooms. She carefully deposited her sea glass treasure in a bowl from the kitchen and set it under the glow of the pendant light on the glass coffee table. To Lisa it looked as artful and precious as a priceless work of art produced by one of the masters.

Peeling off her swimsuit, Lisa caught sight of her reflection in the mirror. The sun and wind dried her hair into crispy, wavy tousles. Flaming red sunburn on her shoulders outlined the white skin beneath her swimsuit. She sported a red nose to match.

Yikes! I'll have to be more careful.

Showered, moisturized, and dressed, Lisa was famished. She grabbed her tote and sun hat, slid her feet into sandals, and trotted off to the taverna. She requested a table in the shade and eagerly awaited the catch of the day.

Sadly, Chef served no whitebait or octopus. Instead, a delicious prawn salad, grilled bream with lemon and oregano, and for dessert, galatoboúreko, a golden, buttery, custard pie baked between layers of phyllo pastry, which she enjoyed with a bríki of heavy coffee.

Lisa celebrated her own magnificent catch of the day, the beautiful sea glass. With her notebook opened to the hotel stationery, she read her mother's love letter with greater understanding.

Like the surge of the ocean, the roll of the waves,
So is My love for you . . . relentless.
My love is like the sand on the shore,
Multi-faceted and plenty.
You are My sea glass,
Polished by My nature . . . My jewel . . . My love.

The words came alive and leapt from the page. Having walked the beach and experienced the surge of the ocean, the roll of the waves, having watched the sea glass tumbled to perfection in the rubble of sand, she understood, *"You are My sea glass, polished by My nature . . . My jewel . . . My love."*

With the second bríki of coffee, Lisa made a new list:

1. Call Cate, Peri, and the gang and give sea glass update.

2. Ask Zenda questions about hotel history and access hotel archives.

3. Update Lyra on my relocation and findings, and get update on her research.

4. Get research update from Nico.

5. Visit and research Giórgos Hill Winery and toast Professor Diákos.

After her first morning on the beach at the Thálassio Kósmima Xenodocheio, Lisa quickly fell into a new routine. She woke to the sound of Bee-Eaters chirping at her windowsill, swam in the sea, and combed the beach for sea glass, which she added to the collection in the bowl on the coffee table.

On her third day at the Sea Jewel Hotel, Lisa met with Zenda and drew her into the mystery of Cynthia's treasures. Zenda took her time studying each Greek item. Realization dawned in her eyes at the examination of the Hotel Mákari stationery and love letter. She picked up the crystal bottle and re-examined the sand and sea glass.

"You found sand and sea glass on my beach, and you wonder if my hotel is Hotel Mákari?"

"Yes."

Zenda placed the items down, deep in thought.

Zenda said, "I purchase abandoned hotel property in 1997. Neglected for over twenty years, and run down. I cleaned it out, and renovated it three times through the years."

Lisa's heart plunged. Was the Sea Jewel Hotel to be another dead end?

"I think attorney say at least two owners of property before me. It was used as hotel, or guest rooms long time ago."

Rollercoaster. Buckle-up. "May I ask who you purchased the property from?"

"I do not know name. It was private sale from undisclosed seller represented by law firm."

Dead end-ish . . . think, Lisa . . . ask the all-important follow-up questions.

"Can you give me the name of the law firm? Perhaps enough years have passed they would disclose the seller's name."

Zenda shook her head. "I got curious a few years ago. Tried same thing. No longer in business."

Lisa scratched her head. *Dead end . . . think, think, think. Records . . . chain of custody.* "Maybe I could research their old records."

"I tried that. They were all disposed. Destroyed."

Lisa asked, "Zenda, after so many years, why did you get curious and look into this?"

"Marketing. Designing new website. Wanted to give some hotel history, or maybe say, 'Aníkos Pavlís, or Audrey Hepburn stay here.' Then when I find nothing at all, it make me wonder who build this? What was former hotel name? Why was sale to me private? Why all the mystery?"

Lisa clicked her tongue. "Ah. So, there are no clues at all in local lore?"

"It is like a hole in history."

"Before I showed you the stationery, you never heard of the Hotel Mákari?"

"I never hear words Hotel Mákari. That is another hole in history."

Zenda's eyes met Lisa's. Lisa asked, "Are you thinking what I'm thinking?"

Hot on the trail, Zenda said, "Too many mysterious coincidence."

"Plus, I found the matching sand and sea glass on your property. Were there any old hotel records left behind?"

"I was told there were boxes of paper in underground wine cellar."

Lisa's heart leapt. "Are they still there? Have you seen them?"

Zenda looked pained. "I want to know if Aníkos Pavlís slept here, but not that bad. When I first take hold of property, I unlock wine cellar door, scream, and run away. Too scary. Like dark cave." She shivered. "Spiders."

"So, some old boxes from the previous owners are still down there?"

"Yes, they sleep in dark with spiders."

"Would you allow me to look through them?"

"I don't know . . . the records is private. Hotel cannot disclose guest information. Cellar is not safe, and I think spider still there."

Lisa's skin crawled. She kept her game face on and stifled a shudder. It was time for a pep talk. *C'mon, Lisa, you have not come all this way to fail, or be afraid of the dark and spiders. Put your big girl pants on. If you don't go look, you will always wonder.*

With confidence Lisa said, "I really want to explore that cellar. Maybe I could find the answers to questions we both have. What if I sign a Nondisclosure Agreement for records review, and a Non-Liability Waiver for injury and spider bites? My friend Mia has agreed to translate for me. I'm sure she will sign the agreement and waiver, too. We will do all the work. You will get all the answers." Lisa dangled one last carrot. "You might be able to advertise some famous people stayed here."

Zenda narrowed her eyes. "Lee-zah, you very tough, savvy business woman. Strong purpose. Determined. Not scared of spider. I like that."

Lisa suspected Zenda was much the same way, with the exception of the spiders.

"Okay! I have a deal for us. You sign papers. I let you and Mee-ah explore cellar. If you find papers I need for hotel, I keep them. If you find papers you need, you keep them, or a copy if we both need them. Agapitos will burn what no one need, and spray for spider. At the end, my cellar is ready for fine wine, and we both have answers. Deal?"

"Deal."

Again, Lisa could not imagine the reason she was allowed into Zenda's private world . . . but God. On the front end, Gianna, bless her hotel-lovin' soul, cleverly provided Zenda just enough of a teaser that she eagerly welcomed Lisa into her private hotel, at an absurdly reduced rate. Once Lisa got her foot in the door and Zenda held the Hotel Mákari stationery—read the love letter—she was as curious as everyone to unearth the answers.

CHAPTER 22

One never knows what a day will hold.

"Lisa? It's Lyra."

"Hi!"

"I've found something significant."

"Shall I come to you?"

"Actually, I'm at your hotel. I came right over on the chance you'd be here."

"Room three."

Lisa leaned out the doorway waving to Lyra. It was early Saturday morning, and though the hotel was full for the weekend, the terrace was still quiet.

"I hope I'm not too early. I just couldn't wait."

They exchanged hugs.

"It's never too early to see you, sweet girl. Come in."

Lyra immediately settled herself on the sofa as Lisa joined her.

"Coffee or business first?"

"Business." Lyra deposited her portfolio on the coffee table, pushed

ELIZABETH TOMME

her designer sun glasses onto the top of her head, and looked about the suite.

"Oh . . . *tres chic!* Zenda's done a marvelous job with this place."

"I like her style for sure."

"Is this the sea glass you found on the beach here?" Lyra fingered the sparkling glass in the bowl. "Jewels from the sea?"

"Yes, such a treasure." Lisa realized her mother, for whatever reason, must have spoken the exact same words over her collection of sea glass. "What have you found?"

Lyra drew the portfolio onto her lap. Apprehension shadowed her expression. "I found this among old hotel papers from when my pappoús and giagiá ran the Mountain Inn. Prepare yourself for a shock."

Lyra handed Lisa a large, flat envelope. Lisa opened the clasp and withdrew a single 8 x 10, black-and-white glossy photograph. She gasped and stared at it.

"You see why I could not tell you about this over the phone?"

"I . . . would not have believed you . . . could have never . . . no . . . not over the phone."

Lisa and Lyra stared at the old photograph of a young woman who bore an uncanny resemblance to Lisa.

"It's like looking in a mirror."

"I gasped, too, when I found it. It put shiver on my spine."

Lisa turned the photograph over. It revealed no information. The clothing and hairstyle of the woman were timeless.

Lyra said, "She's beautiful—you're beautiful."

"Any clues to how old this photograph might be? Were there any others with this one?"

"This was the only one. The box was a jumble of twenty or thirty years of souvenirs and paperwork."

"Who is she?"

"I showed it to my Ángelos and my mitera. They do not know."

Lisa stared at the younger version of herself in the old photograph. Dissociation left her numb. *Another Greek clue.*

"How could this photograph fit in with the olive wood cross, the Hotel Mákari, the letter, the crystal bottle, wine cork, sand, sea glass, and my locket?"

Lyra measured her words. "The day you came to our hotel, do you remember you show us picture of your mother?"

"Your father stared at it for a long time. He looked from me to the photo. He was thinking something he did not say."

"I noticed that, too. I respected his silence and did not ask him in front of you. After you left, I asked him, but he did not say."

Lisa ventured, "I believe he was thinking I do not look like my mother." Lisa shrugged. "I was told I look like my father's side of the family."

Lyra nodded, unable to argue Lisa's claim but offered a thought. "Maybe this woman is your aunt? Did your father have a sister? Maybe she traveled to Greece. Maybe she brought your mother the Greek things."

"Oh . . . maybe," Lisa laughed with relief. "Whew, I can breathe again—except, my father said he was an only child. But, you know, at this point, I would not rule out any possibility. I've never researched the family genealogy. I think it's time."

"Perhaps you will find your father had a sister. Or, perhaps you will find that it is only a coincidence you look a lot like this woman."

"My mother always said everyone has a look-alike somewhere out there in the world. Can I make a copy of this photograph?"

"We give you the photograph. I made copy for us."

Lisa leaned in to hug Lyra; however, it was Lyra who wrapped her arms around Lisa and held her tight. "My papa is right," she promised, "Míos have answer." She added with confidence, "God always have the answer."

"Amen. Let's celebrate with coffee and Sweet Almond Cake."

* * *

"Mom?" A very drowsy Cate answered the phone and yawned. "It's five in the morning. Is everything okay?"

Oops, and on a Saturday. Lisa chuckled, "No, it's two in the afternoon. Please forgive me for calling so early. Go back to sleep, honey. Just give me a call later. I love you."

"Mom, wait. I love you, too. I want to talk to you now."

"You sweet girl. You sound good, but so sleepy. I miss you."

"I miss you, too. Tell me the latest news from Greece. Find any more sea glass?"

"I find new pieces every day. I met with Zenda. She bought the hotel in a private sale, and has no idea if it was the Hotel Mákari."

"I'm sorry. Are you discouraged?"

"No, Evandir says that Míos and God always have the answer. And, Zenda's agreed to let me explore her wine cellar for old hotel records. Mia and I start on Monday. Maybe we'll find something there." Lisa did not mention Lyra's visit nor the shocking photo of her look alike. She had another plan in mind.

Cate yawned. "Good. Keep me posted. Have you seen any celebrities at the hotel?"

"A few."

"Take some photos for me."

"They come here to get away from all that. I can't blow their cover. Any updates on the wedding?"

"The alterations on Grandmother's dress are finished. It's just perfect."

"I can't wait to see you in it. I think it's time to start calling it *your* wedding dress. Have you picked out the flowers for your bouquet?"

"I wanted to talk to you first. What did Grandma carry?"

"I'm not sure. Maybe you should let that be your 'something new.' What flowers do you have in mind?"

"Something vintage. Pale pink cabbage roses, white snap dragons, and sprigs of silver leaf."

"Mmmm. Lovely choice." Lisa closed her eyes, wishing she was with Cate.

"So you called me up early on a Saturday. What's going on?"

"Actually, I'd like your help with the investigation. I have a big favor to ask. Could you do some genealogy research on our family?"

"I'm your girl! Hold on, let me get a notepad." Lisa heard Cate opening drawers, rustling papers, pulling out a chair. "Okay. Ready. I'll start a research notebook, too . . . maybe a spreadsheet." Lisa smiled. This sweet apple had not fallen far from the family tree.

"What branch do you want me to research?"

"Everyone."

"What?"

"Well, it's a big order, but we need anything you can get your hands on. The more I look into everything here, the less I realize I know about our family. Especially my grandparents, their family histories—etcetera. I need you to dig up the 'etcetera.'"

"Sure. The etcetera sounds like a *really big* category. How deep do I dig, and how far back do I go?"

"Start with my mom and dad and dig backwards into *their* parents and follow all the ancestral lines back as far as you can. Not centuries, but enough generations to uncover anything that might directly impact our known history. Think in terms of anything that could explain why mom had these things from Greece. Look for the usual stuff."

"Cynthia . . . Wells . . . their parents . . . their parents' parents, families . . . ties to Greece . . . the usual stuff . . ." Cate scribbled notes. "Wait! Define 'usual stuff.' Let's make sure we're on the same page."

Lisa smiled. She loved working with Cate. "Anything you can find on your grandmother Cynthia Carter Brenner, grandfather Eduard Wells Brenner, and their parents, so both sets of your great-grandparents, the Carters, Frank and Joan, *and* the Brenners, Beatrice and Eduard.

"And, if possible, your great-great grandparents. They all lived in the Denver, Colorado, area so the information should be fairly centralized, at least for these first few generations back. You can do a cursory look on Cynthia and Wells, but I don't think there's much need to look too deep— we already know they were both born in Denver, grew up there, attended school there, and eventually met and married there in 1965, the year after Mom graduated high school. Then, they moved to Alpine Lake, Colorado, as newlyweds."

"And, Granddad was something, like, ten or fifteen years older than Grandma?"

"Fifteen."

"I can't imagine marrying a man fifteen years older. I mean, Derek's five years older than me. If he were fifteen years older he'd be, like, *forty*! Oh, my gosh! That's *so* old."

"*Ouch* . . . watch it," Lisa cautioned.

"Oops . . . sorry, Mom. I don't think of you as being that old . . . I mean, I don't think of you as being an older woman . . . not that you are . . . old, that is—"

"Cate," Lisa interrupted, laughing, "Just stop digging. You're only getting yourself in deeper and deeper. Cut your losses. And, for the record, I'm only forty-nine . . . years that is, not decades, not centuries. I'm still considered middle-aged."

"Well, you certainly look young for your age."

"Thanks, I think."

"*Anyway*, I think it's sad Granddad ended up outliving Grandma even though he was so much older. That's a strange twist of fate, you know?" Cate stopped talking and tapped her pen again on her notepad. Lisa knew it's what she did with her nervous energy when she processed her thoughts. "Okay, so, speaking of age, you were born September 1967. What was Grandma and Grandpa's wedding date?"

"June 18, 1965. They lived in Alpine Lake their entire marriage. Our family's been there ever since. So, you should be able to find all those records for them and my grandparents in Alpine Lake and around Denver. Our family tree kind-of dried up and withered. My parents were each an only child, I'm an only child . . . you're an only child. It's up to you and Derek now to have babies and fill out the branches.

"Grandpa and Grandma Carter died in a car wreck in 1968. My Grandpa Brenner died in 1972 and Grandma Brenner died in 1976. I was too young to remember any of them, or if they had siblings, which I don't think they did, because Mom and Dad never talked about having any aunts or uncles. If you find any siblings, especially female, I definitely want to know, and get any photographs you can.

"The usual stuff will be birth and death records, educational records, home addresses, siblings, census records, names and numbers of people in the households, their ages, employment status, professions, and photographs. You should be able to find most of this online and download it."

"Piece of cake!"

"Oh, cake. That sounds good." Lisa realized she was hungry. "Oh . . . and passports! Check if any of them had passports and traveled or ever lived outside the country, Greece in particular. Look for any connections to Greece or Greek ancestors. Who knows? Maybe we're descendants of Zorba the Greek."

"Who?"

"Zorba the Greek. Never mind. That's not really possible. He was a fictional, happy-go-lucky character. It seems our family is well-rooted in real-life drama."

There was a long pause. Lisa feared they had lost connection. "Catie, are you there?"

"Yeah." Lisa could hear Cate tapping her pen on the notepad again. "Mom, what have you found? Why this sudden interest in our family genealogy?"

"Let's just say I still have more questions than answers, and I wonder if there's more real-life drama to our family than meets the eye. It would be good to know for sure. Oh, and if needed, I have some birth and death certificates in the safe at my house. You know the combo."

"Gotcha. I'm on it. I'll get started."

"But don't start now. Wait until morning."

"Mom, it *is* morning."

"Oh, yeah. I can't keep this time difference thing straight. But you know what I mean. Maybe you can go back to sleep for a bit before you have to get up for work."

"Mom, it's *still* Saturday. Are you sure you're alright?"

"I'm fine." Lisa was more rattled than she realized by the sight of her look-alike in the old photo.

"Be sure to call me any hour of the day or night with your findings. I don't care what time it is in either time zone."

Cate laughed. "I'll start now. I can't go back to sleep—my mind is already making lists. You do your part there. I'll cover the bases here. I'm so excited. I've been hoping to help with the actual investigation. Who knows? Maybe I'll find some interesting nuts in the family tree."

Lisa bit her lip. *Be careful what you wish for.*

CHAPTER 23

*One really, really never knows
what a day will hold.*

Unable to sleep, Lisa checked the time—again. *Five 'oh-wow' three a.m. Ugh. Forget sleep— Coffee. I need coffee.*

She ventured onto the terrace with a tray, drank cup after cup, and watched for the dawn. Stiff, tired, and caffeine-buzzed, she hit the shower, dressed and grabbed her keys, Bible, and tote. Today Thalia was hosting the gathering. She longed for the reunion.

The photograph from Lyra was secured in her research binder, next to the one of Cynthia. She couldn't wait to show it to everyone and watch their reactions.

Lisa's cell phone buzzed. She fished it from the side pouch of the tote. It was Gianna.

"Lisa?" All she heard was tears, crying . . . fear struck the pit of Lisa's stomach. Gianna sniffed. "Have you left your hotel?"

"I was just going out the door. Gianna, what's the matter?"

Gianna sobbed. "It's Nico. He's . . . gone."

"Nico's missing?"

"No. He passed . . . he *died*."

Too shocked to cry, Lisa sobbed on the inside. "He died? *But—*"

Gianna told the story between sobs. "Jack . . . went to get Nico . . . to take him to . . . Thalia's for church . . . found him . . . *dead*."

"Oh, no, no, no, no, no."

"Nico didn't come to the door. Jack searched the house, found him in bed . . . holding a picture of Maria. Jack thought he was sleeping, but he was . . . "

Together in their shock they cried over the phone. Nico was a grandfather-figure to Gianna. She was heartbroken.

"I'm on my way."

"Good. I'm here alone. Skender took Thalia to Nico's. He stayed to help them. The authorities are coming to investigate and get Nico's . . ." she sobbed, "*body*."

"I'll be there soon."

Lisa drove as quickly as she dared on the winding west coast road. In the hour it took to arrive at the Aegean Hotel, a deep sadness settled over her heart with the knowledge Nico was gone from them.

Happy tears flooded her cheeks at the thought of Nico in God's presence and his spirit reunion with Maria. She envied him in that. One glorious day she'd be with John again.

In her memory, she would forever see Nico as she had just weeks before, captivated at the sight of her locket. Her "very expensive Greek jewelry." Lisa placed a hand over the locket at her neck. They were to solve the mystery of her locket together—find the jeweler. More than that, she liked Nico and counted on, rather, taken for granted the many more times they would spend together. This deep friendship she longed for with all her heart could now never be.

* * *

MIA ASKED LISA, "Did Zenda give you a skeleton key?"

"An entire ring of them. She said the one for the cellar is on here. Step carefully. The stone steps are primitive." Lisa pitched to one side on a narrow, uneven step.

Lisa juggled her notebook and camera. Mia carried a grip filled with flashlights and light bulbs.

Mia said, "This is exciting. I feel like those explorers I teach the girls about."

"Me, too. We need miner hats," Lisa mused.

They reached the bottom step and began the process of elimination with the rusty lock. On the fifth try, the lock mechanism yielded. Lisa cranked the handle, and musty, dank air assailed their nostrils as she pushed the door inward.

"Oh, wow," they both exclaimed, their words falling on top of one another.

They inched their way into the dark cellar, dust particles suspended in the beam of the flashlight.

"Right. Let's try the light switch."

Mia located the switch and pushed the antique button that resembled a bell call. Braided cord ran from the switch up the wall to a single bulb hanging at the ceiling. It flickered and died. Others in the sequential rooms remained illuminated.

Lisa cheered, "Hooray! Not total darkness. I'll find something to stand on and replace that bulb in a bit. Let's orient ourselves first."

Mia agreed. "Good plan. This cellar is huge."

The rough-hewn walls were unevenly excavated from the subterranean rock. Rickety wooden shelves that once held wine bottles were filled with haphazard heaps of yellowed paperwork and over-stuffed, worn-out boxes.

"We have our work cut out for us. Are you willing?" Lisa asked.

"It's a little creepy, but I'm in. I bet we find some interesting things down here."

"Let's prop the door open and get some air exchange."

Lisa progressed into the next room. More of the same. "More missing bulbs, but the structural integrity of the walls and ceiling looks safe. We'll have to be cautious when shifting weight loads on these rickety shelves."

"Have you done this before?"

"Not exactly . . . I think I've seen too many movies. This reminds me of *Indiana Jones*."

Wide-eyed Mia asked, "When was the last time someone was in here?"

"Ummm, I think 1997."

"So, we need a system."

Lisa proposed, "Like at the Records office?"

"Exactly. Let's pull a few samples and determine if there is any chronological order to this mess, or if it's just been dumped." Two hours later, lightbulbs replaced and worktable set up, Mia gave her diagnosis. "No dewey decimal system here. We'll just have to scrap it out."

"Alright then. Let's take a break and then dig in."

They resurfaced and breathed the fresh air in deeply. An immaculately dressed Zenda emerged from the back door of the hotel office. She noticed them and froze dead in her tracks at the sight of them.

"Lee-zah . . . Mee-ah! Is this what my wine cellar do to you? You are dusty, and you have spider in your hair."

For the first time Mee-ah was unable to keep her full composure. A restrained squeal escaped her lips. "*Eeewwww* . . . get it off me . . . *pleeeeeease*."

Lisa brushed her hand through her own hair as she turned to inspect Mia. "Good news!" Lisa said, "It's mostly cobwebs. The spider on your head looks quite dead."

The news did not have the calming effect Lisa expected.

"Get it off meeeeee."

Lisa dusted the debris from Mia's head. "So, you can handle a swarm of bees, but not a dead spider?"

"Hey, I wear a special suit for that," Mia retorted. "And, bees are cute."

Lisa raised her hands in surrender and mouthed, "*Sorry.*"

"Come!" Zenda commanded. "I fix this." She led them to her private powder room, gave them each towels and tiny bars of luxury soap, and—without licking her thumb and rubbing their faces—cleaned the dirt smudges away with sisterly care.

"Now, we go have lunch together before you come out with dead rat on your head . . . or something worse."

Wide-eyed, Lee-zah and Mee-ah exchanged a look.

Lisa asked, "What in that cellar could be worse than a dead rat on my head?"

Zenda stomped her foot and announced, "Zenda decide right now, you no go back down there. I do not allow!"

Unwilling to surrender her cellar key, Lisa pushed it deeper into her pocket.

"Zenda . . . we made a deal. It's dusty and dirty down there, but it's not that bad. We're already making progress. Mia and I have a plan."

"No."

"But—"

"Zenda have a plan, too. After lunch, I send man to that dungeon. He bring papers out to you. He can wear dead rat in his head. I give you an office. You see papers there. No spider, no rat, no dungeon. No for you."

Zenda named the faithful maintenance man, Agapitos, worthy to wear a dead rat in his head. Lisa agreed to the plan with the caveat that she could go back down to the cellar on occasion, if needed.

Lisa and Mia followed along like ducklings in Zenda's flowy wake as she led the way to the taverna for lunch. Fresh salt air, the catch of the day, and a round of morello liqueur were the antithesis to the dank wine cellar. That, and the distraction of Zenda's purple, orange, and red African print caftan and black-and-white, zebra-framed eyeglasses.

In Zenda's charismatic presence, and with the promise of Agapitos' assistance, Lisa could feel the wind of excitement filling the spinnaker of her spirits and pushing her forward once again. She was certain the cellar would yield something important.

"I put you in this office," Zenda flipped the switch that illuminated the conference room. "See. Agapitos already deliver some boxes for you."

Lisa and Mia rolled up their sleeves and plunged in.

Lisa asked, "Shall we do like we did at the records office? I have my cheat sheet. I will sort papers into what appears to be "like kinds" of letters, statements, etc. I'll read the English ones and hand you the Greek ones?"

Mia agreed. "Perfect. I'll pull anything Hotel Mákari. I'll cull out the insignificant paperwork. You or Agapitos will ferry it to Zenda, who either files it or burns it."

In addition to his usual duties, the resilient Agapitos traveled in a never-ending circle. Cellar to Lisa with more boxes, from Zenda to the incinerator, and back to the cellar to start the cycle over again, and not once with a dead rat in his head, or something worse.

Late Thursday afternoon Zenda and Agapitos entered the conference room looking grim.

Hat in hand, looking at the ground, Agapitos stood next to Zenda. "Agapitos say he is very sorry, but no more box in the cellar. It is empty."

Lisa and Mia both pulled their reading glasses from their faces and sighed.

Agapitos spoke, and Zenda translated for Lisa. "Agapitos say he is sad for you, sad no more boxes. He ask if you sure you not find what you look for."

Lisa shook her head. She managed a smile for him though she wanted to cry.

"Mia, please tell Agapitos that I am sad we did not find what we were looking for. I thank him for working so hard to help us. Without him, we would have to live in the cellar for years, growing old, with spiders in our hair."

Agapitos laughed at the translation and wiped tears from his eyes.

Lisa stood, and hugged Mia, Zenda, and Agapitos. "Thank you all for everything."

Mia squeezed Lisa's hand. "We are sisters. Here for each other."

They all fell silent. Zenda stared into space, then snapped back to life. "So, you no find paper in cellar that say Mákari Hotel. So what? I say this not over. It not over!" Zenda pointed at Lisa and lodged a challenge. "This not over unless you quit."

"You're right," Lisa said with more confidence than she felt at the moment. She raised her chin. "I did not come all this way to quit. I'm not going to quit. My friend Evandir Vlochos says, 'You ask questions. Míos gives answers. Most important, God gives the answer.'"

Zenda nodded her approval. "You find your sand and sea glass here at Petrádi Beach. Petrádi mean jewel. Your mother love letter say,

'You are My sea glass . . . My jewel . . .' My *Petrádi*. See? That is something."

Lisa kicked herself into gear. *Wake up, Lisa! Ask the all-important follow-up question.* "Zenda, did you give this beach the name Petrádi?"

"Me? No. That is name of beach when I bought it. I have no idea who name this beach Petrádi."

Lisa and Mia exchanged glances.

"Mia, are you thinking what I'm thinking?"

"We need to investigate who named this beach, and when."

CHAPTER 24

∞

O death, where is thy sting?
O grave, where is thy victory?
—1 Corinthians 15:55 (KJV)

Wrapped in a bath towel, Lisa let Zenda in. Zenda breezed through the door, her arms full of clothes.

"You have wardrobe emergency? It okay. Zenda is here."

"I have no idea what to wear to a casual funeral on a Greek island."

Zenda sorted the hangers into groups. "Is funeral in church?"

"No. It's going to be at Nico's house."

"*What?*" Zenda raised her eyebrows and furrowed her brow with suspicion. Blinking away her confusion she discarded four garments.

"Indoors or outdoors?"

Lisa shrugged. "Probably both. You know, doors opened onto the terrace, guests going in and out. Thalia said casual. Mia and Sophia could not say how casual. Nobody knows what this means. Everything I have either looks like a day at the beach, or a pool party. Should I wear black?"

"No." Zenda picked through the hangers and discarded another two. She hung the remaining four garments on the closet doors.

"All these are safe choice."

One was a muted floral one-piece jumpsuit; another, a white wide-leg pantsuit; the third, an ice blue knee-length sleeveless sheath; and the last, a full-length turquoise caftan. Zenda admired the outfits. "These are perfect for a casual outdoor funeral."

"Have you ever been to a casual outdoor evening funeral? Aren't most funerals held during the day in a church, followed by a burial at the cemetery?"

Zenda put her hands on her hips. "Be happy it not in stuffy church." She pointed at the line-up. "Which one you like?"

"They're all pretty."

"You hold each one up to you. I look from over here and tell you what I think."

Zenda scrutinized each. "Clear winner. Wear blue sheath with your gold sandals, and gold locket look perfect in that neckline. Honor Nico with your stunning Greek jewelry."

An hour later, Lisa navigated her way to Villa Maria on the east side of Míos. With each passing mile Lisa's trepidation grew. She dreaded arriving and seeing Nico's casket in the living room, or worse, finding Nico laid out on the terrace in the warm afternoon sun. *At least there's a cool breeze.*

Lisa pulled into the gate. To her surprise, the car park was full and the overflow of vehicles spilled across the property. She finally found a place to stash the Fiat.

Lisa climbed the steps toward the terrace. A crescendo of conversation spilled over from the gathering crowd. Topping the steps she froze in disbelief. As with the church gathering two weeks prior, Nico surprised everyone yet again. There was no casket, no rows of chairs, no weepy people in black. This was not a funeral; it was a *party*.

The terrace was decorated with strings of party lights, balloons, candle lanterns, streamers, flowers, a Greek band, and tables piled with food and drink. The terrace was filled with chatty people erupting with laughter. It was the liveliest party Lisa ever attended.

She remembered Nico's response when she asked if he had done the church party decorations. His proud response, *"I know people."* In death as in life, Nico *knew* people. He had known exactly who would carry out his last wishes. His friends, Jack and Thalia.

"Lisa! Over here." Among the crowd, most of the church gang circled up at the edge of the terrace. They waved her over. She picked her way through the guests.

Gianna kissed her on the cheek. "Isn't this *wonderful?*"

"It is. I've never seen anything like this. I couldn't imagine what a casual funeral was. Was Nico part Irish. . .is this a wake—or a Greek thing?"

Everyone laughed. Peri said, "Not wake. We not know what casual funeral was either. This is not Greek thing. This is *Nico* thing."

"Well . . . whatever it is, it is perfect for Nico."

Demetri said, "Nico left instructions for Jack. Since he not attend Greek Orthodox Church, he not want boring funeral in empty church. Nico was buried in wooden coffin next to Maria the day he died. Nico no want funeral, eulogy, obituary. He want friends celebrate him living in heaven, not dead body on earth.

"He want one last big party for his friends. He say bring them all in for food and dance. Like parable of Jesus, Nico say, 'Go invite everyone on Míos from highways and byways to come for my party.'"

Lisa joined Gianna and Skender at the buffet. They loaded their plates and ate with Sophia and Hali. Meanwhile, Mia, Javi, their girls, Peri and Demetri formed a circle and danced to the band. By the end of the night, under strings of party lights, Lisa met more new friends than she could count, laughed more than she could ever remember, and with happy abandon, flung her arms heavenward singing her heart out to "Never On Sunday."

Sandwiched between Peri and Demetri, she danced "Zorba the Greek," and learned folk dances where they swirled in circles at high speed as the bouzoúkis played frenetically. Together the crowd celebrated Nico, his arrival in heaven, and his zest for life.

She raised her glass in toast to Nico in the company of rousing cheers, "Opa!" It was another glorious night that would forever change her outlook on life *and* death.

In addition to sleeping under the stars, swimming in the ocean, ditching the high maintenance hairdo, losing a few pounds, and becoming more spontaneous, Lisa added a few new things to her list:

1. Lose the boring clothes. Get blingy and get glamorous. *Think Zenda!*
2. Shred the funeral arrangements and make party arrangements instead.
3. Remember life is a song best sung with a bouzoúki.
4. Hire a Greek band on retainer.
5. Throw some really great parties.
6. Invite people from the highways and byways.
7. Party often and party like the Greek.
8. Dance to "Zorba the Greek" at least once a week. Dance in a crowd, dance alone—just

dance!

In the wee hours of Sunday morning, Peri gave Lisa a candle. "Come, we go to water, say bye-bye to Nico."

Together they followed the gathering crowd down to the beach.

Leaving their shoes on the shore, they waded into the sea. Standing beside her in the water, Peri said, "The band play farewell song. We face east, symbolize dawn of new day in heaven for Nico. We pass the flame, candle to candle, show God's light overcomes darkness of world. We stand in sea, symbolize baptism, and salt and light of God's children in the world."

* * *

MONDAY MORNING LISA sipped coffee and reviewed her to-do list. On the brink of her fifth week on Míos, she longed to solve the mystery surrounding her mother's treasures. Cate and Derek's wedding date was growing closer. She felt the pull. She must return home soon.

That she had jumped off the merry-go-round for a month was an experience she would never forget. Somewhere along the way between Gianna's faith and friendship, Thalia's strength and goats, Sophia's purity and bakery, Peri's kindness and morello liqueur, Lyra's faithful follow-through, Mia's interpretations of the Greek life, and Zenda's savvy flamboyance, Lisa's own thoughts got re-calibrated.

She learned to let go of a lot. Like the Greek people on Míos, she was content to flow with the uncomplicated wind blowing in from the sea. Her inner spirit, peaceful. Even if she never explained her mother's treasures, she was thankful they led her to Míos Island.

Humming "Never On Sunday," Lisa downloaded some Greek music to her phone. Enthused from Nico's party, Lisa decided to throw a Greek-themed pre-wedding party for Cate and Derek, complete with a Greek band and Greek caterer.

* * *

Cate's long-awaited call came on Tuesday just after three p.m. Míos time. Lisa counted backward nine hours.

"Hi Catie. You're up early."

"You said to call at any hour, so here I am."

Though Cate's voice was chipper, Lisa detected an undertone of something else. Something was up. After an update on Lisa's cat Sam, the wedding plans, and an assurance that business was doing well, Cate finally took the plunge down the rabbit hole and, ready or not, took Lisa along with her for the ride of her life.

CHAPTER 25

*Trust in the LORD with all thine heart
and lean not unto thine own understanding.
In all thy ways acknowledge him,
and he shall direct thy paths.*
—Proverbs 3:5–6 (KJV)

"So, I've been looking into the genealogy thing like you asked. I've worked on it every spare moment."

"Um-hmmm." Cate's nervousness transferred to Lisa, and her heartbeat quickened. With an edge of nervousness in her own voice, she asked, "What have you found?"

"Okay . . . well, actually, it's what I *haven't* found."

"That sounds interesting. Well, like I said, our family tree seemed to wither and die on the vine. Oh, wait, that's a mixed metaphor, isn't it? Hold on, let me get my notebook. I've added a section for genealogy." Lisa clicked her pen open and set it on the page.

Cate began her methodical presentation. "So, you said your Grandpa Eduard Brenner died in 1972 and Grandma Beatrice Brenner died in 1976?"

Lisa noticed Cate led with the Brenners. Were they the only significant finding, or was she saving the big stuff for a strong finish?

"Yes. That's what your grandmother told me about her in-laws. That's what I have written in the few notes I have on our family history."

"And, that they lived and died in Colorado?"

"Yes."

"And you never met them and have no memory of them?"

"Right."

"So . . . ummm, Mom, this is *really* bizarre. Are you sitting down?"

"No, I'm pacing the floor and growing more anxious by the second. Tell me. Whatever it is. Just say it." After all the surprising findings in Greece, she figured she was ready for anything.

"Okay . . . just don't forget, you asked for this." Cate finally dropped the bomb over the target. "I found no records of that. *No records!*"

"No records? No records of which part?"

"No records that your grandparents, my great-grandparents—the Brenners—*ever* lived or died in Colorado."

"No records?" Long pause. "Hmm. Well, their births were in the early 1900s. Maybe their records are just not there to be found, or incomplete—for whatever reason."

"No . . . no, that's not the case. I found no birth records, no death records, no school records, no driver license records, no marriage records, no census records, no tax records. Nothing. No records for Eduard Alfons Brenner, Jr., and Beatrice Marie Wells Brenner in *Colorado*."

This announcement was followed by crickets on both ends of the call. Moments ticked by.

"Okay, honey . . . so you did not find anything in Denver . . . maybe the records just didn't get filed at the County Clerk's Office. Maybe they were filed somewhere else in the state."

"Mom, picture this. I'm rubbing my temples and staring at the ceiling, hoping my words sink in."

Lisa laughed. Cate was such a darling when she tried to break news gently. "Catie, just rip the bandage off. One swift, painful motion."

"I didn't find any records for them in Denver, or *anywhere* in the state of *Colorado*. I pulled your grandparents' death certificates, and your father's birth and death certificate from the safe as you asked. They include everyone's information, names, Social Security numbers, dates of birth, addresses, etc., and it is consistent with your knowledge of the family history. The problem is, when I searched for Eduard, and Beatrice Brenner, I found no record of them in *Colorado*. I was so sure there must be a glitch in the system, I drove to Denver and spent an entire day in the Clerk's Office at the courthouse. I accessed all their records, dug for hours, got on their computers, sliced through the info in every possible way. I searched, they searched, and we all came up with zip."

"Oh. Well . . . oh. But we have the birth and death certificates."

"Yes. *We do.* We have the Colorado birth and death certificates for Eduard and Bea, but no one else does. Get ready. I'm ripping the bandage off *now*. The certificates we have are. . .fakes."

"Fakes?" Lisa gasped. "I'm sorry, sweetheart, the connection went bad. It sounded like you said fakes."

"I did."

"That can't be. There must be some mix-up, some reasonable explanation. Surely my grandparents are just lost in the system somewhere." Lisa could hear Cate flipping through papers in the background.

"Mom, I didn't want to believe it either. Trust me, I checked every possible source. In the state of Colorado there are no known graves for your grandparents, no obituaries in the newspapers, no addresses, no affiliations of any kind associated with their names. It's like they never existed . . . in Colorado." Cate sounded tired. "That's not all I discovered. I need to tell you more. A lot more. The fact that there was no evidence of your Grandpa Eduard and Grandma Bea in Colorado has a greater implication . . . their son Wells, your father."

Lisa suddenly realized that Cate had pitched a pebble in the pond. It did not trigger a ripple effect, rather a tsunami.

Lisa felt heartsick. "Oh, no . . ." The tide was sucking away from the shore at an alarming pace, and the tsunami was about to obliterate everything in its path.

"There are no records in Colorado for your father either . . . until 1969."

"1969? Catie, that's impossible. Dad grew up in Colorado. He and Mom married and moved to Alpine Lake in 1965."

"There are no records. Wells was off the grid until 1969. Then, I did find all the usual records for him that reflect the life he lived in Alpine Lake, Colorado, from 1969 until his death in 2010."

Lisa's heartsickness turned to dizziness and nausea. "So . . . where?" Lisa breathed deeply to stifle the nausea. "Where was my father for the first thirty-eight years of his life?" After she asked the question, she realized Cate already knew the answer. She dreaded hearing it. She wished for a do-over. She would take back her genealogy request. Ignorance was indeed blissful.

"When I got home from Denver, I started a nationwide online search for Granddad and his parents. It was like looking for needles in a haystack. Eduard and Bea's Social Security numbers were dead ends. Fakes. It was like they did not exist . . . but I believe I've finally found a match."

Lisa stared strangely at the room around her as if she just landed in an alternate universe where everything was the same, only different. The reality she lived in and this new reality collided in a surreal mish-mash. Her cognitive mind slammed into an unseen wall and slid to the floor in a messy heap. Her life-clock ticked slower and slower, and then . . . Time. Stood. Still. Her heart was in freefall as the basis for every memory dissolved.

Tunnel vision closed in, narrowing her world to a pinhole. The room around her became very small, the air close and thick. It pressed on her lungs, and she could hardly breathe. She could not comprehend what she heard.

Cate continued. "So I *did* finally find records for an Eduard Alfons Brenner, Jr., and a Beatrice 'Bea' Marie Wells Brenner, *and* I found the birth record for your father, Eduard Wells Brenner." Cate stopped.

Lisa did not feel capable of speech but heard her own weak voice ask, "Where?"

"Trenton, New Jersey."

Lisa's incredulous voice came out in a disbelieving whisper. "New

Jersey? Are you sure it's them? Sometimes other people have the same name."

Cate explained how she spent hours searching, verifying, and reverifying records. She obtained true copies of birth and death certificates, and all the "usual stuff" they expected to find in Colorado.

Cate proceeded slowly. "Mom . . . there's three more very important things I have to tell you about the Brenners."

Lisa heard herself ask, "There's more?" And then realized how preposterous it was to hope there wasn't.

"First, your Grandpa Eduard did not die in 1975, nor your Grandma Bea in '72 like you thought. Oh Mom! I'm sorry, this part is so tragic! They died in a house fire in 1942 when your father was only eleven years old. I found the records, I downloaded everything, even the newspaper articles about it. And, as I said, I have their death certificates and found their graves —everything. I found all their records in New Jersey."

Lisa's heart went out to her resilient daughter who traversed the heartbreak of this broken path that led to tragedy, heartache, and shock. She was thankful Derek was there for Cate as she processed these findings.

"And my dad's records?"

"Yes. Everything from his birth certificate in 1931 until he relocated to Colorado in 1969."

"The second thing?" Lisa was now officially in shock and functioning on autopilot.

"According to census records, after his parents' death, your dad lived with his paternal Grandmother, Willa Marie Guthrie Brenner. She raised him. Willa Marie died in 1965."

"The third thing?"

"Mom . . . I found a silver lining . . . your dad had a younger sister! Her name was Elise Marie Brenner Scott. You have an aunt. And, get this, her name is significant. Elise *Marie*. Her middle name, *Marie*, was her mother's middle name, and it is *your* middle name. You received your grandmother's and your aunt's middle name."

Lisa stood in front of the open window facing the Aegean Sea but did not see it. She was beyond stunned to think she had an aunt whom she was named after, in addition to having a significant

GREATER LOVE

Greek name. Lisa was afraid to ask the next question. "Is she still living?"

"Yes!" Cate said. "At least I found no records to the contrary. She was also born in Trenton, New Jersey, in 1933, two years after your dad. She is eighty-three years old and apparently lives in Connecticut with her husband, Dr. Charles Scott."

"Have you found any photos of her?"

"Not yet. I'll get one to you ASAP. I just have to find some first."

"And, we need to know if she ever traveled to Greece or lived in Greece."

"Do you want me to contact her?"

"Yes . . . no . . . not yet. I'll have to think about all the implications of that . . . and everything else you've found out. And, it might depend on what I find out about your grandmother's treasures. My mind's a blur; I can't think straight. I'll have to process all this. It changes everything I knew about my parents. I don't understand any of this."

Lyra's words echoed in Lisa's brain: "Maybe this woman in the photograph is your aunt. Did your father have a sister? Maybe she traveled to Greece—maybe she brought your mother the Greek things."

Lisa had assured Lyra her father was an only child. But agreed she could not rule out any possibility. At that time, she was so desperate to explain her resemblance to the woman in the photograph, she actually hoped for it to be a reality. It could solve the entire mystery in one fell swoop. But now that the search revealed everything it had . . . she was not sure. And, of course Cate had no knowledge of the mysterious photograph or of Lisa's conversation with Lyra.

Cate was quiet. She let a long pause go by, then said, "I know you asked me to dig into this, but honestly neither of us expected to find anything. You know, the whole withered family tree and all. It's a lot to take in all at once. I've been researching these shocking truths for days. I've had a little time to wrap my brain around it, and I'm still blown away. Do you want me to keep going?"

"There's still more?" Numb, Lisa's mind tumbled in on itself again, landing somewhere in her psyche with a surreal thud, but her voice managed to urge her daughter onward. In a moment of private horror, Lisa realized that Cate had only shared information on the

Brenners. They had not even talked about the Carters or her mother's genealogy.

Cate took a deep, shaky breath and asked, "Are you sitting down?" She sounded serious. "If you're still pacing, I really think you should sit down now."

Just as Lisa suspected, the Brenners were the warm-up. If the Brenners were a soft-pitch Lisa realized she'd better ready herself for some hardball. Instead, she just felt sick. Nauseous and sick.

"I'm sorry, Mom. I also found absolutely no records in Colorado for your grandparents, Frank and Joan Carter."

"And my mom? What about birth records for my mom in Colorado?"

"No."

Plunged under the surface by the force of another savage undertow, Lisa gasped for air as her mind numbly began to fill in the next set of blanks. She asked, "New Jersey?"

Sounding frustrated, Cate sighed. "I don't know. Another needle in a haystack. Same problem with Social Security numbers, etcetera. I've started a nationwide search for them as well. But so far, nothing."

Nationwide search. Lisa winced as her brain folded in on itself yet again. She quickly transitioned from disbelief, to overwhelmed, to totally numb, to deeper shock.

Lisa mumbled to herself. "Where on earth did my mother and her parents live? Why was it different from what she told me? Did they live in Greece? Did they come from Greece . . . ?"

"Mom—" Cate tried to interrupt.

"If so, why did Mom never tell me?"

"Mom—"

"Maybe they were all in the Witness Protection Program. But that would be weird. Was the Witness Protection Program even a 'thing' back then?"

"Mom—"

"Oh, no! Maybe we're all in danger now and just don't know it. Maybe we all need to hide."

"Mom . . . stop talking for a moment."

"I wonder if Grandpa Frank and Grandma Joan really died in a car wreck in 1968? But . . . if they didn't, they'd be like—ninety-something years old."

"Mom? Can you hear me?"

"I wonder if Mom has siblings somewhere out there, too? Maybe I have more aunts or uncles."

"Mom, are you okay? You're talking to yourself. Please—talk to *me*. Are you sitting down? Maybe you need to drink some water?"

". . . I am sitting down . . . I don't have water at my sitting down place. I could go get some water, but I'd have to stand up. Should I be sitting down or standing up and drinking water?"

"Mom, you're seriously worrying me. I think you're going into shock."

"Oh, uh, maybe I should eat some chocolate. I got some the other day, you know, to have on hand for stress . . ."

"Well . . . okay . . . if it would make you feel better."

"I don't remember where I put it. I hope it didn't melt in my purse—that's so messy."

"Oh, Mom, I wish I were there with you. I can't believe I told you all this over the phone. I mean, like, this is huge. I could hop a flight—"

"I could put it in the refrigerator—"

"Mom! Forget the water and the chocolate. You need something stronger. Do you have any whiskey?" Cate stammered. "Or cold air. Stick your head in the freezer."

"On my hands and knees," Lisa said.

"What?"

"I'll have to get down on my hands and knees."

"Oh, no! Because you're passing out?"

"No. Because it's a micro-fridge."

CHAPTER 26

Honour thy father and mother;
which is the first commandment with promise;
That it may be well with thee,
and thou mayest live long on the earth.
—Ephesians 6:2–3 (KJV)

Cate pleaded, "Promise me you'll find Zenda and spend the evening with her."

"I promise."

"The second we hang up?"

"The very second."

"I just don't want you to be alone."

"I promise. I love you, sweetheart. Everything will be alright. God is with us. He already knows everything about our family, and He's got this. And, remember, you're just the messenger. None of this is your fault."

"I wish I were there with you."

"Me, too. Now, go find Derek and let him take you out for a

romantic dinner. Get lost gazing into his eyes. Don't think about this for a while."

Cate giggled. "Mom, it's still breakfast time here. Love you. Bye . . . but call me later to let me know you're okay."

Lisa knocked on Zenda's door. She did not remember leaving her suite or walking there.

"Lee-zah! Oh, no. What happen? You so pale. Look spacey."

Zenda took Lisa's arm, and pulling her inside, said, "Sit down. I get you whiskey."

"That's what Cate said to drink. Maybe just some water."

"No water for you. What happen to you? Bad news find you?"

Numb with shock, Lisa nodded.

An hour later, Chef delivered dinner to Zenda's. She ladled soup from the tureen and handed the bowl to Lisa.

"Eat. After the story you tell me, you need food to help with shock."

Lisa sipped the soup. Zenda tore a piece of crusty bread, buttered it, and put it in Lisa's hand. "Eat."

"My mother told me Dad's parents lived in Colorado and died there in the 1970s, but they died in a house fire in 1942, in New Jersey. She said her parents lived in Colorado and were killed in a car wreck in 1968, but there are no records."

"So you wonder if they no die in car smash. You think all is lies. And, you no ever meet any of them?"

"Not that I remember. I was only a year old when Mom's parents died." Lisa pursed her lips and repeated the word, died, motioning air quotes.

"And you wonder why your mother tell you wrong thing?"

Lisa nodded, closing her eyes.

"Your family history is a wipe-off. And, you never know you have aunt, but it must be true, you have her name." Zenda's eyes narrowed shrewdly. "No. I say Cynthia's parents *not* die in car smashing."

"Cate's researching it. If anyone can get to the bottom of it, she can."

Zenda shook her head dramatically.

"I can't believe it. All those years I could have known my aunt and uncle and spent time with them. I guess I'll try to make contact with them."

"Is that so good idea?" Zenda looked wary.

"I don't know," Lisa said. "I don't understand any of this."

"Are you angry with your mother and father? They not tell you the truth."

"I'm shocked, and I don't understand," Lisa rubbed her temples. "It hurts."

"I think you should wait for God to give you answers before you make reunion with new aunt."

"I feel like my heart's in free-fall. Like I'm dangerously close to doubting my parents. Did they lie to me?" Lisa shuddered. "No . . . Jesus, help me, I won't go there. I trust them."

"But, you must be realistic. Weigh the evidence. After what Cate found, do you still trust them?"

Motionless, Lisa closed her eyes. "I love them. I don't want to be realistic. I want to rewind the clock to the moment before I learned this and it changed everything. When they died, I lost them. I don't want to lose them again, not like this." Tears slid down her cheeks. "My mother and father gave me a lifetime of selfless love. They sacrificed themselves to provide for me. They loved and nurtured me. They dedicated their lives to God and to me. This revelation does not fit with that. The evidence is tearing my brain in two." *God, help me.*

Zenda sat with her friend, holding her as she sobbed.

Lisa wiped her eyes. and shook her head in defiance. "I refuse to trash my parents. I trusted them before, and I trust them now. I won't let doubt steal them from me. The enemy wants me to lose faith in them. Well, this family is not going down without a fight. I know my parents. They would never do anything without good reason. I just have to keep investigating and find out what that reason was." Lisa raised her chin. "Remember when we didn't find anything in your cellar, you said, 'It's not over unless you quit.'"

"Okay, Lee-zah. *We not quit.* We keep looking. Together, we find answers."

"You are a good friend, Zenda. Thank you for everything."

Late that night, Zenda walked Lisa to her suite.

GREATER LOVE

"I make hot bath for you. Soothing salts. Make herbal tea. You soak, you drink tea, you get relax and drowsy. Then you sleep."

Once in bed, Lisa opened her journal to the words God gave her at the beginning of her search.

"You are My beloved daughter, I Am in all, and I know your story from beginning to end. I will answer your every question, and bring you full circle. I am a Covenant-Keeping God."

Lisa turned to the promise she penned to God on the ferry to Míos. *My God and steadfast Companion, I promise to listen for Your voice, and open my heart to the answers You provide. I trust You to lead me safely back home with a renewed heart. In Jesus' Name, Amen.*

Now neck deep in the shocking and cryptic answers, they swirled ominously like a cyclone. Had she not promised to open her heart and listen for God's voice, her bruised heart would easily have abandoned her and God at this latest turn.

Lisa turned out the light and drew the covers up close. *Father, You are the first place I should turn when I lose my footing. You always catch me and still my heart.*

In her mind's eye, she imagined Jesus rescuing her. She was thankful to be the *one lamb* He sought and carried to safety. In His loving arms, she drifted into deep sleep.

Lisa slept until eleven o'clock the next morning. For one half second it seemed like any other day. Then she remembered Cate's call. She tried to make sense of the new family history, but her mushy brain refused to help. The day before—now all seemed a smeary blur of distorted memories. She quashed the temptation to call Cate and ask, "Are you sure about all that?"

Still skittish of reality, Lisa opted for Gianna's remedy after the long week at the Records office. She would act like a tourist, rest, and swim in the sea. She would listen for God's voice and open her heart to the answers He provided.

Without a thought to her appearance, she pulled on a swimsuit, cover-up, hat, and flip-flops, and headed to the beach. She swam in the ocean, walked the beach, and collected sea glass. With each piece she gathered, she felt a unique kinship with Cynthia, though she still had no idea why her mother had the sand and sea glass from *this* beach. Lulled by the sound of surf washing onto the shore, Lisa napped all afternoon under an umbrella.

If her mind circled back to troubling thoughts, she remembered her promise to trust God and His admonition to take every thought captive. A wise counselor once taught her an effective way to redirect her racing thoughts.

She recited the verses she'd memorized from Colossians, "If then you have been raised with Christ, seek the things that are above, where Christ is, seated at the right hand of God. Set your minds on things that are above, not on things that are on earth." (ESV)

CHAPTER 27

There is gold, and a multitude of rubies:
but the lips of knowledge
are a precious jewel.
—Proverbs 20:15 (KJV)

"I've been trying to reach you all day." Gianna sounded excited.

"Hey! I followed your advice and acted like a tourist today. I spent the day at the beach."

"Hooray!" Gianna cheered. "So, Thalia called, and I've got good news for you. Jack was going through Nico's things and found a folder addressed to you. And . . . you've been on my mind since yesterday. I feel in my spirit that something unsettling happened. Did you get some big news?"

"Oh, my, yes. Cate called with some really big news. It's rocked the foundations of my world."

"You should have called me. You know I will always come. Is it emergency-meeting-with-the-ladies kind-of-big?"

"I just hated for you to drive all the way over here so late in the day, so I went to see Zenda. And, yeah, this information is emergency-meeting kind-of-stuff. I need to be with everyone and talk things out."

"I'm on it! How about lunch tomorrow, poolside at the Aegean Hotel for everyone who can make it. Will that work? I already know Thalia can come, and she'll bring the folder from Nico."

"Perfect. I'll bring Zenda and Lyra with me, if that's okay."

"Sure. See you then. Promise you'll call me if you need me before then?"

"I promise."

The next morning Zenda insisted on driving Lisa and Lyra to lunch in her hotel lee-moh-zeen. Lisa did not burst Zenda's bubble by explaining the SUV was not technically a limousine.

Upon arrival, Lisa led her friends down the landscaped path to the terrace and pool. They were impressed with the Gataki's oasis of a hotel on the brown, terraced hillside.

Remembering Gianna's spiritual introduction of the ladies, Lisa introduced them to Zenda and Lyra in the same fashion.

"This remarkable lady is Zenda Roussos. She is an encouraging example of strength, beauty, and enterprise. Her zest for life is infectious. Her charismatic spirit soars with joyful delight. She's been there for me during difficult moments.

"This precious young lady is Lyra Vlochos. She is faith-in-action, steadfast, loyal, as constant as the North Star, and a beacon in the storm. She is a Mikrí Mélissa . . . a Little Bee, intent on her Father's business."

With that, the hen-party swung into high gear as if they'd all been friends forever. Lisa loved how God united people as only He could.

They lunched on dolmadákia yialanzí, the stuffed vine leaves, and moussakás, a savory eggplant dish with minced beef, olive oil, onion, tomato, white wine, cheese and béchamel sauce.

Gianna served Lisa's favorite Greek dessert, galatoboúreko and coffee. Lisa devoured every crumb of the buttery, golden-brown flaky phyllo pastry layered with custard and drizzled with lemon syrup. It was the comfort food her body craved after the difficult past few days.

Over a second cup of coffee Lisa and Zenda filled everyone in on Cate's phone call and unbelievable genealogy discoveries. The information hit everyone like a jolt of current that electrified the conversation. They took turns pitching theories, punctuated by a zillion questions, to which Lisa shrugged and said she had no answers.

For Act II, Lisa and Lyra stunned everyone by revealing the old photograph of the young woman, Lisa's look-alike. Like Lyra and Lisa before them, everyone gasped when they saw it. For once, all were speechless.

Peri broke the stunned silence. "Lisa, hold the photograph next to your face."

They stared at the side-by-side, comparing the two likenesses.

Lisa said, "Does anyone know who she is?"

Wide-eyed, they stared and shook their heads.

Peri said, "If we did, we would have said when we met you that you look just like this other woman."

Everyone snapped photos with their phones. Once again, Mia and Thalia announced they were "on it" and committed to the task of researching until they uncovered the identity of the mystery woman.

Unwilling to miss out on the call to action, Lyra said, "I'm on it, too."

Mia said, "We'll get with you and get the information on where you found it." Mia nodded at Thalia. "Okay, now it's your turn. Show Lisa what you have."

"Jack found Nico's research materials on his desk. His pen was on the page where he last made notes. We think he was probably ready to reveal his findings to Lisa." Thalia passed a thick envelope around the table to Lisa.

Gianna said, "Do you want to open it in private?"

Lisa squirmed at the memory of being alone during Cate's revelation. "No, we're all in on this; let's do this together."

Everyone leaned in as Lisa opened the envelope and placed the notebook on the table for all to see. She flipped through the paperwork.

Impressed, Lisa said, "Nico was methodical and organized his work by sections with tabs."

The first section held a series of enlarged, detailed color photographs of Lisa's locket. The second section contained photos, printouts, and detailed physical descriptions of the Greek Paeonia Parnassus, or peony flowers that held the rubies, the Achillea

Ambrosiaca, or Olympus Yarrow flowers that held the diamonds, the Greek key fret pattern, and the Greek cross.

The third section contained a single sheet. It was Nico's appraisal of the value of Lisa's locket. It included his jeweler's assessment detailing the technical description of the style, weight, and measurement of the locket, the quality of the gold, and size of each stone. All eyes drifted down through the professionally catalogued valuation of each line item. As their eyes settled on the bottom line, everyone gasped once again.

There in black and white, it read: "€10,280.00*. *Valuation Denomination is for precious metals and stones only. Professional Valuation Required: Not included, jewelry-maker/artist's notoriety/masterpiece worth. This could add significant value."

Reflexively Lisa's hand flew to her neck to verify the *"very expensive Greek jewelry"* hung safely around her neck.

After Lisa brought her eyes back in off their stems, she proceeded to the fourth section. It was a thick collection of papers and contained several subsections with lists of jewelers, jewelry-makers, and maps of Míos, surrounding islands, and the mainland.

Nico printed examples of work from a variety of jewelry-makers. He made notes in the margins and drew arrows pointing to different aspects of their work where he perceived similarities to Lisa's locket.

Lisa slowly turned the pages studying Nico's findings. She thumbed over to a group of pages clipped together. As if waiting for her to come to this section, Thalia said, "This page is where Jack found Nico's pen. He was making notes in this section."

The pages were printed in Greek, and Nico had scribbled some notes in the margins, but Lisa's eyes were drawn to one word that Nico had angled across the top of the page for emphasis. Large block letters were circled in red, "ATHÍNA."

Eyebrows raised, Lisa looked over her shoulder at Thalia and Mia. "*Athens!* What is the content of this page about? Did he find the jewelry-maker in Athens? Does it give a name?"

Lisa handed the research folder over to Thalia and Mia. Intently they studied the pages.

Excited, Mia spoke first. "From his notes, look like Nico find custom jewelry-maker in Athens maybe make your locket."

Thalia removed the clip and flipped through the various pages. A folded, yellowed newspaper clipping worked its way free and fell into her lap. Carefully she picked it up, and silently read the headline. Her eyes widened, clearly impressed with something. Lisa watched her eyes dart back and forth scanning the article.

Thalia said, "This jewelry-maker name, Mílos Stávros. Very famous!" She kept reading, "Make only very expensive Greek jewelry . . . how you say . . . only one kind? Only one order."

Lisa said, "One order? He only made one piece of jewelry?"

Zenda came to her rescue. "I think, he make only commissioned works of art . . . one-of-a-kind."

Thalia kept reading and said, "Yes. And, make only for diasimótites."

Mia interpreted, "Celebrities. Commissioned works for special clients, celebrities."

Sophia asked, "What is the date on the article?"

Thalia carefully unfolded the brittle paper, "21 Aprílios 1967."

Lisa murmured, "April 1967?"

"Look . . ." Lyra pointed to a section of the paper that was still folded back on itself. "There's more to the article." With care, Thalia unfolded the last remaining section. It contained a yellowed, grainy photograph of a pendant fashioned by Mílos Stávros. Thalia laid the newspaper clipping on the table before Lisa.

It was not identical to Lisa's locket, but the style was reminiscent. It had the same type of intricate, embossed, three-dimensional gold filigree overlay on the surface. Lisa removed her locket from around her neck and laid it on the table beside the newspaper photograph.

"Look, instead of a floral pattern like mine, it has branches, leaves, and little birds. The artistry and style are quite similar to mine."

Thalia said, "Hard to see in photo, but Stávros always use jewels. This one have sapphire bird eyes and emeralds for leaves on branch."

"Oh, my goodness," Lisa said, "Look at the loop the chain passes through. They're identical. And it has the same Greek fret pattern around the edge as my locket."

"Like artist's signature style," Lyra suggested.

"Wait . . ." Peri remembered something she saw in Nico's notes and looked closely at the newspaper photo. She pointed toward the folder and motioned for Lisa to go back to another section. "Go back to Nico's close-up photo pages of your locket."

Lisa flipped pages until Peri stopped her. "Look!" Peri was beside herself with excitement. On the page before them was a close-up photo Nico took of the front of Lisa's locket. Nico had drawn a circle around the embellished loop that the chain passed through.

"Look!" Peri exclaimed again. They all looked and now plainly saw what Nico had seen: crafted into the pattern were Greek alphabet symbols. Peri said, "It has the Mu Sigma . . . the artist's signature. Mu for Mílos, and Sigma for Stávros."

Sophia said, "Just like Luca Adino's initials on olive wood cross."

Lyra asked to borrow Zenda's stylish magnifying eyeglasses and bent down closer to examine the newspaper photograph. If the Little Bee felt a bit ridiculous in the hot pink frames bejeweled with yellow and green zirconia pineapples at the temples of each ear piece, she did not let on.

"It's grainy and a little blurry, but I'm sure I see the Mu Sigma on the loop in the newspaper."

"Lee-zah! You have a *Mílos Stávros* masterpiece!" Zenda breezed around the table, her pink and green Hawaiian print caftan riding the breeze in her wake. She pointed to Lisa's locket laid on the table, glinting in the sun in all its glory. "You must put that work of art in my hotel safe. You cannot just walk around with Mílos Stávros on your *neck!*"

Visions of wearing the locket in high school gym class flashed through Lisa's mind. She kept them to herself, but said, "Zenda, do you know of this jewelry artist, this Mílos Stávros?"

Zenda dismissed the pointed question with a wave of her well-manicured hot pink nail-varnished hand, "No! I *never* hear of this *Mílos Stávros* in my life. But I think now, he is very famous. *You have masterpiece*. Remember Nico's valuation. Did it add Euro for the famous artist? No! He say you *need* to get this special value amount. Who knows? Maybe your necklace worth *millions*."

Lisa carefully refastened the presumptive Mílos Stávros masterpiece around her neck.

Thalia added her opinion: "Zenda, you have a point." Focusing her attention on Lisa she said, "Zenda does have a point. Jack has international connections and some clients in finance, he might know a guy who knows a guy who knows someone who can appraise it for you."

Zenda questioned, "Is it insured?"

"Umm . . . not that I know of." Lisa squirmed a bit. "Well . . . probably under my umbrella policy. I'll have to check." Again finding herself on information overload, she motioned a "T" with her hands, calling for a time-out.

Thalia looked at her oddly. "Why you do that with your hands?"

Sophia jumped on board, "Oh, I know this! She want to watch American football." Sophia then looked as puzzled as she felt pleased the moment before.

In confusion, the group was immediately divided into a dither of chaos, undecided as to whether Lisa or Sophia was the crazy one to talk about American football at a time like this.

Incredulously Peri said, "Lisa, why you want to watch football now? Sophia, why Lisa want to watch football now, at time like this?"

Gianna snorted. Mia, who had just taken a drink, spewed. Despite herself, Lisa laughed until she cried. Once she recovered, she explained, "I don't want to watch football now, but Sophia is on the right track. That hand signal is from American football. It means, *'time-out.'* Stop the action. I need a minute to think about all this."

Understanding the concept, the circle of ladies cooed in sympathy and agreement.

Lisa sat quiet for a moment and thought, then said, "Why on earth would my mother have expensive jewelry from Athens made by Mílos Stávros who specializes in commissioned, one-of-a-kind work for celebrities? *Why* did she give it to me when I was sixteen? And, why does everything keep circling back to my mother, Greece, and 1967ish?"

"Yes, that is good questions." Peri nodded, and on Lisa's behalf, raised her hands and signaled the "T" at every woman huddled around the table. "You need this American football *time-off*. We give you more minute to think."

Lisa's minute to think lasted about a half-second before Peri added, "You just find out your father, aunt, grandmother, grandfather live in Treen-ton! *Why? You don't know why.* You just find out your mother, grandmother, grandfather live . . . you not know where. *Why? You don't know.* There is picture of this woman. *You don't know who is that?* Why you look like her? *You don't know.*" Peri shook her head, "It's *too* much for you."

In protective motherly fashion, Peri petted Lisa's head and motioned for everyone sitting around the table leaning *in* toward Lisa to lean *out* and give her room to think.

With painful awareness, Lisa felt all eyes riveted on her. With intensity, they watched as if she were about to lay an egg, or something else equally astounding.

Lisa felt the heat rise in her cheeks. She closed her eyes. Maybe if she did not look at them looking at her, she could have a thought.

At last she grasped the faint shred of a thought looming somewhere in the back of her mind. Clearing her throat, she said, "Is Mílos Stávros still alive?"

With that simple question, the vacuum that had sucked the air from around her blew back in with a whoosh and filled everyone's sails. Catching hold of it, they all talked at once again and wondered why they had not thought to ask that question.

"And . . ." Lisa began, all eyes now concentrating on the newspaper photograph, "are there any records of his works and/or who commissioned works from him? If so, we might be able to find out who commissioned my locket."

The Little Bee was on it. With laser focus, Lyra typed fast and furious, nails clicking on the microscopic keyboard of her cell phone. She was still wearing Zenda's magnifiers.

Lisa watched as she scrolled, tapped, and read the tiny screen. Her shoulders sagged. "Mílos Stávros died in 1967. It says most of the records of his work were destroyed."

A collective groan signaled another dead end in Lisa's investigation.

CHAPTER 28

◈

Who can find a virtuous woman?
for her price is far above rubies.
—Proverbs 31:10 (KJV)

Unable to sleep, Lisa called Cate at one o'clock the next morning, Míos time. For Cate, it was four o'clock in the afternoon the day before.

"Mom? Why are you calling me so early?"

"It's not early. It's late."

"Not for me. For you."

"I can't sleep so I've called to drop a bomb on *you* this time. I'm going to fax some information to you. Can you do me another favor?"

"You bet. A new wrinkle in the case, I hope?"

"Yeah, another big, surprising development. Do you think you could contact my insurance agent today?"

"Health, business, or personal property insurance?"

"Personal property." Lisa heard Cate tapping on the computer keyboard.

"Okay . . . I've already pulled up the contact and started an email."

ELIZABETH TOMME

"We had ladies' luncheon today at Gianna's. Zenda and Lyra joined us. They fit in like they've been a part of the group forever. Oh, and, Gianna served dolmadákia yialanzí . . . you know, the stuffed vine leaves, and moussakás, and galatoboúreko—"

"Yum! Mom . . . insurance?"

"Oh, yeah. Jack found Nico's research on the locket. Thalia brought it and we studied it together. Nico knew jewelry, and, he was right, my locket is *very . . . expensive . . . Greek . . . jewelry.*"

"Like, how expensive?"

"It is a one-of-a-kind, designed for a celebrity, a masterpiece, designed by Greek artist Mílos Stávros in Athens, kind-of-expensive."

"Wow! Seriously? Mílos Stávros. He sounds exotic. Any chance you can meet him?"

"Afraid not. Cursory research indicates he died in 1967—"

"Another tie to 1967? Too many coincidences. Maybe you can find records of his works."

"It appears his records were destroyed. So, we're dealing with another missing records issue."

"Destroyed? How? Why?"

"Don't know yet."

"It's like a big black hole opened and swallowed up everything pertinent in 1967."

"So, meanwhile, I have a Mílos Stávros hanging on my neck, probably made for a celebrity, and we don't have a clue why."

"So, back to the insurance. How expensive?"

"Nico valued it at over €10,000, and that doesn't include historic value, or artist's name value."

"Ten-thousand euros?"

"Yep. Zenda says I should lock it up in the hotel safe."

"Uh-yeah."

"Catie, I've worn this locket around my neck almost every day for twenty-eight years. You'd probably die if you knew all the places I've worn it. Anyway, it's a part of me. I don't care if it was made by Michelangelo. What is important to me is that my mother loved me and gave it to me for my sixteenth birthday. It's value for me is sentimental. But, we will need to get a professional appraisal, and possibly add a rider to my insurance policy."

Cate said, "I can't believe it. I'm totally blown away!"

"Welcome to my club. I'm so blown away with everything I've found out about your grandmother's things . . . let's just say she should have put a wind warning label on her wedding dress box. 'Caution! If you open this box and have any sense of curiosity, prepare to be blown away.'"

Cate laughed mimicking a newscaster, "Colorado citizens are blown away as Hurricane Cynthia makes landfall in Greece—"

Lisa added to the monologue, "The Category 4 storm is making waves—"

"Oh, Mom, she's made such a big splash she's at least a Cat 5."

"Speaking of which, do you have any updates on the genealogy?"

"It's like looking for needles in a haystack. I promise to call the second I find anything new. So, what's left to investigate there?"

"Is that your way of asking when I'm coming home?"

"No . . . not at all. And, don't put words in my mouth. That's your own guilt talking. I'm one of the ones who sent you off, remember? Are you still worried about being gone for so long?"

"Well . . . yes. I should think about coming back home."

Cate interrupted, "Mom—"

Lisa continued, "Your wedding is just around the corner. I want to be there for you. I don't want to miss anymore of this special time together."

"Oh, here we go again. Mom—"

"I need to catch up to speed on things at the office to cover for you and Derek while you're on your honeymoon."

"Mom—"

Lisa finally yielded her ground and simply said, "I miss you, Catie."

"Oh, Mom," Cate sniffed, "I miss you, too."

"I thought so. I can always finish this search later, maybe sometime after the wedding. I'll start looking at flights home."

"I miss you, too, Mom, but I don't want you to come home yet. I'm serious. What's left to investigate? You must be close to the bottom line." Cate sighed, "I can't explain it, Mom, but I think you're getting close to finding all the answers to every one of your mother's treasures. And, who knows? It might also unlock all the genealogy stuff."

"Maybe. Maybe not."

"Don't be negative, Mom. It's not like you."

"I know. I'm just being realistic, honey. So far, it's all dead ends."

Cate reasoned, "Answer me honestly. Have you looked into one clue yet that you haven't found some sort of answer for, some sort of connection to, or some sort of tie to Greece, Grandma, or the time period surrounding the year 1967?"

Lisa laughed. "Wow, you're good at making an argument. And, no. So far, everything has some connection. I still just don't know how it all ties in to your grandmother or why she had these things. Nothing I've learned makes any sense."

"Then your time there is not finished. Please promise me you will stay until you get to the bottom of it."

In the long pause that followed Lisa looked out her window into the deep early morning darkness. In a matter of hours, the light of dawn would illuminate the sky. A voice within whispered, *It's always darkest just before the dawn . . . don't be afraid to look at things in the light of day . . . keep going.* She felt a glimmer of hope dawn in her soul.

"You're right. I need to sojourn a bit longer."

"Whew. Good. Let's recap."

Lisa began, "Okay, we now have information on the locket, but don't know why my mom had it or gave it to me. I found the sea glass and the sand at this hotel, but we haven't found any evidence of the Hotel Mákari or the stationery. We don't know why your grandmother wrote the love letter on the Hotel Mákari stationery. We don't know why she had the cork from the Giórgos Hill winery, and I have not been there yet to check it out or investigate if there is anything special about that cork. Mia and Thalia are researching Petrádi Beach, when it was named and by whom. They are also helping me research the identity of the woman in the photograph Lyra found in her grandfather's archived papers at the Mountain Inn."

"Wait, what?"

"Which what?"

"*What woman?* What photograph from the Mountain Inn?"

Uh-oh. Lisa realized she never told Cate about the mystery woman in the old photograph. Lisa cleared her throat and told Cate of Lyra's discovery.

"That's why you wanted the family genealogy, a photo of your aunt, and passport and Greek travel info!"

"Well, yes. Lyra suggested the resemblance could be because the woman is a relation. It's probably just a fluke."

Cate drilled her. "No arguments, young lady! You are definitely not coming home until you learn the identity of this look-alike woman and more of the other answers, too."

Lisa rolled her eyes, amused at Cate taking charge.

"I'm certain the answers are there. Mom! God will answer your prayers. He'll show you where to look next. You can't stop now. You have to keep looking."

Lisa smiled, thankful for Cate's faith, confidence, and tenacity. Talking to Cate was a cool breeze that blew out the cobwebs in her own busy mind. Lisa took in a deep, refreshing breath and let it fill her soul.

Cate said, "Oh, before we hang up, I almost forgot to tell you. I've taken all the information you've found and the genealogy information I've found, and organized it on a computer spreadsheet. I'll email it to you. Zenda or Gianna can print it out for you. Maybe that will help."

"Thank you. I can't wait to study it. My notebook is full, and I've almost run out of pages. It will be good to see it in a new light. Cate, you are an amazing research assistant, and I'm so proud of you."

"I'm proud of you, too, Mom. I'll send the email about the locket to the insurance agent. Just remember, no matter what you find or don't find in your search, no matter what we learn about our family history, we have God and we have each other and Derek. We're a family, and I love us."

"I love us, too. Mwah, sweetheart. Now, go have a wonderful Friday night date with your handsome fiancé."

"Mwah."

With satisfaction Lisa rested her head on the pillow and snuggled into the bed linens. Drifting into sleep, Lisa thought on Cate, and the gathering of beautiful, Godly women on Míos who had come together to help her.

She prayed, "Father, thank You for Your goodness, Your grace, Your mercy, Your steadfast love. Thank You for surrounding me with these virtuous women. You always provide what I need. I love You and I trust You. In Jesus' Name, Amen."

In her last thoughts before sleep, she wondered why the Mílos Stávros locket with all of its precious gold, diamonds, and rubies had been given to her.

Father God answered, *"You are my precious daughter and your price is far above these few small rubies. I have joyfully paid the price. And, I have kept . . . my . . . vow."*

Lisa whispered, "Oh, my . . . my name means, My God Is a Vow, and my God has kept His vow. God . . . are You saying that You have *kept me?* Am I the vow You have kept? I can't wait for You to tell me the rest of this story."

CHAPTER 29

Hold Fast.
Stay the Course.
I have heard the desires of your heart.
I am Faithful and True.
Love, Abba

Midday Lisa joined Zenda on her terrace. Kissing her on the cheek, she said, "Ooh, Zenda, you look marvelous in that gauzy, white caftan. Your rhinestone eyeglasses and sandals are just too cha-cha for words."

Zenda's mass of dark, wavy hair was twirled loosely and secured to her head in a chic, messy bun. Wispy tendrils framed her face. Dangly pearl-drop earrings bobbed at her lobes. The total effect was soft and feminine. Lisa yawned, "I wish I felt as fresh as you look."

"You look lovely, darling," she wagged a finger, "but those dark circles under your eyes don't go with your outfit."

"Maybe I need some bling," Lisa proposed. "Where *do* you get your beautiful eyeglasses?"

"You like them, Lee-zah?"

"Very much."

"I find some in Athens. Some at chora specialty boutique. I take you shopping and introduce you. Some online."

"Would you mind terribly if I buy a few pairs and copy you? You make an unforgettable fashion statement." Lisa could imagine the look on Cate's face if she wore a pair of red rhinestone magnifiers to the next board meeting. Perhaps she would go wild and pair them with a red slacks suit.

Zenda turned her head demurely to the side in exaggerated humility. "I would be honor for you copy me." Zenda patted the sofa cushion. "Our lunch is ready. Come, sit, eat."

Zenda filled Lee-zah's wine glass. "Chef just delivered lamb pastries and fried tomato balls. Eat while it's hot and crispy."

Lisa filled her plate and tried a bite of each. "These are delicious!" Lisa said in delight.

"You like? I love this lunch."

"It's crispy and savory."

"We have loukoumádes and coffee, too."

"Oh, yum, another favorite. I ate them at your taverna with Peri and Demetri the day we found your beach."

"That Peri, I *love* her—and, all those ladies. I talk to Thalia about enterprise with her for goat products and Mia for honey. Gianna and Lyra, they both in hotels like me. We need to work together with our hotel businesses." Zenda took a sip of wine. "I notice every woman at luncheon is nice, not say one bad thing about each other or any other person. That is rare." She made a gesture across her neck and said, "So many women, cut your throat."

"Every weekend we get together along with the men at someone's house. We study the Bible, pray together, sing praises to God, and encourage one another. I call them my God-gathered family on Míos. Zenda, I have heard you talk about God. Would you like to go with me to our gathering tomorrow?"

Zenda fell quiet. "I will think and let you know."

Lisa smiled. "Lyra is going with me. We'll leave around four, if you decide to join us."

Over coffee they did a deep dive into Cate's spreadsheet.

"Your Cate is thorough. She already updated it with column for

Lyra's photograph, and Mílos Stávros locket. Look, she even make section for your name in Greek, "My God Is a Vow."

"Zenda, do you believe that God speaks to people today?"

Zenda added cream and sugar to her coffee and stirred it. "I do. You hear something?"

"Mmmm. Early this morning. I wondered why I have this jeweled locket. God said, 'You are My precious daughter, and your price is far above these few small rubies. I have joyfully paid that price. *I have kept My vow.*'"

Tears welled in Zenda's eyes. She let them spill onto her cheeks.

Lisa said, "Evandir Vlochos said every Greek word has a meaning and a purpose. Evandir and Mia both believe my parents named me with purpose, *'My God Is a Vow.'* This morning God said to me, *'I have kept My vow.'* I realized that means God has *kept me*."

Zenda looked deep into Lisa's eyes. "You must believe what God say to you. When I was young, God spoke to me and I did not listen. It still make me sad."

"Oh, honey," Lisa squeezed Zenda's hand, "Our God redeems all things. You can always start fresh, His mercies are new every morning."

"You think God give me—let me, do again?" Zenda dabbed at her wet face.

"Yes, He is with you no matter what you go through. Always ready to pick up the pieces of your broken heart and speak to you in love. Would you like to talk about it?"

With a sad, far-off look, Zenda shook her head. "Another time." She blew her nose, pulled her guard back up, and flashed a bright smile. "Today we talk about you."

They studied the spreadsheet and added notes. When finished, Lisa pulled the cellar key from her pocket and laid it on the table between them.

"Zenda, I must ask a favor."

"Ask."

"Agapitos, bless him, he said he brought everything up from the wine cellar. I have honored your request and did not go back down there. But, before I return your key, I ask your permission to let me go down and look one last time."

Zenda nodded her head. "Did God tell you to go look again?"

Lisa ducked her head. "No. This is all my idea. It's my inability to let things go." She laughed, "You know, hope springs eternal."

To her surprise Zenda laughed. "You, too? I have want to go look, too. Told myself to go look when I get key back." Zenda jumped up. "We go together. Two curious friends. Check if Agapitos is right or wrong."

Lisa eyed Zenda's immaculate white ensemble. "Perhaps you should change clothes first."

Zenda returned from her dressing room a changed woman. Lisa stared at the sight of her in denim jeans, a T-shirt, and athletic shoes. She looked ten years younger.

"Ta-da! This is true me."

"Why do you hide your incredible figure under those huge floppy caftans?"

"It's good for business. When I open hotel, I happened to wear a wild caftan outfit. My clientele see this eclectic woman. Somehow my look become part of mystique of private Greek hotel. So, I play the role, give them exotic Greek adventure."

"Well, you're a raving success. I am in no position to judge. I've worn my share of ridiculous business suits, panty hose, and high heels to meet clients' expectations for professional attire. Ugh, the things we do for business."

They descended the steps to the wine cellar. Lisa held the lanterns, and Zenda unlocked the door.

"Thanks for letting me see the real you. I'll keep your secret about the caftans. Only, let's agree to always be real with each other. Deal?"

"Deal."

Once inside, they turned on every dingy overhead light, and set lanterns around on various shelves. They each carried a lantern as they walked room to room examining every empty shelf, nook and cranny. Coming to the end of the cellar, they were forced to admit Agapitos was right. Their search only produced empty wine racks.

Unwilling to admit defeat, Lisa stood, hands on hips, lips pursed. "Well, pooh. I was sure we'd find something somewhere that Agapitos missed."

"Me, too." Zenda sneezed. It echoed off the dusty walls. Lisa prayed it would not trigger a cave in.

Lisa sighed. "Well . . . I guess that's that, but I still don't want to give up."

Zenda dropped her lantern to her side and turned to reverse course. With the floor illuminated, something at the base of a wine rack caught Lisa's eye. "Stop!"

Zenda froze in her tracks. "You see something? Is it scary? Is it spider? Should I close my eyes?"

"It's probably just a shadow. Shine your lantern over here." Lisa lowered her lantern, took a few paces, and knelt down on the floor. They put their lanterns on the ground.

Zenda said, "Oh, it's just broken planks on the floor." She sounded as disappointed as Lisa felt. "They fall off wine racks and nobody pick them up. Probably been there for years."

Lisa bent down, resting her cheek on the dusty floor. "Judging by the layer of dust on the boards, you're probably right. Looks like they've been there for years." Lisa pushed her lantern closer. "I see something behind the planks. It's probably just more broken boards, but I've got to check." Lisa pulled on the splintery, broken planks. "They're wedged in there tight. Ouch." She held her thumb in the light of the lantern, removed a splinter, and reached for the planks again.

"Careful. You might get spider bite, too."

Once Lisa pried one board free, the others pulled away easily. Lisa pushed the lantern closer and bent down once again to explore the shadows under the rack. She was afraid if she reached into the unknown darkness, she would meet Zenda's infamous spider.

"More boards, or you find something?"

In answer to Zenda's question, Lisa called up her courage, reached in, and pulled out two stacks of large, black, leather-bound books.

Lisa straightened. She and Zenda exchanged looks. Zenda rubbed her hand across the surface of the top book, pushing aside the thick layer of dust. Gold-embossed Greek lettering gleamed under the lantern. Afraid to ask, Lisa held her breath and waited for Zenda to interpret. She feared they had only found old accounting books.

Zenda said, "*Xenodochéio Mákari Engrafí.*"

"What? Did you say Mákari?"

"This book title says, 'Hotel Mákari Registration.'"

"Hotel Mákari! We found the Hotel Mákari?" Lisa hugged Zenda, then examined the writing on each of the four books. They were all the same.

"So, at the very least, we have confirmed there was a Hotel Mákari, a hotel with the same name as the stationery where my mother wrote the love letter. And," Lisa exclaimed, "These Hotel Mákari Registration books are in the same location as the beach where we found the sand and the sea glass like my mother had. I can't believe it."

"This is miracle discovery," Zenda smiled wide, shaking her head. "I have hard time to believe it. My hotel was *Hotel Mákari*. No one ever say to me this was Hotel Mákari. All those box of paper we search, nothing. Only sign is this register books."

Lisa opened the cover of the first book. Centered on the facing page in block Arabic numerals, "1965." She turned the page. Line after line was filled with what appeared to be guest signatures, dates, addresses, and assigned room numbers.

"Okay, 1965—that good. That's close to the time period of the other clues."

In turn, they opened the other three books and found 1962, 1963, and 1964.

"No 1966 or 1967 book." Zenda's shoulders fell.

Unwilling to give up, Lisa held out for another miracle. "Zenda, can I borrow these? I would like to look through them." She would pour over them, scour every line of these books looking for clues that related to her mother's treasures. Perhaps she would find her aunt's name or the theoretical high school boyfriend who brought the Greek mementos back to her mother.

Zenda sneezed. "Yes, of course." She shoved the dusty books in Lisa's direction and said, "Knock yourself over."

Lisa grinned. "Oh . . . I think you mean, 'knock yourself out.'"

Zenda nodded and sneezed again. The meager overhead lightbulbs flickered. They both held their lanterns up and looked around.

Lisa ventured, "Are you thinking what I'm thinking?"

"Yes, we need to check for more books."

"Yep."

Lisa and Zenda crawled along the wine cellar pavers, shining their lanterns under every wine rack and into every dark corner and crevice of every room.

Lisa shouted out from the middle room. "Aha! I found two more registration books under the wine racks."

They huddled together over the last two books. Zenda held the lantern, and Lisa opened the front cover: "1966 and 1967."

"Let's take them, get out of here, and go celebrate."

Before moving a step, however, Lisa opened the 1967 registry, brought the lantern in closer, and started flipping through the pages. Zenda sat back down and did the same with 1966.

"What I look for?" Zenda stared at the first page and sneezed again.

"Well . . . I'm not sure." Lisa suddenly questioned herself as to what she expected to find.

She stared at the first page, too. It was mostly written in Greek and other foreign languages she could not identify. As with every step of her journey, Lisa knew she must ask for help once again. She needed translation assistance from Mia, Zenda, or some equally patient friend.

Zenda said, "Let's take all these back with us so you can look through them."

"Good idea. I can sit in a comfortable chair, better lighting . . . glass of wine." She smiled at Zenda. Before she snapped the musty old book shut, she gathered a large section of the pages in her hand and flipped through them. It appeared to be monthly headers, Aprílios, Máios, Ioúnios . . . followed by lists of guest signatures.

Zenda got up from the floor, gathered up three of the books, and started toward the door. "Let's get out of here. I get these. You get those. We say 'bye-bye' to spiders."

Hearing no response, she turned to find Lisa still on the floor, Hotel Registry open before her, one hand over her mouth, the other resting beneath a line in the middle of the page.

"Lee-zah?"

Zenda off-loaded her unruly pile of books onto a wine shelf, knelt down beside Lisa on the floor, and peered over her shoulder.

Stunned speechless, Lisa stared at the hotel registry. The entry on line twelve was written clearly in her mother's unmistakable cursive hand:

June 2, 1967 Cynthia Chadwick U.S.A. Room 2

"Lee-zah?" Zenda followed Lisa's gaze and witnessed the proof on the page for herself.

"She was here . . ." Lisa whispered as the hard proof ripped the veil off her naive mind and exposed the naked reality in ink, on paper. Tears fueled by mixed emotions formed in her eyes, and she ran her fingers over the line as if it was written in Braille. Her fingertips connected with the mysterious moment from the past.

Lisa's eyes bore into her mother's familiar handwriting on the page. It was the same handwriting as the love letter on the Hotel Mákari stationery. It was same the handwriting as the shopping lists, and notes about school milk money, and water bills, and birthday wishes.

The culmination of the long weeks of research and wonder lay before her in black and white. Her mother's signature on line twelve of the registry erased all speculation and supposition. Without a doubt, her mother, Cynthia, stayed at the Hotel Mákari on Míos Island, Greece, in 1967, at the tender age of twenty-one.

There was just one problem. Her mother had not signed the guest registry as Cynthia Carter. She signed as Cynthia *Chadwick*, a name Lisa did not know. Once again, Lisa's life history was rewritten before her eyes.

Lisa stared at the page. In the blink of an eye, the foundation of her life story arced and faded into nothingness as surely as the glistening tail of a brilliant meteor that disappeared in the night sky, leaving no trace of its dazzling existence.

PART TWO

The Covenant
Σύμφωνο

Know therefore that the LORD thy God,
he is God,
the faithful God
which keepeth covenant and mercy
with them that love him
and keep his commandments
to a thousand generations.
—Deuteronomy 7:9 (KJV)

CHAPTER 30

༄

Passport to Adventure

Cynthia's Story
January 1967, Athens, Greece

*C*ynthia Chadwick caught first sight of Athens, Greece, as it crept into her field of view—through the passenger porthole of the Boeing 707 aircraft. With clear skies overhead, the land beneath appeared as folds of brown velvet, dotted with green scrub and sun-drenched, blocky white buildings. The cerulean waterscape that was her traveling companion for the past ten hours relinquished, giving way to a purchase of coastal land that was the Ellinikon International Airport.

Too excited and naive about arriving in Greece, Cynthia did not fret the touchdown at one of the riskiest take-off and landing strips in the world. Hemmed in by the Aegean Sea and surrounding mountains, this landing space required skill. Nose glued to the window, she strained against her seatbelt as the pilot came in hot and hit the brakes to avoid exceeding the short runway.

Looking beyond the runway traffic, Cynthia glimpsed bits of Athens as it popped into view between terminal buildings. In contrast to New York City, the populated Greek landscape was a sprawling mass of low-lying buildings strewn for miles across the arid hillsides. It captured her heart at first glance. Eager to experience it, she released her seatbelt and retrieved her handbag.

Arriving in Greece was the culmination of months of paperwork, foreign study applications, rigorous interviews, and meticulous planning. On Monday, Cynthia would begin a spring semester internship at the Alexander Archaeological Museum of Athens.

For the next five months, she would immerse herself in the Greek culture and sharpen her museology and archaeological skills. On her own for the first time and in a foreign country, she felt a little anxious, but mostly excited.

Once deplaned, Cynthia made her way through the sleek, modern terminal. The edgy, futuristic architecture juxtaposed modern style with ancient surroundings. Unable to read most of the signs, she followed the flow of passengers pouring from the flight, dispersing into the terminal. Odds were, they would lead her to the baggage claim. Close on the heels of the man in front of her, she stopped just short of following him into the men's restroom. *Oopsy!*

Despite the high heels and pencil skirt, Cynthia breezed through the crowded spaces at a steady pace. The leg stretch felt glorious after being cooped up onboard the aircraft for so many hours. Her feet were swollen from prolonged sitting and salty airline food, and she longed to kick off her shoes and peel off the tiresome nylon hosiery. After twenty-four hours in this ensemble, she was ready for a change.

Once her passport was stamped and her stated business approved, Cynthia emerged into the brisk January air, a trolly full of luggage and a capable and admiring skycap in tow. He greeted the cab driver, and they set to work.

"Will you be able to fit all my luggage in?"

"Naí, naí."

"No?"

"Óchi, no. Naí, yes. We make fit." They stuffed everything possible in the trunk and stashed the overflow in the front seat. Cynthia rode in the back seat, train case in her lap and luggage piled on the seat and floorboard beside her. She packed enough wardrobe for at least five months and three seasons.

Clear of the airport, the cab sped along the highway north from Glyfada, toward the Port of Piraeus before entering the congested canyons that led to the city center. Greek music blared from the radio, and the cabby sang along off tune, but with admirable gusto.

Surprised to see ancient ruins interspersed among the modern buildings, Cynthia repeatedly tapped the cabby on the shoulder and pointed out the window. "What is that?"

In good humor, the cabby sang out the answers in Greek as he jerked through the traffic in fits and stops. They chatted and sang the entire journey despite the fact neither understood a word the other uttered.

Cynthia tipped him generously for the safe arrival at her destination, and for him heaving her mass of luggage up the stairs to the door of her third-floor apartment. Eager to see her accommodations, she inserted the key in the lock. It did not turn. She grabbed the knob, pushed and pulled, jarred the door within its frame, wiggling the key from side to side.

A moment later she heard footsteps on the other side of the door and the sound of the door being unlocked from within. Panicked, she jerked her hand and the key back from the knob and fought the urge to run and hide. Surrounded by luggage, she bravely chose to surrender.

A young woman with a baby on her hip opened the door, her eyebrows arched in question.

"Hello . . . I am *so* sorry. I'm new here. I thought this was my apartment."

The woman stared at her as the baby cooed, smiled, and clapped his hands.

"Hello, little one!" Cynthia smiled and cooed back at the baby, then looked to the woman. "Do you speak English . . . mílas Angliká?"

"Ligo—little." Having looked beyond Cynthia and spied the mountain of luggage, the young mother seemed to decide Cynthia was not a burglar. She asked, "What number you look?"

Cynthia held up a piece of paper that contained her rental agreement, and the offending door key. Hopefully it was enough evidence to prove she was in the right place at the right time.

"My lease says, 'Door number four on the third floor.' Maybe I'm in the wrong building."

The young woman shifted the baby on her hip and leaned in closer to read the paper. A shy smile crept across her features. "You make little American mistake. You are in right building, wrong floor."

"I don't understand. This is the third floor."

"This is American third floor. Greece second floor." She pointed down to the lobby. "Street is ground. Up one stairs is *first* floor. Up two stairs is *second* . . ." She pointed up, "Third floor. You are neighbor. Hello to building."

"I am so sorry. Thank you for helping me. I am Cynthia Chadwick."

"Lena Ballas. Baby is Veniamin. He is six mínas . . . month, new baby. Come in."

"I should go. I don't want to intrude."

"Please, come. Sit. We meet." Lena opened the door and motioned her head toward the sparse room. "Are you here for university or for museum study?"

"Museum studies."

"Where you from?"

"New York City."

"Alone? First time Athens?"

"Yes, yes. I can't believe I'm actually here."

"You will happy here. What history you do?"

"Classical Greek Studies."

Through the open apartment door, they heard noisy footsteps and boisterous conversation drifting up the stairwell and growing closer. Lena smiled, "That is husband, Pavlos, and loud friends. Pavlos is professor, Athens International University."

With a wide smile, Pavlos entered the apartment, tossed his briefcase aside, kissed Lena on the cheek, and swooped Veniamin up in his arms. Cynthia gathered it was common for them to have company in their home. After he blew a raspberry on Veniamin's belly, he said,

ELIZABETH TOMME

"Hi, I'm Pavlos, you must be the new museum intern moving into the third floor."

"Cynthia Chadwick."

Getting over her shyness, Lena gave Cynthia a mischievous look and said, "She try move onto our apartment."

Pavlos nodded his head and kidded, "Ah. The American mistake."

Pavlos introduced his two friends. Lena retrieved Veniamin from his father and offered, "Men move your luggage upstairs. You move in, I put Veni for sleep, and you eat here."

Feeling she had imposed enough, Cynthia declined.

Disappointed, Lena asked, "You have other plans for first night Athens?"

"Well . . . no, but I should not impose on you any further."

Lena waved a hand. "You change clothes. Come back one hour. We eat."

Pavlos and entourage relocated Cynthia's luggage to the third floor and left her to sort it out at her own pace. Cynthia closed the door behind them and leaned against it. She savored her first impression of the small apartment that was to be her home through the end of May.

Walking from room to room, she let the space introduce itself. Cynthia liked her assigned quarters. Located near the heart of the city, the student housing building was within safe and easy walking distance to the museum, markets, restaurants, parks, the Metro, and ground transportation. Though dated and austere with meager furnishings, the space was bright and airy with large windows.

She preferred this blank canvas to a cluttered, dingy space. She imagined warming the space with bunches of flowers, stacks of books, candles, and bits of colorful pottery from local markets. Perhaps she would even find an ancient artifact or two. If lucky, she could pick up art for the main wall, from a local sidewalk artist.

The first room had a kitchenette along the back wall. There was a metal and Formica dinette table and chairs. Further into the room, a sofa, chair, and coffee table with a pole lamp in the corner. A writing desk and chair pushed up against one wall were home to an avocado green rotary dial telephone.

A sliding glass door ran the width of the room and opened onto the balcony. The view was of surrounding buildings, but looking up the street she could see a rocky hill topped with a smattering of ancient ruins. The second room was a windowed bedroom with en suite.

Cynthia unpacked a few suitcases. She filled the chest of drawers and closet, organized her toiletries in the bathroom cabinets, and stowed the suitcases under the bed. She shed her travel suit, heels, and hosiery; showered; and dressed in a soft sweater, casual slacks, and flats.

At the top of the hour she revisited the Ballas' apartment. The door was open for her. Soft music and delicious aromas wafted into the hallway. Lena and Pavlos introduced Cynthia to two other couples and two singles. They filled plates and lounged casually amid the sofa and floor cushions. Lena was an excellent cook.

Jet-lagged, Cynthia was grateful for the delicious meal. She was also thankful for new friends. Alone in a foreign country, it was comforting to know she already had "people."

Hunger satisfied and feeling relaxed, Cynthia excused herself from after dinner conversation, drug herself back upstairs, closed the heavy curtains, and crashed. The soft bed was pure heaven. She plunged into deep sleep for the next twelve hours.

She would have the next day to explore before starting her internship. She'd get her bearings, walk the neighborhood, stock the pantry, and prepare to start her new life at nine o'clock Monday morning.

CHAPTER 31

※

> What delight comes to those
> who follow God's ways!
> Their pleasure and passion
> is remaining true to the Word of "I Am,"
> meditating day and night in his true
> revelation of light.
> —Psalm 1:1a–2 (TPT)
> 444 BC

*B*riefcase in hand, Cynthia approached the Alexander Archaeological Museum of Athens on foot. She mounted the sweeping bank of marble steps and passed between the two center Corinthian columns and through the brass-plated revolving doors.

Spellbound, she beheld the cavernous foyer of the great main gallery. She savored her first moments in the impressive space, anxious to absorb the history stored within. The atmosphere around her was heavy-laden with centuries of revelation.

Before her on a massive pedestal, under spotlight in all its naked, full-body glory, the twelve-foot Classical Greek sculpture, *Iákovos*. He was breathtaking. Drawn to it, Cynthia encircled it by two revolutions before remembering the time. She homed in on the concierge desk and checked in.

The docent led her through the atrium of the main floor, great hall, and a series of passages. Distracted, Cynthia fell behind, drawn off task by the world-class displays of ancient history.

The docent urged her, "Please keep up. You can see everything later."

"Sorry," Cynthia pled, rushing to catch up. The docent swiped a card. A private elevator opened.

The glass-front elevator lifted them above the atrium exhibit hall and deposited them on the top floor. It was lined with modern, glass-walled conference suites.

Cynthia checked in at the desk and was directed to a reception room, for assembly and orientation of interns. They completed the requisite paperwork, followed by a dry review of program rules and photographs for access badges. After sworn affidavits and a series of non-disclosure agreements, they broke for a luncheon in the rooftop atrium.

Cynthia basked in the midday sun as they dined amid exotic hanging orchids and large potted palms. The high-rise view of Athens was captivating. From the high perch and with the help of museum staff, Cynthia spotted the Acropolis, the Royal Gardens, the Temple of Olympian Zeus, Filoppoúpis Hill, the Ancient Agora, and the Roman Agora. It was an exciting and memorable lunch.

The first afternoon was dedicated to welcome speeches from the museum head curator, head archivist, and team of conservators. Interns would receive mentor assignments the second afternoon.

Each intern would pair with a conservator with whom they would work for the duration of the museology courses. Rotations would include studies for Archives, Curating Conservatorship, Exhibit Design, and Museum Education.

During introductions, Cynthia learned she was the sole intern from the United States. The other nine interns were from Europe and Asia. Humbled, she was excited to study alongside students sponsored by the Louvre in Paris, the National Museum of Prague, the Art History Museum of Vienna, the Prado of Madrid, the British Museum

ELIZABETH TOMME

of London, the Zhejiang Provincial Museum of Hangzhou, and the Galleria dell'Accademia of Florence.

In addition to the museum work, Cynthia gained unlimited access to all museums and national historic sites throughout Greece, and was slated for field trips and onsite work at archaeological digs. Her ultimate reward for completing the program was full semester credit toward her degree plan and an impressive line-item on her professional résumé.

Museum staff badge on her lapel, Cynthia boarded an elevator for the ground floor. She checked her watch. Twenty minutes until closing. She had just enough time to dawdle in the gallery.

Cynthia sat on a bench at the far end of the great hall, cleared her mind, and studied the spotlighted ancient white marble metope frieze mounted on the wall. It was from the Classical Greek period and dated 450–430 B.C. It depicted a parade of Athenian nobility in horse-drawn chariots.

Though enormous, it was only one of many rectangular panels originally mounted over the architrave above the outer columns of the Archiros temple. It was stunning.

She withdrew her sketch book from her briefcase and a soft charcoal pencil. Working quickly, she completed a rough sketch that captured the essence of the frieze. Footsteps approached as she closed her sketchbook.

"It's magnificent, is it not?"

Cynthia looked over her shoulder. It was a fellow intern, the only other female in the group. Her voice was soft, with a delicious French accent.

"Yes, I could sit here for hours. I'm not ready for this day to end. Once it does, it will mean one day behind us, and one less day ahead. One day closer to the end of the program."

The young woman took a seat on the bench. "I feel zee same way. There is so much to see and so little time. I wish to stay forever."

"Me, too."

"I'm Océane Benoît." Unfamiliar with the luxurious, beautiful-sounding French name, Cynthia repeated it in her head. *Ooo-see-ahn. Ooo-see-ahn. Lovely.*

"I'm Cynthia Chadwick." They exchanged smiles. "You're with the Louvre."

Océane nodded.

"I should think your attention would easily be drawn back to Paris."

Océane shrugged. "Oui, Pah-rhee—and yet . . . I've always dreamed of Athens and zee study of Ancient Greek culture. And you, New York . . . zee Metropolitan Museum of Art, oui?"

"The Chadwick Centre for Classical Art."

Océane raised her eyebrows. "For a small museum, it is a worldwide contributor of notable exhibits. Ah, on zee Museum Mile, Fifth Avenue, Manhattan, oui?"

"Yes, you have a good memory," Cynthia laughed. "By New York standards, it is considered a sizable museum; compared to the Louvre, oui, it is très petit."

"Your name is Chadwick. You have direct relation to the museum?"

"It was established by my grandfather. My father is the chairman of the board and head curator. I hope to secure the academic groundwork to follow in their footsteps."

"An admirable goal, an opportunity that should not be squandered. I should think many doors will open for you."

"It won't be given me because of my name. Nor should it. I'll have to work hard for it, earn it."

"Yes, especially as a woman in zee man's world. I wonder, will you have to make *compromises* to earn it?"

Cynthia realized the true nature of Océane's question. "No. I will earn it academically, and based on the quality of my work, or not at all."

Océane nodded and turned her attention back to the frieze.

Cynthia said, "The Louvre. That's beyond impressive. What are your goals?"

"Oh, to be one of zee many museum conservators. My ultimate goal is exhibit designer, if I can obtain enough advanced degrees in art and design. Perhaps if I, too, work really hard, it is possible."

They both looked over their shoulder as heavy footsteps approached. Cynthia glanced down at her watch. "Our time's up."

The security guard circled in front of them. "Ladies . . . you must excuse yourselves. Museum is closing."

Cynthia rose. "Right. Thank you."

Outside, Cynthia and Océane buttoned their coats against the chilly night breeze. From their vantage point, the city lights blanketed the span of Athens. In the distance, the Acropolis was illuminated spectacularly in golden light atop the temple mount.

Cynthia asked, "Are you living in the Alexander student apartments?"

"Oui. I moved in only yesterday, to zee fifth floor, room deux."

"I'm on the third floor, room number four. If you don't have plans, we could share a cab back, or we could walk and look for dinner in a restaurant along the way."

"Let's walk and look. I'm starving." Océane pressed a hand to her slim waist.

Supper was found in a storefront restaurant called Taverna Loukanis. The savory aromas at this busy cafe pulled them in as they passed by. They shared a corner booth and a kreatópita, a meat pie filled with minced beef, onions, eggs, and white wine baked between buttery layers of pastry; a bottle of red wine; and karidópita, a walnut cake; and coffee for dessert.

Cynthia said, "The Greek food is delicious. I may have to buy a new wardrobe. How do you find it compared to French food?"

"*Non.* It cannot compare to zee French cuisine." Ruefully, Océane made a face, then forked another bite of cake into her mouth. "But, eh . . . it is acceptable."

Cynthia and Océane became fast friends. They agreed to meet up for morning coffee and walk to the museum together.

Back at the apartment, Cynthia deposited her briefcase on the desk, slipped into a hot soak, and then pajamas. Bible in lap, she cuddled up on the sofa and read in the glow of a single bulb illuminated on the corner pole lamp.

Far from home, parents, and New York City, she knew deep contentment with her new life in the heart of Athens. Surrounded by ancient history, she contemplated the timelessness of God. The very God of Abraham, Isaac, and Jacob, and Father of the Lord Jesus Christ, was forever faithful to His children throughout the ages. It was a faithful, eternal love that existed long before these crumbling Athenian temples were built.

From His throne somewhere high in the heavens, He heard the desires of her heart and deposited her on the doorstep of her ancient beloved history.

More than she desired to see any time-ravaged temples erected to mythical gods, Cynthia longed to visit the ancient Biblical sites. She wanted to walk the roads of the Apostles. It was in seeking these things she was certain she would learn everything she needed on her visit to Greece.

CHAPTER 32

⚜

Oh, My! A.K.A. Oh-La-La!

The second morning of Cynthia's internship included an extensive orientation of the entire museum complex. As the only two women in the group, Cynthia and Océane paired up during the tour of the public and private areas of the museum.

The extensive labyrinth of corridors in the basement of the building included the conservatory labs, archives, and design facilities. The tour concluded at the museum cafeteria just before noon.

Cynthia and Océane purchased sandwich boxes and coffees, and lunched outdoors on a sunny bench in the museum courtyard.

Cynthia said, "The sun feels marvelous on my face. It was freezing down there in that windowless basement."

"Oui, magnifique." Océane turned her face to the sun.

"I wish we could work on the same team. Our assigned rotations are completely opposite."

"C'est pitié . . .'tis a pity," Océane pouted, unfolding the wax paper from her sandwich and taking a bite.

Cynthia sipped steamy black coffee from a paper cup and nodded,

"At least we can work together on the group field trips and digs. I can't wait to see more of Greece and get the field experience." She bit into her apple.

Océane said, "I wish we could start with zee field work. Have you participated anywhere in zee digs?"

"Only one small excavation in upstate New York. We recovered some Native-American tools they said dated back about 10,000 years. That's my weakest area of experience. All my experience has been in the museum. I grew up around it. You?"

"Only one site in northwest France. I shuttled buckets of soil for endless hours. They found stone tablets that dated back 8,000 years. Have you chosen an area of expertise? What Greek artifacts do you hope to study while you're here?"

Cynthia smiled and answered, "I'm working toward a SME, a subject matter expert certification in glass amphoriskos from the Classical period, the Greek and eastern Mediterranean cultures. While I'm in Greece, I hope to secure some legitimate recommendations on collections my father could curate for the Chadwick. Then I plan to apply and be selected to work with the Chadwick designer for the exhibit."

Océane raised her eyebrows at Cynthia's well-planned course of action. She was sorry now she asked the question and was relieved she knew what an amphoriskos was.

"C'est impressionnant . . . that is to say, impressive choice. So, your heart is captivated by zee petite amphora . . . zee ancient glass parfum bottles?"

"Mmm-hmm," Cynthia nodded as she chewed a bite of sandwich. With a frown she pulled back the bread and examined the unimpressive innards.

"Your papa makes you apply for jobs in zee musée?"

"Oh, yes. As I said, *nothing* will be given me because of my name, nor should it be, if the Chadwick is to maintain its reputable status. I'll have to work hard for it." Cynthia returned the uneaten sandwich to the box and took out the cookie. "What about you?"

"I don't really like zee sandwich either. I'll try zee salad box tomorrow." Océane tossed her sandwich back in the box and retrieved her cookie, which she held up for critical inspection.

"I meant what are your interests, your area of expertise, and what would you like to study while in Greece?"

"Oh," Océane made a face. "Zee Greek cooks could learn something from zee French pâtisserie chefs. Want my cookie?" Cynthia declined. "I will study Classical Greek Sculpture, in particular, Polykleitos' Canon . . . eh . . . zee proportioning of sculpture, the Hellenistic Period that redefined zee perfect male human body . . . in stone."

Cynthia raised her eyebrows and nodded knowingly. The viewing of the *Iákovos* came to mind. "Ah, so . . . you are looking for the perfect male while you are in Greece?"

"Oh, oui," Océane laughed. "I believe I should conduct a thorough comparative cultural study."

"Of the men or the sculptures?"

"I think both. Zee *Iákovos* at the museum entrance is stunning, do you agree?"

Despite being well-practiced in evaluating and discussing nude sculpture from a purely artistic and historical point of view, Cynthia felt warmth flush her cheeks. Unable to look at Océane, she said, "Yes. It is marvelous."

Océane teased, "Are you blushing?"

"*Nooo*." Cynthia took a long drink of coffee, shielding her face from view. Océane leaned in closer, "Oui, you *are*!"

Busted, Cynthia giggled. "Okay, yes, I'm blushing. I don't know why . . . I mean, I look at these things all the time."

Océane gasped, covered her mouth with her hand, and batted her thick eyelashes, *"Oh-la-la!"*

"No!" Cynthia stammered, "I mean, I don't look at these things all the time . . . well . . . I do, but, I mean I've looked at a lot of male nudes —statues, that is. I mean . . ." Cynthia stopped. No matter what she said, it only made things worse.

Océane just kept laughing and saying, *"Ooh-laa-laa!"*

"Oh, forget it," Cynthia said in good humor.

Océane said it again and again. Each time she stretched the syllables out even more seductively. *"Oooh-laaa-laaa!"*

"Okay," Cynthia said a little ruffled. "You can stop saying that now."

GREATER LOVE

Océane elbowed Cynthia and pointed across the courtyard at a man sitting opposite them on a bench.

Cynthia took one look at him and repeated slowly and with sultry emphasis, "*Ooooh-laaaa-laaa!*" In a heartbeat she decided Océane was already a subject matter expert in her field.

The next day Océane was over her pout at being assigned a different schedule from Cynthia. As well, neither she nor Cynthia purchased another box lunch from the museum cafeteria. The reason for both: Mr. Ooh-la-la.

The afternoon session revealed that Océane's assigned mentor and Mr. Ooh-la-la were one and the same. From the next day forward, Océane lunched with him instead of Cynthia. Without offense, Cynthia either brought a lunch or hiked to Taverna Loukanis for the daily special.

Cynthia's assigned mentor was a no nonsense, middle-aged, matronly spinster with a mole to the side of her nose and black horn-rimmed glasses. Freideriki Kormos was a formidable tutor, and Cynthia was thankful.

Cynthia's number one goal in Greece was to deepen her skill-set and become a force in her own right. A handsome male tutor, while pleasant to gaze upon, was an unwelcomed distraction. Unlike Océane Benoît, she had not come to Greece to find a lover. She came to seek, conquer, and ultimately take the snooty New York museum-world by storm.

Modeling Freideriki's obsessive eye for organization and detail, Cynthia dedicated extra hours to her work and excelled throughout the Archivist, Museum Educator, and Conservator modules ahead of schedule. Based on demonstrated proficiency in all studies, Freideriki promoted Cynthia into the advanced internship program for her final three months.

For the remainder of her study in Greece, Cynthia would focus on the Curator and Exhibit Design modules. Acceptance into this program had profound and immediate consequences for Cynthia and her course study requirements.

Instead of the lectures and lab assignments with the original team of interns, Cynthia became full-time assistant to Freideriki. Inspired by Cynthia's passion, Freideriki received board approval to research, develop, curate, and oversee design of a new exhibit for the Alexander, Amphoriskos of the Classical Greek Era.

In reciprocation for her work on the project, Cynthia hoped to one day procure an on-loan rotation of the exhibit for the Chadwick in New York. In addition to the recognition of her work at the Alexander Museum, Cynthia dreamed that in bringing the exhibit to New York, she could truly make her father proud.

Frank Chadwick, Jr., maintained a long, impressive list of accomplishments. Though Cynthia tried her entire life, she found her father a hard man to impress.

***

AT THE BEGINNING of her fourth month in Athens, Cynthia was hard at work researching and curating artifacts for exhibit at the Alexander. Late on a Tuesday afternoon, Freideriki asked Cynthia to report to her office.

Cynthia knocked and waited to be acknowledged. Back to the door, Freideriki swiveled in her chair, motioning Cynthia to enter and take a seat. When she hung up, she smiled and uttered Cynthia's three favorite words.

"Pack your bags."

Cynthia took that to mean Freideriki succeeded in contacting the owners of an amphoriskos collection Cynthia helped locate the week before. She resisted the urge to clap and jump up and down in celebration.

"We got the Xenos collection?"

"We got it. Rather, *you* got it."

"I can't believe it. So, where are we going?"

"Dr. and Mrs. Xenos invited us to a private viewing at their gallery located on their estate in Thessaloniki."

"Whoopee! And, I get to go?"

Freideriki beamed proudly and nodded. "Congratulations. It's one of the perks."

"I'm *so* excited. I can't wait to see it."

"Dr. Xenos' attorney indicates they are amenable to loaning their collection to the Alexander for exhibit . . . and, *if* the Alexander can meet their terms, they will consider gifting the Alexander permanent display."

"*What?* Are you serious?"

"They are so pleased to know of our interest in their amphoriskos they will consider parking their collection here where it can be shared with the public and appreciated on a daily basis."

Cynthia's mind raced ahead to the exhibit. She could picture the stunning display shining within the gallery of the Alexander, and eventually, the Chadwick.

"We leave first thing in the morning for Macedonia. Pack professional dress for two days of travel and three days of meetings, and cocktail dresses and heels for three nights of events. We can expect meetings, tours, and dinner invitations. Also, our visit coincides with the Macedonian Museum of Antiquities Annual Gala. We will attend and represent the Alexander."

The private viewing of the Xenos' Amphoriskos Collection at their opulent estate overlooking the Thermaic Gulf was an extraordinary event that surpassed Cynthia's expectations. The Xenos collection was more extensive than first believed. If exhibited in conjunction with two other leads Cynthia was researching, the exhibit would be remarkable and could, perhaps, receive international recognition.

Cocktail dress number one was worn the first night. Freideriki correctly anticipated the events of the procurement expedition. The Xenoses celebrated the new alliance with the Alexander with a cocktail party that evening. The multi-millionaires of Thessaloniki circulated among the display, with champagne and hors d'oeuvres in the Xenos' private gallery.

Cocktail dress number two was worn the second night. After a day of meetings between Dr. and Mrs. Xenos, the Alexander head curator, and legal teams, Freideriki and Cynthia were wined and dined, courtesy of the Xenoses, at Thessaloniki's finest restaurants and night spots.

Cocktail dress number three was worn the third night to the museum gala. After a full day of touring Thessaloniki, Cynthia rested in the quiet of her hotel room, bathed, and dressed for the evening. She saved her most elegant evening attire for the gala.

In sheer black hose and high heels, Cynthia stepped into the sleeveless, A-line cocktail number. The layers of black chiffon swished and swung three inches above her knees as she walked. She slipped on a set of pearl bangles, a pearl-bobble necklace, and secured a pearl headband in her golden blonde bouffant do. Her bobbed hair encircled her shoulders in a perfect flip. She added extra bold winged eyeliner and heavy mascara to her lashes, and applied a pale pink shade to her lips. She grabbed her clutch and headed downstairs to the waiting car.

To her surprise, Cynthia observed a rarely seen facet of Freideriki on the trip. Freideriki also dressed for success. She punctuated her wardrobe for the business meetings and evening events. It reminded Cynthia of the story of the ugly duckling that turned into a beautiful swan.

Once away from the basement of the museum, Freideriki dressed fashionably, applied make-up, and wore contact lenses in lieu of the black horn-rimmed eyeglasses. Cynthia respected Freideriki all the more. Though quite attractive, she intentionally downplayed it during normal business hours. Cynthia suspected Freideriki found she was taken more seriously that way.

Once at the gala, Freideriki introduced Cynthia to the who's-who of the Greek and European museum world. Cynthia paced herself with the free-flowing champagne and canapés and met more titled people than she could ever hope to remember.

Once her diplomatic representations were fulfilled, Cynthia snuck into the deserted recesses of the museum to study the exhibits. The museum was phenomenal, and she could not count on returning to Thessaloniki. Sipping champagne, she immersed herself in the Ottoman exhibit.

"There you are. We've looked all over for you."

Oh, pooh. Busted. Dr. and Mrs. Xenos advanced on her position, a third party in tow. Dr. Xenos kissed Cynthia on the cheek.

"We thought we would never find you. We want to make introductions."

It turned into a tag-team event. Mrs. Xenos kissed Cynthia on both cheeks, took her hand, and did not let go. "My dear, we've looked throughout the museum for you. We could not leave until we introduced you to our dear friend." Mrs. Xenos placed Cynthia's hand in that of the poised man standing with them.

Dr. Xenos said, "Miss Cynthia Chadwick, we introduce you to Dr. Isidor Christopoulos."

Cynthia looked up into the eyes of Dr. Christopoulos, who steadily met her gaze. He said, "It is a pleasure."

Cynthia felt herself flush at the intensity of his attention toward her. His soft hazel eyes penetrated directly into her soul.

Dr. Xenos announced, "Isidor is the curator of our amphoriskos collection."

In the surreal moment, Cynthia wondered why she had pictured their curator as a snobby, aged museologist. She forced herself to stop thinking about the shade of Dr. Christopoulos' eyes and pay attention to Dr. Xenos' introduction.

"Isidor is a tenured professor of archaeology at Athens International University, curator consultant for the Alexander Museum, and our close personal friend and confidant."

A tuxedoed server orbited their position. Dr. Xenos drew him in with a wave of his hand.

"We should toast this momentous occasion. We are indebted to you both." They each received a fresh glass. Dr. Xenos led them in the toast. "To Isidor's keen eye and unparalleled skill in curating the illusive amphoriskos. And, to Cynthia's love of amphoriskos and her inability to take 'no' for an answer, which brought the Alexander Museum to our door. You are of shared passion. It is fate you meet at the gala tonight. Stin ygeiá sas . . . cheers!"

Cheers, indeed. Cynthia was over-the-moon with excitement at this chance meeting. She was dying to ask Dr. Isidor Christopoulos a million-and-one archaeological questions that swirled somewhere in her brain. But, one look at the impressive, perfectly proportioned Greek mortal standing in front of her, and the only words that came to mind were, "*Oooooh-laaaa-laa!*"

CHAPTER 33

Kindred Spirits and Buckets of Soil

*D*r. *Isidor Christopoulos, shared passion, fate . . . indeed.*
After another toast or two and a courteous chat, Dr. and Mrs. Xenos excused themselves for the night, leaving Cynthia in Dr. Christopoulos' company. Cynthia prayed their chance meeting did not come to an abrupt end.

Dr. Christopoulos looked toward the noisy swarm of patrons in the main hall, then toward the quieter galleries. He rubbed his jaw.

"Miss Chadwick, would you care to join me for a tour of the Toumba Thessaloniki exhibit?"

"Yes . . . I'd love to."

He lightly guided her by the elbow into the expertly exhibited collection of domestic vessels and utensils. Well-aimed spotlights illuminated the ancient fragments against black backdrops.

In a casual, confident tone that hung intimately close between them, Dr. Christopoulos spoke. "This exhibit opened in 1962 following significant findings from excavations located at Toumba Thessaloniki, near the Thermaic Gulf. This archaeological site was discovered in 1895 and included conical hills, with sequential building sites from the Bronze Age around 1100 BC, through the Iron Age up to 800 BC and forward."

He shadowed Cynthia as she moved among the displays. The description cards were written in Greek with very few English subtitles. She turned, noting his trim frame, and tilted her head upward to achieve eye contact. His head was haloed by a spotlight overhead. His intent gaze was trained on her. She felt self-conscious. He was observing her observing the exhibit.

Cynthia squared off in front of a display case containing a single artifact. "Dr. Christopoulos, I have a question—"

"Please, call me Isidor." His easy use of the American English language suggested extensive Western exposure. The articulation of his words was softened to percussive perfection by his Greek accent. The effect was exotic, sensuous. Cynthia forgot her question at the flutter of butterflies forming a Congo line in her stomach. Peeling her eyes from Isidor's thick, dark hair and strong jawline, Cynthia refocused on the exhibit.

"Isidor, my Greek is not adequate to read these descriptors; I believe this one is significant. Please, tell me about it."

Isidor faced Cynthia and leaned his arm casually on the display case. "In fact, it is the most significant artifact in the exhibit. Take a closer look. Tell me what you see and what you think."

Taking a deep breath, Cynthia studied the artifact. "Well, of course it is a vessel for liquids—a jug, but the shape is unique . . . quite distinct from the other pieces." Unhurried, Cynthia continued with her critical classification. "The rounded shoulders distinguish the main vessel chamber . . . the neck extension is narrow yet flared at the top with a . . . trefoil mouth. Based on the curve of the handle extending from the shoulder to the lip . . ." She paused, working out her final analysis. "It is a wine pitcher, specifically, an oinochoe."

He nodded, prompting Cynthia to continue. "Fashioned and used in the . . ."

"In the Archaic period . . . the mid 7th to 6th centuries BC."

"Well done, Miss Chadwick—"

"Cynthia, please call me Cynthia—"

ELIZABETH TOMME

"Cynthia. What led you to conclude it was Archaic, rather than Classical?"

Sipping her champagne, Cynthia gave him a sidelong look. "Isidor, I'd say the professor in you is coming out. Is this a pop quiz, or a casual evening among colleagues at a museum gala?"

Isidor laughed. "Please forgive me, Miss Chad—Cynthia. I suppose I did rather sound like a professor." Isidor rubbed his forehead. "I've got to get out of the classroom more often." He took her empty champagne flute and placed it on a tray with his own. "And, it is quite nice to discuss exhibits with someone who has a genuine interest in them."

"It is. Thank you for taking my interest seriously." Cynthia gestured at the display case. "I say it is Archaic because though the Classical period exhibited some similar structure, the overall material composition differs from the Classical vessels "

"You have an educated eye, and a tenacious spirit. No wonder you were able to sniff out the Xenos private collection."

Self-conscious of the blush that rose in her cheeks, Cynthia turned her attention to the next display case filled with a number of smaller cooking utensils.

Isidor said, "Since 1960, the Greek Archaeological Foundation has maintained no less than forty different excavations. One of the most notable findings was a Persian helmet, believed to be from the battle of Marathon."

"Oh, cool. That would be around 470 BC?"

"Close, 490 BC."

"The Thermaic region is rich in heritage. I'm impressed with the exhibits here. It's a well-kept secret. If not for the trip to see the Xenos collection and the gala tonight, I wouldn't have known to visit this jewel of a museum."

Isidor smiled, "For some reason, color photos of the Acropolis are more popular on postcards than Archaic oinochoe."

Cynthia shook her head and clicked her tongue at the tragedy. "Well, the Parthenon dishes up some pretty tough competition." She stopped at the end of the gallery and surveyed the room. "By any chance, is the Persian helmet on exhibit here?"

"Sorry to disappoint. The helmet lives in the National Greek

Museum in Athens, and it's on tour in Europe for a year. Perhaps I could interest you in another more boring exhibit?"

They entered the great hall. Cynthia said, "I'd love to see the Vergina exhibit."

"Ah, excellent selection." He pointed in the direction of the exhibit gallery. "This way."

Cynthia smiled inwardly as Isidor once again took her elbow, and he ushered her through the Great Hall. He leaned close to her ear to be heard over the noise of the reception and narrated as they made their way.

"The Vergina exhibit opened a decade ago, and due to active excavation, is updated regularly. In the 1850s, Napoleon III supported the excavation of burial mounds near what is now known as Vergina. It was believed to be the site of the first ancient Macedon capital, Valla. This is, of course, where Phillip II was assassinated in 336 BC, after which his son, Alexander the Great, became king. Excavations through the years were interrupted by a number of things . . . a malaria outbreak, the war with Italy, lapses in government funding, you name it.

"In the 1950s, portions of the capital were uncovered. The excavation continues, and recent papers report the finding of what appears to be the theater where Phillip II was murdered. Current theories suggest they will find burial sites there for Phillip II and other Macedon kings in that area. It's a work long in progress. There is still much excavation to be done."

"What an amazing project. Have you participated in this excavation?"

Isidor released a long, steady breath. "Not yet. I applied and was accepted, so I'm slated to join the team next summer."

"Congratulations. That is *so* cool. Can I apply to be your assistant? Shuttle away your buckets of soil onsite?"

Isidor stopped walking and faced Cynthia. He appeared thoughtful and rubbed his jaw again. Cynthia decided this was his reflexive mannerism for contemplation.

Cynthia flushed. "I'm sorry. That was forward of me. I can't believe I said that out loud. I just got so excited thinking how marvelous it would be onsite at an excavation of that magnitude."

Isidor took Cynthia's hand, raised it up between them, and frowned. "You wish to carry buckets of soil with this delicate hand? Your background is museum administration, at the Chadwick Centre, no less." Slowly, she raised her eyes to meet his. She feared at least a mild look of derision in them. She searched and found none.

"I do. I wish to roll up my sleeves, work in the thick of it, and carry buckets and buckets of soil."

He raised his brows and cocked his head to one side. "Then, you should apply for the team." Isidor shook his head and said, "Miss Chadwick, heir to the Chadwick Centre for Classical Art of New York City, there's certainly a lot more to you than meets the eye."

* * *

TANGLED in bedcovers from sleepless tossing and turning in the wee hours of the morning, Cynthia stared at the hotel room ceiling. Somehow it doubled as a movie screen and replayed all the scenes from her chance meeting with Dr. Isidor Christopoulos the night before.

Isidor Christopoulos was the quintessential tall, dark, and handsome man she always heard was out there. He was Greek. He was an expert on amphoriskos. He was the reason Cynthia did not return to her hotel until after midnight.

After the Vergina exhibit, they toured the Karabournaki Hall, pouring over the pottery, iron, and bronze antiquities excavated from the ancient harbor of Therme on the Thermaic Gulf region of the Northern Aegean.

From there, they continued their discussion of the merits of the Macedonian Museum of Antiquities over coffee in the then deserted museum lobby. When event staff finally pushed them out the door, Isidor tucked Cynthia into a cab bound for her hotel, driver paid and tipped, and a dinner date set for Sunday afternoon.

In their time together, Cynthia learned Dr. Isidor Christopoulos completed his undergraduate degree abroad at New York University. He said the best thing that came out of it was the sports car he shipped back to Greece and the opportunity to perfect his English. He completed both his graduate and doctoral degrees in Anthropology Archaeology, at the Athens International University.

Dr. Christopoulos' archaeological fieldwork was impressive. It included excavation sites such as the Giza Pyramids of Egypt, Petra in Jordan, Tikal in Guatemala, and Karabournaki in Macedonia. He was well-educated and well-traveled.

He was a professor of graduate and doctoral-level archaeology studies at Athens International University. In addition, he curated special interest artifacts for personal collectors and served as a curator consultant for the Athens Alexander Archaeological Museum.

He was ten years her senior, a man with stellar experience, expertise, and credentials, so easy to talk to and just as easy on the eyes. Yet, Cynthia was not daunted by him. No, she was beguiled by him.

Cynthia imagined all the young female students in his classes gone ga-ga, staring at him, and not hearing a single word of his lectures. A horrific thought occurred to her—as an undergraduate, she was even younger than his students, and just as ga-ga. "Ughhhh!" she groaned, covering her face with a pillow.

Cynthia turned off the alarm before it blared at her. She sat up on the side of the bed. *Remember Océane and Mr. Oh-La-La. Stay focused while in Athens, work hard at the museum, return to New York, and make my mark on the world.*

Cynthia dressed in record time, zipped her suitcase, and drug it to the lobby in search of strong, hot coffee and breakfast. She landed both, and was wolfing down her second pastry when Freideriki slid into the opposite side of the booth.

Cynthia asked, "Why the sunglasses? You can't be hungover. That champagne glass in your hand last night was a mere prop. Do you have a headache?"

Freideriki whispered, "No. I'm pretending I'm still asleep."

"Can I get you a plate of food and a coffee?"

Freideriki yawned, "Coffee."

Cynthia returned with a cup and a full carafe, poured it, and pushed it toward her sleepy travel companion.

Freideriki announced, "I think I'm dead."

"Drink, and give me an update after your first cup." Cynthia dug in her purse for lipstick.

Freideriki downed the first cup and amended her status. "Good news. I'm not dead; I'm only exhausted." She pulled the sunglasses from her face, stretched, and yawned again.

Cynthia noticed Freideriki was back to her usual self: no make-up, hair pulled into a bun. No doubt the contact lenses were packed away and the black horn-rimmed eyeglasses were at the ready.

Cynthia refilled Freideriki's cup. "A second round of caffeine should do the trick. I'll have you travel-worthy in no time."

Freideriki said, "What a week." She rose from the booth and headed for the buffet as if it drew her in with a homing device. Returning with an impressive portion of food, Cynthia decided Freideriki might not be travel-worthy after all.

CHAPTER 34

~~~

Stand at the crossroads and look;
ask for the ancient paths,
ask where the good way is, and walk in it,
and you will find rest for your souls.
—The Prophet Jeremiah, Jeremiah 6:16 (NIV)
627–586 BC

*C*ynthia dressed casual and wore comfortable walking shoes for her date with Isidor Sunday afternoon. He promised a diverse tour of interesting sites around Athens. He arrived early and loaded her into his red sports car.

"Your car is marvelous."

He turned the key, and the powerful engine roared to life, purring at a low rumble. Isidor smiled at Cynthia, "The only way to truly experience Athens in the spring is in a convertible." He revved the engine. "Do you have a scarf?"

"Yes."

"You'd better put it on."

Cynthia untied the colorful abstract print scarf from the strap of her handbag, folded it in a triangle, wrapped her head, and knotted it at her chin. She donned a pair of large, round, orange-rimmed sunglasses. The sunshades coordinated with her scarf, double-knit pantsuit, and handbag. She felt mod and glamorous from head to toe.

"Hold on!" Isidor let off the clutch and sped into the lane of traffic. He shifted gears, accelerating. Jolted to life with a crazy infusion of adrenaline, Cynthia felt giddy. Spring had sprung, the sun was high, and the day was glorious and warm. She absorbed the vibrant city that was Athens, Greece.

"Besides your trip to Thessaloniki, what have you seen since you arrived?"

"I've been to the Royal Gardens, Syntagma Square, and a field trip to the Ancient Agora."

Isidor took his eyes off the road and stared at her, his brow furrowed behind his sunglasses.

"Oh, and the Byzantine and Christian Museum, and Aristotle's Lyceum. We start our intern field work at the end of this month."

"But you arrived in January. No weekend trips? No house parties with friends?"

"I've kept my head down studying and working extra hours at the Alexander. I haven't found the time to be a tourist."

"Freideriki Kormos tells me you are a dedicated, serious student, to the point of extremity, and have excelled in all areas of museology." Isidor rubbed his jaw, then drummed his fingers on the steering wheel. "Have you found any restaurants you especially enjoy?"

"When I leave the museum in the evening, I usually have supper at Taverna Loukanis or Taverna Miltidis on the way back to student housing. On weekends, I shop for groceries at the Aikaterini Farmers Marketplace. I eat in some and take a lunch most workdays."

Isidor pursed his lips and gunned the engine. "We've got to get you out more. We have much territory to cover. There are many important things about life you will never learn in a museum. When do you return to New York?"

"The first of June."

Isidor shook his head. "That's a mediocre plan. Your visa, educational, yes?"

"Yes."

"Good. You have some time, then. We can work with that."

The butterflies in Cynthia's stomach fluttered to life at Isidor's repeated use of the word, "we." Cynthia was willing to find out what "we" meant, and what Isidor had in mind.

Isidor maneuvered the car through the congested streets toward open highway. He began a running narrative describing points of interest with a casual ease. His depth of knowledge would make any tour guide envious.

"Of course, I will eventually take you to the Acropolis and the most iconic tourist areas, but today, we enter into a dance with the Acropolis. We will look upon it from many angles as we see other important sites.

First, we drive southeast of Athens to the Kaisariani Monastery. It is located on the wooded western slopes of Mount Hymettus, the sacred mountain of Attica. You will see a unique perspective of Athens from that elevation."

Once parked, Isidor led Cynthia to a precipice overlooking the sprawling mass of white structures. Isidor stood squinting against the sun and taking in the view. Cynthia leaned over the edge of the railing, enthralled with the panoramic scene.

Isidor said, "Athens is spread before you, as far as your eye can see."

Far beneath them, the sounds of the teeming city evaporated on the hot, dry wind that whistled around the rock formations towering around them.

Cynthia said, "Tell me every fascinating thing you know about this place."

"The orientation of this mountain is crucial to its unique appearance at ground level, especially when viewed from the west at dawn. Sunrise often creates red streaks in the sky that appear to emanate from the mountain. It's a magnificent experience."

"Sounds glorious. Please add that to our list of things to do."

"Archaeological discoveries claim this mountain was inhabited in the Neolithic age. Throughout time, the Greeks predicted the weather by watching the cloud formations on the peak. They called it the 'crazy mountain' because the peak confused the clouds and actually caused unpredictable weather. In the ancient world, Mount Hymettus was the center of god worship, surrounded by mythological tales of Zeus, Apollo, and Aphrodite.

"Let's go farther up the mountain to the Kalopoulaone, and on up to one of the oldest Byzantine Monasteries in Athens. It dates back to the eleventh century, AD, and has frescos from the sixteenth century, AD."

Eager, Cynthia retreated from the lookout point. They hiked through the forest surrounding the Monastery and visited some smaller chapels as they ascended the mountain.

They arrived at an area with a cluster of primitive huts. "This place is called the Kalopoula. They sell snacks and jars of honey. Would you care for something to drink?"

"Yes, I'm parched."

"What is your preference?"

"Surprise me."

Isidor pulled two ice cold bottles of fizzy mineral water from an ice-filled barrel and claimed a jar of honey from the shelf. After he paid, they took a table in the shade.

"Thank you," Cynthia smiled. "Thank you for bringing me here. It's beautiful. I'm having a wonderful time. What a perfect day."

"I come here as often as I can. It's peaceful, away from the crowds, and the forest is cool. Rejuvenating."

"And the view of Athens is magnificent."

They sat for a few long moments in companionable silence. After a bit, Isidor pulled the jar of honey from the brown paper bag and wedged the cork free. He held the jar under Cynthia's nose. She closed her eyes and breathed in. A subtle smile spread across her face. "Mmmm. That is tantalizing."

"Try it."

Cynthia dipped her finger in the pale golden honey and touched it to her lips. "Oh, my, that's amazing. It's so . . . so . . . " She licked her lips, tasting it again, searching for just the right words to describe it. "It's sweet, yet herbal and earthy."

Isidor said, "The flavor is unlike any other honey in the world. There's a natural spring here that feeds the local vegetation. The thyme, the source of their nectar, grows in abundance on this mountain, and attracts the bees. The result is this delicious honey that tastes fruity and fills your senses with the thyme herbs."

Isidor recorked the honey bottle, returned it to the brown paper bag, and offered it to Cynthia. "For you."

She nodded accepting it with grace. "A gift I shall treasure. I can't wait to spread it over crispy, buttered toast, and stir it into my hot tea. It's so delicious, I could just eat it by the spoonful."

They revisited the overlook on the way to the car park. The late afternoon sun arced lazily toward the Athens skyline. As Isidor and Cynthia descended Mount Hymettus and motored toward the city center, the orb gradated into an ombre of rusty orange and red as it lumbered, sinking into the horizon.

"Next, I am taking you to my favorite part of Athens, the Plaka. Have you been there?"

"No," Cynthia shook her head, "I'm truly the worst tourist ever. I wanted to see Athens and much of Greece while here, but I have to stay focused. Prioritize my future."

"What do you mean? What does that have to do with seeing the sights while you are here?"

"If I don't impress my father with my work here, I don't stand a chance of advancement at the Chadwick Centre."

"I know the qualifications required to advance in museology, and you demonstrate proficiency. So, what are you trying to prove to your father? What exactly is it you are trying to earn?"

"My father's respect. He is not easily impressed. One day, if I work hard enough, I hope to earn his respect." . . . *and his love.*

Frowning, Isidor shook his head. "Your father is not already impressed with you? You are an excellent student, the only American selected for this internship. Is that not impressive enough for him?"

Staring at the road ahead, Cynthia said, "Tell me about the Plaka."

Isidor navigated the crowded streets in the heart of Athens and parked the car on a smidgeon of pavement.

"This ancient area is best experienced on foot. Let's walk in."

He cut the engine and turned to Cynthia. "So, my beloved Plaka—it cannot be told about; it must be experienced. You will begin that journey in a moment." He reached for her hand. "Cynthia, when it

ELIZABETH TOMME

comes to your future, it's important you understand your father's approval is not the measure of your success. If you confuse the two, you *will* reach your potential, but you will *never* experience the joy of it."

"So, what should I do? The Chadwick Centre is my heritage, and my father is the gatekeeper."

"Does your father love you?"

Cynthia clung to the lifeline that was Isidor's hand. "He says he does."

"If he did not say those words, would you know that he does?"

Cynthia shrugged. "I . . . I . . . please, show me the Plaka."

"Alright," Isidor smiled gently.

Cynthia mentally shook off her anguish and smiled brightly. "So . . . teach me how to be a proper tourist. Help me regain balance in my life, to learn how to breathe again, to truly see the sky above and the beauty of Greece beneath my feet."

Their eyes met and held. Isidor nodded.

Isidor helped Cynthia from the car and led her into the intricate labyrinth of narrow lanes that made up the Plaka. They wound through canyons of Neoclassical architecture that rose up several stories on each side.

Isidor shared a little history to introduce her to the area. "The Plaka is called 'The Neighborhood of the Gods,' because it is near the Acropolis, built on top of the ancient town of Athens at the northeastern slopes surrounding the base of the Acropolis. It has survived periods of war and ruin, but for the most part has been inhabited since the Neolithic age. It is the oldest part of Athens, with many visible archaeological remains. So, as we walk these ancient streets, take your time, acquaint yourself at your own pace, listen for what the Plaka has to say to you."

As in the Macedonian Museum, Cynthia found that Isidor shadowed her as she walked slowly through the maze of passageways. This time, there were no pop quizzes from the professor. Cynthia pushed aside her internship, museum work, and father, cleansed her palette and experienced her surroundings.

Though some areas were old and crumbling, she sensed the vibrance and significance of the place. It was evident the ancient and the new married happily here, and meaningful revitalization was in the works. The old buildings that crowded the narrow lanes housed a mixture of residences, shops, markets, sidewalk arcades, tavernas, bakeries, and businesses.

Cynthia wandered down a lane that was broader than the others and uneven under her feet. The buildings that lined the street were older and in serious disrepair.

She said, "These pavers are from a different period . . . this street has a different character."

"You have found the ancient street of Laskaris . . . it is a Greek word meaning, 'a tribute to a fighting soldier.' It's named in honor of the brave soldiers who fought battles to protect Greece. These are not the original pavers and structures, but they date back further than others in the Plaka. The course and name of most other streets have changed throughout history to accommodate the developmental progression of the city. But, Laskaris is significant in that the name of this street, and its course, have remained unchanged for at least 2,500 years. Archaeologists hope to receive permission to dig down to the level of the original street."

Cynthia turned in a slow circle, viewing her surroundings, studying every detail, searching for clues, and beckoning the perception of the feel of this ancient site to settle into her consciousness. The street descended in front of her and, in the distance, rose again. She followed the ascent of it with her eyes. It led to the Acropolis. Her heart beat faster.

Amid the dwindling foot traffic, Cynthia knelt down in the middle of the street and placed the palm of her hand on the ancient pavement.

"Isidor, is it possible that the Apostle Paul walked this route? Perhaps as he went to speak on Mars Hill?"

Isidor was taken aback by Cynthia's question. He wondered if he heard her correctly.

"The Apostle Paul?"

"Yes. Is it possible he walked here on his way to Mars Hill?"

Isidor rubbed his chin. ". . . it . . . is *possible*." Isidor knelt beside Cynthia and placed his palm on the pavement next to hers. "That is important to you?"

Cynthia nodded. Surprised by her emotions, her eyes brimmed

with tears. "It is very important to me." She looked from Isidor to the Acropolis and said, "While I am interested in ancient artifacts, I am only *drawn* to one thing, the True and Living God of the Holy Scriptures. I am not interested in temples built to other gods. The history of the Bible calls to my heart—that is my passion. The history of the Bible is what I want to experience while I am in Greece." A tear spilled down her cheek.

When Isidor met her gaze, she felt his eyes probe deeply into her heart. He said, "Yes. I can see that." He gently reached up and wiped away the tear, his fingertips warm from the pavement.

"Isidor, I must know—"

"Yes, I, too, am a believer and a follower of Jesus Christ."

Cynthia smiled joyously through her tears.

Isidor stood, reached for her hand, pulled Cynthia to her feet, and said, "Then we have important work to accomplish while you are here. I will explain over dinner."

CHAPTER 35

*Commit your way to the LORD;
trust in him, and he will act.
—Psalm 37:5 (ESV)*

With sunset and the lengthening shadows, the heat of the day yielded to the cool breath of evening, and the Plaka grew quiet and mellow. Families shuffled homeward to put children to bed and prepare for the week ahead. Lamp posts illuminated the dusky pathways. Strains of Greek music played on the breeze and married with enticing aromas wafting from tavernas and residences.

Isidor and Cynthia ascended the picturesque Steps of Mandrapílas to the intersection of Lambrós and Pagonís streets.

"We shall dine here, at the Taverna of Ankistrévo. It's one of the oldest restaurants in Greece."

Cynthia was captivated at the sight of it. Tables and chairs surrounded an enormous tree in the center of the intersection and spilled down the broad terraces of Lambros Street beside the restaurant.

Under the broad canopy of the tree, candles flickered against white linen tablecloths. Red bougainvillea spilled over slanted terra cotta tiled roofs, hanging over blue doors and window shutters, along the exterior walls of the restaurant. Trees rooted in enormous clay pots flanked the entrance and dining areas.

"Isidor, this is lovely." *And so romantic.* "It's everything Greek, past and present, at this one street corner in the heart of the Plaka."

Isidor waved at the host, who rushed over. They greeted each other warmly.

"Isidor, brother! I see you bring beautiful guest."

"Miki, brother! This is Miss Cynthia Chadwick, visiting from New York City. Cynthia, this is my lifelong friend, Miki Galanis."

Miki took Cynthia's hand and bowed. "Miss Chadwick, welcome to Taverna Ankistrévo. A friend of Isidor is a friend of my family and our Taverna." He motioned toward a table. "Paraklό, eh . . . please . . . this way."

"Efcharistό, Miki." Hand at the small of her back, Isidor guided Cynthia to a table for two under the canopy of the tree, at the top of the Steps of Mandrapílas. At their table, Cynthia turned and studied the view from the direction they had come. Their table overlooked the Steps, the red tiled rooftops of Athens, and the city lights twinkling in the settling darkness. Crowning it all was the Acropolis, high on the hill across from them, bathed in golden light, the hue of a golden beryl gemstone.

Cynthia's heart skipped a beat. She said, "This is a breathtaking view in Athens."

Isidor held the chair for Cynthia as she was seated. Miki smiled at Isidor, "This is special occasion, yes?"

"Naí, naí," Isidor smiled warmly.

"Eh, you care for menus tonight, or you want the usual?"

"I will have the usual; a menu for Miss Chadwick, please."

Cynthia declined, "No . . . thank you, no menu. I will have the usual as well."

Miki looked to Isidor for confirmation. Isidor nodded, "As the lady wishes."

Miki rubbed his hands together. "I am, how you say, eh, delight with this. You will enjoy."

Isidor looked at Cynthia and raised his eyebrows. "You *are* a brave one."

Cynthia regarded Isidor with a playful, daring expression. "I live life on the edge." She unfolded her napkin and draped it across her lap. "Tell me about Taverna Ankistrévo."

"Ankistrévo, this means 'The Ancient Tavern of the Angler.' They serve all classic Greek dishes. However, their specialty is delicacies from the sea."

"And, which of these delicacies are your favorites? . . . Wait, don't tell me. Surprise me. Tell me more about the Taverna."

"This is one of the oldest restaurants in Greece, in operation since 1892, by the Galanis family. It is Athens' most loved treasure, frequented by locals." Isidor lowered his voice to a whisper and spoke in a serious tone. "If you enjoy this restaurant, *do not* tell your friends about it. We do not wish it overrun with tourists."

Cynthia laughed, "Your secret is safe with me." She realized with fresh clarity, Isidor was allowing her into his private world. If he simply wished to take her to dinner, a thousand other restaurants would do. Cynthia looked toward the Acropolis. Tears filled her eyes. Wiping them away, she hoped Isidor had not noticed.

"It seems I make you cry often."

"Not at all. I rarely cry. It's just . . . this day has been so perfect. And . . . I just realized that I've fallen in love with Greece." Cynthia laughed, "I suppose I have spent too much time in the museum."

She turned her head studying the view. "The city of Athens, the cuisine, the people, the old rooftops, ancient pathways, Mount Hymettus, the Aegean Sea, thyme honey, riding in your little red sports car, the sunsets, the Acropolis at night, Taverna Ankistrévo . . . I'll never be the same." She looked around, "I want to savor every detail, commit it to memory . . . remember these moments forever."

She turned her attention back to Isidor. His gentle expression was soft with kindness. Their eyes met.

"Isidor . . . the Plaka . . . this restaurant . . . this night. It is all just as life should be. I wish I could stay here forever."

Clearing his throat, Miki approached the table. He opened a bottle of Greek red wine and offered Isidor the cork. He nodded, placing it on the table between them. Miki poured a sample for Isidor, who swirled, wafted, sipped, and pronounced his approval. Miki filled their glasses and gave them crusty bread along with a bowl of dark, rich olive oil.

Isidor raised his glass, and Cynthia followed. "Se eséna! Se aftó vrády! . . . To you! To this night!"

Cynthia repeated, "To you! To this night!" They clinked their glasses and drank to seal the toast.

Cynthia indulged in another sip. "Mmmm. The wine is delicious!"

"It is from the *Giórgos Iófos Oinopoieío*—Giórgos Hill Winery, an old family vineyard on the Greek Island of Míos. The terroir, the vineyard . . . it is remarkable." Passion filled his voice. "The tendrils of the ancient vines emerge from the dry, rocky soil on the brown, terraced hillside. During the day, the hot sunshine inundates the grape with sizzling heat. During the night, well, the cool darkness gives the grape the cold shoulder, and *ekeí to échete!* —there you have it! It makes for magnificent wine."

Isidor handed the cork to Cynthia. "Look, this is the hill of the vineyard." Cynthia took the cork and studied the abstract drawing encircling it, depicting a steep hill with boxy buildings upon it.

Her eyes danced at the sight of it. "How clever! There is writing on the cork. What does it say?" Cynthia took a sip of wine.

"Wine sings a love song to the soul."

"Ah . . . lovely, and so true. Tell me more of Míos Island."

Isidor leaned in. "It is the island of my birth, the island of my family. It is a place always alive in my heart." Isidor tore a piece of bread and soaked it in the olive oil. He ate the bread and took a sip of wine.

At this revelation, Cynthia placed her elbows on the table and leaned in closer, listening.

"There is so much to tell you of Míos, most of which cannot be said with words. It must be experienced."

"Is it an Ionian island, close off the coast of Greece?"

Isidor shook his head. "It is a small, Cycladic island in the Aegean Sea, southeast of Athens. It is farther than Santorini, not as far as Crete."

"It must be remarkable. I would love to experience it."

"I will take you there."

"Is that a promise?"

"Yes, Lord willing!" Isidor closed Cynthia's fingers around the wine cork in the palm of her hand. "Keep the cork as a symbol of my promise." Cynthia held the treasure against her breast, over her heart. She prayed the promise could be kept.

Miki frequented their tableside often to refresh their glasses and present the courses of the meal. As he brought one delicious course after another, Cynthia learned something new of the Greek culture, culinary wonders, and tastes of the complex man sitting opposite her at dinner.

Zealous with enthusiasm, Isidor explained each dish and why it appealed to him. By joining him in "the usual," she stepped back in time with him on a journey of memories from his childhood and meaningful family celebrations.

"The appetizer is bakaliáros kroketákia with skordaliá, cod croquettes with creamy garlic sauce. My giagiá, my grandmother made this same recipe. It is a taste of home for me. It's casual food, pick this up with your fingers and dip it in the sauce. It's meant to be shared among friends."

Isidor offered his hand to Cynthia, "But first, will you pray with me for our meal?"

Cynthia placed her hand in Isidor's and, together, they offered thanks.

Isidor's chosen salad was fasólia saláta, a haricot bean salad with onions, parsley, olive oil, vinegar, and herbs. The soup was psarósoupa, a creamy soup with mild fish, potatoes, carrots, onions, tomatoes, and rice. The main entree, lithrínia sti scára, grilled bream served with fresh lemon, parsley, and rigani.

Cynthia savored each bite. "Isidor, your 'usual' is exquisite, pure culinary perfection."

Miki cleared the table announcing, "Finally, I serve the exquisite epidórpio!"

Isidor mouthed, "Dessert."

Miki said, "Miss Cynthia, as you see, in Greece, we savor the meal. We eat, we drink wine, we talk, we savor. We enjoy it as experience. Also, important to allow food to settle, make room for Mr. Isidor's favorite recipe of the night. This will steal your heart. It is the galatoboúreko. Golden brown, flaky, buttery phyllo pastry layered with delicate custard served warm with honey-lemon syrup. You have it with the bríki kafés varýs glykós, eh, a pot of the heavy coffee."

Miki set all this before them on the table, poured cups of the strong black coffee, and with a flourish announced, "I go. Eat. Enjoy."

Isidor waited as Cynthia took her first bite of the galatoboúreko.

"Oh, that is the most magnificent epidermis-eee-o ever!"

Isidor tried to let it go by, but finally laughed heartily.

Uh-oh. "Wrong word?"

"A valiant effort. I give you a million sincere affirmations that you tried. I hope you never lose your love of life and your bravery to try."

Cynthia beamed, "Please teach me the correct word. Of all words, I must learn the word for dessert."

Isidor pronounced the word with a thick Greek accent, "Epidórpio."

Cynthia repeated the word after him a number of times until she produced an acceptable version.

Isidor took several bites of his dessert, followed with coffee. "My mitéra made this every year to celebrate my birthday. It is my favorite."

"I want this for my next birthday, too. Surely, I can find a Greek restaurant in New York that serves it. Still, it won't taste the same as it does here, tonight. What does it mean, a 'bríki of heavy coffee'?" Cynthia took a sip from her cup.

"This is the traditional way to serve coffee. It is made according to an old Eastern custom as it came to our country from the Arabians, to the Greeks of Constantinople through Asia Minor."

Cynthia interjected a comment as Isidor took a sip. "So, I can't believe the conversations I have with you. That simple sentence, made so off-handedly, just rolled off your tongue. You just covered thousands of years and at least four major cultural groups in the blink of an eye. A semester's worth of history, uttered between sips of coffee. Yet another thing I love about Greece, a cup of coffee isn't just a cup of coffee." Cynthia smiled at Isidor. "Forgive me, I interrupted you. Please, professor, continue. I do want to learn the full history of the coffee."

Isidor looked mischievous and continued without missing a beat.

"In the old days, for the Greek men in the villages, coffee-making was a ritual. They gathered at coffee houses, roasted the beans, ground them by hand, and brewed the coffee in a brass bríki," he motioned to the long-handled pot on the table. With a sly smile and twinkle in his eyes, he added, "Then they put the bríki in the embers of a fire, add sugar, heat it almost to a boil, and when frothy—they pour it into the cup, drink it, read newspapers, and talk politics."

With a bit of her own mischief Cynthia asked, "Dr. Christopoulos, by any chance, was this the subject of your doctoral dissertation?"

"As a matter of fact, it was." Isidor looked serious. "That, and the instructional methodology for foreign language pronunciation, specifically instruction of clever American undergraduates in pronunciation of key Greek words like *epidórpio*."

They laughed. Cynthia relaxed, comfortable with the easy banter. *Or was it flirting?*

Not to be outdone, Cynthia raised her cup in salute to Isidor. "Well, this clever American undergraduate finds this bríki kafés varýs glykós strong, smooth, and delicious. A worthy companion to this heavenly epidórpio."

Isidor nodded, "Impressive." Chuckling, he raised his cup in salute to Cynthia. "It appears my coffee and dessert dissertation methodology was successful."

Meeting his eyes, Cynthia asked, "So, professor, what's next?"

Elbows on the table, Isidor rested his chin on his hands, maintaining eye contact he said, "Miss Chadwick, you cannot imagine what's in store for you."

CHAPTER 36

❁

> Have you forgotten that your body
> is now the sacred temple of
> the Spirit of Holiness, who lives in you?
> You don't belong to yourself any longer,
> for the gift of God, the Holy Spirit,
> lives inside your sanctuary.
> You were God's expensive purchase,
> paid for with tears of blood,
> so by all means, then,
> use your body to bring glory to God.
> —The Apostle Paul, I Corinthians 6:19–20 (TPT)
> AD 53–55

Together, they sipped coffee. A cool breeze fluttered across the courtyard, and Cynthia shivered. Isidor shrugged from his sport coat and asked, "May I?"

Grateful, Cynthia nodded. Isidor rose from his seat and placed the coat about her shoulders.

"Thank you." She pulled it close and caught the scent of his cologne. Closing her eyes, she breathed in the masculine scent. Cynthia wished for Isidor's arms around her rather than his coat.

Isidor interrupted her thoughts with a question. "So, tell me, Miss Chadwick, of the Chadwick Centre for Classical Art in New York City, how did you come to find a special interest in Glass Amphoriskos of the Eastern Mediterranean Culture, from the Classical Period?"

"May I be painfully honest?"

"Please."

Cynthia eyed Isidor, making sure. "But, you're a professor, with a doctorate in archaeology. I'm afraid I'll lose all credibility."

Isidor nodded his encouragement. "Please, speak your mind. Trust me."

Cynthia clasped her hands together, placing them on the table. "Here goes. I find most archaeologists dwell on the amphora, ad nauseam."

Cynthia felt safe with Isidor's response. He frowned, but he laughed with his eyes. "Okay, you have my attention. Do go on."

"While amphorae are an undisputed archaeological treasure, they are beyond a doubt, *boring!*"

Isidor laughed. "That's a bold statement. I shall have to cross-examine you on the subject. Are you prepared to defend your position on this topic?" His tone was playful. Cynthia was thrilled at the prospect of another discussion on archaeology with Isidor: the professor and her dinner date.

"Absolutely. Amphorae are representative of the form, function, and art of their period. But—"

"But?" Isidor quickly parried, "and, your explanation better be good."

Shrewd argument at the ready, Cynthia's eyes narrowed. "But, if you've seen one amphora, you've seen them all."

Isidor shook his head. "Hardly an adequate apology on your position."

Undeterred, Cynthia began her diatribe. "Amphora. A clay pot. Tall and slender, short and round, nondescript. Broad shoulders, slender shoulders, *no shoulders.* Tall neck, skinny neck, no neck. Big handles, broken handles, no handles. Egyptian pottery, Grecian pottery, Attic pottery, Turkish pottery. And, the artistic themes . . . done to death. Red-on-black figures, black-on-red figures, men driving chariots, men driving carts, men playing drums, lutes, lyres, and flutes. Palm trees, fruit trees, and flower bees. Dancing ladies, dancing chimps, dancing tigers, and dancing nymphs! Shall I go on?"

Humored by her wit, Isidor threw his head back and laughed. He drew her further into the conversation.

"So, as an expert in . . . as an expert in . . . please remind me again of your credentials?"

Cynthia feigned humility and gushed, "Well, I hate to flaunt my credentials, but I am a certified Archaeological SPE."

Isidor cocked his head with a quizzical look. "SPE? I am unfamiliar with the designation."

"S—P—E. Self-Proclaimed Expert."

"Ah, so, you, a Self-Proclaimed Expert, are not impressed with the ancient amphora, revered by historians, museologists, archaeologists, and valued by the international expert community as a priceless artifact?"

"That is correct."

Isidor stood and slowly paced around the table, hands behind his back, deep in thought. In time, he stopped, leaned over the back of his chair, and all kidding aside, asked, "What makes you so passionate about amphoriskos? What about them inspired you to study and pursue them? What created such boldness in you to recommend that the Alexander Archaeological Museum of Athens curate an exhibit of such?"

Cynthia pointed the question back at him, "Why are you driven to curate them?"

"I asked you first."

Cynthia's eyes gleamed with the passion that drove her. "Every individual amphoriskos is a unique, colorful work of art reflecting the workmanship of its creator. Every amphoriskos is a vessel created for a sole, distinct purpose."

"And that purpose?"

"To be filled with something greater than itself."

Isidor shrugged, "Amphorae were also created to be filled with water, wine, grains, a variety of uses. Why does the amphoriskos set your soul on fire?"

"Because, they were created to be filled with oils and perfumes that are precious, life-giving, healing, fragrances . . . purchased at a great price. I find great beauty in the symbolism.

"Tell me of the symbolism you find."

"We, God's children, believers and followers of Jesus Christ, are God's workmanship. We are individual, unique works of art, made in the image of our Creator, for the exact same purpose as amphoriskos. God created us as vessels to be filled with something greater than ourselves. He wants to fill us with His precious, fragrant, life-giving, healing presence. Like the oil that fills the amphoriskos, He purchased us at a great price. We are meant to be filled with the grandeur of God Himself."

Isidor, professor of archaeology and curator of private amphoriskos collections, looked at Cynthia for several long moments. He sat down and let out a long-held breath. He ran his hands through his hair, rubbed his jaw, looked at the ground, and shook his head.

"Cynthia—" he stopped, then began again. "Cynthia, you are probably the most interesting, curious, tenacious, passionate, surprising woman I have ever met." He leaned forward, resting his arms on his knees and tented his hands. To Cynthia, he appeared to be thinking through a big problem.

"You may very well be my personal and professional undoing." He rubbed his chin. "I can't believe I'm going to admit this, you're right. Amphorae *are* boring, but you," he pointed at her, "you have the courage to say so. And, you have the ability to see a deeper, profound truth. You have the uncanny ability to look upon the created and see the Creator."

Isidor stood and paced again. "You so aptly dismantled the obscure and articulated it as a profound, life-changing parable." He gave her a suspicious look. "How do you do that?"

Cynthia decided it was a rhetorical question because Isidor kept talking. "I mean, I've studied artifacts for years. Written in-depth papers. Defended complicated, disputed positions. And you just breeze in out of nowhere, announce amphorae are no big deal, and it makes perfect sense. Huh." He smiled at her. She smiled back. They held eye-contact. It was a comfortable moment. A moment in which life felt like a favorite coat that fit just perfectly.

Isidor sat down. Cynthia refilled their cups, and they sipped coffee to the sounds of the city in the background.

Isidor said, "It's been a long time since I've spent the day with someone and just talked."

"Me, too."

"You know, for the first time, I finally understand why I was so driven to research and curate the Xenos Amphoriskos Collection."

Cynthia urged, "Tell me about your passion and drive to curate amphoriskos."

"Well, until now, I could not have said why I was driven. Now that I've heard your parable, I can see I was also drawn to the Creator by the beauty of the created. My soul longed for something stunning, breathtaking, purposeful—something with deeper meaning. And, like you, I long for it. To be filled like an amphoriskos, with the precious, life-giving presence of my Creator. To be filled with something greater than myself. More than anything else, I want to be filled with the presence of God."

Isidor stared at the Acropolis. "As an archaeologist, I've been too wrapped up in temples to the wrong gods." He gestured, "The Parthenon, the temple to the goddess Athena."

He leaned forward, "Again, in one brave expression of truth, you dismantled all the hype and mysticism of the glorified ancient history. Your faith in God is deep, yet uncomplicated, pure, and inspiring. You may have come to Greece for an internship, but I think God brought you here for another purpose."

"Really? Like what?"

"I can't say. But I think it's something important. Something life-changing."

"Hmm."

Cynthia could not imagine what could be more important than advancing her career at the Chadwick in New York City.

She said, "Earlier as we stood in Laskaris Street, you said we have important work to do while I'm here. Is this what you were referring to?"

"No." Isidor shook his head, "No, that would be *another* life-changing purpose."

Cynthia raised her eyebrows and teased Isidor. "I'm not sure how many of those I can take in one night. Is this one going to require another one of your cross-examinations?"

Isidor stood and offered Cynthia his arm. "Walk with me, and I'll tell you."

Isidor and Cynthia waved across the way to Miki and started down the Steps of Mandrapílas.

"Whether you realize it or not, you've made a big splash at the Alexander Museum. An intern is rarely fast-tracked in the program. They're impressed. I'm impressed. You came on my radar when you came after the Xenos Collection.

"I've had you in mind for a while. Now that I've met you, I'm certain you're the right one for the project. I'm leading an excavation team to the Island of Crete to study and excavate amphoriskos."

Cynthia stopped walking. "What? Excavation of amphoriskos on Crete?"

"We leave at the beginning of May. I want you to join our team."

"Yes, oh, my . . . *yes!*" Cynthia couldn't believe her fortune. "Oh . . . except, my Alexander internship is not complete until the end of May."

"Given you're actively assisting the Alexander in the curation of amphoriskos for their new exhibit, I believe you could fulfill both your museum study and field trip requirements with this expedition."

"Are you serious? You think the Alexander will accept it?"

"With your permission, I will speak to Freideriki first thing. Cynthia, this team would value greatly from your knowledge and perspective. They need to experience your passion and hear your parable of the amphoriskos." Isidor looked serious. "Most importantly, our team lacks a crucial member. If we can't fill this position, we may have to cancel the expedition."

Cynthia's heart was pounding. "Oh, no! What is it?"

"We need an SPE."

Cynthia rolled her eyes and socked Dr. Isidor Christopoulos on the arm.

CHAPTER 37

Give your dreams to me
And you will see
They'll all come true
Forever and ever and ever

Monday morning Cynthia attended a debriefing with Freideriki. The Alexander head curator congratulated them on their procurement of the Xenos Amphoriskos Collection in Thessaloniki. During the meeting they outlined the status of their work in also curating two additional collections.

Late Monday afternoon Freideriki sent for Cynthia. As usual, she was on the phone when Cynthia reported to her office. Head down, scribbling notes, Freideriki waved Cynthia in and smiled.

"More good news."

"Did we get the Kalfas Collection?"

"Yes. And a ninety-nine percent commitment from Jonas Savas. I believe by the end of the week he will propose a private viewing of his collection. Well done, Cynthia, thanks for doing all the leg work on these."

"Thank you. That *is* good news."

Freideriki studied Cynthia for a moment, and a sly expression played across her features. "That's not the only good news."

Cynthia thought of Isidor's Crete expedition, and her heart beat faster.

"The museum has received a special request."

"Oh?"

"It appears your work on the Xenos Collection made quite an impression on Dr. Christopoulos. He's asking for you to join his Crete Amphoriskos Expedition in May."

Despite foreknowledge, Cynthia's head spun at the pace Isidor worked to secure her invitation to the team.

Freideriki said, "This is an amazing opportunity for you and would fulfill your internship obligation for course of study and field experience."

Cynthia took a seat. "The museum would agree to that? What do you think?"

"Selfishly, I'd like you to stay and finish your internship here with me, but I won't require that. Honestly, this is the opportunity of a lifetime. You'd be crazy to turn it down."

"So, you really think I should do it?"

"It's up to you, but it is amétriti apófasi—a no-brain decision."

Then, yes! I say yes."

* * *

FRIDAY EVENING ISIDOR presented a box of long-stemmed roses to Cynthia when he arrived for their date. He greeted her with a kiss on each cheek.

"You look stunning."

"Thank you. Come in. The roses are exquisite. I'll just put them in water and collect my things."

On Tuesday, Isidor visited Cynthia's desk in the basement of the Alexander. He congratulated her on making the Crete team and asked her for a date on Friday. He hinted at a special evening full of surprises, saying they would attend a formal theater event. Arriving at her doorway in a tuxedo and black-tie, he quite took her breath away.

Thursday afternoon, Cynthia invited Océane on a shopping expedition to find a dress for the big date. With Océane's expert fashion advice, she chose a tailored, powder pink, satin gown, sleeveless, with an empire waist, and matching opera gloves. Cynthia coiffed her hair into a Hepburn-esque, half-beehive, bouffant up-do, with full-fringe bangs. She accessorized with diamond and pearl earrings. She felt glamorous on his arm as they arrived at the Petrakis Theatre by private car and driver.

A uniformed page met Isidor and Cynthia at the palatial entrance of the opulent theater. He ushered them through the gilded grand salon, where they ascended the wide marble steps. To her surprise, they were seated in a private box overlooking the stage. Rows of red velvet seats lined the floor. Semi-circles of gilded opera boxes rimmed the house.

"Isidor, this hall is majestic, and our seats—I'm beyond words. I feel like royalty."

"My darling, you are."

Puzzled, Cynthia searched his face.

"You are a beloved daughter of the most high King of Heaven."

"Ah." In awe of the thought, she humbly internalized Isidor's words. "This is the most beautiful night of my life."

"I hope this night becomes a treasured memory."

Cynthia's eyes met Isidor's, and she assured him, "It already has."

The lights flickered, and Cynthia looked at her program, which was printed in Greek. The lights dimmed as Isidor leaned close and whispered, "The play is called *Farewell to Nikolo*."

When the heavy, red velvet curtains swept aside, the stage came alive. Though the dialogue was in Greek, Cynthia was captivated by the performance. The skill of the actors drew her in, and she experienced the emotion of the drama.

Halfway through the First Act, Cynthia whispered, "The actress playing Phoibe is magnificent. So talented, so compelling, so beautiful."

Isidor whispered, "She *is* magnificent. She's my baby sister, Alexandra."

Uncertain she heard correctly, Cynthia looked at Isidor. He

repeated, "She is my sister, Alexandra." His eyes gleamed with pride. He smiled at Cynthia and returned his attention to the stage.

During intermission, over glasses of champagne in the crowded lobby, Isidor explained that Alexandra was married to his best friend, Gregor Andras, the celebrated Greek playwright. *Farewell to Nikolo* was his latest critically acclaimed success.

"I'm thankful I met you in time to catch one of the last performances before they go on hiatus. I'll take you backstage, introduce you to Alexandra and Gregor, and then we'll have dinner together at Zolakis."

The Third Act brought Cynthia to tears. Isidor reached for her hand, brought it to his lips, and kissed it gently. He held it firmly in his own. Cynthia felt electricity pulse through her veins. The chemistry between them quickened, melding them together. His touch exuded the warm compassion of a friend—and the searing passion of a would-be lover.

At the final curtain, they sprung to their feet for the standing ovation. Giddy with emotion, Cynthia savored the beauty of the gilded concert hall, the splendor of the evening, the artistry of the performance, and the handsome man by her side. Placing her hands over her heart, she consigned it to memory.

In that moment, Cynthia understood what she was born to do, and where she was meant to be. Her heart and her hand were destined to be held by Isidor Christopoulos.

As the theater emptied, Isidor placed Cynthia's hand in the crook of his elbow and escorted her backstage. The atmosphere was energetic and buoyant with the triumphant performance.

Comfortable with the backstage scene, Isidor's interactions with cast and crew were dynamic. Introducing Cynthia to everyone in sight, Isidor led the way to Alexandra's dressing room. Entering the lead actress' inner sanctum, Cynthia found the crowded space filled with floral arrangements, buckets of champagne, gifts, and racks of wardrobe and dressing table mirrors outlined in light bulbs.

Still in costume, Alexandra stood in the center of the room, surrounded by admiring fans, the who's-who aristocracy of Greek high society. They looked well-monied and important. One woman wore a sash and tiara. The man at her side, in dress uniform with a chest full of colorful medals. Alexandra bobbed in curtsy before they embraced.

Once deference was paid to the aristocracy, Alexandra spied Isidor and reached her arms toward him, beckoning him closer. He swooped her up in his arms, and she nuzzled playfully at his neck and blew a raspberry.

"My favorite sister!"

"Stop it, you scoundrel. Put me down," she laughed, ruffling his hair. "I'm your *only* sister!"

"Your best performance yet!"

"Did you sleep through the whole thing again?"

As stunning as Alexandra was on stage, she was more so in person. She turned her attention to Cynthia.

"You must be Cynthia." She drew Cynthia in with a warm embrace, "You are so lovely. *Oooooh*, my big brother has a girlfriend, yay!" With perfect aim, she punched Isidor's arm. "I've been outnumbered far too long." Hands on hips, Alexandra gave Isidor a shrewd look, "It took you long enough." She turned her attention to Cynthia, "Isidor has not stopped talking about you since he met you last Friday."

Isidor did not appear embarrassed at Alexandra's comments. It was obvious he loved his baby sister. Cynthia was thrilled Isidor had talked about her, and amazed at Alexandra's genuine excitement toward her.

A stunning, robust figure of a man, even taller than Isidor, ducked through the doorway of the dressing room. Everyone quieted, making way for him. He stared at Alexandra, approached, and stood before her. Raising her chin, she summed him up. Arching her eyebrows, she gave him a smoldering look. He took her in his arms, dipped her, and kissed her deeply. Cynthia watched the dramatic scene unfold.

He said, "I want to make passionate love to you."

"Take me, take me now," Alexandra swooned.

He kissed her again. "Excellent performance, My Darling. I love you with all my heart."

"I love you, Gregor, with all my being."

Everyone in the dressing room clapped and cheered. Gregor righted Alexandra and placed her squarely back on her feet.

Gregor greeted Isidor with a huge bear hug. "Brother!"

"Brother! Your best masterpiece yet."

Gregor turned to Cynthia. "You must be the beautiful, the captivating, the lovely goddess of a woman called Cynthia." He kissed her cheek. "It is an honor to meet you."

*　*　*

Cynthia found dinner at Zolakis a superior dining experience—paralleled only by the meal at the Ankistrévo, as it was her first date with Isidor. Seated in a large semi-circular booth with white table linens and a small lamp, they settled in for the victory dinner.

Framed, glossy celebrity photographs lined the walls of the iconic Athens dinner club. Couples danced to live music, and the restaurant buzzed with the energy of the late-night scene.

Once again, Cynthia declined a menu. She turned to Isidor, raising her eyebrows in challenge, "Surprise me."

The waiter delivered a silver bucket stand, and popped the cork on the bottle of champagne. "Compliments of the Count and Countess of Sagona." He motioned with his head toward a table along the far wall as he charged their glasses.

Acknowledging the gift, Alexandra blew kisses in their direction. Gregor nodded and delivered a casual salute.

Isidor proposed a toast to the success of *Farewell to Nikolo*. Sitting next to Alexandra, Cynthia noticed she brought the flute to her lips but did not sip from it.

Cynthia whispered, "Do you not care for champagne?"

Smiling, Alexandra placed a hand at her belly, "We are pregnant with our first baby."

"Congratulations! That's wonderful." Cynthia kissed Alexandra on the cheek.

Alexandra glowed. "I am so happy, and Gregor is beside himself. I am four months along and starting to show." She put both hands down against her dress, and Cynthia could see her baby bump. "We have one more week of performance, and I will go on hiatus. It is best not to be hugely pregnant on the stage. It does not fit into the storyline, and soon it will not be easy to conceal." Her eyes twinkled with joy. "Gregor and I would be happy for the whole world to see me with child. But I suppose no one wants to see a dancing hippopotamus in a polka dot tutu, though I am confident that my Gregor could write a play for that!"

Gregor kissed the top of Alexandra's head. "My Darling, my plan is for you to lounge in the shade of a grass-roofed pavilion on the beaches in Míos while you grow a big, healthy baby."

Alexandra kissed Gregor, "Thank you, My Darling."

Isidor chided his sister, "She is *finally* going to make me an uncle," "We had all counted on Leonidás, but—"

Alexandra interrupted Isidor, "but Leonidás and Isidor compete to see who will get married last. So far, it's a tie."

Cynthia felt a stab to the heart. Was Isidor's goal to remain single? She looked from Alexandra to Isidor. "Who's Leonidás?"

Isidor said, "Leonidás, in Greek this means lion, Leonidás, is our wild, older brother, the Lion. He's abroad somewhere, off to see the world, up to who knows what. We have not heard from him in some time."

"Oh. So, are you close?"

Isidor and Alexandra answered simultaneously, "Yes."

Alexandra said, "Whenever he comes home, it's like he was never gone. It's impossible not to love Leonidás." She smiled, and her eyes danced. "We let Leonidás be Leonidás, the wild lion who prowls the globe. It would be cruel to try and pin him down. His territory is large, and he is like the wind, everywhere and not anywhere. Life gets boring for us, and then, he arrives and everything is a party."

Isidor nodded his head, a warm, knowing expression on his face.

Cynthia said, "I wish I had brothers and sisters."

Alexandra said, "Then let's be sisters. I've always wanted a sister."

"I'd love that." Cynthia was captivated by Alexandra's genuine nature. "Tell me about your parents. They must be something special to raise the three of you."

"Oh, yes." Isidor, Alexandra and Gregor agreed, exchanging glances. "They live on Míos," Isidor replied.

Alexandra said, "Our papa, Theódoros, his friends call him Theo, his children call him Teddy because he is sweet and lovable like a big Teddy Bear. Our mitéra, our mother, is Elisávet. We call her Mimi. Isidor started that. When he was a baby, he would not say mitéra. He'd cry and reach for her saying, 'Mi-mi-mi-mi-mi-mi,' so we call her Mimi."

Cynthia cupped Isidor's chin in her hand. "Awww. What a precious baby boy you must have been."

Alexandra chirped, "Isidor thinks he's her favorite, but we all are. Mimi is a good mother to us. She cannot wait for me to come home for the summer so she can spoil me and watch her first grandbaby grow."

Cynthia pictured this loving family coming together for the summer. The thought of returning to her own family in New York filled her with a measure of emptiness. She would rather spend the summer on the Greek island with her new friends. She craved the warmth in their hearts and their happiness with life.

A photographer came to the table. As he raised the large camera, Isidor put his arm about Cynthia's shoulders. Alexandra reached over and placed her hand over Cynthia's as it rested on the table. She playfully squeezed it and held on. They all smiled, and the flash bulb flared with a percussive "poof" capturing a glorious moment in time that would no doubt be mounted on the wall amidst the clutter of photographs.

After the meal, Isidor asked Cynthia to dance. She met him step for step in a lively dance. The band shifted gears. Isidor took Cynthia in his arms. A smooth baritone crooned into the microphone. They danced slow.

"Isidor, this song is beautiful. What are the words?"

Isidor sang the words in English for Cynthia, his voice close in her ear, "Darling, dance with me . . . let me be . . . the keeper of your heart . . . forever and ever and ever." Isidor drew Cynthia in closer. "Give your dreams to me . . . and you will see . . . they'll all come true . . . forever and ever and ever." He swung her around in time to the music and their eyes met, "Darling, dance with me . . . make romance with me . . . forever and ever and ever."

Cynthia's heart beat wildly. She laid her head against Isidor's chest, willing her heartbeat to sync with his own strong, resolute rhythm, and she prayed the song would never end.

CHAPTER 38

We are like common clay jars
that carry this glorious treasure within,
so that the extraordinary overflow of power
will be seen as God's, not ours.
—The Apostle Paul, II Corinthians 4:7, 9 (TPT)
AD 56–57

*E*arly Sunday morning, Isidor's red convertible carried them through the streets of Athens toward open highway. Carefree, with the top down and sun at their backs, they raced away from the city and hurtled across the countryside. Cynthia tied the knot of her headscarf more securely as they flew like a lark on the wind.

They skirted around the blue waters of the Gulf of Elefsina and the Gulf of Megara, northwestward toward the Isthmus of Corinth, a diminishing reflection of mainland Greece in the rearview mirror. They crossed the Corinthian Canal by bridge, passing the Hexamillion Wall as they wandered deeper into the Peloponnese peninsula toward Ancient Corinth.

When he was not revving the motor and shifting gears, Isidor held Cynthia's hand on the console between them. Isidor explained the rich history of the Corinthian region as they drove. Five minutes beyond the new city of Corinth, they arrived at the Archaío chorió Korínthou, the village of Ancient Corinth. Cynthia's pulse surged with excitement at the sight of the ornate Corinthian columns amidst the ruins. She jumped from the car before Isidor could come around to open the door for her.

"Isidor, it's amazing!" She raced ahead and stopped at the edge of the ruins allowing him to catch up.

She said, "Wow! I can't wait to hear about these ruins."

Isidor moved near her. Cynthia turned her face to him. The light breeze ruffled hair. His handsome features melted her heart, stirred her emotions. He held a well-worn leather Bible in his left hand. He squinted his hazel eyes against the bright sunlight and regarded Cynthia with a relaxed expression.

"We are now roughly ninety kilometers from Athens. The Isthmus of Corinth separates the Corinthian Gulf of the Ionian Sea and the Saronic Gulf of the Aegean Sea. Because of its fertile land and proximity to the sea, Corinth was an entrepôt, a center of commerce and trade, for its own products—wood, agriculture, and high-quality clay—as well as the produce and industry that was trafficked through here from other regions. It was a busy commercial hub. Of course, it would take hours to tell you of the history, rulers, and possession of the land through the ages," He tapped her nose, "but, I happen to know you don't want to hear all that boring history. I know where your true passion lies. So, I'll start with that. Let us walk in the footsteps of the Apostle Paul."

This time, it was Isidor who took off, his long stride catching Cynthia by surprise. She hurried to keep up.

"So, we will start with recent history. In 146 BC, the Romans destroyed much of Corinth. In 44 BC it was rebuilt under Roman Emperor Julius Caesar. Paul came here from Athens in AD 52. The population was estimated at around 800,000 at that time. Many people, many sins, much sexual immorality. There was a Greek phrase, 'Korinthiázomai.' This meant, 'to act like a Corinthian,' in other words, to commit sexual immorality."

Isidor took Cynthia's hand and led her onto a public path amongst the ruins.

"There were over a thousand prostitutes in the temple of the goddess Venus. With the wealth and the immorality of the city, Paul had much work to do. In the book of Acts, the Scriptures tell us that Paul openly spoke in the synagogue every Sabbath, to the Jews and the non-Jews—the Gentiles, telling them about Jesus Christ.

"The Jews brutally slandered him, so he finally 'shook the dust from his clothes,' left the synagogue, and devoted his teaching to the conversion of the Gentiles. Paul stayed here a year-and-a-half with his new Jewish friends, the tentmakers, Aquila and Priscilla, who came here when driven from Italy. He worked alongside them making tents and establishing the church here in Corinth.

"Of course, when Paul left the synagogue, he spent time with Titus and his family, who became believers. Also, with the leader of the synagogue, Crispus and his family. When people in Corinth heard of the conversions of Titus and Crispus, many others became believers and were baptized as well."

Cynthia immersed herself in the Biblical account of Paul, as Isidor led her through the ruins. He reached a point, stopped walking, and gestured for Cynthia to look around.

"This area is believed to be the site of the Bema, an elevated area in the Roman Forum. This is where Paul stood trial when the Jews brought him before the tribunal of Lucius Junius Gallio Annaeanus, proconsul of Achaia. They charged him with trying to persuade the people to worship God in opposition to the law. Before Paul could utter a word in his own defense, Gallio threw the case out. He refused to rule on the matter, stating Paul had committed no crime. Rather, it was a matter pertaining to their religious laws. Gallio threw the Jews out of the tribunal. The Jews then turned on a ruler of the synagogue, Paul's friend, Sosthenes, and beat him before the tribunal. Gallio turned a blind eye to this."

Cynthia said, "Paul's courage blows my mind. Can you imagine trying to teach the Corinthians about Jesus? His conviction was strong."

"Indeed," Isidor said, pointing toward a natural rocky formation that steeply rose 1,800 feet above Corinth. "Paul literally preached

Jesus Christ in the shadow of the Acrocorinth, the site of the Temple of Aphrodite, Greek goddess of love, lust, and sexual immorality."

Cynthia said, "I am so weak, I'm ashamed of myself. I want to be as courageous, brave, and bold in my faith as Paul."

Isidor's eyes met Cynthia's. "I believe you already are. Look at you. You traveled around the world by yourself. You took on the Alexander Archaeological Museum and made a success of your internship. You had the courage to stand up to me and teach me how we are vessels filled with God Himself. You were so bold about your belief in your passion that you convinced everyone, me included, in the value of an amphoriskos exhibit. If that is not bravery, I am at a loss for its definition."

Cynthia argued, "That is different than sharing the message of Jesus Christ in a place it could cost you your life."

Isidor turned to face Cynthia squarely, studying her. "I'm not convinced. I'm certain you have it within you to be brave for the cause of Christ. I believe if you ever had to take a stand and put your life on the line for Jesus, you would not flinch nor shrink back."

Wanting it to be so, Cynthia asked, "How can you be so sure of it?"

Isidor took Cynthia's face in his hands, "I can see it in your eyes. I see an uncommon strength and courage within you."

Isidor turned Cynthia to face the area of the Bema. He held up his Bible, gestured toward the Bema and said, "In Acts it says before Paul went on trial, the LORD spoke to him and said, 'Don't ever be afraid. Speak *the words that I give you* and don't be intimidated, because I am with you.' (TPT)

"So now, Cynthia, *you* stand in the place where Paul stood so boldly. You are God's workmanship, His beautiful amphoriskos. Remember, as you said, you are filled with the grandeur of God Himself. He has filled you with His courage, His boldness. You can do all things through Jesus Christ Who is your strength. Come with me."

Isidor led them to a bench, and they sat. He opened his Bible, turned through the leaves, and ran his finger down a page, stopping at a verse. "King Solomon said, 'Death and life are in the power of the tongue.' Cynthia, words are important; *names* are important. Here we are in this place of ruin, in the shadow of the goddess of immorality, the exact thing Paul preached against. Did you know that in Greek mythology, your name, *Cynthia*, was associated with the Greek moon goddess Artemis, twin sister of Apollo, born on Mount Cynthus?"

Cynthia listened with rapt attention. Her eyes grew large. "I had no idea."

Isidor continued, "but, the Greek name *Cynna* means one who is *strong*, one who is *courageous*."

"Oh," Cynthia frowned. "It's like my name came close to something of greatness, but unintentionally, I missed out. Do you think that . . . maybe . . . ?" She left the unspoken question hanging in the air.

"That is exactly what I think," Isidor brushed a strand of hair from her eyes. "Words of life should be spoken over you. You have such courage and want to be even more courageous still. I think I should call you *Cynna*."

Cynthia's heart quickened. "Oh, yes, please, from this moment on." Isidor nodded.

"Would you pray for God to seal it with His blessing?"

"Yes, of course."

Cynthia moved from the bench and knelt. She folded her hands in prayer over her heart and bowed her head. Isidor knelt before her, laid his hands on her head, and prayed:

Our God and Father, Creator and Redeemer, Bless Your child, Cynthia, now called Cynna, Daughter of Strength and Courage. Fill Your amphoriskos, Cynna, with Your presence and create in her a courageous and steadfast heart, as she calls upon You as her Ever-Present Help in times of trouble, as she walks in Your will for her life. In Jesus' Name, Amen

* * *

Upon their return to Athens, Isidor and Cynna met Gregor and Alexandra for Sunday evening dinner at the Taverna of Ankistrévo. Miki Galanis welcomed them to their table and began the usual meal service.

Alexandra was anxious to know the details. "Tell me about your day. What archaeological expedition did my handsome brother give you?"

"He surprised me with a trip to Corinth and the Bema of the Apostle Paul."

"Mmmm. The land between the two seas. And, how did you find Corinth?"

"Sun-drenched and glorious. More meaningful than I could have imagined." Cynna beamed at Isidor. He reached for her hand.

After Miki served the wine and delivered the bread and olive oil to the table, they joined hands and Isidor blessed the meal.

Isidor tapped his spoon on his glass. "It is time for a toast." He raised his glass. "You have known her as Cynthia. Because of her strength and courage, she has received her new Greek name today. To *Cynna*."

"To Cynna!"

Alexandra kissed her on the cheek. "It fits you perfectly, my sweet sister."

Gregor agreed. "Names are important. It is good for us to speak to your strength of spirit and God-given path."

"Thank you, all. I rather like my new name. It makes me feel quite special to you and to God. I feel new courage already."

As they broke bread together, a question popped into her mind. She asked, "Isidor, what is the meaning of your name?"

"I'll answer this," Gregor said. "In the Greek, Isidor means fairness and equality. It is associated with intelligence, compassion, diplomacy, and the ability to solve complex issues as a trailblazer, always with fairness and care for others in mind."

"Impressive," Cynna winked at Isidor, "it fits you perfectly."

Gregor dipped a piece of bread in olive oil and raised it to Alexandra's lips. She accepted it, savored it, and looked at Gregor with adoration. "Agápi mou."

Cynna said, "That sounds beautiful. What does it mean?"

Not taking her eyes from Gregor's, Alexandra touched him on the cheek. "It means, My Darling."

Isidor asked, "How was the performance last night?"

Gregor boasted, "Alexandra was magnificent. Three curtain calls."

"Bravo!" Cynna clapped her hands. "I wish I had been there again."

Gregor took Alexandra's hand, "Only two more performances and we are off for the summer. She and the baby can rest."

ELIZABETH TOMME

Alexandra said, "Gregor is still receiving excellent reviews for *Farewell to Nikolo*, New York is after him again."

Isidor asked, "Will you consider returning to New York?"

Cynna looked puzzled, "*Returning* to New York?"

Alexandra explained, "Gregor has lived in New York off and on during his career as a playwright. He is in high demand there."

Cynna had not previously considered the broad scope of Gregor's career.

Gregor gave a reassuring glance in Alexandra's direction. "No, I do not plan to return to New York. I will stay here with Alexandra and our baby. I will write from here. If there is a return to New York, it would be the three of us together sometime after the baby is born. But, of course, we would rather the baby be raised in Greece."

Isidor nodded with relief.

Learning of Gregor's success explained his near perfect English.

She asked Alexandra, "Have you been to the United States as well?"

"Only on extended visits with Gregor."

"Just think," Cynna proclaimed, "you have all been to my hometown. And now, we are all together here. God is in all and through all."

After the galatoboúreko and coffee, Cynna said, "It's the LORD's Day. We have bread and wine. Shall we commune together?"

Alexandra said, "That's a glorious idea."

Isidor lifted the bread from the basket and said, ". . . Jesus took the bread, and after blessing it broke it and gave it to the disciples, and said, 'Take, eat; this is my body.'" (ESV)

Isidor raised his glass of wine saying, "And, he took a cup, and when he had given thanks he gave it to them, saying, 'Drink of it, all of you, for this is my blood of the covenant, which is poured out for many for the forgiveness of sins.'" (ESV) Isidor passed the cup among them saying, "Let's share it now to remember Him and His sacrifice."

After they had done these things, they prayed together, kissed one another on the cheek, and bid Miki Galanis good night.

Back at her apartment, Isidor unlocked Cynna's door. The lamp on the desk cast a pale glow about the living room. They entered the small space, and Isidor closed the door behind them. They faced each other.

Isidor placed his hands on Cynna's shoulders. He leaned slowly forward. Their lips met and lingered. Cynna savored the feeling of the new, intimate nearness. Isidor kissed her slowly, sweetly, gently, and drew back slightly. Their eyes met, and she answered the question in his eyes. It was the question she hoped he would ask since the moment they were introduced. She invited him deeper.

Isidor cupped Cynna's chin in his hand and gently pulled her closer until their lips touched again. He kissed her, searching for the depth of her passion. She breathed him in, his masculinity, his strength, his essence, and it awakened an aspect of her heart she had not known existed. She was awakened by a longing that reached to the core of her being.

Isidor kissed her deeper, and deeper. She responded, knowing as fully as she could know anything that she loved Isidor Christopoulos.

Isidor held Cynna close, kissing the top of her head. He sighed, "I must go."

Cynna knew this, too. Their beautiful day together must draw to a close. "Thank you for today."

They drew apart. Isidor held Cynna's face in his hands, looking into her eyes. "Cynna, never underestimate yourself again. From this day forward, and with God's help, you will forever find the strength to rise with courage, on wings of eagles."

He kissed her forehead. "Goodnight, my love."

From her balcony Cynna watched Isidor emerge from the building onto the sidewalk below and drive into the night.

CHAPTER 39

> Truly, my heart cannot find a way
> to say good-bye.

The weeks between Corinth and their departure for the Crete Expedition passed as quickly as sand through a sieve. Amid packing for the expedition, packing the remainder of her things for storage, and finishing her work at the Alexander Museum, Cynna's days were filled with sad farewells.

Cynna and Océane Benoît said their good-byes in the spot their friendship began, sitting on the bench in the great hall, admiring the white marble metope frieze from the ancient Archiros temple. Océane would depart for Paris before Cynna returned from Crete.

On their last day of work together, Cynna and Freideriki celebrated their accomplishments with a nice dinner. Cynna did not consider it a farewell since their shared amphoriskos curation guaranteed ongoing dialogue. Freideriki did her best to extract a promise from Cynna she would return to the Alexander for the exhibit opening in the fall.

At last, Isidor and Cynna saw Gregor and Alexandra off at the Port of Piraeus where they boarded a high-speed ferry for Míos. Isidor and Cynna waved from the dock as Gregor drove their car into the hold of the ship. It was packed to the gills with summer clothes, presents, and of course, Gregor's typewriter and reams of paper. With a successful run of *Farewell to Nikolo* in the bag and their baby growing by the day, their summer reprieve would be all the sweeter.

During their last three weeks together in Athens, the two couples spent frequent time together. Gregor and Alexandra welcomed Cynna into their intimate circle of friends. Alexandra and Cynna grew particularly close.

Knowing they would not see each other again this trip, Cynna and Alexandra's farewell at the dock was heart-wrenching. They promised to write letters and splurge on occasional phone calls. The departure was even more painful for Cynna knowing Isidor would spend the summer with Gregor and Alexandra on Míos, after Crete. She longed to spend the summer with them rather than return to New York.

Cynna overheard Alexandra tell Isidor, "Do *not* let her leave after Crete, bring her to Míos with you." She remembered the wine cork and Isidor's promise to take her to Míos. *Oh, if only.*

The next day Isidor and Cynna departed for Crete. Isidor led the team, which consisted of two other archaeologists, one was Pavlos Ballas from the apartment below Cynna's, and five archaeology interns, including Cynna. Lena and baby Veni saw Pavlos off at the airport, promising to join him for a holiday in Crete at the end of the expedition.

Isidor did his best to prepare Cynna for the primitive conditions he expected at the archaeological site. He warned the field work was demanding, a true test of her mettle and passion for archaeology.

Before they left for the airport, Isidor kissed Cynna long and hard. "Our time together will be sparse once we join up with the team," he cautioned. He explained that she was not his student and thus their relationship was not prohibited. However, they both agreed that as leader of the expedition, favoritism toward her would compromise his leadership role.

Once deplaned in Crete, the team and their mass of luggage was bused to the village of Áthanásiou, located on the southern coast. Their assigned quarters were primitive dormitories on the outskirts of the village—a modest compound erected in close proximity to the archaeological excavation and field office.

The six men on the team were consigned to a large, one-room bunk house. They were quartered with the men from three other on-site teams.

Cynna and Bía Nasso, the other female intern and archaeology student from Alexander University, were quartered in a dormitory on the compound's far side. Together, they lugged their gear up the stairs to the first floor and down the hallway to their assigned room.

Newly acquainted Cynna and Bía stood together at their room's entrance and assessed their lot. Their small room had two twin beds, a desk, a toilet, and a sink and mirror. With concrete walls and its toilet's lack of privacy, it more resembled a jail cell than a dorm room.

Cynna reported, "At least there's toilet paper."

"But that sign above it says not to flush it," Bía pursed her lips. "We'll have to empty the waste bin often."

"No prob," Cynna assured.

A small window with a faded, ragged curtain hung from a few rings on a rickety rod. At least it afforded some privacy. Cynna pushed the curtain aside. Sunshine and stifling heat flooded the room.

Cynna said, "I'll try to open the window."

With no budging it, Cynna and Bía exchanged a look. A pair of roommates passed their doorway in the hall. One of them, in a proper British accent said, "Welcome to the Ritz, ladies!"

They all burst out laughing. One woman began introductions. "I'm Margaret Townsend, and this is my cellie, Evelyn Murphy, UK. We're your across the hall neighbors."

"Hi, I'm Cynna Chadwick, United States."

"Bía Nasso, Greece."

Margaret announced, "Good news, there is a communal shower at the end of the hall. Evie and I found with the last set of neighbors, if you'll open your glass pane and leave your door open, and we do the same, we can conjure up a breeze. Makes the heat tolerable. That is, if you're not too private about your business with the loo."

Once again, Cynna and Bía exchanged a look and wiped the perspiration from their foreheads, shrugging amicable consent. Bía cast their vote, "We're in."

Cynna said, "Only problem, I can't get our glass pane open."

Margaret offered, "I'll show you the trick."

Bía used the rock stationed at the baseboard for a doorstop. Margaret and Evie did the same, and a warm breeze fluttered the curtains and delivered air exchange. Given no closet or dresser existed, Cynna and Bía organized their gear to the degree possible. Then they opened their suitcases and shoved them under their beds. They would share the array of hooks on the wall.

When finished, Evie and Margaret crossed the hall, nodding their approval.

Evie said, "Well done, you. We're off to the dining hall." In proper British phraseology, Evie said, "I should consider joining us. The best grub is out first. After that, you are subject to scraps, and there's not much for it. Come along. We'll give you orientation and survival tips."

Isidor and team were outside the dining hall when Cynna, Bía, Evie, and Margaret arrived. They were engaged in dynamic discussion with the other team members. Cynna watched as Isidor and another man pointed toward the field site, exchanging information.

Isidor looked in Cynna's direction. Smiling, she looked directly at him. Isidor pulled his sunglasses down, assessed her appearance, and nodded. In an effort to show she took the work seriously, she'd changed into khaki utility pants and shirt, scrubbed her face clean of the dramatic eyeliner, and combed the bouffant tease from her hair. It hung thick and silky at her shoulders and moved with the breeze.

Isidor came alongside her. "Miss Chadwick."

"Dr. Christopoulos."

"You never cease to amaze me."

"I came here to do some serious work."

Isidor raised his eyebrow and smiled at her. Cynna's cheeks grew warm at the passion in his stare. He whispered, "You would blend in with the others if you were not the most alluring blonde I ever saw in field khakis."

Introductions were made all the way around. Each team composition mirrored their own. Much to her delight, Cynna learned Margaret was actually *Dr.* Margaret Townsend, archaeologist and team lead for the UK delegation. With courage, Cynna raised her chin at the thought, *if she can do it, so can I.*

Dinner was followed by a meeting in the dining hall that doubled as a conference room. Cynna learned that Margaret and her team were the one constant during the April through July excavation season.

Isidor's team and the other teams rotated in for the month of May, to be replaced by three other teams in the successive months. They would take their direction from the oversight team and work the tasks and shifts assigned them. Their scheduled shifts allowed for every fifth day off.

A glance at the schedule for the first week revealed half of their team, Cynna, Pavlos, Bía, and Dion, were set for the early shift, which meant they must arrive at the dining hall by 5:15 each morning and check in at the dig site no later than 6 a.m. They would work until 1 p.m., at which time they would give report to the oncoming team, who would work until 6 p.m. The afternoon shift was abbreviated due to the sun exposure and heat. Isidor, Haris, Yiorgos, and Ermis were set for the afternoon shift. Every week the teams flipped from morning to afternoon.

The first day on-site, Cynna remembered Océane with fondness as she shuttled away buckets of soil. By the fourth day, Cynna was assigned to work alongside Pavlos in a deep trench. He trained her in whisking away extraneous materials, unearthing the treasure beneath — in this case, an ancient domicile.

On the fifth day, the team took a much needed break. Isidor arranged for a van, and by mutual determination, they all piled in atop one another for sightseeing. With Isidor in the pilot seat and Pavlos as the co-pilot, they bumped along the primitive southern coastal road. Isidor drove until he ran out of road, parked, and got out. Everyone disembarked, following as he hiked the rugged terrain. They crested a bluff overlooking the shoreline. What happened next became another memory Cynna would forever treasure in her heart.

Isidor looked pointedly at Cynna as he spoke, careful to accentuate key words. "Crete is significant to the history of *the finest amphoriskos, the beautiful vessels that held the precious perfumed oils.* The rarest, most priceless amphoriskos were produced in the second half of the fifth century, BC, by artisans on Crete.

"Their *workmanship* was far superior to that from other producers along the Mediterranean Rim. The reason being, their workshops were located specifically in this area of the coast. With the sand on this shore, they created far superior glass, making their amphoriskos with a process called core-forming."

Tears filled Cynna's eyes. Not only did she glimpse Isidor—the professor—at work, but there, in front of everyone, he demonstrated his love for her. He gifted her the passion of her heart: amphoriskos. As their eyes connected, they alone experienced the true meaning of that sacred moment. Placing her hands over her heart, Cynna mouthed, "Thank you."

Nodding, Isidor turned, leading the group along the bluff. The next point of interest was an abandoned dig.

Isidor cautioned, "Approach the lower level with care—erosion makes the descent precarious. Excavation was terminated in 1965 due to lack of funding. It won't be reopened until the Crete government secures more funds. This unfortunate as it's a confirmed site of production for the Crete amphoriskos, specifically, the Sofoklis Amphoriskos, now on display at the Metropolitan Museum of Art in New York City. It's one of their most prized exhibits."

Isidor looked again to Cynna. She beheld a rare fire in his eyes. His words were meant for Frank Chadwick, Jr., of the Chadwick Centre for Classical Art in New York City. For Frank, who lacked the foresight to curate them as the Met had. For Frank, who should value amphoriskos—on many levels, not the least of which was that his daughter loved them.

When the team returned to their shifts at the excavation, their tired, aching muscles did not deter them from working with renewed vigor. As part of his lecture about the Crete Sofoklis Amphoriskos, Isidor announced the UK team had found a shard from an amphora. He impressed on them the possibility they could unearth artifacts such as tools used in the core-forming process, if not an actual amphoriskos.

Over the next two weeks Isidor and Pavlos led the group on their fifth-day outings. They explored Crete at length and enjoyed the cuisine in the local tavernas. Occasionally, a schedule was flipped, and Cynna worked alongside Isidor. Together they uncovered and identified a glass ingot typical of those melted down for amphoriskos production.

As ecstatic as Cynna was with their find, sadness settled over her heart. Her time in Greece was drawing to a close. She dreaded the thought of leaving Isidor and the remarkable country that was Greece.

No matter the courage she infused into her heart, returning to New York felt like a death sentence. A return to New York would mark the end of her time with Isidor. The end of freedom to be herself. The end of the contentment she knew in Greece. She was desperate to feel Isidor's reassuring arms around her, his lips on hers.

Cynna perceived a heaviness in Isidor as well. More often than not, she found a serious, preoccupied look on his face.

On their last day off before their final five days on shift, Cynna emerged from the dorm to join the group for their outing. She saw the back of the van, driving out the gate without her. Left behind, her heart sank. She checked her watch. She was early as usual. Defeated, she walked back toward the dorm.

To her surprise, Isidor was waiting for her. Keys in hand he motioned toward an old car parked to the side. They got in and sped off opposite the direction of the van.

Reaching for her hand, Isidor brought it to his lips and kissed it. With a sideways glance he said, "I hope you don't mind not going into town with the group today."

"Not in the least."

"Good," he winked, "I have a special surprise for you."

Traversing the arid hillsides, Isidor navigated dirt roads leading to a cove. The clear water, and the promise of the day, both a glistening sapphire in the sun. Isidor parked the car. Hand in hand they descended the path to the beach. Wrapping Cynna in his arms, Isidor held her close. They kissed.

"Mmm, I've missed you." He breathed her in. "These weeks have been harder than I imagined. It's been—"

"*Agony.*" Cynna nuzzled her head against Isidor's chest. Isidor buried his face in her hair, kissing her head.

Isidor said, "But, being here *together* with you has been worth every moment of being here apart. Our experiences here have been so rich, I would do it all again."

"A million times. Working with you in the field is my dream come true—"

"For me, as well. Our two great passions united: our love for each other, and our love of archaeology."

Meeting Isidor's eyes, Cynna held his face in her hands. "Thank you for believing in me and adding me to the team."

"That was an emotional and professional no-brainer."

"And, this is a wonderful surprise. Thank you for kidnapping me today and bringing me here."

"So, My Love, do you know where you are?"

"I am in the only place that matters. I am in your arms."

"True, but I have something very special for you here." Turning her to face the water, he wrapped his arms around her shoulders, and rested his chin on her head. "Tell me what you see."

"A beautiful cove, a beach, a dock, some buildings."

"I brought you to Kaloí Liménes—Fair Havens."

Squealing with delight, she faced Isidor, eyes wide with excitement. Standing on tiptoe, she smothered his face with kisses.

"You. Are. *Marvelous!*" Kiss, kiss, kiss. "This is the best surprise ever! The Apostle Paul in Crete. I've read this story over and over since we arrived."

Isidor said, "So, tell me the story."

"Paul was a prisoner on a ship to Italy. They were blown off course, sailed in the lee of Crete, struggling along the coast. They found safety *here* at Fair Havens. They stayed here a while until the Jewish feast was over—" Cynna paused, realizing the next part of Paul's story was like her own, "then they had to leave this place of sanctuary—" her voice broke.

Not wanting him to see her tears, Cynna turned her head from Isidor. The thought of leaving this time of sanctuary, Isidor's side, Greece, Alexandra and Gregor, of never seeing them again was more than she could bear.

Isidor broke into her thoughts, finishing the story. "Though Paul was determined to make his appeal before Caesar in Italy, he advised against leaving Fair Havens because of the weather. But they left and were blown off course by a bad storm and shipwrecked."

Turning her face toward his, Isidor said, "Cynna, look in my eyes. Like Paul, your faith in God is strong. You came to Greece, and, like Paul, you ended up at this safe harbor, and now must leave. So, like Paul, could you survive being blown off course, knowing it could end in shipwreck?"

Cynna looked at Isidor in confusion. "Off course? Shipwreck? What are you—"

"Cynna, I love you," Isidor took her hands. "Don't return to New York. Come with me to Míos for the summer."

Cynna stared at Isidor in disbelief. "Isidor, I love you, too. I adore the idea of getting blown off course with you to Míos."

"Even if it makes your father angry or wrecks your plans for the future?"

Ah, the shipwreck. Cynna opened her mouth to speak, then closed it again. Her thoughts raced, calculating the possibilities. She knew her answer. She was meant to be with Isidor, her life course was reset the moment she met him.

"Yes!"

"*Yes?* Are you sure?"

"I'm *very sure*. Father God is so extravagant. He has given me, His daughter, the desires of my heart."

For the first time in her life, Cynna didn't care if her decision angered Frank Chadwick, Jr. Cynna inhaled deeply. Her first unpolluted breath of freedom charged her lungs with purity and life. Without a backward glance, Cynna pulled her trust from her earthly father and reassigned it to her Heavenly Father.

Smiling at Isidor, Cynna said, "Holy Spirit, blow me off course wherever you will."

Isidor whooped, lifting Cynna off the ground and spinning her around. Twirling in a dance of laughter and joy, she lifted her arms heavenward in pure joy and praise.

CHAPTER 40

༄

> Love is a safe place of shelter,
> for it never stops believing the best for others.
> . . . So above all else,
> let love be the beautiful prize for which you run.
> —The Apostle Paul, I Corinthians 13:7a, 13b (TPT)
> AD 53–55

From the window, Cynna watched Isidor pace outside the field office at the Áthanásiou archaeological site. The phone call to her parents took some time. Crying, she emerged from the office and ran into his arms. He cradled her head against his chest, praying she had not relented under pressure.

Cynna pulled back and wiped the tears from her face. "There *was* a shipwreck, but—" she squealed and said, "I can spend the summer on Míos."

"So, why are you crying?"

"Tears of joy—and relief."

"Thank God." Isidor kissed her. "I'm so proud of you. You have lived out your name today, my precious Cynna. I promise, your strength and courage will bring you the most unforgettable summer of your life."

"I am sooooo excited. I can't wait to meet the rest of your family."

"You know, when Paul was blown off course and shipwrecked, he swam to shore, and the people there welcomed him and lavished him with love. It will be the same for you. When we reach the island of Míos, my family will welcome you and lavish you with love."

Isidor, Cynna, and the expedition team finished their last four days on-site at Áthanásiou. The following day the team was bused back to the airport in Heraklion. Eager for his reunion and vacation with Lena and Veni, Pavlos rushed off to meet their incoming flight.

Haris, Yiorgos, Ermis, Dion, and Bía boarded a flight to Athens, minus Cynna. She buried her unused airline ticket to Athens and New York in the depths of her suitcase. Piling into a rental car, Isidor and Cynna sped away for a day of exploration on Crete. The next morning they would board the ferry for Míos.

Isidor held Cynna's hand as they drove east from Heraklion.

"I'm taking you across the northern coast toward Malia, Agios Nikolaos, and Sitia. This route is awesome. The mountains are rugged. They rise from the sea and reach elevations over seven thousand feet."

In Sitia, they pulled into a taverna for lunch. Their table overlooked the sea. Cynna watched the white seabirds drift like kites over the blue water. Her heart soared with them, her spirit feeling as free and light as a feather on the wind.

After lunch, Isidor navigated the shoreline road around the harbor of Sitia and entered the gate of a private estate. The palm-lined driveway led to a porte cochère with a gated entrance to a courtyard filled with lush foliage, potted trees, and cascades of bougainvillea.

"Isidor, this place is grand. Where are we?"

He brought her hand to his lips and kissed it. "It's another special surprise for you."

A valet met them promptly and assisted Cynna from the car. Isidor came around and offered his arm. He led her through the courtyard, past a fountain, to a set of massive wooden doors. Isidor rapped the heavy metal knocker against the wood.

A man in a dark suit greeted them. "Dr. Christopoulos, welcome. It is good to see you again." He turned to Cynna, "And you must be the lovely goddess, Miss Cynna. Dr. Christopoulos tell me you stole his heart. Welcome to Árgyros. I am Michaelídes Marinákis. Please, follow this way."

Mr. Marinákis ushered them into a private salon and seated them in plush chairs in front of an ornate wooden desk. The walls and floor were paved in dark, glossy slabs of marble, studded with Corinthian columns.

Mr. Marinákis took a seat behind the desk. He and Isidor exchanged a brief dialogue in Greek. Isidor nodded. Mr. Marinákis retrieved a key from the inner breast pocket of his suit coat, unlocked a drawer, and placed a handsome wooden box on the velvet desk pad. Isidor sat forward in his chair. Unsure what was happening, Cynna did the same.

Mr. Marinákis opened the wooden box, withdrew a purple velvet bag, and set it before Isidor.

Isidor turned to her. "Cynna, with all my heart, I long to give you your own beloved amphoriskos. As you know, they are quite rare." With a mischievous expression, he patted his empty jacket pockets. "I don't happen to have one on me at the moment." Cynna regarded Isidor with love, her eyes brimming with tears. He picked up the velvet bag. "I promise you this: I will spend the rest of my life trying to fulfill this dream of yours. Until the day I curate an amphoriskos for you, I humbly ask that you accept this gift as a token of my love." He placed the velvet bag in her hands.

Cynna loosened the tasseled, gold-braided drawstring and withdrew a crystal bottle. The light glinted off the sleek crystal bottle and decorative crystal stopper. Cynna traced her finger over the silver label and elegant black lettering. θυμίαμα Αργυρος.

Isidor translated, "Árgyros Thymíama . . . Árgyros Incense."

Inside the bottle, pale gold nuggets tumbled as Cynna turned the bottle in her hand.

"Isidor, it's exquisite."

"May I?" Isidor took the bottle and pulled the stopper free. He whispered, "Close your beautiful eyes."

Cynna did so. Isidor raised the bottle to her nose. As she breathed in, the fragrance awakened her senses. "Oh, my, it's glorious." Cynna's eyes popped open sparkling with joy.

Michaelídes Marinákis rubbed his hands together with pride.

Isidor explained, "This is, if you will, a modern, crystal amphoriskos. The crystal is a unique work of art that reflects the workmanship of its creator. The crystal has a sole, distinct purpose." He opened her hand and poured a few nuggets into it. "It is filled with something greater than itself."

Cynna raised the incense once again to her face and breathed in the earthy, woody, slightly sweet fragrance.

Isidor said, "These are Frankincense tears. It is the most precious of incense, in its most pure form, harvested from the rare *Boswellia Sacra* tree found only in the Dhofar Valley of Oman, on the Arabian Peninsula."

Isidor nodded at Mr. Marinákis, who opened the wooden box once again. He placed a silver bowl with an embossed, perforated dome in front of them on the velvet pad. Isidor nodded his approval.

Cynna said, "Such a thing of beauty. What is it?"

Isidor raised the lid, "This is used to burn the incense."

Cynna reached for the magnificent bowl. "May I?" Isidor nodded. Picking it up, she admired the exotic design. Isidor replaced the dome.

Cynna's eyes met Isidor's and she kissed him, "I love you. This is the most meaningful, beautiful, extravagant gift I have ever received. It is another memory I shall treasure forever. Thank you."

* * *

THE NEXT MORNING Isidor and Cynna met in the hallway outside their hotel rooms, kissed good morning, and headed to the lobby, a bellman in tow with their luggage. A waiting cab whisked them away to the Heraklion harbor.

Familiar with the routine, Isidor checked their luggage and led Cynna onto the ferry to cross the Aegean Sea to Míos. The engines revved to life as they savored one last look at the Isle of Crete from the upper deck. Cynna clung to Isidor as the boat maneuvered from the dock amid a wake of frothy whitewater. Thrilled with the experience, Cynna memorized every possible detail.

An alarm sounded. Isidor said, "We must go inside now. The ferry is headed to open sea and will accelerate to high speeds."

The crowded deck emptied, and Isidor led Cynna down the stairwell to a lower deck, locating their seats. Cynna sat in the window seat. Next to her, Isidor turned his back to the aisle, looked out the window, and studied the rolling, blue Aegean.

He smiled at Cynna. "We arrive on Míos in about two hours. I am honored you chose to come home with me."

Cynna kissed Isidor, "I will always choose you."

Partway through the journey at sea, Isidor gathered coffee and warm pastries from the concession.

"This should tide us over until dinner tonight."

"Where will dinner be tonight?"

"Mimi and Teddy are having a small family party for our homecoming."

"So, Alexandra and Gregor will be there?"

Isidor shrugged. "Yes, and about eighty other aunts, uncles, cousins, and friends. It will be fun."

Cynna's eyes grew big. "That's not a small party—that's huge."

Isidor laughed, "For my family, it's a small party."

"Oh, how fun! I'm so excited. Tell the boat captain to hurry it up."

An hour later, the ferry reduced speed and made a wide turn toward a mass of island. Cynna's face was glued to the window at the first sight of Míos. The shoreline was dotted with white, boxy buildings. A blue-domed church topped a hill overlooking the harbor. It was idyllic.

"Oh, Isidor, Míos is *gorgeous*. I want to explore every inch of it. Can we?"

"Every inch."

The ferry approached the dock.

Isidor said, "Stick close to me. If we happen to get separated—"

"Separated? How?"

"It's possible. The ferry runs on a tight schedule; things can get a little crazy. When they lower the ramp, everything happens fast. The cars driving off, people getting luggage, and everything and everyone at once going down the ramp. So, if we get separated, go straight down the ramp to the dock. I promise, I'll meet you there."

"Um . . . okay, but I'm sticking to you like glue."

"Don't worry, I've got you, and a porter will get our luggage."

Filled with nervous excitement, Cynna embraced the thrill of the moment.

Together they made it down the crowded stairwells and through the exhaust and screeching brakes of the vehicle traffic. As they were halfway down the ramp, the alarm blared. A moment after they set foot on the dock, the ramp raised and the ferry was seabound again.

Cynna smiled triumphantly at Isidor, "We made it."

"Look, there's your welcoming party." Isidor pointed to a large group of people on the dock. "Your Míos Family."

Cynna stopped in her tracks. *Family.* A lively mass of twenty or thirty people were waving, clapping, and jumping with excitement.

Alexandra and Gregor hurried in their direction. Cynna let go of Isidor's hand and ran into Alexandra's arms. Gregor joined their embrace, followed by Mimi and Teddy and a million aunts, uncles, and cousins.

CHAPTER 41

～

Every spiritual blessing in the heavenly realm
has already been lavished upon us as a love gift
from our wonderful heavenly Father,
the Father of our Lord Jesus – all because
he sees us wrapped into Christ.
This is why we celebrate him with all our hearts!
—The Apostle Paul, Ephesians 1:3 (TPT)
AD 6–62

Once their luggage was loaded, Isidor and Cynna piled in the car with Gregor and Alexandra, and joined the family caravan headed to the west side of the island. The convertible top was down on Gregor's spacious sedan. The 1960 Chevrolet Impala was turquoise blue, with whitewall tires and white inset stripes running from the tail to the back fender. The chrome trim flashed in the Greek midday sun.

Cynna sat in the back left passenger seat. Isidor sat close with his arm around her waist as she leaned her head over the side of the car like a happy dog. Hyped with excitement, Cynna chattered away, asking dozens of questions about the island, harbor, people, and the ancient windmills. As they drove along the coast, Cynna remarked at the deep blue of the Aegean and the thrill of the precarious road that hugged the cliff overlooking the coastline far below.

"Isidor and Alexandra, your family is wonderful! I can't wait to learn everyone's names and get to know them." Gregor's eyebrows shot up behind his movie-star sunglasses, and he shook his head.

Seeing him in the rearview mirror, Cynna poked Gregor on the shoulder. "What?"

Gregor looked back at Isidor. "The child really has no idea what she's in for, does she?"

Isidor hugged Cynna's waist even tighter. "No idea."

Undeterred, Cynna said, "I can learn the names of your family that met us at the dock."

Gregor threw his head back and laughed. Isidor whispered in her ear, "That was just the greeting committee."

"Oh." Still confident, Cynna asked, "What are we going to do next?"

Alexandra cast a broad smile over her shoulder in Cynna's direction. Resting her hand on Gregor's shoulder, she caressed his ear. "We get you first! Gregor and I own a hotel on the coast. We spend our summers and holidays there. We have a room for you. We will get you checked-in and settled. Later we go to Teddy and Mimi's for a family celebration."

"Oh, yay! Is your hotel close to a beach?"

"It has a *private* beach."

"Sweet. Isidor, do you like to swim in the ocean?"

Isidor nuzzled her neck, and she took it as a yes.

The road descended into a small village. Isidor leaned his head over Cynna's shoulder and spoke close in her ear so the wind could not snatch his words away. "This is the seaside chorió. 'Chorió' is the word for village. The village has no name, just refer to it as the chorió, or seaside chorió. There are a few houses, markets, and shops here."

Driving along the coast road from chorió, Gregor pointed out an impressive driveway flanked by tall rock walls, where massive wooden gates stood open. "That is my family home."

"It's grand. Can we stop and meet your family?"

"We'll take you there soon. My mitera passed away last year, and my papa is very old. His nurse will bring him to the party tonight. I'll introduce you then."

Gregor negotiated a series of hairpin curves and continued along the coastline. He turned onto a one-lane, unmarked road. They jostled down an overgrown track that meandered around scrubby berms and rocky outcroppings. It led them away from the main road, and northward, parallel to the shore. After a half mile, the road curved westward toward the sea, crested a steep hill, and Cynna gasped with delight as a breathtaking vista opened up before them.

On the seaward side of a crescent-shaped hill, a hidden half-mile strip of sandy beach glistened in the sun. Rocky ridges of hill extended into the sea on the north and south ends of the beach, creating a natural cove.

A sprawling flat-roofed structure occupied the ledge overlooking the north end of the beach. Bougainvillea poured over the shady arbor that ran the length of the hotel and framed the doors and seating areas.

A set of stone steps led to a lower terrace, the beach, and a walkway that meandered northward some fifty yards to another small cluster of buildings sheltered by the hill at the end of the cove. Gregor parked the Impala, and they got out.

Cynna said, "This is the most beautiful place on earth. Thank you for bringing me here."

Alexandra hugged her. "Welcome to the Hotel Mákari. Come, let's get you checked-in."

Together they went to the hotel office. Gregor and Alexandra greeted the clerk and stepped behind the desk. Alexandra made introductions. "This is Silas Artino. If we are not around, and you need anything, Silas will help you. You'll be in room number two."

Cynna signed the black leather-bound guest registry. Alexandra pulled the key from the desk. "Let's get you settled."

Alexandra led Cynna to her room as Isidor and Gregor retrieved Cynna's luggage.

Alexandra motioned at the first door they passed, "Gregor and I stay in this one. You will be next door to us."

She unlocked the door to Cynna's room and dropped the key in Cynna's hand.

"And, this, my darling, is your home for the summer. You are our guest for as long as you are on Míos, which we hope is forever."

"Oh, Alexandra, it is so gracious of you, but I cannot accept. I will pay you for my room and—"

"Hush that nonsense, and don't mention it again. We are family. You are staying in our home."

"Thank you," Cynna hugged Alexandra.

"I am so happy Isidor brought you home to Míos. Tell me, did it take much convincing?"

"No, I'm very much in love with your brother."

"He's in love with you. I've never seen Isidor so in love. You are good for him. You know, the professor in him can get a little stuck in the museum, if you know what I mean. He's serious about his work."

"We have that in common. It's one of the things I love about him."

"Me, too." Alexandra opened a window ushering in the sea breeze. "So, now it is summer, you both swim, you eat, you drink Greek wine, you go to parties. You relax. You can go back to your stuffy museums when summer is over."

Cynna stretched. "That sounds luxurious."

Alexandra walked Cynna through her suite. "This is the living room, over there, small kitchen, table and chairs, in here—bedroom and bathroom."

"It's perfect. The views of the Aegean are amazing."

"That's my favorite part, too. You have a private outdoor sitting area, and the beach is private. Knock on our door anytime, or join us on our terrace."

"You, too."

"We will, but if you need quiet time, take it. The most important thing about your time here is to rest, replenish, and fall in love with Míos, my brother, and grow closer to Father God."

"A lovely plan. How long have you had the hotel?"

"Gregor and I snatched it up several years ago. We need our own place when we come home. We love our parents, but we do not want to move back in on top of any of them, though Gregor's father, Teddy and Mimi would love it. One or two days is fine, but all summer?" Alexandra waved the thought away.

"We all need our space. Plus, Gregor and I like to entertain. We invite friends from around the world to come holiday with us. You will see our friends coming and going all summer. There'll be a big party at the end of the summer."

"Sounds glorious. I can help you entertain."

"Absolutely . . . that is, if you do not run away after meeting the rest of our big, boisterous family tonight. They are loud and fun-loving. Between them and our friends, it is one big Greek party all summer long."

"If the rowdy gang at the dock today was any indication, this will be the most fun summer of my life."

Gregor and Isidor burst through the door with Cynna's suitcase from the car. Isidor and Gregor disappeared out the door and in again with more luggage.

"Surprise!" Isidore announced. "We got your things from storage in Athens sent over on the ferry."

Cynna looked at the heap of luggage in disbelief. "Oh, my goodness! How did you manage that?"

"We know people," Gregor said as he carried two heavy suitcases into the bedroom.

Cynna kissed Isidor. "You sweet man. I'm so happy to have my things. I can wear clean clothes tonight. Let's make a bonfire and burn my filthy field clothes."

After a bubble bath and shampoo, Cynna did a mani-pedi and put on make-up. For her family debut, she dressed in a cool summer dress and sandals. She used a colorful silk scarf as a headband to secure her bouffant shoulder flip in place. After a month of fieldwork, she was thankful to have her wardrobe back.

A little anxious, she checked her appearance several times. She was ready to ride to the party with Gregor and Alexandra when the knock came at the door.

"Come in, Alexandra, it's open. You can tell me if I look okay for the party."

Another knock. She opened the door, surprised to find Isidor there, looking sharp in slacks and a crisp, white, open-collar shirt.

Cynna raised a provocative eyebrow. Isidor stepped into the doorway, pulled Cynna into his arms, and kissed her.

At last he drew back. "Mmmm. You look stunning."

"Mmmm. So do you."

"Do you know how hard it was to see you in the field and not take you in my arms?"

"Actually, I do. It was torturous."

"Are you ready to meet more of the family?"

Cynna nodded.

"I told Gregor we would meet them there." Isidor led Cynna to the parking lot.

"Your car!"

"I had them put it on the ferry along with your luggage. I wanted us to have it for exploring Míos this summer."

"You clever man."

A golden sun smoldered over the dusky, slate-blue waters of the Aegean as the evening deepened. Overhead, a star twinkled as they drove north climbing the coast road. Isidor turned westward toward the sea, onto a private driveway. He proceeded a quarter mile to a large compound of boxy, whitewashed buildings lodged on a promontory near the edge of the cliff. The driveway was filled with vehicles.

"Do all these cars belong to your family?"

"Mmm-hmm. Most of them."

Isidor led Cynna through the house to the terrace. Laughter and live Greek music filled the air. Teddy and Mimi pushed through the crowd greeting them with kisses and hugs.

Mimi took Cynna's hands. "Mimi welcome you to her house. This party," Mimi gestured at the Greek band, the food tables, and the wild crowd eating and dancing, "is for you and Isidor. Mimi so happy you come home. Eat, sing, dance, meet peoples. First rule, have fun."

Cynna hugged Mimi again, "Efcharistó. It is a beautiful party."

"This your first Greek family party?"

"Yes."

"Oh, I tell them." Mimi clapped her hands and yelled, "Everybody, this is Cynna first Greek family party. You teach her how to make Greek party. Opa!"

The crowd yelled out, "Opa!"

Isidor grabbed Cynna by the hand, "Let's dance."

"I don't know how."

"It's easy. Just link arms, follow me, and yell out, 'Opa!'"

They joined a circle, dancing in the glow of party lights strung over the terrace. Candles flickered in tabletop lanterns, surrounded by tables piled with food, and rotisseries filled with succulent skewers of meat.

Flushed and breathless from dancing in circles, Cynna fell into Isidor's arms. "I love your family."

"They love you, too . . . oh, especially Uncle Constantine. Watch out for him, he might pinch you."

"Seriously? Is he a flirt?"

Isidor shrugged. "No, he's just a little off-target these days. He gets confused around beautiful blondes who remind him of the young Aunt Varda. If she catches him doing it, she'll throw him off the balcony by his ear."

Cynna laughed, "Oh, poor Uncle Constantine. This party is the most fun ever. I don't want it to end."

"Oh, it never does. We pretty much go from one celebration to the next all summer. But, pace yourself. The night is young, and there is more excitement to come."

Cynna's eyes grew wide with anticipation. "What kind of excitement?"

Isidor tapped her on the nose. "You must wait and be surprised with everyone else."

During the middle of their meal, Isidor jumped up and cued the band. They launched into a loud, rhythmic song. *Dun, dun, dun-dun-dun.* The crowd looked around in expectation and erupted with cheers as a young man jogged in, fists pumping the air like a prize fighter. Cheering, everyone rushed him like a rockstar.

Mimi sobbed, "Leonidás, to moró mou, my baby, Leonidás!" Hanging on his neck, she and Teddy smothered him with kisses.

Cynna worked her way through the crowd to Isidor. He took her hand, pulled her in close, and introduced her.

"Cynna, this is my older brother, Leonidás. At last, he has come home."

Leonidás took Cynna's hand. "Where did you find this gorgeous goddess? Well done, little brother!"

Leonidás embraced Cynna, kissing her on the cheek. "If things do not work out with Isidor, remember, he has an older, wiser, more handsome brother." Isidor socked him on the arm, not a playful jab. Rubbing his arm, Leonidás scowled at Isidor.

Cynna asked Isidor, "How did the family know he was here when the band played that song?"

Isidor explained, "Remember we told you Leonidás was the wild lion? I told the band to play, 'The Song of the Lion.' It's kind of his theme song."

Impressed, Cynna asked, "He has a theme song?"

Mimi took the stage and grabbed the microphone. It squealed and the band stopped playing.

"This is most special family celebration. All Mimi babies came home. My Gregor, Alexandra, and pregnant baby come home." She blew kisses at them.

"The prowling Lion—" she whacked Leonidás on the head. "You in trouble with Mimi! You gone too long." Everyone laughed. "Mimi love you anyway."

Mimi blew kisses at Cynna, "Isidor bring Mimi and Teddy special new daughter to love. For all of this, I thank God in heaven." Mimi raised her glass, "To God who make this happen!"

"To God!"

Mimi declared, "Now we happier, we dance more, *faster!*"

The bouzoúkis strumming in quick tempo, the family joined hands, dancing in concentric circles. Holding Cynna's hand, Isidor led her around in circles, laughing and yelling out, "Opa!"

The hour was late; the night of celebration was young. Cynna's thankful heart grew younger still, lightened with laughter, overflowing in exuberant love for God and her new family.

After midnight, Teddy and Mimi brought forth unleavened bread and wine, placing it before them, and they all gathered around the LORD's table.

Isidor brought forth the wooden box of incense as Teddy read from the Holy Scriptures. Isidor and Cynna set a Frankincense tear smoldering in the silver bowl, its fragrance rising as a prayer unto the LORD, in a gossamer column.

Raising his hands, Isidor said, "Let my prayer be set forth before Thee as incense; and the lifting up of my hands as the evening sacrifice."(KJV)

The family lifted their hands in praise to God, "Amen."

Isidor continued, ". . .walk surrendered to the extravagant love of Christ, for he surrendered his life as a sacrifice for us. His great love for us was pleasing to God, like an aroma of adoration—a sweet healing fragrance."(TPT)

"Amen."

Teddy led the family in the breaking of bread together, commemorating the broken body of Jesus Christ, and they shared the cup of wine symbolizing Jesus' shed blood—the sacrificial lamb, covering their sins.

Uncle Ómiros led a song of praise, and their joyous voices joined in, lifting it up. From the hill above the Aegean, their song drifted heavenward—a sweet-smelling sacrifice to God.

Heart overflowing with love for the Christopoulos family, Cynna looked from face to face. From the youngest to the oldest, their countenances shone with love, like beacons lighting the darkness. Joining them, her own high, clear voice lifted her praises, celebrating God's unfailing, steadfast love.

CHAPTER 42

*And the sea shall bring forth
her many treasures in great abundance.*

Pushing the curtains aside, Cynna opened the French doors, luxuriating in the late morning sunshine. Barefoot, she padded to the kitchen and foraged for breakfast. She brewed coffee, toasted bread, and spread it with butter and thyme honey.

Mug and plate in hand, she cuddled into a cushy nook in the outdoor living area. With a postcard view of the Aegean Sea and shaded by a veil of bougainvillea, she considered this pure heaven.

All was quiet. Next door, Gregor and Alexandra's curtains were drawn. The three of them had not left the party until one o'clock that morning. A chugging motor drew her attention to a boat entering the cove. It docked at the marina near a dinghy bobbing at its mooring. The deserted beach and luscious blue water begged a visit. Stashing her dishes in the sink, Cynna pulled on her swimsuit and cover-up, and scrambled down the steps to the shore.

She crossed the dry sand and dropped her beach towel at her feet. Watching the waves crash on the shore, Cynna shrugged from her cover-up. Surprised by a wolf whistle, she turned, shielding her eyes and looking up the beach. A barefoot Isidor was walking toward her, in swim trunks, a white T-shirt, and sunglasses.

Stopping a few paces away, posturing he said, "This is a private beach."

Raising her chin in defiance, she said. "Yes, it is. If you do not have permission to be here, I'll report you immediately."

Lowering his sunglasses, Isidor took in the sight of her in the swimsuit. A smile spread across his lips. Pulling his T-shirt off overhead, he threw it on the sand near her tote.

He challenged her, "So, are you going to call the authorities and have me removed?"

Closing the distance between them, Cynna stood before him.

"Well, that depends."

"On what?"

"On how good of a kisser you are."

Without touching her, Isidor leaned in placing a sweet kiss on her cheek.

Shaking her head, Cynna crossed her arms and rolled her eyes. "That won't do."

Isidor frowned. "No?"

"No. I'll give you one more chance."

Raising his eyebrows, Isidor's expression turned mischievous. "Okay then, I think I'll give you a big, sloppy, wet kiss."

Realization dawning, Cynna squealed, turned, and ran. "Oh, no, no, no—*noooo!*"

Grabbing her by the waist and picking her up, Isidor carried her into the surf. Chest deep, he tossed her into the water. Laughing, Cynna bobbed to the surface, splashing Isidor. He splashed back. She swam to him, laughing and splashing.

Pulling her close, he kissed her. "Good morning, My Love."

"My Love . . ." She kissed him again.

They swam parallel to the beach until they grew tired. Walking ashore, hand in hand, they pushed through the frothy breakers and onto the wet sand. In companionable silence, they walked the length of the beach at the edge of the water.

Isidor brushed Cynna's shoulder. "You're starting to sunburn. Let's get out of the sun."

Cynna smiled and wrinkled her nose. "I don't like that idea."

Isidor kissed her nose, "Come on. Your beak is pink, too."

"What if we got back in the water? We could swim back."

"It's against the current going back. And you will still burn." He took her hand and started back up the beach ankle-deep in the surf. Cynna bent down to retrieve a colorful shell at the edge of the water. Swishing it in the water to wash away the sand, she raised it for a closer look.

"This is not a shell. It looks like a rock—or a jewel." Cynna held the frosted, ice blue nugget up to the sunlight for Isidor to see.

"Ah. Well done, My Love. You just found your first piece of sea glass."

"It's beautiful. I've never heard of sea glass. What exactly is it?"

"It's formed from glass that finds its way into the ocean, like from shipwrecks, or bottles thrown overboard from boats or washed out to sea from a beach. The glass gets broken and tumbled in the ocean currents amid the sand and coral at the bottom of the sea and in the waves on the shore. The chemical properties of the salt water and the tumbling give it this smoother, frosted, jewel-like appearance."

"How long does it take to become like this?"

"Thirty, forty, perhaps fifty years to become this beautiful."

"So, it's rather special."

"Indeed, it is."

"I've only been to a few beaches, but I've never heard of it or found it before."

"It can be found worldwide, but only on certain beaches. It depends on the ocean currents and ship traffic, among other things. It's a rare find. Some collectors travel the world to visit beaches known for sea glass."

Cynna admired the nugget in her hand. "A jewel from the sea."

"They do make jewelry with it. We could take it to a jeweler and have something designed for you. A ring or a necklace, perhaps?"

Thinking of the long summer ahead, Cynna's eyes sparkled with delight. "I'd love that. I'll spend every day on this beach looking for more."

Isidor kissed the top of her head. "Then, I shall spend every day on this beach looking for you, my little sea jewel."

When they returned to the hotel, they found Gregor and Alexandra sitting in the shade of the arbor on the terrace.

Alexandra put down her book. "Hello, you two. Isidor, where did you come from? Your car's not in the lot."

Cynna eyed Isidor. "We had a security breach on the beach. I was going to call security," Cynna laughed, "but we entered into successful negotiations."

Smiling at Cynna, Isidor said, "I came around the coast in the boat. I'm docked at the marina."

"Ah, I figured," Alexandra batted her eyes. "Negotiations, indeed. I watched you two through the telescope. The water looks glorious today. After that swim, I figured you'd like some lunch." Alexandra motioned to the table and chairs.

Cynna said, "Yes, please. I'm starving."

"It's just a light meal to tide us over until dinner tonight."

They sat, joined hands, and blessed the meal.

Gregor asked Isidor, "You pulled off quite a surprise last night. When did you find out Leonidás was coming home?"

"I was as surprised as everyone else," Isidor admitted. "Somehow he knew we all arrived, and he rushed home for the party." Isidor shook his head, "I'd swear that guy's a spy with underground connections. Anyway, he called late yesterday afternoon, used some phony accent to get me on the phone, swore me to secrecy, and made me accomplice to his surprise entrance."

"He can never just walk through the door like everyone else," Alexandra laughed. "There is only one Leonidás."

"Thank goodness," Gregor said amused. With a tinge of annoyance he added, "When he found out Alexandra was making him an uncle, he kept picking her up and swinging her around. Three times I told him to put her down. If this baby fancies flying or wants to be a pilot, it's Leonidás' fault."

Alexandra laughed and patted Gregor's arm. "It will be fine, Sweetheart. Besides, I think this baby will play soccer or football. Right now, he's kicking a lot." She straightened and massaged the side of her belly.

"No, My Darling, that means *she* will be a ballerina. She is practicing her plié and pirouette piquée."

Alexandra kissed Gregor. "Most men want a son first. But Gregor, no. He wants a daughter. I think this baby is a boy. Gregor is convinced she is a girl."

Alexandra added some grapes and cheese to her plate. "Gregor wants a baby girl so much, he named the hotel after her."

Cynna was confused. "You will name her Mákari?"

"Not quite. After we bought the hotel, we were here for the summer. We were trying to get pregnant, and at the same time, trying to think of a name for the hotel. Gregor said, 'I wish for a baby girl.' The Greek word for 'I wish' is *Mákari*. We liked the sound of that, so in faith and as a prayer to God for Gregor's wish to come true, we named it Hotel Mákari."

Gregor leaned in and kissed Alexandra sweetly on the lips. "What a meaningful story it will be when we tell our *daughter* that we named our hotel this because of our wish for her."

Isidor smiled mischievously, "And, if the baby is a boy?"

Alexandra giggled. Gregor laughed, "That's simple. I would also love to have a son, in which case, I will wish for the second baby to be a girl."

A booming voice suggested, "I think you should rename it the Hotel Leonidás." Once again, Leonidás appeared out of nowhere.

Cynna was amazed at the uncanny timing of this phenomenon called Leonidás. He appeared and disappeared without warning. Later, she asked Isidor, "One day he'll just disappear again, won't he?" She hoped for Mimi and Teddy's sake Leonidás lingered a bit.

Alexandra jumped up from the table, "Pull up a chair; I'll get a plate for you."

Kissing Alexandra on the cheek, Leonidás said, "Sit, sit, sit. I'll get it."

Making the rounds, he kissed Cynna on the cheek and slapped Isidor and Gregor on the shoulder.

"Actually, I don't think I can eat again. Mimi's been feeding me since I got out of bed this morning. Breakfast, more breakfast, snacks, lunch, more snacks. She never stops pushing food in front of me and saying, 'Eat! Eat!' So, uh, maybe just a glass of wine."

Gregor filled his raised glass.

Leonidás rubbed his hands together. "So, what's the plan?"

"Plan?" Isidor asked.

"The plan. What are we going to do next? I'm sure you have something fun planned for tonight, right? I need some fresh air, a little breather from Mimi and Teddy."

Isidor, Gregor, Alexandra, and Cynna exchanged looks.

Leonidás looked from one to the other, "*What?*"

Isidor checked his watch. "You're in luck. We have big plans for tonight. We're going to Mimi and Teddy's. She's making a family dinner for you."

"Ughhhh." Defeated, Leonidás groaned and hung his head. "Okay—I give up. All I ask is one thing."

Gregor asked, "Which is?"

"We take a day off tomorrow."

Isidor parried, "A day off? You're off every day."

"A day off from the women."

Cynna and Alexandra complained in unison, "Excuse me?"

Conspiring, Leonidás rubbed his hands together, looking at Gregor and Isidor. "You know, we need to call all the guys and do that thing we do, you know, *the Men of Míos* thing."

Gregor tilted his head and nodded. "It has been a while."

Isidor said, "I don't think—"

Leonidás punched him. "Little brother, it will be good even for you." He eyed Cynna. "Think how much sweeter your reunion will be after a day apart."

Isidor gave Leonidás a ferocious scowl.

Leonidás persisted, "Just like the old days, we recruit Teddy and Uncle Ómiros, Geórgious from the winery, and—" Leonidás snapped his fingers trying to summon a name from memory, "eh, Evandros, you know, Vlochós, from the hotel on the mountain."

"Oh, yeah, yeah, yeah!" Gregor said, moving to the front of his seat.

Despite himself, Isidor nodded and smiled. "I hate to admit it, older brother, but you actually have a good idea."

Cynna asked, "What is the Men of Míos?"

Leaning close, Alexandra whispered to Cynna, "I'll tell you in a minute."

Leonidás asked, "Teddy's big boat is in working order?"

Both Gregor and Isidor nodded with enthusiasm.

Leonidás got up. "No time to waste. I'll make the calls." He swaggered to the hotel office, fisted hands raised high in victory.

Cynna said, "The only thing missing is his theme song—"

"Yeah, the 'Song of the Lion,'" Alexandra said.

Isidor and Gregor belted out the rhythmic tune, "Dun, dun, dun-dun-dun!"

At the office door, Leonidás turned, and raising his arms like a victorious prizefighter, he boomed, "Men of Míos! We leave at dawn!"

Alexandra pushed back from the table, "*Oh, brother.*"

Cynna laughed.

Gregor pulled Alexandra onto his lap. In his best stage voice he bellowed, "Fear not, fair maiden, the Men of Míos shall conquer the fish of the high seas and return in triumph to claim our women."

Alexandra laughed and cuddled in Gregor's embrace.

Cynna sat on Isidor's lap and put her arms around his neck. "Go, Man of Míos, go with the men to the sea and conquer the fish!" Cynna kissed Isidor lightly on the lips. He responded to her kiss, and she pulled back. He clearly wanted more. "You may collect the rest of my affections when you return from the sea with a fish." With that, Cynna got up and helped Alexandra clear the dishes.

She asked Alexandra, "So, the men are going fishing?"

Putting the dishes in the sink, Alexandra turned to Cynna, "Yes, but you don't know what this fishing trip really means."

Cynna ventured, "A bunch of sunburned, sweaty, smelly men who come home, want us to kiss them, clean, and cook fish for them?"

Alexandra shook her head, a playful expression in her eyes. "It means 'Mimi's Rules' go into effect."

"What are Mimi's Rules?"

"Our Mimi is a very clever woman. She *encourages* the men to go on their fishing trips as long as they honor Mimi's Rules, which means we get equal time."

"We have to go fishing?"

"No," Alexandra did a sassy little dance in the kitchen, "we get a girl's day. We go on a *really* good shopping trip, buy new dresses, pamper ourselves, and lunch in a nice restaurant."

"Oh, I love Mimi's Rules!"

"And, at the end of the day, the men return, clean their own fish, clean themselves up, and serve dinner to the women."

Cynna did her own little dance. "Oh, I *love* Mimi."

"The women wear their new dresses for the men. We make it a point to look alluring." Alexandra raised her eyebrows seductively. "At the end of the day, everyone is happy. The men feel manly and handsome. The women feel feminine and beautiful. It is a magical day off from routine." Alexandra gave Cynna a sultry look, "Let's just say the night ends well for all us old married couples."

Cynna thought a moment, then blushed. "Oh . . ."

CHAPTER 43

∞

> Behold, you are beautiful, my love,
> behold, you are beautiful!
> Your two breasts are like two fawns,
> twins of a gazelle,
> that graze among the lilies.
> —Song of Solomon 4:1, 5 (ESV)
> 970–931 BC

Monday morning the guest shuttle, a minivan with the logo of the Mountain Inn emblazoned on the side panel, careened wildly around the hairpin curves of the coast road, Kyveli Vlochós at the wheel. She volunteered to drive the ladies to town for shopping when the Men of Míos went fishing.

In the rear seat, Cynna and Alexandra alternately held hands and let go in self-defense, bracing themselves against the windows and ceiling of the bouncing van. Amid shrieks of fear and waves of excited laughter from her passengers, Kyveli drove with one hand and gestured with the other.

Cynna said to Alexandra, "I'll give Kyveli credit, this ride is more thrilling than any roller-coaster."

"I know. I'd fear for my life, but I can't stop laughing."

Strapped into the middle seat were Isidor's Aunt Ioxánio, Barba Kostas from Giórgos Hill Winery, and her daughter, Dina Kostas. They chatted as casually as if they were visiting in Mimi's living room. Holding on to Alexandra, Cynna watched the shoreline whiz by a hundred feet below. It seemed a surreal blur. She squealed, *"Eeeeeeeee!* I don't think all four tires are on the ground."

Alexandra took a deep breath. "I can't watch."

Mimi rode shotgun, participating in all conversations without missing a beat. She told Kyveli, "This is wild ride for baby. Slow down or you bounce the baby out of Alexandra too soon."

Cynna said, "Too soon? So, it's an option for later?"

To her credit, Kyveli reduced speed by at least ten knots while racing through the sleepy little chorió by the sea. Cynna imagined doors blown off the quiet residences in their wake. Once they cleared the little town, Mimi in the front passenger seat commanded, "Spévdo! Kyveli! Spévdo! Hurry, *go faster!*"

Cynna blinked, wide-eyed at Alexandra, and giggled, "Yes, by all means, *go faster!* If we're all going to die, let's get it over with." Alexandra clutched her hand and burst into nervous laughter.

Kyveli obliged, punching the accelerator.

Alexandra re-checked her seatbelt. "Mom and Kyveli have the shopping *zoomies*." Burying her head in Cynna's shoulder, she added, "Just wake me when we arrive in heaven."

Cynna put her arm around Alexandra's shoulders. "I think Kyveli just broke the sound barrier on the straight-away. She'll be popping the chute for landing soon. I see the chora up ahead."

Kyveli snagged a parking space and halted the minivan with a loud screech of the brakes.

Cynna announced, "Good news, Alexandra, we survived."

"Oh, my Lord!" Alexandra breathed shakily, wiping the tears of laughter from her cheeks.

Relieved, Cynna took a deep breath and asked, "Has her driving always been this bad?"

"Oh, no," Alexandra assured her, "it used to be much worse."

Incredulous, Cynna stared at her. "And, we got in the car with her?"

"Yes, wasn't it exciting?"

The gaggle of ladies staggered from the vehicle and began their trek toward the mound of white, boxy buildings that wound around the hill by the harbor. It looked like a wedding cake, decorated in bougainvillea blossoms and topped with a magnificent, blue-domed church.

Coming alongside Cynna, Mimi looped her arm through the arm of her potential new daughter-in-law. "Wasn't that exciting drive?"

"The most exciting ever."

"Kyveli scare the underpants off you with her horrible driving, didn't she?"

Cynna burst out laughing. "Yes."

Patting Cynna fondly on the cheek, Mimi said, "You probably think, 'Why you get in car with her?' I answer this. She drive worse than this her whole life, and she survive. So, we all decide she not meant to die in car, we are safe to ride with her."

"Well, I can't argue with that."

Mimi said, "You survive this drive to town. You feel more alive now, don't you?"

"Oh, yes, and thankful, too."

"See? Kyveli's wild driving was good for you. Kyveli's driving is one thing we love most about her," Mimi pronounced proudly. "She has big gusto for life. She make us feel *alive*."

Walking arm-in-arm with Isidor's precious mother, Cynna felt alive and happy. Mimi said, "Isidor want to be first to show you his town. So, I tell him it okay because I can only show you town as his *mother*. He is only one can show you his town as a *lover*."

"Thank you for that, Mimi."

Walking ahead of them, Alexandra and Dina talked incessantly.

As if reading her thoughts, Mimi said, "Alexandra and Dina have been friends since they were born. Same for me, Kyveli, Ioxánio, and Barba. We all born and grow up on Míos."

They climbed the narrow stone pathway winding through the cluster of buildings.

"I tell you now about the older generation. I marry my Teddy.

Kyveli marry her Evandros Vlochós. They have the Mountain Inn in mountain chorió. They have son, Evandir. He is like Leonidás, off to see the world. Tonight, we have our dinner at the Mountain Inn, and Sunday we go to there for church together. Barba marry her Geórgios —her George. He inherit family vineyard, Giórgos Iófos—Giórgos Hill Winery. Dina is their daughter. Ioxánio—Roxane, we call her Roxie for short, it is cute name. She marry to Teddy brother Ómiros. We all grow up together. Go to school together. Get married and have babies together."

They threaded their way past shops and tavernas. Mimi said, "Leonidás, Isidor, Alexandra, Gregor, Dina, Evandir . . . their generation, they all grow up together, but leave Míos, go out to see world."

Cynna covered Mimi's hand with her own and held it tight. She knew the summer would pass all too quickly, and she and Isidor, and Gregor and Alexandra would return to Athens. She knew Leonidás' days at home were few by any standard.

Mimi said, "Like birds from the nest, only time will show if this young generation return home to live on Míos, or if they scatter on wind."

They reached their destination and were seated at an upscale sidewalk taverna. Luncheon was a feast of champagne, saláta melitzánas—aubergine salad, saláta choriátiki—village salad, and revíthia soúpa—chick-pea soup. The entree was kotópoulo yemistó—chicken stuffed with rice, butter, tomato, cinnamon, almonds, raisins, and potatoes, served with patátes fournou ladorígani— potatoes roasted in olive oil, lemon, and rigani. Dessert was one of Cynna's favorites, loukoumádes —honey puffs.

Telling one hilarious story after another, they laughed even more over lunch than during the van ride. Unlike the cultured ladies' societies in New York, Cynna found these ladies vibrant and brimming with zest for life and compassion for one another. Not one unkind word was spoken.

After lunch, they waddled to the ladies' boutique. Standing outside, they huddled-up.

Mimi said, "Cynna, this is your first ladies' day. We explain to you how this next part work. We always eat first. Don't ever buy dress when you feel skinny; it might not fit after lunch."

All the ladies nodded.

Roxie explained, "First rule in boutique: No trust sales clerk. She say, 'Honey, that look beautiful on you.' This not always true. One time she say dress matches your eyes. It was *plaid!* How can plaid match eyes? And, she not know our men. So, we help each other find dress. Number two rule, always tell truth. If I try on dress that make me look like cow, you tell me, 'Roxie, you look like cow.' No tell me I look like beautiful . . . kamilopárdali."

Cynna nodded seriously. "Okay. Then, I need to know, what is a cameo-party-doily?"

Dina snorted, "Kamilopárdali, a giraffe."

"Okay, I promise to tell the truth."

Kyveli plunged in next. "My Evandros, he no like anything with stripe like tiger. Animal prints, they no start his motor, if you know what I mean. I will not try this on."

Mentally blinded by the picture, Cynna refocused.

Running her hands down her torso from armpits to hips, Barba stood taller, thrusting her chest forward. "My Geórgious . . . he is *breast man.* No worry, this is *biblical.* I must find something that show off my twin fawns for my lover. Like in Song of Solomon."

Dina snorted even louder. "Okay, Mom. We get the picture."

The mental picture of Barba's twin fawns now rivaled that of Evandros' motor. Shaking it off, Cynna feared she'd never be able to face Geórgious or Evandros again. Subconsciously, she slumped her shoulders forward, and her own breasts all but disappeared behind the fabric of her top.

Mimi went next. "My Teddy, he is leg man . . . and, he likes red dress." She raised an eyebrow, for him, this red is a, "Vrooooom-vrooooom!"

Okay, now I know way too much about Teddy. Despite herself, and in the spirit of things, Cynna asked, "So, do you want a short dress that shows off your legs, or do you want a longer dress with a slit so you can tease him with little glimpses?"

Everyone chimed in with appreciation, "Oh, good question."

Mimi thought for a moment. "We married for long time . . . I think it is time to tease him little bit. Show him whole leg at once and he might make up mind quickly, that he not interested. Show little bit, maybe he think he want to investigate." She laughed, giddy at the thought. "You might need to teach Mimi how to do *'little glimpse to tease with leg.'*"

Everyone promised to teach her how.

All eyes turned to Alexandra. She ran her hands over her large middle. "We will have to see, they may not have any maternity clothes."

Roxie chimed in, "Well, it's obvious you wore something in past Gregor really liked." Alexandra blushed.

Kyveli made goo-goo eyes and batted her lashes at Dina. "Perhaps tonight you wish to interest Leonidás? You are home, he is home. You are beauty woman, he is handsome man. Time for your love to blossom like flower. We help you find something very beautiful." Mimi clapped her hands and smiled, pleased at the thought.

Dina shook her head, "Thank you, Kyveli, but no. I am dating someone in Athens."

Barba gave her daughter a look. "Really? That's news to me, your own mitéra. Why you no tell your own mitéra? Who is this *'someone in Athens'*? Does this *someone* have name?"

Alexandra piped up, "Dina does have a boyfriend. Gregor and I know him."

Barba gave Alexandra a hurtful look. "Why you no tell Dina's mitéra she dating someone?"

Looking back to Dina, hand on hip, Barba waited for her daughter to divulge the goods.

Dina said, "His name is Mílos Stávros. He is a celebrity jewelry designer."

"*Oooohoooo!*" Everyone cheered.

Barba said, "Next time, you *tell* your mitéra."

Cheers dying down, Dina surrendered. "Okay, Mom, okay."

Cynna felt all eyes on her.

Roxie said, "You met Isidor short time. We met Isidor when born. I think we tell you what you buy to catch him."

Cynna did not point out she'd already *caught* Isidor.

Agreeing, they sized her up from head to toe. Cynna felt the heat rising in her cheeks. She reached for Alexandra's hand. Alexandra squeezed it, telegraphing all was okay.

Roxie said, "You have beautiful blue eyes. I think blue dress lure Isidor."

Kyveli narrowed her eyes. "Isidor like archaeology . . . maybe he like animal print?" Failing to see the connection between archaeology and animal prints, Cynna let it go.

Barba suggested, "Stand up straight." Self-consciously Cynna pulled her shoulders back and her chest rose. Barba pointed at Cynna's chest and said, "We find your best feature!"

Mimi and Kyveli "Ooooed" in agreement.

Roxie frowned, "She have very good leg, too."

Dina weighed in, "Look at that gorgeous long neck and shoulders, I think something off-the-shoulder."

Barba asked, "Has Isidor seen glimpse of cleavage?"

Placing a modest hand over her chest, Cynna said, "Ummm, no." She slumped her shoulders again.

Barba said, "Isidor needs to get a peek of the twin fawns! If he see this, I guarantee marriage proposal."

Mimi said, "I'm not sure—"

Barba reassured, "It's *biblical,* Mimi, like Song of Solomon."

Despite herself, Dina snorted yet again.

Alexandra took charge, "Ladies, let's go in. We have our game plan. We need one sexy giraffe outfit, one outfit—no tiger stripes, one red dress with a teasing leg slit and lessons on how to use it, one maternity dress, and two lowish-cut outfits for biblical fawns."

A few hours later when finished at the boutique, they recovered and debriefed over coffee and dessert.

Alexandra said, "Next stop, shoes and accessories. I'll buy earrings for everyone, my treat."

Arms filled with shopping bags, they meandered down the hill, collapsing into the minivan. The ride grew quiet as they neared home. Exhausted, Alexandra fell asleep with her head on Cynna's shoulder. Anxious to wear her new dress for Isidor, Cynna anticipated the magical evening ahead.

CHAPTER 44

And now, dear brothers and sisters,
one final thing. Fix your thoughts
on what is true, and honorable, and right,
and pure, and lovely, and admirable.
Think about things that are
excellent and worthy of praise.
—Philippians 4:8 (NLT)

Dressed for the evening, the ladies assembled in the salon of the Mountain Inn at eight o'clock Monday night. Ready to join the Men of Míos for dinner on the terrace, they modeled their new outfits for each other.

"Mimi, you do have great legs!" Barba said. The slit in the formal length gown opened modestly at the knee. Coaching her, Dina showed her how to angle her hip and foot so the fabric draped open on each side of her calf. Though awkward in high heels, Mimi struck the pose and owned it. Blushing like a schoolgirl, Mimi announced "This make Mimi feel pretty. Hope Teddy like it."

Kyveli said, "With your dark hair and skin tone, you look amazing in red. Teddy know more than you give him credit for. Alexandra, great job with her hairdo and make-up. Mimi, I've never seen you fluffed, teased, lacquered, and lipsticked before. You look like beautiful model."

Mimi said, "Somebody catch Mimi if I fall off my shoes." She pointed. "Look at Roxie, so pretty in little black dress!"

Cynna said, "You certainly don't look like a cow, and you're prettier than a kamilopár—giraffe."

A group effort saved Kyveli from herself at the boutique—she was drawn to animal prints like a magnet. Regardless, she looked fabulous in a sleeveless, emerald green dress with an embossed collar.

"Pretty lady," Alexandra said, "green is your color. It goes with your eyes."

Roxie said, "If that dress not start Evandros' motor, it's time to call the mechanic."

Everyone hooted.

"Look at my Alexandra." Mimi crooned with pride, "My beautiful daughter look gorgeous in pink."

The empire waist gown with its gathered skirt draped perfectly over her mid-section. She swooped her long, thick, dark hair into an updo of ringlets that adorned the back of her head like a crown.

Admiring Dina in the gold lamé halter-top jumpsuit, Alexandra said, "You look smashing. After I have the baby and get my figure back, can I borrow that outfit?"

Eyebrows raised, Barba eyed Dina and said, "Leonidás going to follow you around all night like puppy dog, eating from your hand. Maybe you give him chance?"

Dina rolled her eyes. "Mama, I'm in love with Mílos."

"Oh, so now you tell your mama you in love with this Athens jewelry man. Earlier you say he is boyfriend. In five minutes, you tell your mama you get married?"

Roxie drew her off. "Barba, give matchmaking a rest. Let young ones figure it out."

Kyveli coaxed, "Look at you, Barba, Glamorous! When Geórgious see peek of biblical fawns, he be happy man."

Drawing her shoulders back, Barba boosted the bodice of her electric-blue, satin dress with the keyhole neckline.

Alexandra said, "Cynna, you chose the perfect dress. Isidor will love it."

Cynna's ice blue dress somehow met all their criteria. The spaghetti strap, chiffon, A-line cocktail dress matched her eyes and showed off her legs, long neck, elegant shoulders, and bonus, the slinky cowl-neck occasionally revealed a modest peak at her cleavage. Plus, the liquid-silver loop earrings and necklace from Alexandra mirrored the folds of the cowl-neck. She felt rather pretty and a little shy about seeing Isidor.

En masse, they entered the terrace on a cloud of perfume. The Men of Míos, waiting for their dates, stood handsomely spit and polished and appearing all the more masculine from their day at sea.

Candles flickered on white linen tables flanked with china, and silverware. Jazzy Greek music played softly in the background. It reminded Cynna of prom night, only a million times more magical.

Isidor approached Cynna, his sun-kissed face vibrant and healthy-looking. Taking Cynna's hands in his own, he whispered, "You are beautiful, My Love." He kissed her on each cheek. "You look stunning in that dress."

"Thank you, it's biblical."

An odd look came over Isidor's features. "Excuse me?"

Smiling, Cynna met Isidor's eyes. "My handsome Isidor, the man of my dreams."

His lips touched hers and lingered. "I missed you today."

"I missed you, too."

Joining the others at the table, Cynna noticed that Leonidás and Dina paired up. Serving the wine, Geórgious described the vintage and tasting notes, and raised a toast to the women. Kyveli then proposed a toast to the Men of Míos.

Gregor and Evandros served the bread, olive oil, soup, and salad plate. Teddy, Isidor, and Leonidás served their specialty, fish a la spetsiota, striped bass broiled in olive oil, onion, tomato, white wine, garlic, and parsley. Ómiros served the dessert, karidópita, walnut cake.

After dessert and coffee, Evandros loaded a new stack of records on the turntable. Everyone slow danced until midnight.

Swaying to the music in Isidor's arms, Cynna said, "This is the loveliest party. Let's dance forever."

"Yes, forever." Guiding Cynna around the dance floor, Isidor spoke intimately into her ear. "You belong in my arms. I am incomplete without you."

After the party, Isidor drove Cynna to the Hotel Mákari. At her door, Cynna pulled her key from her clutch. Isidor unlocked the door for her. Awkward, they faced each other in the doorway, halfway between two scenarios: intimate privacy and public scrutiny.

Cynna withdrew something from her clutch and held it between them.

Isidor recognized it immediately. He did not take it from her. Rather, he closed his fingers around hers, and together they held it between them. It was the Giórgos Hill Winery cork Isidor gave her on their first date.

"This is from the first bottle of Giórgos Hill wine we shared when you told me of Míos. You said, 'Míos is the island of my birth, the island of my family. It is the place that always lives in my heart.'"

Isidor nodded. "You said you wanted to come to Míos."

"You promised to bring me here." Cynna reached her arms around Isidor's neck. "On this, another one of the most memorable nights of my life, I wanted to thank you for keeping your promise. Thank you for bringing me to Míos."

Isidor stepped forward and backed Cynna against the doorway. He held the back of her head in one hand and with the other he touched Cynna's face. He kissed her and drew back to look at her. He traced the line of her jaw with his finger, and let it drift down the side of her neck and along her collar bone, to the hollow of her neck. He sighed, closed his eyes, and pulled his hand away, planting it firmly on the door frame to the side of her head.

"You are irresistible in that dress. It is very hard for me to leave you at the doorstep tonight."

Looking into Isidor's hazel eyes, Cynna longed to run her hands through his thick brown hair and pull him close. Instead, taking a deep breath, she put her hands behind her back. Isidor did the same and leaned against his side of the doorway. They smiled at one another. It broke the heated passion and tension pulsing between them.

In a husky voice Isidor said, "I will never dishonor you or God's perfect will for our lives."

"Thank you for that, and for the most perfect evening, Isidor. I shall never forget it."

"Nor shall I. I love you, Cynna."

"I love you, Isidor."

He kissed her forehead. "Goodnight."

CHAPTER 45

⤞

Every single moment you are thinking of me!
How precious and wonderful to consider
that you cherish me constantly
in your every thought!
O God, your desires toward me
are more than the grains of sand on every shore!
When I awake each morning, you're still with me.
—Psalm 139:17–18 (TPT)
1048 BC

*I*ntrigued by its simple beauty, Cynna fingered the bowl of sand and sea glass on the coffee table. Sparkling softly in the glow of the pendant light, the simple collection represented a glorious summer filled with morning swims, walks on the beach, and the beautiful love she and Isidor shared. The largest piece of sea glass, a pale blue oval, was harvested the magical Monday the Men of Míos went to sea and the women went shopping.

Falling into a carefree rhythm of sunny days and starry nights, the summer rushed past her, eluding her grasp like sand through her fingers. The first month already spent, Cynna sighed with contentment, unwilling to count the dwindling days left her on Míos.

The days drifted by unchecked, the weeks delineated by the Sunday routine. The Christopoulos, Andras, Vlochós, and Kostas families gathered for house church. Cynna rather preferred this over the austere, liturgical services she attended in New York.

Here, these gatherings meant a celebration, a heartfelt worship and connection with her God and Father, and this God-gathered family. It was through these relationships, she learned their individual joys and sorrows, the truth behind the praise flowing from their lips.

When Cynna asked Isidor why the families met together for church, he explained the Greek Orthodox church buildings were many, and the priests few. Opportunity to attend church was limited to once or twice a year. Seeking more, these lifelong friends met like the Christians in the Bible, coming together the first day of the week and sharing life together.

By the end of June, Leonidás' visit dissolved into a delightful memory. The Lion was once again on the prowl, exploring territories unknown, an empty void left in place of his charisma. In exchange for Leonidás' sad departure, they gained Mílos Stávros, Dina's Athens boyfriend. Mílos took up residence in room number three at the Mákari.

"I loved the ruins we explored today," Cynna said, taking Isidor's hand. "And, I love our quiet evenings together here on the Makari terrace."

They often dined at her bistro table and relaxed on the outdoor furniture. Cynna sat next to Isidor on the sofa. "I can't believe it's July already. Will we have enough time to finish exploring the island before summer's over?"

Isidor twirled a lock of her hair. "Most of it, I think, short of personally visiting every household."

"Oh, don't disappoint me," Cynna laughed. "I'd planned on meeting them all, every last citizen of Míos."

Cuddling up to Isidor, Cynna laid her head on his chest, his relaxed breathing soft and percussive in her ear.

"Well, if we're launching a door-to-door campaign, we'd better get an early start tomorrow."

"Actually, I'm selfish. I'd rather just spend the day with you."

Isidor put his arm around her, lowered his head, and kissed her.

Cynna traced the outline of his lips with her finger. "I love our evenings together here. I tell myself if we sit quiet, we can make time slow down, perhaps even stand still. I want this summer to last forever."

"But nothing lasts forever, does it?"

The breath caught in Cynna's lungs. "No, sometimes it even reaches beyond." She closed her eyes and prayed for *beyond forever* with Isidor. When it came to life with Isidor, she always wanted more.

Isidor kissed the top of her head and said, "I think we should explore the mountain ch*o*rió tomorrow; it's their market day. We can shop, eat, and I'll tell you of their history."

The day after the mountain chorio tour, Isidor took Cynna to a quiet rock beach cove on the east coast. The water was warm and calm, perfect for floating on the swells and sunning like turtles on the enormous boulders.

That night, Isidor loaded stacks of records on a portable suitcase turntable, and they listened to music, ate, talked, and danced for hours under the summer stars. Isidor surprised Cynna with an LP of Dorian Onassis singing their song, "Darling, Dance With Me." Softly, he sang the words to Cynna and kissed her goodnight.

Many other evenings, they gathered with Alexandra and Gregor, Dina and Mílos, and another of their childhood friends, Luca Adino, Jr., his wife, Tessa, and their little son, Luca, III. They shared meals on the terrace at the Mákari or under the arbors at Gióros Hill Winery.

During the full moon, they walked on the beach, hypnotized by the ribbon of golden moon glow stretching across the water. The enormous pearl orb, kissing the horizon.

Likewise, Cynna considered every moment of her remarkable Greek summer a sweet kiss from Father God. He heard the desires of her heart, and fulfilled every dream, even more than she dared hope for.

At the end of the week, Isidor gathered the whole Mákari gang into Teddy's big boat. Navigating into open water, he accelerated to a comfortable cruising speed steering south along the coast.

Mílos asked, "What is our destination, Captain?"

"Lunch at Psarás and a swim on the beach."

Everyone cheered.

Dina explained to Cynna, "Psarás means fisherman. Their seafood is fresh and delicious. It is one of our favorite places to eat when we come home."

Isidor pulled in to the marina, and everyone bailed out. The dockside taverna was brimming with a boisterous lunch crowd, but they got a table in the shade of a stick roofed arbor overlooking the surf. A crude wooden sign hung on the wall advertised the daily special, "χταπόδι."

Cynna asked Isidor, "What does that say?"

Isidor pointed to the fresh catch of the day hanging on the line and said, "Octopus."

Cynna looked at the squiggly legs covered in suction cups dangling on the line beside their table.

Noticing Cynna's wary expression, Alexandra kicked Isidor under the table, motioning her head toward Cynna. Isidor laughed. "This is the girl who always asks me to order for her." He asked Cynna, "Shall I order for you?"

Cynna summoned her courage and once again said, "Yes, surprise me!"

The result was a rich octopus stew with tomatoes, onions, and a red wine sauce.

All eyes at the table were on Cynna as she took her first bite.

She chewed and beamed, "Oh, my! That's *delicious*."

After lunch they retrieved their things from the boat and walked across the expanse of powdery sand to the beach. The men planted umbrellas in the sand and drug out ice chests of cold drinks. Dina and Mílos plunged in immediately for a swim.

Drowsy, Alexandra napped in the shade of their umbrella while Gregor scribbled in a notebook.

Cynna whispered, "What are you working on?"

"I'm outlining ideas for a new play."

"Oh, that's marvelous. Can I be in it?"

"Of course." Gregor stuck his pen between his teeth and turned the page. He smiled at Alexandra, "You just can't be the leading lady. Perhaps a French laundry maid?"

"Oui, bien sûr."

Isidor pulled Cynna to her feet. "Let's get in. I'll race you to the water." They splashed in, swimming out to Dina and Mílos. The warm rollers tumbled relentlessly onto the shore.

When Alexandra awoke, Gregor walked with her on the beach. They sat at water's edge. Cynna and Isidor swam to shore and sat with her. Gregor swam out to Dina and Mílos who floated on their backs atop the swells.

A big wave washed up and knocked Alexandra and Cynna over. They both laughed and sputtered.

Seven months pregnant, Alexandra struggled to right herself, laughing. "I feel like a beached whale."

Cynna and Isidor sat her up. Cynna said, "You tiny thing, you're more like a beached minnow."

Isidor regarded his sister with love. "I'd say you look like an olive on a toothpick dunked in a martini glass." They all got the giggles and laughed until they cried.

Before they could recover, another rogue wave tumbled them over. The ever-encroaching tide was coming in. Cynna and Isidor helped Alexandra scoot backward on the wet sand so the splashes gently kissed her toes.

Cynna said, "Look, there's another group just up the beach."

Watching them prepare for a swim, she realized they were busy shedding their clothes. Covering her eyes she shrieked, "They're *naked!*"

Familiar with culture, Alexandra said, "Oh, the nudes."

Cynna said, "The *nudes?* They can do that?"

Alexandra shrugged, "Sure. You can too, if you want."

Isidor raised an eyebrow.

Cynna shook her head, "Oh, no thank you." Again she peeped through her fingers in the direction of the spectacle. "I still can't believe it."

Alexandra teased her, "Oh, come on, try it."

"Ummm, no."

Alexandra coaxed, "I will if you will."

"No."

"It's invigorating."

Gregor, Dina, and Mílos joined them, plopping onto the wet sand.

Mílos said, "That swim was invigorating. I love getting back to nature."

"Oh, really?" Alexandra asked.

Alexandra, Cynna, and Isidor burst into giggles again.

Dina, Gregor, and Mílos stared at them. Mílos asked, "What did I say that was so funny?"

Quick witted, Alexandra said, "Nothing. You just told the naked truth."

* * *

That evening, Mimi and Teddy dined with Cynna and Isidor on Cynna's terrace at the Mákari.

Cynna said, "It's just a simple meal, I hope you like it."

Looking at the spread, Teddy said, "Bread, fish, and vegetables broiled in olive oil, onions, and garlic. What's not to like?"

For dessert, Cynna served a plate of cookies, fruit, and chocolates for nibbling with their coffee.

"Cynna, food was delicious. You must give Mimi recipe."

"Oh, Mimi. It can't compare with your magnificent meals. The important thing is to share a meal together. I haven't seen you for days. I've missed you. Have you heard from Leonidás?"

Mimi shook her head.

Teddy shrugged with a knowing twinkle in his eye, "Eh, you know, our Leonidás, our Lion, he is wild animal. A papa, even Greek papa no tell his Lion when to call home. The Lion call when the Lion is ready."

Mimi smiled at her husband, "Teddy know this because before he was Teddy Bear, he was the Lion, too."

Cynna looked at Teddy, "Ah—"

Mimi continued, "My Theo, he kiss me first time when I was twelve. He was seventeen. He tell me he marry me when I grow up. Then, like real lion, he have wild side. He disappear in the jungle, out on prowl. I grow up. I look around. No Theo."

Mimi grew more animated, continuing the story. "So this handsome boy, Konstantin, he ask me to marry him. I say, 'Yes, I marry you.' We make big wedding. Big white dress. Big feast. Big cake. Big band for party."

Teddy began to chuckle. Isidor had a rueful smile on his face. Cynna moved to the edge of her seat.

Mimi put her hand on her hip. "I walk to front of church to marry my handsome Konstantin."

Cynna asked, "What happened?"

Teddy laughed, slapped the table, and said, "Ha!"

Mimi looked at him and cautioned, "Don't you 'ha!' to me." Though she sounded tough, Mimi's eyes twinkled with love for her husband. Teddy reached for her hand.

"I was beautiful bride at front of church, and this, this—*lion*," she spatted Teddy's hand away, "this lion, he prowl through the church. The priest ask, 'anyone know reason Konstantin and Elisavet cannot marry?'"

Teddy chuckled.

"This *lion* jump out of crowd and say to priest, 'I know of reason Elisavet cannot marry Konstantin.' The priest ask this reason. The lion say, 'because Elisavet going to marry *me*.'"

Cynna clapped her hands over her mouth. "Oh, my! Then what happened?"

"Konstantin tell me to choose. In front of God and everyone, I compare these mens. Pros—cons." Mimi narrowed her eyes, "I take my time, make the lion squirm."

Mimi cupped Teddy's face in her hand. "I pick *my* Teddy. Priest marry us right then."

Mimi and Teddy cuddled and nuzzled playfully. Cynna decided Mimi had no need to tease Teddy with a "glimpse-of-leg dress"; she had him totally wrapped around her little finger.

"Teddy," Isidor asked, "don't you think you cut that a little too close?"

"Close, suspense, perfect timing. I won the beautiful bride."

Teddy kissed Mimi sweetly on the lips and finished the story. "Big wedding, big white dress, big feast, big cake, big band, big party, big surprise for everyone . . . and for us, big honeymoon." He raised his eyebrows, "Eh, we still on big honeymoon."

Mimi patted Teddy on the cheek. "And from big honeymoon

comes big beautiful family. Mimi and Teddy have two handsome sons and beautiful daughter. Soon, grandbaby."

Teddy rose from his chair, "I think, nice walk on beach before we go home."

In the moonless night, the myriad of stars winked amidst the nearness of the heavens that lay close to the earth as a mantle of black velvet. They kicked off their shoes, padding along the wet sand.

Teddy offered Cynna his arm, and she looped her hand into the crook of his elbow. Arm-in-arm, Isidor and Mimi followed. Teddy and Cynna meandered by the water's edge in comfortable silence. Teddy patted Cynna's hand and covered it with his own.

"You are lovely girl, Cynna. You come to Míos and honor our family. We happy you with us."

Cynna patted Teddy's hand. "This is the most beautiful summer of my life. Thank you for welcoming me into your home, your lives, and your hearts."

"I see you have deep love for Heavenly Father. You honor Him with your life."

"I love Him with all my heart, soul, mind, and strength. If I do not have love I am nothing."

Teddy said, "Ah, yes, Corinthians—faith, hope, and love—the greatest is love.'"

"Yes." Cynna laughed, "I don't want to be the tinkling cymbal."

Teddy patted her hand and chuckled. "People are careless with this word '*love*.' What you think is love?"

"To love others as Jesus loves us."

"And, what Jesus say is special about his kind of love?"

"Jesus said, '. . .the greatest love of all is a love that sacrifices all.'" (TPT)

"Hmmm. So, yes, I agree, without this kind of love, we are nothing."

They walked on to the sound of swishing waves.

After some time, Teddy ventured, "Speaking of love, I can see that my middle son, Isidor, is in love."

"I am in love, too."

"So, what kind of love is this love you have for my son, Isidor?"

"The greatest kind, the love that sacrifices all."

"I am pleased about this, Cynna." Teddy faced her. He took her hands and smiled. "I give you both my blessing."

Teddy kissed Cynna on each cheek and laughed softly, "Isidor is not a restless lion. He does not prowl around foolishly as his old man and his brother. You will not have to wait for him to come to the altar at last moment."

Cynna kissed Teddy's cheek, "You dear man, I am so thankful you rescued Mimi from Konstantin at the last moment."

Teddy and Cynna turned to look back at Isidor and Mimi.

Teddy said, "I was young and foolish. Now . . . eh, I am *old* and foolish. But this I know, Mimi, my beautiful Elisavet, she is *good* woman. I thank God every day she chose me. She love me. She lay down her life for me and walk by my side. Most important, she love God with her whole heart."

Isidor and Mimi caught up with them. Teddy took Cynna's hand and placed it in Isidor's, and he reached for his Elisavet. "Come, my bride. Let us go home and leave this romantic beach to the young ones."

CHAPTER 46

〰️

> Who could ever find a wife like this one—
> she is a woman of strength and mighty valor!
> She's full of wealth and wisdom.
> The price paid for her
> was greater than many jewels.
> —Proverbs 31:10 (TPT)
> 950 BC

*I*n August, the summer holiday on Míos climaxed with the arrival of the Andras' international friends in the Performing Arts community. Actors, actresses, playwrights, directors, musicians, and artists filled the Hotel Makari, the Mountain Inn, Giórgos Vineyard, and the Christopoulos household. Every evening, the gang gathered at the Mákari terrace for parties, dinners, and dances with live music.

Alexandra explained to Cynna, "This is why Gregor and I bought the hotel. It started several years ago as a small group on holiday with us. We all camped out at Teddy and Mimi's the first few years.

Our circle of friends grew, more people wanted to come, and it became a thing. Now it is a *huge* thing. They come from all over, friends who have performed together through the years. It's a family reunion of sorts at the end of hiatus. Then we return to the stages and the galleries."

"You have great friends. Everyone's so nice and easy to talk to."

"I'm glad you enjoy them."

Isidor smiled at his sister. "And this year Dina and her parents are hosting a party at Giórgos Hill Winery for Alexandra's twenty-fifth birthday. The Men of Míos, plus a bunch of these guys, are going to sea again. We will provide the seafood for the feast."

Cynna asked, "Is Leonidás coming?"

Isidor shook his head, "I don't know, but I'm afraid not."

Cynna had a vivid flashback to the magical Monday in June when the Men of Míos went to sea, and the women went shopping. Remembering Kyveli at the wheel of the minivan careening around the coast road gave her pause. She asked Alexandra, "Mimi's Rules, again?"

"This time," Alexandra patted her belly, "Mimi's Modified Rules. At eight months pregnant, Mimi refuses to let me ride to town with Kyveli. And my feet are so swollen I can't hike the hill in this heat to the boutique and restaurant."

Cynna offered a silent prayer of relief.

"Kyveli's hosting our Ladies' Day at the Mountain Inn. We'll have a luncheon and spa day. I hope you're not disappointed. Do you mind wearing your dress from last time?"

Isidor slid his arm around Cynna's waist and answered, "I would be delighted for her to wear that dress again. And she assures me it's biblical though I have no idea why."

Cynna and Alexandra exchanged glances. Cynna blushed.

Cynna said, "What about *your* dress?"

Alexandra's eyes twinkled. "The baby's so big I can't fit into it. Mimi and Roxie pulled out patterns, fabric, and their old sewing machines. They're dressing me en couture."

Isidor raised his eyebrows and rubbed his jaw. He opened his mouth to comment. Cynna gently nudged him in the ribs and said, "What a treat. You'll look gorgeous."

The evening of the party, Cynna helped Alexandra slip into her new dress and fastened it for her in the back. Mimi and Roxie had indeed created a gorgeous dress for the very pregnant Alexandra.

"I can't see my feet. Can I hold onto you as I step into my shoes?" Offering her arm, Cynna steadied Alexandra. The rhinestone jeweled slippers were beautiful with her dress and perfect for her swollen feet. Cynna peered over Alexandra's shoulder at their reflection. They smiled at one another in the mirror.

"You look beautiful. Happy birthday, Alexandra, my sister,I love you dearly."

Alexandra reached for Cynna's hand. "I always wanted a sister, and look, here you are!"

"I always wanted a sister, too."

Alexandra rubbed her hands around her enormous midsection. Cynna reached over and placed her hand on Alexandra's baby bump.

"You are going to have the most gorgeous baby ever. I wish I were going to be here for the birth. Promise me you'll send photos the first possible moment."

Alexandra pled, "Are you sure you can't stay longer until the baby comes? *Please.*"

Cynna shook her head. "I promised my parents I would come home the first of September, and that I would not ask for another thing on this trip. Anyway, the fall semester starts right away. I'll barely get home in time as it is."

Seeing the tears in Alexandra's eyes, Cynna changed the subject, "Come along Birthday Girl, we must get you to the party. Gregor, Isidor, and your adoring family and friends are waiting."

Gregor's turquoise Impala crested Giórgos Hill and parked at the entrance. They entered the party with a fanfare from the band and cheers for the guest of honor. As they mingled with the crowd, Cynna recognized the lead actor from the performance of *Farewell to Nikolo*. Gregor said film stars were there as well. As Cynna was unfamiliar with Greek celebrities, Gregor and Alexandra made introductions for her.

The glamorous party was an amazing event with festive lights strung about the arbors, flowers, candles, and sparkling streamers. Caterers prepared the Men of Míos' catch from the sea. Servers in

ELIZABETH TOMME

black slacks and crisp white shirts circulated, charging glasses and offering canapés.

Seated at the center of the head table, Alexandra was flanked by Gregor, Teddy, Mimi, Cynna, Isidor, Ómiros, Roxie, Dina, Mílos, Barba, and Geórgious. Professional photographers circulated through the crowd capturing the celebration of Alexandra's birthday. It was a joyous occasion, the party of the year.

At the head table, Isidor, Cynna, Dina, and Mílos leaned close to Gregor and Alexandra for a photograph. With a percussive pop and whine, the flashbulb illuminated their smiling faces, freezing the moment in time and consigning them to a black and white glossy image.

Upon entering the venue, Cynna noticed the gallery of celebrity photographs lining the walls in the great hall, near the wine cellars. It reminded her of the celebrity photographs on the walls at *Zolakis* restaurant in Athens. This photograph was certain to reside among them. She hoped to get a copy of it.

The meal over, the band played a rousing rendition of the "Happy Birthday Song" as everyone sang to Alexandra and caterers wheeled in an enormous cake aglow with sparklers. During the serving of cake, Teddy gave a tearful birthday speech in honor of his baby girl. Following Teddy, speeches were made by everyone at the head table.

Gregor spoke last. "My Darling Alexandra, you are my love, my life, my everything. I have a special gift for you. Like you, it is beautiful and unique. A one of a kind. It is a symbol of the extravagant love we share.

"I give you the stunning ruby red Paeonia Parnassica, the peony from Mount Parnassus that flourishes high above ancient Delphi. I give you the white Achillea Ambrosiaca, the Olympus Yarrow from Mount Olympus. I give you the Greek fret symbolizing our infinite love, and a cross symbolizing God at the center of our marriage.

"My Love, like the Peony Parnassus and the Olympus Yarrow, you thrive at lofty heights under difficult conditions. Your stage performances are magnificent. The more challenging the role, the higher you soar to rare and lofty heights at which you, My Love, flourish.

"I am spellbound by your talent. As your playwright, I am thinking, *'she is the most amazing actress.'* As your husband, I am thinking, 'this *most beautiful goddess is my wife.'* I am in awe. You, My Love, My Beautiful Goddess, descended from Mount Olympus, to become my *wife*. Of all men and husbands, I am most blessed. I love you."

Gregor placed a wrapped package on the table before Alexandra. Dabbing away their tears, everyone watched Alexandra untie the bow and open the box. She gasped as she beheld the jewelry inside.

Cynna leaned closer to catch a glimpse. It was a gold locket embossed with a floral overlay studded with rubies and diamonds.

Alexandra held it up for all to see. Dangling from her hand, it glimmered in the party lights.

The guests cheered. Alexandra wept and wrapped her arms around Gregor's neck. He kissed her and wiped her tears. He hung the locket around her neck.

Gregor gestured toward Mílos. "Friends, I give you the artist, the man with the vision, the creator of this masterpiece, the incomparable Mílos Stávros." Alexandra rose, putting her hand over the locket and her heart. She kissed Mílos on the cheek.

Following the gift ceremony and cake, the party erupted into dancing and singing. When everyone danced in frenetic circles, Gregor, Alexandra, Teddy, Mimi, Isidor, and Cynna danced arm-in-arm in a family circle, at a safe pace for Alexandra.

The band played folk songs and the popular tune, "Never On Sunday," and they all danced and swayed and sang at the top of their lungs. Cynna learned to dance to "Zorba the Greek." She thought it was marvelous. Everyone danced with such attitude. She loved how the bouzoúkis started slowly and ended in a frenzied finale, with everyone dancing faster and faster.

When they finished with "Zorba the Greek," Alexandra caught her breath and said to Cynna, "The baby wants more birthday cake!"

"Me, too!"

Threading their way through the crowd, they found the cake cart and steered it to a quiet table and sat down. Cynna found plates and forks.

Alexandra held up a plate, "The baby wants a corner piece with lots of frosting."

Cynna cut a huge corner of the cake for Alexandra and the baby. She cut the other remaining corner for herself. They sat together, feet up in chairs, shoveling in the cake and guarding the cart against predators. They learned early in their friendship that they each had an insatiable love of buttercream frosting. From that point on, they were partners in crime when it came to party cakes.

Mimi found them and cut a piece of cake. She kissed her baby girl on the head, sat down, putting her feet up as well. The slit of her dress fell open, exposing her nicely shaped legs. One by one, Dina, Barba, Roxie, and Kyveli drifted in and cut slices of cake.

Mimi recounted the story of Alexandra's home birth as she did every year on Alexandra's birthday. Barba followed suit and told how she was in excruciating labor for three days with Dina. Alexandra, knowing her time for labor was drawing near, put her hands over her ears and sang to drown out the gory details, "La-la-la-la-la-la-la!"

Dina shoved another piece of cake at her mother and said, "Eat!"

CHAPTER 47

> Who could ever wrap their minds around
> the riches of God, the depth of his wisdom,
> and the marvel of his perfect knowledge?
> Who could ever explain
> the wonder of his decisions
> or search out the mysterious way
> he carries out his plans?
> —The Apostle Paul, Romans 11:33 (TPT)
> AD 55–57

By the third week of August, the Hotel Mákari fell quiet once again. Except for Mílos, the holiday-making friends were gone. Mílos and Dina would return to Athens the next week. Cynna's days in Greece were numbered. Soon she, Isidor, Gregor, and Alexandra would return to Athens, and Cynna to New York.

Unable to sleep, Cynna rose from bed, padded down to the beach, and waited for sunrise. After walking the beach almost every day since arriving on Míos, the beach was a comfortable companion, a treasured friend. She knew the details of the rocky outcroppings, the depth of the tidal pools as well, the sand beneath her toes, and the cadence of the tide.

Sitting in the predawn darkness, she sensed the energy of the sun, waiting to illuminate the new day. But for now, the darkest point before dawn prevailed. The inky blackness deepened and enveloped her. The water murmured softly as it washed upon the wet sand.

Cynna asked, "Father God, how can I return to New York when my heart is here?"

She laid back on the sand, not caring it stuck to her clothes and dampened her hair.

"Isidor believes You brought me to Greece for a unique purpose, a reason deeper and more important than my internship. Was it to spend the summer on Míos? Was it to learn how loving a family can be? Was it to fall more in love with Isidor? Was it to spend this special time with You?

"Whatever Your purpose, I trust You, God."

At the thought of boarding the ferry the next week, tears filled her eyes and ran hot down her cheeks. She let them flow.

"Isidor named me *Cynna*—one who is *strong and courageous*. I echo his prayer for me, Father. Give me an unfailing heart, to look to You as my Source of strength and courage, my ever-present Help. Fill me with Your presence, and bless me with resilience and resolve to carry out Your will for my life.

"Father, I know You are with me. Show me a sign from Your hand, just a little wink or a nod. A little something extra-special to cling to as I go through these next days."

A warm breeze stirred. It dried her tears and tickled her skin. A meteor blazed across the sky in a dazzling display. Its sparkling tail glistening in its wake.

Both laughing and crying, Cynna sprang to her feet, heart bursting with joy. She lifted her hands, dancing before the LORD, and splashed into the water.

As the sun rose, she swam in the pale light of morning, savoring the warmth of the sun on her face. Combing the beach, she found God's voice was not limited to a breeze and a meteor. The beach was strewn with His love letters. He surrounded her with dozens of sea glass nuggets in a rainbow of rare colors.

Running from one piece to the next, she gathered them. Cradling them against her heart, Cynna celebrated God's extravagant gift to her. It was as precious a gift as the jeweled locket Gregor gifted Alexandra.

When Cynna found no more sea glass, she returned to her room, showered, breakfasted, and waited for Isidor. He was taking her, Gregor, Alexandra, Dina, and Mílos for one last outing in Teddy's big boat.

When Isidor arrived at Cynna's room, he came inside, took her in his arms, and kissed her.

"Good morning, you," Cynna whispered in his ear.

"Good morning. I missed you." He drew back and looked at her, "I wish we could spend the day alone together."

"But you have already promised the others one last great adventure."

"Yes—" he rubbed his jaw, "let's not make any other commitments after this. I want to spend our remaining time on Mios together. With our return to Athens next week, I feel more selfish by the minute."

Cynna agreed. To keep her tears at bay, she thought about the early morning meteor and the sea glass from God.

Once everyone was aboard the boat, Isidor navigated into open water, accelerated to a comfortable cruising speed, heading north along the coast.

Dina asked, "Where are you taking us today?"

"It's a surprise, I've saved the best for last. I promise you'll carry this memory with you forever."

They rounded the northern tip of the island and turned southward. Cynna sat in the stern with Alexandra and Dina. Carefree, they turned their faces to the sun, and chatted. The men piloted the craft from the flying bridge.

When Isidor reduced speed, the bow of the boat lowered in the water. At slow idle, he guided the boat inward near a large rock formation. Some thirty yards off shore he cut the engine while Gregor dropped the anchor. The boat rocked with the mild swell of the sea in the protected cove.

Cynna peered over the side of the boat. The turquoise water was clear. Rock formations peppered the sandy bottom. Longing for a swim, she slithered from her cover-up.

Gregor outfitted Alexandra and himself in life vests. Helping Alexandra to the diving platform, he eased her into the water. Rolling her onto her back, Gregor wrapped his arms around her from behind. She laid her head back against his chest, and he pulled her through the water like a tugboat escorting a lovely yacht.

Alexandra called back to the boat, "Everyone get in the water! This is pure heaven."

Isidor climbed down from the bridge and joined Cynna.

Captivated by her surroundings, Cynna said, "Isidor, it's magnificent! The water's so clear. I love this cove."

Isidor smiled at his accomplishment, pulled his T-shirt off and cast it aside. He pointed toward the apex of the small cove. "See how the rock wall extends down into the water there, with no beach? It's shallow there. And, there's natural rock bridges there . . . and there." Cynna nodded. "Those are the entrances to a cave behind that rock. You want to see it?"

"Indeed, I do."

"Are you strong enough to swim to the shore?"

"Absolutely!" Kicking off her sandals, Cynna followed Isidor to the diving platform. They dove in, swimming for the cove. Dina and Mílos followed close behind. Reaching the rock structures, the four of them climbed onto a flat rock, panting.

Dina combed her fingers through Mílos' wet, dark, curly locks. Smiling at her, he kissed her hand. Dina said, "This is my favorite place on Míos. I rarely get to come here since it's only accessible by boat."

Isidor suggested, "Let's come here first thing next summer."

Cynna nudged Dina, "And, you get to come to Míos all during the year, lucky you."

Dina smiled, "It's glorious to hop the ferry and spend so many weekends at home. Plus, I make special trips for events at the winery, I come help mama and papa."

Cynna prompted, "And you, Mílos? Do you come with her?"

"'I'll come for the weekends with Dina when I can. If I'm creating a special order I can't always get away."

Cynna said, "The locket you made for Alexandra is gorgeous."

Mílos smiled humbly and looked in the direction of Gregor and Alexandra floating around by the boat.

Dina said, "That's my Mílos. Phenomenal artist."

Mílos asked Isidor, "Did you see the newspaper today?"

"No, I take the summers off from the news. Why?"

"The King called for a special election."

Isidor's head snapped around and he eyed Mílos, "*What? Seriously?*"

"Yeah, surprising, huh?"

"When?"

"In a couple of months. I guess he hopes to finally replace the interim government."

Isidor frowned. "Hmm. Well, maybe that will settle things down a bit."

Cynna said, "What do you mean? Is the government unsettled?"

Dina shrugged. "When is the government *not* unsettled?"

Mílos shrugged, "True."

Isidor looked at everyone, "Ready to swim through the cave?"

They all slid off the sunny rock and into the water like a bale of turtles. Mílos and Dina took the lead. Isidor swam alongside Cynna to the rocky outcroppings. They floated through the archway into the cave.

The ceiling of the cave vaulted twenty feet above their heads. Shafts of sunlight streamed in through the arches. Playing off the water, it reflected onto the walls, and illuminated the depths of the crystal clear pool inside. Dina and Mílos swam through the cave and out the other side.

Isidor motioned Cynna toward a ledge along the back wall. He held on and hovered shoulder deep in the water. Cynna swam toward him. Grabbing onto the ledge she faced him. His gaze traveled over the features of her face. Serene in the moment, he smiled at her.

"What?"

"I enjoy looking at you."

She held his gaze. Her eyes smiled back at him.

"Cynna, you are the most beautiful, capable, fearless, surprising, amazing woman I have ever known. One moment, you're dazzling me at the museum gala—the next, you're in the trenches beside me, covered in soil—the next, you're speaking of your faith in God, your passion for amphoriskos, or you're captivated by a Greek play, or dancing to "Zorba the Greek." The next moment you're risking your life in a minivan, Kyveli at the wheel, or you're jumping into the sea, swimming into caves . . ." His voice drifted off, the expression in his eyes, loving and tender. "But in every single moment, you're wrapping my heart around your little finger—like just now when you look at me like that with those beautiful, blue eyes."

Isidor traced the curve of her jaw with his finger. Cynna wished the moment to last forever.

Searching her eyes, Isidor asked, "Cynna, will you marry me?"

Cynna held his gaze. "Yes, Isidor."

"Will you be content to live the humble life of a professor's wife in Greece?"

"Yes, Isidor, *yes!*"

He pulled her close, and they kissed with the passion of two hearts committed to loving each other forever and beyond.

CHAPTER 48

～⌘～

Sing to Yahweh a brand-new song!
Sing his praise until it echoes
from the ends of the earth!
... Islands and all their inhabitants,
sing his praise!
—Isaiah 42:10 (TPT, *Isaiah: The Vision*)
740–700 BC

On the last Sunday before returning to Athens, Isidor and Cynna, Gregor and Alexandra, and Mílos and Dina gathered with everyone at the Hotel Mákari terrace for church, an engagement party, baptism celebration, and baby shower. Silas, from the hotel office, and his sons roasted a lamb on the spit, and Gregor provided a band.

First thing Monday, Dina and Mílos were departing for Athens, followed by Isidor, Cynna, Gregor, and Alexandra on Thursday. With Isidor's marriage proposal, and Cynna's decision to stay in Greece, Cynna's happiness was boundless. Her sense of belonging told her she had found her home.

ELIZABETH TOMME

For one of the last times that summer, Cynna stood on the terrace overlooking the sea and the beach. With the promise of a new life with Isidor, Cynna's courage was buoyant. The storm of disapproval sure to come from her parents was no match for her invigorated strength of spirit.

Cynna did not need her parent's approval to marry Isidor, nor did she crave it. In their time together, Isidor, his family, and the God-gathered family on Míos lavished her with a transforming, redeeming love. It was a love independent of her own merit, a love not dispensed according to her accomplishments. It was a love so steadfast and merciful that her earthly father's so-called love was exposed for what it was: A lifelong administration of severe judgment. An illusory prison in solitary confinement, for which she was meant to beg for every shred of meager affection.

Over the summer in Míos, God filled her amphoriskos with something far greater than itself. God filled her to overflowing with His Fatherly love. He lavished it upon her. He taught her what it meant to be welcomed into a Father's loving arms.

Through the Christopoulos family, God put a face on His love for her. Through the sunshine, surf, and glistening pieces of sea glass on the beach, God demonstrated His redeeming love for her. Like the sea glass, from something broken and discarded—her heart—something beautiful was forged—certainty of her Heavenly Father's unconditional love. By God's grace, during her time on Míos she was filled with something greater than herself, she was transfigured and reborn.

Joining Cynna at the overlook, Isidor wrapped his arms around her from behind, resting his chin on her head.

"Happy?"

"Mmmm-hmmm. My heart is shimmering within." She turned her head toward him. Their lips met in a sweet kiss. She said, "Is it terribly hard for you to leave Míos and your family at the end of summer?"

"Farewells sadden me, and I'll miss seeing Mimi, Teddy, and our friends here. But this time, it's easy knowing what is ahead. For the first time, the end of summer means new beginnings. Our future together, and a wedding to plan. Our niece will arrive soon.

"And, I'm looking forward to archaeological expeditions with my new field partner—I met a gorgeous woman at the Macedonian

Museum gala. She begged to shuttle buckets and buckets of soil for me."

Cynna's eyes narrowed. "Dr. Christopoulos, if you're trying to make me jealous, it won't work. I am engaged to marry a handsome and prestigious world-renowned archaeologist—" Isidor kissed her.

His eyes rested on her. "No . . . I don't mind leaving Míos. My heart is at home anywhere in the world as long as I am with you."

Content, Cynna said, "Wherever in the world we find ourselves, I promise to take care of your heart."

"And I yours, My Love."

Once everyone was assembled together for church, they made their way to the beach and gathered at the water's edge. Luca and Tessa Adino told everyone of their new faith in Jesus. They waded into the water with Isidor and Gregor, who baptized them. Their God-gathered family cheered and splashed into the water, hugging and kissing them.

Together on the beach, the circle of believers communed with bread and wine, celebrating Jesus' birth, death, burial, and resurrection.

Back on the terrace, they feasted on lamb with all the trimmings. After the meal, the women gathered around Alexandra and blessed her with a baby shower, and party cake piled high with frosting.

Mimi's gift for her first grandbaby was a sweater, booties, and cap she knitted in delicate yellow yarn. From Great Aunt Roxie, receiving blankets; Kyveli, a stuffed lamb with a satin ribbon about its neck; Barba, a cloth baby book; Dina, a cozy onesie; Cynna, Baby's First Bible; and Tessa, an olive wood rattle carved by Luca.

After the baby shower, Isidor led Cynna to the middle of the terrace, and knelt before her, taking her hand.

"Cynna, please accept this ring as a symbol of my love and our engagement. I promise to always honor you and cherish your life and the happiness of your heart above my own."

Isidor slid a diamond solitaire on Cynna's finger, rose, took her in his arms, and kissed her. Everyone cheered. The circle of family widened around them as the band played "Darling, Dance With Me." Isidor and Cynna danced.

Gazing into his eyes, Cynna whispered, "I love you, Isidor, I love you completely, and I love you forever. I can't wait to be your wife. Let's not waste time on a long engagement. Let's get married as soon as possible. Athens or Míos?"

"At home on Míos, surrounded by our family."

Isidor held her close and sang in her ear, "Darling, dance with me . . .let me be . . . the keeper of your heart . . . forever and ever and ever . . . give your dreams to me . . . and you will see . . . they'll all come true . . . forever and ever and ever." Swaying with the music, Isidor kissed her lips. "Darling, dance with me . . . make romance with me . . . forever and ever and ever."

Cynna kissed Isidor again and again, "Oh, Isidor, I *have* given my dreams to you. I know that with you, they will all come true."

Cynna's hand rested on Isidor's shoulder as they danced. Admiring the sparkling diamond on her finger, she smiled at Isidor, "Thank you for choosing me. The ring is beautiful."

After the party, Cynna and Isidor burned another precious nugget of Frankincense to celebrate their official engagement. Together they prayed, asking God to consecrate their marriage and fill them with selfless, steadfast love.

Her head was so filled with wedding daydreams, it took Cynna the remaining days to pack for their departure. She spent every other moment admiring her engagement ring, dreaming of wedding dresses and wedding cakes, and practiced writing, "Mrs. Isidor Christopoulos" across the pages of her journal.

With care, Cynna packed her precious collection of sand and sea glass, and secured it in her luggage with the wooden box of incense from Crete. As well, she packed some of the Hotel Mákari stationery as a keepsake of her stay in Gregor and Alexandra's hotel that summer.

Cynna wished the magical summer on Míos could last forever, but she no longer dreaded leaving since she and Isidor were together. As well, she looked forward to the days ahead with Alexandra, Gregor, and the new baby in Athens. And of course, she and Isidor would return often to visit Teddy, Mimi, and their God-gathered family on Míos.

And now, there was a wedding to plan. They would set a date for

December, during Isidor's Christmas break. Pushing all possible negativity aside, she and Isidor agreed to call her parents upon their return to Athens. They would break the news of their engagement and Cynna's decision to stay in Greece.

Cynna hoped her parents would come for the wedding, and prayed they would accept Isidor, but knew it was unrealistic to expect either. It did not meet their criteria: a high-society marriage in New York City.

Over breakfast with Alexandra and Gregor on Wednesday, she and Isidor firmed up their departure plan for the next day. They strategized getting both cars and luggage onboard the ferry, as well as living arrangements for Cynna in Athens. Gregor and Alexandra invited Cynna to live in their home, at least until she transferred back to university housing, if accepted for her senior year.

If unable to enroll for the fall semester, Cynna would contact Freideriki and explore job options at the Alexander Museum. Another possible scenario, Cynna would find work and rent an apartment until she and Isidor married.

Over coffee, Alexandra slid an envelope across the table to Cynna. "This is an early birthday present for you."

Cynna opened the envelope and withdrew an official form. It was printed in Greek. Excited, she said, "Quick, tell me what this means."

With a tone of importance and an air of ceremony, Alexandra said, "This government form declares the private beach located on the property of the Hotel Mákari is named, and will henceforth be recognized by the government and peoples of Greece, as "Petrádi Plaz. All entities shall officially recognize this name, and it shall henceforth be represented as such on all cartography."

Pleased, Alexandra and Gregor exchanged meaningful looks.

Cynna's mouth fell open in surprise.

Alexandra explained, "Since acquiring the property, we've been at a loss as to what to name our beach. It was not until you joined us here, this most special summer of our time here, that it became clear. We saw how this beach captivated your heart, how your love for it grew every day as you walked the sand, swam in the water, and collected its sand and sea glass.

"Your passion filled it with special meaning for all of us. We fell in love with it all over again, through your eyes. Your love for it reminded us of the true treasure we have here in this magical place.

"The Greek word *Plaz*, of course, means beach. The Greek word *Petrádi* means, pebble jewel. We named our beach after your beloved and rare sea glass—a treasured pebble jewel from the sea."

CHAPTER 49

⁂

> Don't answer the foolish arguments of fools,
> or you will become as foolish as they are.
> —Proverbs 26:4 (NLT)
> 950 BC

On the last Thursday in August 1967, the ferry docked at the Port of Piraeus, Athens, Greece. Cynna's glorious summer on Míos, now a memory that shimmered in her mind as brilliantly as the afternoon mirage on the Aegean.

Once disembarked, the two couples drove to the Andras' residence in the prestigious Arts District. It was near the Petrakis Theatre, the Plaka, Syntagma Square, the Acropolis, and a stone's throw away from the Taverna of Ankistrévo̱.

Gregor helped Alexandra from the car and into bed. She was exhausted from the heat, seasick and nauseous, and her back ached. Isidor and Cynna distributed the luggage and moved Cynna into her guest quarters at the front of the house, with a view of the street and the Acropolis beyond.

The Andras' townhouse was one of six three-story units lining the block, each with a unique street-front design, and double front doors flanked by potted trees. The interior was spacious with polished herringbone wood floors and high ceilings trimmed with intricate molding.

Alexandra's decorator achieved the perfect balance of spare space, pristine white walls, sleek furniture, interesting artwork, superb lighting, and rich draperies. The bedrooms were plushly carpeted sanctuaries, with designer, room-darkening window treatments, luxury bed linens, comfortable sitting areas, and a modern, gleaming en suite. The master suite occupied the second floor, and Gregor's glass-walled office the third floor, overlooking city landmarks.

Cynna followed her nose to the kitchen. The housekeeper left dinner warming in the oven, salads and dessert in the refrigerator. The pantry and wine racks were full. Cynna set the table and prepared a tray for Alexandra.

Unloading complete, Isidor and Gregor joined Cynna in the kitchen. Gregor opened a bottle of wine and poured three glasses.

Isidor said, "To a magnificent summer, our safe return, Gregor's new play, Alexandra and the baby, Cynna's relocation to Greece, and the beginning of a new semester! Evíva!"

"Evíva!"

After dinner, Isidor and Cynna cuddled on the sofa in the living room strategizing their plan for the coming days.

Cynna said, "I promised Alexandra help with finishing the nursery and running errands for her. There's not much left to do."

Isidor said, "I'll contact the university Registrar first thing tomorrow. I'll call in all my favors."

"I'll call for my transcripts first thing. What else?"

Isidor examined the engagement ring on her hand. "We need to apply for our marriage license and apply for your citizenship."

Isidor handed Cynna a thick envelope with a travel agency insignia. "This was in the pile of mail on the hall table."

Cynna opened it with reluctance. "Airline tickets to New York, courtesy of my parents' travel agent." She reviewed the itinerary. "Well, they didn't waste any time. They scheduled my departure for early Saturday morning."

Isidor said, "Let's call your parents right now and get it over with."

Cynna shook her head. "No, timing is everything. Tomorrow around eight p.m. New York time is better, after my father gets home and starts the weekend. He forbids personal calls at work. And, he won't answer the phone during the dinner hour. Intrusions on his routine put him in a foul humor."

"What doesn't?"

"True."

"You don't expect them to take the news well, regardless of when we interrupt them. Why not get it over with?"

"Let's not poke the bear unnecessarily."

"Cynna, is there anything your parents could say that would make you change your mind and go back to New York?"

"Not one thing."

Isidor kissed the top of Cynna's head.

"Not even a threat of disinheritance or bribery of a position at the Chadwick Museum?"

"My father does not negotiate or make bribes, only threats followed by action. Disinheritance is a given. So, if you're marrying me for money, you need a Plan B."

Isidor groaned. "I don't care about money. But, will *you* regret it one day?"

"No."

"So, if your father won't give you a position at the Chadwick, and they don't want you to follow your dreams, what *do* they want for you?"

"They want me to be the obedient daughter, do nothing to disgrace the Chadwick name, climb the New York social ranks, and marry someone wealthy of *their* choosing."

Aghast, Isidor asked, "An arranged marriage?"

"Not in the usual sense; it's strongly stated and firmly expected. I left for Athens amid a hard sell for marriage to the son of a major patron of the museum."

"Did you date him? Were you in love with him?"

Cynna looked at him sideways. "You can't be serious."

"You're right, I'm not," Isidor laughed. "I was just curious what you'd say."

Cynna fake-punched him in the stomach. "Anyway, if not marriage to him, then they require someone equally beneficial to the museum. The names of the monied players appear to be interchangeable."

"So, how will they view me?"

"My Darling, in their eyes you have two problems. You're not a millionaire, *and* you weren't their idea."

Scowling, Isidor sat forward, unbuttoned the top of his shirt, and vented the space around his collar. "What about what *you* want?"

"That's irrelevant, Sweetheart."

Isidor growled, "Not to me."

"Just prepare yourself for his temper fit and threats . . . and from my mother, tears and pleading."

Isidor sat forward and faced Cynna. "When it comes to abusive behavior, I don't negotiate either. We'll make the call together. I will not allow them to disrespect you. We will remain on the call as long as they are respectful of you. If not, I'll tell them we will only resume the conversation if and when they can be. Are you prepared for me to respond to them in this way?"

Cynna's heart melted with love and gratitude. "Oh, Isidor . . . you are my knight in shining armor." Cynna wrapped her arms around Isidor's neck. He was literally hot under the collar.

She held his gaze. "Thank you for defending my honor. I love you, Isidor Christopoulos."

"I love you too, the future Mrs. Christopoulos." Isidor held up her hand and admired the engagement ring. "Cynna, strong and courageous. Thank you for choosing me."

"My Darling, I will always choose you. Whatever you ask of me, I will happily do."

Isidor pulled Cynna to her feet. "Time for me to go. Get some rest. Big day ahead of us tomorrow."

Cynna watched Isidor drive away, dreaming of the day she did not have to watch his tail lights disappear into the distance. She drifted to sleep with the sensation of Isidor's kiss on her lips, the feel of his touch on her skin, and the sound of his loving voice in her ear.

CHAPTER 50

⁑

> Put on God's complete set of armor
> provided for us, so that you will be protected
> as you fight against the evil strategies
> of the accuser!
> Your hand-to-hand combat
> is not with human beings, but with the
> highest principalities and authorities
> operating in rebellion under the heavenly
> realms, for they are a powerful class
> of demon-gods and evil spirits
> that hold this dark world in bondage.
> —The Apostle Paul, Ephesians 6:11–12 (TPT)
> AD 60–62

At six o'clock the next morning, Cynna was awakened from deep sleep by the sound of loud rumbling outside her window. The glass carafe on her night table rattled with the deep vibration. The glass window panes and every surface of the house shuddered.

A porcelain dish fell from the shelf in the bathroom and shattered on the floor. Confused, Cynna bolted upright in the bed, pushed the covers aside, and turned on the bedside lamp. She heard Gregor and Alexandra's door open and their voices and footsteps, moving about the upstairs hallway.

Cynna's sleepy brain sifted through the possibility of an earthquake—or perhaps an explosion. In terror, she rammed her feet into her slippers and pulled on her robe with shaking hands. As the tremors lessened, Cynna realized the rumbling sounded mechanical. Running to the window, she pushed the heavy curtains aside.

Disbelieving, she watched military tanks roll past her window and down the street. Alexandra burst into the room and rushed to look out the window. They clutched each other, staring out the window, frozen in confusion. Columns of armed soldiers marched in the streets amid the tanks. They heard bursts of gunfire in the distance.

Gregor entered the room, pulled them from the window, and closed the curtains. Another tank rolled by, and the house shuddered again. A speaker mounted on the tank blared a public broadcast.

Cynna said, "What are they saying?"

Alexandra began crying and shaking. Gregor wrapped his arms around her, and said, "They're instructing citizens to remain inside and tune into the radio for instructions."

Gregor reached an arm around Cynna, too. "Come with me," he gently said, shepherding them to the living room sofa. He closed the curtains and switched on the radio. He rolled the dial through the bands of squibs and static until he zeroed in on a station. As they listened, a chill ran down Cynna's spine at the sound of the sinister, disembodied voice.

Gregor translated the broadcast, *"Revolution! Revolution! Revolution! Coup d'état! Greek Armed Forces now control the country. The government was overthrown at midnight. Politicians and Generals were arrested. Constitutional Articles protecting civilian liberties, freedom of speech, and freedom of movement were revoked. Citizens remain in your homes until further notice. Armed Forces are arresting all politicians and citizens considered in opposition of the new regime. If you resist you will be shot."*

Cynna jumped up, "I must find Isidor." She crossed the room, grabbed the telephone receiver. "There's no dial tone. The phone is dead." She slammed it down. "I'll go to his apartment."

Gregor took her by the shoulders. "Cynna, no. Listen to me. We must remain inside, and stay together. We have to be careful—consider every option." Closing her eyes, she nodded. Summoning her courage, she forbade her tears to fall.

Gregor said, "If I know Isidor, he's already figured a way to come to you. The best thing you can do is pray for his safety."

Cynna sank onto the sofa. Gregor was right. "Yes . . . of course." She clenched her hands together and prayed.

Alexandra stood, grabbed her abdomen, doubled over, and cried out. A puddle drained onto the rug at her feet. Panic-stricken, she looked at Gregor and Cynna.

"Oh . . . no . . . no!" she cried. "The baby is coming."

Gregor eased her onto the sofa. Unsure what to do, Cynna arranged pillows around her. Alexandra seized with a contraction.

Helpless, Cynna looked at Gregor. They exchanged a look of equal concern as Cynna murmured assurances to Alexandra. "Here, hold my hand. Squeeze it as hard as you can. Let's concentrate on your breathing."

Gregor went to the window, parted the curtain, and checked the street. The house shook with vibration once again as another tank rumbled past.

He instructed, "Cynna, start timing the contractions."

Alexandra moaned with a strong contraction. "Gregor—get me to the hospital. The baby is coming."

Closing the curtain, Gregor stepped away from the window. He moved throughout the house before returning to Alexandra's side.

Cynna looked up from her watch reporting, "Her contractions are coming about eight minutes apart and lasting about thirty seconds."

Alexandra was seized by another strong contraction. She grabbed his arm. "Gregor—*I've got to go to the hospital.*"

Gregor caught Cynna's eye, and tilted his head toward the street with a grave expression. Cynna nodded her understanding.

Gregor kissed Alexandra on the forehead, met her eyes, and smiled. He whispered something Greek in her ear. Alexandra smiled back at him and concentrated on her breathing.

Gregor brushed the hair back from her forehead and took her hand. He gained eye contact. "My Darling, you must be brave for us, and for the baby. I can't get you to the hospital. If the baby must be born at home, can you do it?"

Eyes filled with panic, Alexandra looked at Cynna and back to Gregor. She quickened with resolve. "Yes, My Love," pant, pant, "God is with us. I can do it—for our baby—for all of us."

"That's my girl. I'll prepare a birthing room, and then I promise, I will not leave your side. Stay with her, Cynna."

Cynna watched Gregor disappear down the hallway, listening as he moved about through the house. When he returned, he was dressed. He withdrew a gun from a desk drawer and slid the holster into his waistband.

Cynna heard sounds in the back of the house. Her heart jumped to her throat, hammering in her ears. Gregor gave her a cautionary look. Putting a finger to his lips, he motioned for them to keep quiet. Cynna nodded and whispered to Alexandra. Clinging to each other, they whispered prayers. Drawing the gun, Gregor held it behind his back, and crept toward the kitchen.

Another strong contraction came. Clenching her teeth, Alexandra pulled a pillow over her face, muffling the sound of her labor. Cynna whispered in her ear, "Breathe, breathe." In the background, she heard male voices in the kitchen. Remaining at Alexandra's side, she prayed it was Isidor.

After some time, Gregor returned to the living room alone. Tapping her on the shoulder, he took her place and motioned for Cynna to go to the other room. Waiting for her, Isidor gathered her in his arms, holding her tight.

"You're safe. Oh, thank you, Father. Thank you, thank you."

Isidor kissed her, cradling her head in his hands. They kept their voices low.

Cynna said, "Alexandra's in labor. She wasn't due for two weeks."

"Gregor told me. I think the shock of the military in the streets sent her into early labor, though her back was aching yesterday, and she was unwell after the trip."

"How bad is it out there? Can we get her to a hospital?"

"It's bad. The city's crawling with military. Major roads are blocked with tanks. They've locked down the city. They're policing the streets, forcing everyone inside."

"How did you get to us?"

"On foot, and with the help of friends—over some rooftops, through underground passages, crawling house-to-house, and through back alleys."

"What would've happened if you'd been caught?"

"I made it, and we're together."

Cynna searched his eyes. Isidor had a good poker face. "The broadcast said, 'Revolution.' Are we in civil war?"

"So far, it's one-sided. The people were blindsided by this military takeover—never saw it coming. They don't have the means to fight back."

"But why is any of this happening? I don't understand."

"Political unrest's been brewing for years. After the Apostasia in '65, the King installed an interim government—trying to stabilize the far left and far right factions." Isidor shook his head. "Remember Mílos told us the King set a special election for next month? The left was favored to win. Last night, right wing military colonels overthrew the interim government to prevent that." Isidor ran a hand through his hair. "We never saw it coming."

"Oh, Isidor, did they execute them? Are they killing people?"

He met her eyes, his expression serious. "We promised to tell each other the truth, no matter how hard."

"Yes." Cynna closed her eyes and steeled her anxious thoughts. By Isidor's side, she had the courage to face anything. She looked him in the eye. "God is with us. Tell me. We will meet this together."

They sat at the kitchen table. Isidor rubbed his stubbly chin. "The Prime Minister, President, and top Generals were executed at midnight."

Cynna shivered. "God help us. Are we safe? Surely the military would let us take Alexandra to the hospital to give birth."

Isidor drew a deep breath. "We—"

Gregor burst into the kitchen. "We need to get Alexandra to the bedroom. The contractions are closer together, longer and stronger."

Gregor turned to Isidor, "One of us needs to go down the alley and get the neighbor. If she is willing to come, she can help deliver the baby."

"I'll go." Isidor was already at the back door. "Which house?"

"Marina, two doors down to the east. Make sure she understands the consequences if—"

Cynna looked from Gregor to Isidor. "The consequences?"

Isidor said, "The Lord will provide." He was out the door.

Cynna and Gregor helped Alexandra into the guest room next to Cynna's. Cynna collected towels and sheets from every linen closet in the house and organized them in stacks near the bed. She wheeled the bassinet in from the nursery. She set water to boil in the kitchen because they always did that in the movies, but she suspected it only served to keep people busy when they did not know what else to do.

Isidor and Marina crept through the back door. Cynna led them to the birthing room.

Cynna asked Isidor, "Is Marina a nurse or a midwife?"

"She said she has the best qualifications; she is a grandmother ten times over."

Marina checked Alexandra and pronounced the baby was coming soon. She stationed Cynna and Isidor at the head of the bed on each side of Alexandra. She enlisted Gregor's help with the delivery at the foot of the bed. At 2:32 that afternoon, Gregor witnessed the birth of his baby girl. His *Mákari* had come true.

Marina and Cynna cleaned and swaddled the baby. Cynna placed the baby in her father's arms. The first kiss she received was from her father's lips. Gregor placed their daughter in Alexandra's arms.

Alexandra smiled at Gregor and kissed him. "You got your *Mákari*, your beautiful wish, My Darling."

"*My Mákari*. I always say, 'Names are important.'"

Alexandra pulled the swaddling cloth back and peered at their baby's face. "What shall we name our precious daughter?"

CHAPTER 51

*. . . Before we were even born,
he gave us our destiny;
that we would fulfill the plan of God
who always accomplishes
every purpose and plan in his heart.*
—The Apostle Paul, Ephesians 1:11 (TPT)
AD 60–62

Isidor kissed Alexandra. "Thank you for making me an uncle today. I am so proud." He cupped his hand around the baby's head. "She's beautiful."

Alexandra exchanged a look with Gregor. He said, "We'd like the two of you to be her Godparents. Will you accept?"

Isidor reached for Cynna's hand and nodded. Isidor said, "Yes, we are honored. We accept."

Cynna kissed Alexandra and the baby. "We'll step out and give you time alone."

Cynna and Isidor retreated to the living room. The tank rumbling down the street failed to draw their attention from the miracle in the next room.

Isidor embraced Cynna. "I look forward to having babies of our own."

Cynna caressed his cheek. "Me, too. Just think of the fun we'll have watching the cousins play together on the beach on Mílos. And Mimi and Teddy spoiling them all—"

Cynna flinched at the sound of distant gunfire. She looked at Isidor. He looked toward the window, his expression grim.

"Why the gunfire? Is that the military?"

Isidor went to the window, pushed the curtains aside, and stole a glance at the street. They both jumped at the shrill ring of the telephone.

Cynna said, "The phones are working again!"

Isidor answered the extension at the table by the window. Cynna could not make out his hushed tones. Rubbing his brow, he bowed his head. With a look of utter devastation, he replaced the receiver. Cynna stood frozen, waiting. He turned toward Cynna, tears running down his face.

Cynna went to him. "What is it?"

"That was Dina. The military came for Mílos this morning."

"*Came* for Mílos?"

"He resisted. They shot him in the street and destroyed his studio."

"No, no!" Cynna could not comprehend the horrific thought. "Why? Why did they come for him? Why would they shoot him?"

Taking Cynna by the hand, Isidor led her to her room. They sat on the bench at the foot of her bed. Cynna sobbed into his chest. "Mílos is dead? Why would anyone kill sweet, gentle Mílos?"

"Because his name was on the list—"

"What list?"

"It is called the Black List. This morning, in one district, I saw soldiers going into houses, making arrests. I talked to one man who fled his home. He was terrified, running for his life. He said the military has a 'Black List' with thousands of names on it. He saw it. They hit the streets early this morning, rounding up the people on the list, taking them away. They do not hesitate to execute anyone who resists —or speaks against the new regime."

In horror, Cynna asked, "Is that the gunfire we've been hearing?"

Isidor took Cynna's hands. "Yes. This morning I saw an execution in the street. An old man stepped outside his home and wandered into the street. They said he violated the government order to stay inside. They shot him." Isidor closed his eyes.

Cynna said, "The *consequences* . . . Gregor was worried about Marina getting caught outside?"

"That is why I did not allow Gregor to go for Marina. I would not risk him not being here for Alexandra and the baby."

Cynna touched the face of this man, her man, who selflessly offered his life in place of another.

Cynna considered the encroaching evil. "Earlier you said the military coup was to prevent the country from falling into leftist hands. Mílos was not a leftist."

"No, and neither are we."

Cynna's eyes grew big. "Are *we* on the Black List?"

"I don't know. I'm afraid many of our friends are, and Gregor and Alexandra, which also puts the baby in danger."

"What about us, are we in danger?"

"Perhaps I am."

A cold fear washed over Cynna. The color drained from her face. She tightened her grip on Isidor's arm. In a heartbeat she realized it was one thing to say you had courage. To face imprisonment or death was a true test of it.

Isidor kissed her shaking hands. "I heard the Black List has at least 16,000 names on it, so it would include more than just the government and political figures. Word on the street is also writers, actors, artists, musicians, composers, journalists . . . academicians—"

"But why?" Cynna shook her head refusing the thought. "Why innocent musicians and . . . *professors?*"

"Because they can influence the people against the regime with their words, their public voice, lyrics, and teachings."

"You're an archaeologist. You don't teach politics. It doesn't make sense."

"My Love, we're caught in the middle of a coup d'état. They've taken over power and will suppress all possible threats . . . anyone who has a voice."

"But how can they just arrest or kill anyone they want to? What about due process? Don't they have to show evidence or prove guilt?"

Isidor scoffed, "Remember the broadcast? They said they revoked the Constitutional Articles. We no longer have civil liberties, freedom of speech, or freedom of movement. We have no rights. No legal protection."

Gunfire erupted again. Cynna flinched. Isidor stood, opened her closet, and rifled through it. He pulled a small suitcase out and threw it on the bed.

"What are you doing?"

He dumped out the contents. "Dina's looking for a way out of Athens, out of the country. I must get you to safety. She agreed to take you with her. Quick—pack a small bag, uh, something easy to carry. Essentials only. In fact, a purse or tote is best . . . less suspicious." He returned to the closet. "Do you have one of those?"

"No, Isidor, no—wait, stop. Don't send me away."

"It's not what I want—but what we must do."

"I won't leave you, and *we* cannot leave Alexandra, Gregor, and the baby."

"I'll try to get all of us out together, but if I can't, I'll find a way to get you out. I will not risk your life."

"Isidor, my life is my own to risk."

Knocking on the door, Gregor entered the room. "Alexandra and the baby are resting." He exchanged a serious look with Isidor. Gregor said, "Cynna, would you sit with Alexandra and the baby?"

"Of course. Take as long as you need."

Isidor kissed Cynna and followed Gregor up the stairs to his study.

Sitting between the crib and the bed, Cynna looked from mother to daughter, each sleeping peacefully in the darkened room. That Teddy and Mimi did not even know their granddaughter entered the world saddened her. The shock of Mílos' death and Dina on the run—as well as their own imminent danger—cast a ruthless pall and numbed her mind.

Her shoulders sagged at the weight of the dark-hearted evil lurking outside the house. Without reason, it gunned down the innocent, gentle Mílos in the street, shattering their unsuspecting naiveté. Their world had turned to chaos in the blink of an eye.

Their lives now, in jeopardy. And for what reason? What had they done?

Will the military come to our door? How will I react if I'm hauled into the street, arrested, or worse? God, help me to live up to my new name—Cynna strong and courageous. Jesus, Jesus, Jesus . . . help.

The baby cried, and Alexandra stirred, trying to sit up. Cynna calmed Alexandra and placed the baby in her arms to nurse. Pushing her morbid thoughts aside, she smiled at Alexandra, sitting next to her on the bed, cooing at the baby.

"Beautiful baby, just like her mother. And, to think I'm an aunt—well, almost. Isidor and I will be married soon."

Alexandra said, "Absolutely you are already an aunt, we're sisters. I can't believe she's already here and that I gave birth at home."

"You are a brave one." Cynna asked, "Was it terribly painful?"

Alexandra shook her head, "I'd do anything for her." She searched Cynna's face. "What's happening out there? Gregor won't tell me what's going on. He's protecting me. It's worse than knowing."

Cynna fought the urge to say she was wrong on that count.

"I keep hearing gunfire, and tanks. Did Isidor have any trouble getting here? Please tell me what you know."

Cynna busied herself straightening the bed linens. "Isidor arrived safely."

"Are the phones in service again? Who called?"

Cynna bit her lip to keep from sobbing at the thought of Dina and Mílos. "Isidor answered it—"

Alexandra grasped Cynna's hand. "Cynna, I have a bad feeling about this. I am worried for all of us."

The bedroom door opened. Gregor and Isidor entered, their expressions grave. Gregor turned on the bedside lamp dispelling the evening shadows.

Alexandra reached for Gregor pulling him closer. "My Darling, what's wrong? What's happening?"

Gregor wrapped his arms around her and the baby. "Darling, you are still weak, and my words will frighten you, but you must know, we are in danger."

Cynna felt Isidor close beside her. She turned to look at him. He nodded, wrapping his arm around her waist.

Gregor said, "The city is crawling with military. The military have some sort of list. They're hunting down certain citizens and arresting them. It's already too late, but we must try and hide or flee the country."

Alexandra asked, "Leave the country? Why?" Alexandra's look of confusion turned into that of clarity. "You think *we* are on the list?"

Gregor met her eyes. "Yes."

Tears filled Alexandra's eyes and spilled down her cheeks. Bravely, she quickened herself. "You're a writer, and I'm an actress."

"They're arresting people with public influence. Artists, composers, musicians, *professors . . . writers . . . actors.*"

Alexandra pushed the covers away. "Oh, Isidor, too? I'm strong enough. Let's go now. Where can we go?" Gregor eased her back against her pillows.

"We must be quick, but we must have a plan. The city is locked down. It won't be easy to get out."

Alexandra said, "Actors and writers—are you sure?"

"Darling, Dina called to warn us that they came to arrest Mílos."

"He's in prison?"

Gregor shook his head. "It's cruel to tell you this, but I need you to understand. Mílos resisted and they killed him. Dina's also trying to find a way out."

Alexandra stared in shock. "We can all go to Míos."

"Darling, listen. From my office window, Isidor saw the soldiers a few blocks away, moving from house to house. They are coming this way. We saw them arrest the Drakoses."

Alexandra shook her head. "No . . . no . . . this isn't happening."

Isidor whispered in Cynna's ear, "The Drakoses are husband and wife. They both played supporting roles in *Farewell to Nikolo*."

The air evaporated from the room. Cynna could not draw a breath.

Gregor looked at Cynna, "The Greek Armed Forces issued a new broadcast. All foreign visas will be revoked in two days. Every foreign visitor must leave the country in the next forty-eight hours—or face imprisonment."

Cynna tightened her grip on Isidor's hand. She shook her head and quoted Gregor's words from that morning back to him. "We must stay together and act with care."

Gregor and Isidor exchanged another solemn look. Cynna realized they already had a plan to save them all, and it did not include staying together. Cynna felt a piece of her heart die as surely as if the military had put a bullet in her.

Gregor kissed Alexandra and whispered in her ear. Alexandra tightened her arms around the baby and drew back searching Gregor's eyes at length. The light in Alexandra's eyes faded to resignation.

Tears falling, she finally nodded her ascent. Pressing her lips to the baby's head, she gave her sweet kisses, whispering a Greek lullaby.

Eyes glistening, Alexandra looked to Cynna and pled, "My sister, you've been ordered to leave the country. You have an airline ticket . . . Gregor and I are asking you—begging you, *please* . . . take our baby with you. Get her out of the country. Get her to safety."

Cynna shook her head. "Oh, no—no, I can't take your baby—she needs *you*, not me. *You* take my ticket." The room was spinning, and she felt sick with panic. A thousand thoughts raced through her mind. Even if she made it past the authorities with the baby and got out of the country, how could she possibly take this new baby away from her parents who loved her so?

"I don't know how to take care of a newborn baby. I can't risk harming her. I could never forgive myself. You can feed her—I can't."

Alexandra said, "We have formula. We'll send everything you need."

Gregor said, "It's just until we can come join you."

Isidor said, "We'll find a way to get out. We'll join you as soon as possible. If we're arrested, we don't know what they might do with her. We can't leave her to chance."

Cynna's mind raced. If she somehow made it through, the next hurdle would be her parents. She had been away from New York for about nine months. She knew how it would look if she stepped off the plane with a baby. Her parents would disown her. She had no means to provide for the baby until Isidor, Alexandra, and Gregor arrived—*if* they ever arrived?

Cynna said, "What if the authorities take her away from me when I try to take her out of the country? What will happen to her then? If we all stay together, there would be four of us working together to fight for her safety, and she would still be with you. She needs her parents. You need to be with her."

The look of pain in Gregor and Alexandra's eyes at the thought of separation from their baby was more than Cynna could bear. She was desperate to help the family stay together.

"Teddy and Mimi! We could board the ferry and get back to Míos. Or, I could take her to them. She should be with her family."

Hopeful, Alexandra looked at Gregor. He said, "We considered that scenario. Míos does not get us out of the country. We doubt the ferries are running, and if we're black listed, they'll arrest us there. And, we can't risk leading authorities to Teddy and Mimi. We can't even risk calling to tell them of the birth. It's better they have total deniability should they be questioned, or searched."

Alexandra squeezed Cynna's hand, "You are right, Cynna. Our baby should be with family. You are family. We are sisters in Christ. And," she looked at Isidor, "soon we will be sisters-in-law. I can't think of anyone I trust more than you to take care of my daughter; Cynna—strong and courageous."

Isidor moved from the bed, knelt beside Cynna, and took her hands in his. "Cynna, the odds of the five of us making it out of the country together are too low. The odds of you getting out are higher. It is a risk we have to take. We must split up, go different directions, and find ways to get out. Then, as soon as possible, we will all meet up again with you in New York.

"Will you take *our* niece with you and keep her safe until she can be reunited with her parents?" He held up her hand with the engagement ring. "As soon as I join you in New York, we will be married. We will start a new life together wherever you want. Then, one day when this madness is over, we will all return to Greece."

Alexandra and Gregor each placed a hand on Cynna's arm, "*Please . . .*"

Cynna covered their hands with her own and nodded, "Yes. I will, with God's help."

Together, they sobbed.

Gregor pled, "God, our Provider, make time stand still long enough for us to get our baby to safety."

Alexandra said, "Gregor, do you have a name for our precious daughter?"

Gregor nodded and took the Bible from the nightstand. He opened the Holy Scriptures and read, "Know therefore that the LORD thy God, He is God, the faithful God which keepeth *covenant* and mercy with them that love him and keep his commandments to a thousand generations." (KJV)

Gregor and Alexandra held the baby together, and Gregor named her, and blessed her. "Our Faithful God and Father who keeps *Covenant* with those who love you, we place from this next generation of our family, our baby girl, into Your Merciful Hand. We thank you for your safe care and keeping. We ask you to reunite us again, if not in this life, then in the life to come. As a family, we enter into greater *Covenant* with you in giving our daughter the name *Lisa*, which means, *My God Is a Vow*."

Gregor withdrew a small glass vial from his pocket. "Lisa, we anoint you with oil, in the Name of the Father, the Son, and the Holy Spirit." With Alexandra's hand over his, they made the sign of the cross in oil on her tiny forehead. "May you always walk in love as Jesus Christ loved us, and gave his life for us. May you one day understand that your God Is a Vow who kept His Covenant."

CHAPTER 52

⚜

> Greater love hath no man than this,
> that a man lay down his life
> for his friends.
> —The Apostle John, John 15:13 (KJV)
> AD 80–85

Isidor and Cynna left Gregor and Alexandra to spend their last moments alone with their daughter. Isidor helped Cynna pack a small suitcase with one change of clothes, a nightgown, a few toiletries, and the Árgyros Thymíama box. Cynna ignored her mountain of suitcases filled with beautiful clothes, focusing only on getting baby Lisa to safety.

Cynna would check her bag, step onto the plane in Athens, and step off the plane in New York. Worst case scenario, she would work out alternate transportation, drop the suitcase if necessary, and travel with only what was needed for baby Lisa.

Meanwhile, Gregor packed Lisa's diaper bag with diapers, formula, bottles, pacifiers, and sleepers. Alexandra insisted he pack the knitted baby set from Mimi, the onesie from Dina, the baby book from Barba, the receiving blankets from Roxie, the olive wood rattle from Tessa, the stuffed lamb from Kyveli, and the baby Bible from Cynna.

In their last moments together, Isidor sat with Cynna at the foot. He gave her a small package.

"I was going to give this to you on your birthday."

Cynna untied the twine and unfolded the brown paper. Her eyes filled with tears at the sight of the handsome olive wood cross.

"It's beautiful. I shall treasure it always."

"I send this to remind you of our summer on Míos, my love for you, and God's steadfast, unfailing love. This is the first thing Luca carved after his baptism."

Cynna brought the cross to her lips, kissed it, and cradled it to her heart. Isidor pulled her hands to his lips. He kissed the cross and her hands as together they held it.

Isidor said, "Our Lord Jesus Christ is the most important thing we have in common."

"Yes. Without Him, all would be empty and meaningless."

"On our first date, you said you would rather walk in the steps of Paul and the Apostles than the temples of mythological gods and goddesses. You told me of your passion for amphoriskos . . . I said your faith was deep and pure, and that I was certain God brought you to Greece for a unique purpose—a purpose deeper and far more important than your internship."

Isidor held Cynna's face in his hands. "I see now that God sent you to Greece, renamed you for strength and courage, and prepared you for such a time as this . . . to carry this precious baby to safety. *That* was your purpose for coming to Greece. To lay down your life for others doing something that *only* you could do."

Cynna's tears fell, ". . . and to meet my husband. In my heart, I am already married to you."

Isidor kissed her tears.

"Isidor, I promise I will get Lisa to safety or I will die trying."

Isidor nodded. "Of that, I am certain."

Cynna looked at the wooden cross. "I wish I had a gift for you."

"Cynna, you have given me—and my family—the greatest gift of all —yourself. You've laid down your plans, freedom, and reputation— for us and this child."

Cynna touched Isidor's face. "My Darling Isidor, I said I would always choose you, whatever you asked of me, I would happily do."

With tears Isidor said, "Jesus said, '... the greatest love of all is a love that sacrifices all. And this great love is demonstrated when a person sacrifices his life for his friends.' To read the verse is one thing. To behold it is another. My Precious Cynna, you truly are God's most beautiful amphoriskos, His most beloved vessel, filled with His presence."

"Isidor, you sound as if we'll never see each other again."

"No, My Love, I only wish to leave nothing unsaid. In the days ahead, I never want you to question my love for you, or how you chose to spend your life when you said 'yes' to me, 'yes' to my family, and 'yes' to God."

Isidor and Cynna kissed, and lingered one last stolen moment.

"Now, let me pray over you." Isidor placed his hands on Cynna's bowed head.

"May you know with unfailing heart, God is your source of strength and courage, your ever-present Help in times of trouble. Be blessed with resilience and resolve to carry out His will for your life. I pray this over you in Jesus' Name, Amen."

Gregor knocked on the door to Cynna's room and entered.

"Cynna . . . it's time. The soldiers are moving this way. We must get you out while we can. Alexandra and I are ready for you."

Cynna folded the brown paper around the cross and retied the twine. She secured it in the zippered compartment of her handbag with a photograph of herself and Isidor, the Giórgos wine cork from their first date, the Hotel Mákari stationery, and a small glass jar with the sand and sea glass from the Petrádi Beach.

Isidor carried her suitcase from the room. Cynna stopped at the door, turned, and looked back. The bedcovers just as she left them when she bolted from bed that morning at the sound of the tanks in the street. Numb, she sensed so many dreams escaping her grasp.

She shook her head at the earthly possessions she left behind. None of it mattered. Her heart only yearned to take Isidor, Alexandra, Gregor and Lisa with her. The sound of nearby gunfire shocked her back to reality, and she hurried down the hall to the birthing room.

Isidor met Cynna at the door, and they entered the room. Gregor stood behind Alexandra, who sat in a chair holding the baby. Alexandra said, "Come quickly."

Handing an envelope to her, Gregor said, "We keep cash on hand for emergencies. We have only kept out enough to cover our expenses to get to New York. We are sending the rest for you and Lisa. It is enough to take care of you both for a while, until we join you."

Cynna took the envelope. Alexandra reached for Cynna's hand. Cynna knelt beside her. She saw that the baby was dressed and was swaddled in one of Roxie's receiving blankets.

"Take this with you." Alexandra pressed her birthday locket from Gregor into Cynna's hand.

"Use it for a bribe to get the baby out if you have to. Sell it to take care of the baby if you need to. If not, you can return it to me when we come to New York." Tears welled in Alexandra's eyes. She wiped them away. "Otherwise, give it to Lisa for her sixteenth birthday."

Cynna's tears fell.

"Cynna, promise me that if I do not make it to New York, you will raise Lisa as your own daughter."

"Yes . . . I promise. I could not love her more if she *was* my own daughter."

"And be very careful. Tell no one who she is. Leave no trace, do not let these animals find her."

"I promise."

"Now," Alexandra handed Cynna a pair of scissors and a razor blade. She motioned toward the en suite. "Quick—go in. Cut a slit in the inside padding of your brassier. Hide the locket on one side, and most of the money on the other. Only put a little money in your purse for immediate needs. This way, the money and locket will only be found if you are personally searched."

Cynna rushed into the en suite and did as Alexandra instructed. She could feel the items safe against her body, but they were not visible. She emerged back into the room.

Gregor confirmed, "You have your passport and airline ticket?"

Cynna opened her purse and showed them, and put the small handful of cash in her wallet.

Cynna said, "The flight boards at 5:30 a.m."

Gregor said, "Quickly, you and Lisa must go—"

Cynna said, "Wait, how will we meet up in New York City? I don't know where I'll be. How will you find me?"

Isidor rubbed his jaw, "Pick a landmark."

"Oh, um—" She sorted through options. "Gregor, you know the theaters on Broadway, right?"

"Yes."

"Faith Chapel, in Manhattan. It's a small historic church tucked between buildings, near Columbus Circle and Central Park South—between Broadway and 8th. It's open everyday for prayer. I'll be there every other morning praying waiting for you—"

They all jumped at the sound of vehicles and commotion in the street. They drew together in a circle and prayed, "The LORD bless you and keep you; the LORD make his face to shine upon you and be gracious to you; the LORD lift up his countenance upon you and give you peace."(ESV)

Gregor, his face wet with tears, kissed Lisa on her forehead. Alexandra kissed Lisa and wept. Gregor reached for the baby. Pulling away, Alexandra shook her head, tightening her arms around her tiny daughter.

Insistent banging at the front door startled Alexandra into action. She pushed Lisa into Cynna's arms, and Isidor rushed her and the baby from the room. Cynna's heart broke at the sound of Alexandra's mournful wail as they ran down the hallway to the back door.

Isidor wrapped his arms around Cynna and kissed her. "I love you. I will meet you at Faith Chapel as soon as possible."

"I love you, Isidor. God be with you."

Marina's husband, Tobías, was waiting in a car in the dark alley, motor running, lights off. As Isidor put Cynna and Lisa into the car, she heard loud male voices shouting harsh orders from within the house. Isidor slammed the car door closed. Tobías took off. Cynna turned and looked back. Isidor disappeared inside the house, and she heard gunshots.

CHAPTER 53

His massive arms
are wrapped around you, protecting you.
You can run under his covering
of majesty and hide.
His arms of faithfulness
are a shield keeping you from harm.
—Psalm 91:4 (KJV)
1015 BC

"Stop the car! Stop! *Stop the car!*" Frantic, Cynna unlatched her seatbelt, reaching for the door handle. "Tobías, stop. I have to go back. *Stop!*" Cynna sobbed, *"Please, stop the car."*

Clenching the steering wheel, Tobías kept driving.

Grabbing his sleeve, Cynna pulled at his arm. "I'm begging you. Take me back. I can't abandon them. Tobías, Isidor needs me. Gregor and Alexandra need me. *Please!*"

Tobías looked at her, his face wet with tears. "No! They need you *here!* This baby, she needs you here." Tobías wiped his face with the back of his sleeve. "You cannot help them by going back. You must do what *only you* can do."

Sobbing, Cynna released her grip on his arm, cradling Lisa closer to her chest. In darkness, the car crept forward, block after block through the back alleyways. Tobías faced forward, sternly watching the road ahead. Gunshots echoing in her mind, Cynna concentrated on the road ahead, praying that Isidor, Gregor, and Alexandra were alive.

"Tobías, have the soldiers come to your door?"

"The soldiers arrested our son tonight—for writing books."

"Oh, no, I am sorry. Do you know where they took him?"

"To prison. We don't know where."

"And, Marina?"

"She is heartbroken, angry, frightened. But I am certain she will go to the Andras' home to see what happened, and help them."

"You are both so brave, and selfless. Thank you for helping us."

"We have lived through war and civil war. You learn to be brave and do what you have to do."

Cynna considered this.

Tobías said, "If I do not talk much, it is because I am praying for all of us."

"I am praying for all of us, too. We can pray together out loud, if you want."

Eyes on the road and scanning their surroundings, Tobías nodded.

Cynna considered the immeasurable mettle of this man and his wife. Fresh from the horror of the soldiers taking their son, they took part in this dangerous mission. Marina risked her life to deliver the baby into her parents' arms. Tobías was risking his life to deliver Lisa and the baby to the airport.

Tobías said, "If the soldiers stop us, keep your door locked, hold the baby close, and let me do the talking. And, pay attention. No matter what I say, follow my lead."

At the end of each block, Tobías edged toward the street. If no activity was detected, he proceeded to the next alley. The metal of the gun on the seat beside him glinted under the occasional streetlamp.

When clear of the Arts District, they breathed a sigh of relief. Several blocks farther, Tobías turned on the headlights. A few miles farther, they encountered barricades that forced them out of the alley and onto the road. At the next intersection, a tank blocked the road. They were trapped. An armed soldier walked toward their vehicle. Tobías slid the gun under his leg. He raised a finger to his lips, signaling for Cynna to keep quiet.

The soldier trained the weapon on them, stopped in front of the car, and gruffly barked an order. Tobías motioned to Cynna to stay in the car and pushed the gun across the seat.

"Hide it."

She slid the gun under her pant leg as Tobías got out, hands raised.

Tobías and the soldier stood in the headlights talking. Tobías assumed an erect military posture, rendering his identification papers. They talked for some time. Tobías gestured toward the car. Taking a long look at her, the soldier approached Cynna's side of the car.

Weapon pointed at her, he ordered, "Visa, passport, tickets."

Cynna's heart sank. Surrendering the paperwork, she awaited arrest.

The soldier compared her likeness to the photos, grunted, and returned to Tobías. Cynna held her breath. They talked again. The guard reached into his pocket and gave Tobías a card and returned the paperwork.

Tobías saluted the guard and returned to the car. He stuck the card in the windshield, put the car in gear, and drove on as the tank eased out of their way.

Tobías gave Cynna her paperwork, and she slid the gun back to him. Tobías pointed to the card in the windshield.

"We're clear to drive to the airport."

"What happened?"

"He asked for my papers. I gave him my papers, my old military card, and a generous bribe. I told him I, too, was a foot soldier for Mother Greece when I was his age. I said as a former soldier, it was my military duty to purge the country of the American woman here on visa. I said you cannot get cab to airport, so I violated curfew to take you and throw you out of the country. He gave me pass to drive through the check points. They'll move over for *us* now."

"Tobías, you're brilliant."

During the drive, Lisa awakened for a feeding and diaper change.

Tobías drove on unflinching, even when Lisa cried at the top of her lungs.

An hour later, Tobías parked outside the departure terminal. At 2 a.m., all vehicle lanes were full, and the terminal was overrun with passengers desperate to flee the country.

Tobías slid his gun under the seat and gave Cynna a card containing a series of numbers, and his pocket knife.

"Make a slit and hide this card in the lining of your purse. That is our phone number. Only call if Isidor, Gregor, or Alexandra do not arrive in New York. Give it time."

"God bless you and Marina. And, thank you for purging me from the country."

Tobías gave her a fatherly smile. "You are brave girl. God is with you. You will make it to New York."

"God be with you, Tobías. He will return you home safely. Give Marina my love. When you see Isidor, please tell him I love him, and give him this."

Tobías received the piece of sea glass, held it up to the light, then tucked it into his pocket. He pulled the military card from the windshield.

"I will now make show of throwing you out of the country. Are you ready?"

Cynna nodded.

Tobías pulled Cynna's suitcase from the trunk, came to the passenger door, opened it, and waited for her to get out. She slung the diaper bag and purse onto her shoulder and held Lisa firmly in her arms. Tobías grabbed Lisa's suitcase, took her by the shoulder, and marched her into the terminal. It was crawling with armed soldiers and crowded with long lines of passengers. Afraid she would never get through the lines in time, Cynna prayed.

Scowling, Tobías pulled Cynna through the crowd to the front of the line at the ticket counter. Processing another passenger and at his wit's end, the clerk unloaded a barrage of Greek at Tobías.

An armed guard stepped forward and leveled his weapon at Tobías. Undeterred, Tobías saluted, slapped the military pass card on the counter, and commanded, "By order of the military, I deliver this

American to your custody. She must leave the country immediately as ordered by the regime."

The soldier shifted his weight, read the card, and handed it back to Tobías. He stared at Cynna. "Visa, passport, ticket?"

Cynna jerked her arm free from Tobías' grip on her shoulder, glared at him, opened her purse, and rendered her documents. The soldier demanded, "Where are papers for baby?"

Panicked, Cynna projected a cool exterior and prayed for swift wisdom.

She said, "The baby does not require an airline ticket."

"Then the passport and visa?"

Holding her ground, Cynna said. "The baby was not here on visa. She was born here. The regime ordered me to get out—" Cynna looked at her watch, "in less than forty-eight hours. The baby was just born. It would take months to get the papers. Which law do *you* want me to obey? To leave the country as ordered, or apply for papers and break the law waiting for papers?"

The soldier reddened. Seething, he raised his weapon. As if on cue, Lisa began to fuss, then wail. With contempt, the soldier ordered the airline clerk to process Cynna's ticket with immediate effect. Cynna dug in the diaper bag for a bottle.

The soldier commanded, "Move to passport control."

Over Lisa's screaming cries, Cynna said, "I need to check my suitcase."

The airline clerk scrutinized the small bag and declared, "Carry-on. Next."

Tobías stood at attention, saluted the soldier, and snarled, "Make sure that American woman is thrown out of country."

Tobías gave Cynna one last look, waved the military pass in her face, turned on his heel, and stomped out. Cynna vowed to nominate Tobías for a Tony Award.

Cynna grabbed all her papers, pushed her suitcase to the side, collapsed against the wall with relief, and fed Lisa the bottle. Now to make it through the passport check, board the plane, and take off.

Cynna's arms ached with fatigue from shouldering the bags, cradling Lisa, and carrying the suitcase. Shuffling through the mass of passengers, she queued up, passport at the ready. Weary, she eyed the long line ahead. In time, she cleared passport control without incident.

Cynna located her departure gate and lined up for the ladies' restroom; Lisa needed a diaper change. They made it to the gate as the flight was announced. Standing in the line of passengers, Cynna waited, anxious to cross the tarmac and climb the stairs into the Boeing 707. Twenty minutes passed, and still they were not released to board.

The gate agent received a phone call, conferred with the other gate agent, and announced a flight delay. Frantic, everyone looked about, moaning with frustration. Resigned, they shuffled back to the waiting area. The seats quickly filled. One man gave Cynna his seat. Thankful, she accepted and sat, exhausted. She cradled Lisa in her arms. The baby slept unaware of it all.

Four armed soldiers approached the gate agents. After an exchange, they studied the waiting passengers. Breaking into pairs, they patrolled the waiting area. Cynna felt the oppressive atmosphere descend—instilling palpable fear.

One pair of soldiers singled out a husband and wife and ordered them to a cordoned off area against the wall. Cynna watched in terror as the soldiers separated the couple, confiscated their paperwork, and pocketed their tickets.

They opened the carry-on bags and rummaged through them. The wife cried and shook with fear when the soldier slashed the inner lining open with his knife, and withdrew papers. One soldier wiped the luggage and contents off the table like trash. The soldiers compared the papers with a list, confronted the couple with their finding, and arrested them.

The woman next to Cynna whispered, "Must be on Black List, trying to leave with false I.D.s."

Cynna thought of Isidor, Gregor, and Alexandra. That could have been them. A cold shiver traveled down her spine.

"Keep your head down," the woman whispered.

Cynna concentrated on Lisa and fussed with her blanket. Two pairs of soldiers' boots entered her field of vision. They stopped in front of her. One kicked at her suitcase with his boot and gave a command in Greek.

Cynna looked up and asked, *"Mílas Angliká,* English?"

Rather than answer, the soldier jerked his head in the direction of the area against the wall. One soldier took her suitcase to the table, dumping it out. Cynna stood, gathering her things. Pointing his weapon at her, the other soldier motioned her to stand at the wall. He ripped the diaper bag and purse from her shoulder. She stood, frozen with fear, her lungs burning, constricting every breath. White noise rose in her ears. Again, the only prayer she could utter was, "Jesus . . . Jesus . . . *Jesus, help."*

The soldiers signaled the gate agent, who announced the flight and opened the door. The passengers rose, amassing at the door, anxious to avoid further military scrutiny. Patting down every surface in Cynna's suitcase, the soldiers checked for hidden compartments.

Dumping her purse and diaper bag onto the table, they rifled through the diapers, bottles, and formula. They slit open the toy lamb, pulled out the stuffing, and tossed it aside.

Terrified, Cynna watched the line for boarding dwindle. One soldier unzipped the compartment in her purse, tossed the cork aside, studied the photo of Cynna and Isidor, compared it to her likeness, tore it into shreds, and threw it on the floor. He examined the bottle of sand and sea glass, shook it, and pitched it onto the pile of Cynna's clothes.

Giving her a lusty look, he handled her bra and panties. Unflinching, she held his gaze. He tore into the brown paper parcel. Finding the olive wood cross, he eyed Cynna suspiciously. Cynna raised her chin and stuck out her hand. "Please . . ."

Shrugging, he tossed the cross aside, "Cheap trinket."

Resuming his search, he unzipped her wallet, and checked her identification card against her passport, visa, and ticket. Showing the other soldier, they talked and pointed at her and the documents. Cynna prayed as they made their decision.

One soldier took the money from her wallet and pocketed it. Alexandra, bless her, had the foresight to have her hide the remaining money and locket in her bra. The other soldier was intrigued with the wooden Árgyros Thymíama box and opened it a second time. It appeared he was going to take it. Cynna held her breath.

As precious as these things were to her, they were nothing

compared to their lives. She started to offer the box to him, but feared she would appear too eager and raise suspicion. If she could only leave with the baby in her arms, it would be enough. Lisa woke, crying.

The other two soldiers came up. One ran his hand along the lining of the diaper bag. Finding nothing, they waved for the other two soldiers to move on. The final boarding call came over the speaker. One of the soldiers made fun of the soldier with the incense box and motioned for him to leave it.

Looking over his shoulder, he set the box on the table, pulled out the velvet pouch, and tried to stuff it in his pocket. It did not fit. He took the crystal bottle from the velvet bag. He tossed the beautiful crystal stopper aside. It fell to the floor, shattering. He poured the incense nuggets into his pocket, chunked the crystal bottle on the table, and walked off.

The moment his back was turned, Cynna dashed to the table, quickly stuffing the baby's things back into the diaper bag. She rummaged through the pile of her clothes, found the gutted lamb, and saved the satin ribbon for its neck. She pushed them into the diaper bag.

The soldier returned to the table. Frantically grabbing her things, Cynna ignored him. He seized her left wrist. Holding her hand mid-air between them, he said, "Diamánti."

Cynna tried to pull her hand away. He was strong, and she could not risk dropping Lisa. He reached for the ring. Cynna clenched her fist. His grip tightened.

"Diamánti!"

Relenting, Cynna unclenched her fist. He pulled Isidor's engagement ring from her finger. Turning on his heel he was gone.

Cynna looked to the gate—the agent waved her to come. Through her tears, she found the wine cork, wooden cross, stationery, sand and sea glass, the incense bottle, and velvet bag, and shoved her treasures into her purse. The photograph was destroyed. Without a backward glance, she left the pile of clothes and suitcase on the table.

Breathless, she scrambled for the gate. The agent closed the door behind her. Without the suitcase slowing her down, she scurried across the tarmac and scrambled onto the plane. The flight attendant sealed the aircraft door behind her, separating Cynna and Lisa from the terrors of the Junta, but the closed door also separated them from Isidor, Gregor, Alexandra, and her new God-gathered Greek family.

Passing down the aisle to her seat, Cynna searched the faces of fellow passengers. The collage of emotions represented all she felt. Terror, grief, sadness, shock, and relief. She passed by the woman who sat beside her in the terminal. This woman's face brightened with relief, meeting Cynna's gaze, she crossed herself and put her hand over her heart. Certain the woman had been praying for her to make it, Cynna smiled back at her and said, "God bless you."

Cynna took her seat at the back of the plane. The flight stewardess helped her push the diaper bag and purse under the seat in front of her. She put her hand on Cynna's arm and said, "Poor thing. You're exhausted. It's a long flight for a baby. We will help you."

Only after the plane was in the air, Cynna allowed her tears to fall. In shock, her mind and heart could not process all that happened in the past twenty-four hours. There was no way to explain how they made it—but God. She nuzzled Lisa, lavishing her sweet head with kisses. The first lullaby she sang to her was, "Jesus loves me, this I know..."

CHAPTER 54

> The LORD is my light and my salvation;
> whom shall I fear?
> The LORD is the strength of my life;
> of whom shall I be afraid?
> When my father and my mother forsake me,
> then the LORD will take me up.
> —Psalm 27:1,10 (KJV)
> 539 BC

Arduous. The ten-hour flight to New York was arduous. Lisa woke about every two hours for a feeding and diaper change. In between, Cynna received two meals and drowsed in abbreviated snippets. Afraid of falling asleep and dropping the baby, she fashioned a sarong from Roxie's receiving blankets, securing Lisa to her chest.

After interminable hours, the incessant drone of the engines changed pitch, and the jet descended for final approach into New York City. Cynna felt queasy at the thought of seeing her parents. No telling what they had heard, if anything, about the military coup in

Greece. As well, she could imagine their shock at her arrival with a baby. How she wished Isidor was by her side.

Cynna prayed, "Jesus, my ever-present help in time of trouble—I need you."

Keep your eyes on me . . .

"Yes, LORD."

Cynna processed through customs, stopped to feed and change Lisa, and emerged from under the "Foreign Arrivals" sign to meet her waiting parents. Cynna spotted Frank and Joan Chadwick in the distance, scanning the crowd.

Tugging on Frank's sleeve, her mother pointed in her direction. Moving through the crowd, pace quickening, they stopped dead in their tracks at the sight of her. Joan put a white gloved hand to her mouth and grabbed Frank's arm with the other. The crowd dissipated, leaving them standing face-to-face.

Staring at his daughter, Frank's expression soured. Fidgeting, Joan moved forward to hug her daughter, then didn't. She chose to adjust her Jacqueline Kennedy-esque pill box hat instead. Holding his position, Frank crossed his arms over his chest. The line in the sand had been drawn.

Joan moved toward Cynna, reaching out, almost hugging her again, and stopped short at the sound of Frank clearing his throat. Stranded in the awkward space half-way between father and daughter, Joan said, "Ummm . . . Honey . . . we heard on the news there was a little situation somewhere in Greece. We're happy you weren't affected by it and got home on schedule. So . . ." Looking around at the other arriving passengers, Joan continued, "So, which one of these women is its mother? I'm sure she appreciates your help and wants it back now . . ."

Cynna's two worlds collided fast and hard. She felt her brain and heart rip apart—it was brutal. Cynna reeled.

Keep your eyes on me . . .

Cynna forced her thoughts to focus—to survive. There was so much to tell; they would not want to hear any of it. They preferred clean, seamless transitions. This was not only filled with seams, but—was an utter mess.

She was meant to step back into her old life as if she never left.

Dinner at the club, church on Sundays, museum galas, a mention on the society page of the *New York Times*. Feeling claustrophobic at the thought of squeezing back into her old life, Cynna shook off the thought.

Blunt and to the point, Frank said, "Cynthia, have you come home with a baby?"

"Yes. But with good reason."

His shrewd eyes narrowed. "We are so disappointed in you." Motioning in disgust at the baby, he admonished, "We raised you better than this. We raised you in church. We let you out of our sight for one minute, and you run off with some Greek and get pregnant. I see now why you were so determined to spend the summer with 'friends.'"

Fidgeting with her hat again, Joan looked about. "Frank, keep your voice down."

Cynna pleaded, "Daddy, it's not what you think—"

Frank barked, "Don't tell me what I think."

"I'm sure seeing me with a baby is a shock."

"It's not a shock, it's *unacceptable*."

"There's a good reason for this. If you will just listen . . . *please*."

"There are *no* good reasons, but go ahead, I'm listening."

Eyes on me, keep your eyes on me.

Cynna steeled her nerves. With clarity she realized telling them anything put Lisa at risk. Her father was angry and volatile. She remembered her words to Isidor, "My father does not negotiate, he only makes threats followed by action." Cynna took a deep breath and tightened her arms around Lisa.

Telling her father anything would empower him to take action. She promised Alexandra she would be careful, tell no one who Lisa was, and leave no trace. Mind racing, Cynna figured he would send the baby away if he thought it was not hers. She knew how it looked. Her father would not suffer the disgrace of even one person thinking she got pregnant out of wedlock.

He barked again. "Well, I'm waiting."

"Daddy, I can't tell you the reason. I'm asking you to trust me."

He scoffed, "*Trust you?* You're gone for nine months and come home with a baby, and you want me to trust you?"

"Daddy, I love God, and I have not dishonored Him . . . or you in any way."

Frank's head snapped around so fast, Cynna flinched back in fear it might torque off. "Don't tell me you got married over there." He stared at her, his eyes narrow slits. "Did you get married over there?"

Cynna shook her head, her heart overrun with sadness at the thought of Isidor. "No."

He turned from her, pacing in a circle. Cynna waited.

He stopped, moving in for the kill. "Cynthia, you must face the consequences of your actions. You've been running all over Greece on my money. The games are over. Time to pay the piper. You have two choices. One, we go directly to Harper Children's Home, you give it up for adoption, you come home, and we never speak of it again. Two, you keep it, you never come home, you are disinherited, and we never speak to you again."

Joan fidgeted nervously and pulled on Frank's arm, "Honey, maybe it isn't what we think, maybe there's a good reason—"

Frank turned on Joan. "So now *you're* going to tell me what to think? I am on the vestry and an elder at the church, *and* I have a professional reputation to uphold. I will not allow a fornicating daughter and her illegitimate child living under my roof." He turned to Cynna and yelled, "And you, missy, you certainly can't walk into church with that baby."

Cynna looked her father in the eye and said, "Jesus said, 'Let the little children come to me.'"

He spat out, "Don't you *dare* quote the Bible to *me!*"

He was so angry, Cynna feared her father would explode. Cynna put a protective hand around Lisa's head.

Joan pleaded, "Cynthia, please, just tell your father the baby is not yours, and we can drop it off at Social Services. No one needs to know you came home with a baby. We can all just pick up where we left off."

Frank, arms crossed over his chest, loomed over Cynna. "Well?"

Pulling off her white gloves, Joan twisted them into a knot. "Cynthia, honey, please do not keep your father waiting."

Cynna promised Alexandra, Gregor, Isidor, and God she would keep Lisa safe, or die trying. She was determined to wait for them to join her, no matter how long it took. Closing her eyes, she pictured

Isidor by her side, their marriage, Gregor, Alexandra, and Lisa together again, Teddy and Mimi with their granddaughter, and their God-gathered family on Míos, dancing in celebration at being reunited again.

Frank demanded, "Well? Surely, you're smart enough to wake up and make one right choice."

Taking a deep breath, Cynna lifted her chin, not in defiance, but with newfound strength and courage. "Yes . . . I have finally woken up, and I have made my choice—the *only* right choice. I am keeping the baby. And, I will forgive myself for not standing up to you sooner. I ask your forgiveness for disappointing you."

Cynna turned and walked away.

Frank called after her, "We will never forgive you—never! You are dead to us."

Cynna walked out of the terminal and into her new life.

CHAPTER 55

⁂

> Here's what I've learned through it all:
> Don't give up, don't be impatient;
> be entwined as one with the LORD.
> Be brave and courageous, and never lose hope.
> Yes, keep on waiting —for he will never disappoint you!
> —Psalm 27:14 (TPT)
> 539 BC

Cynthia's Story
September 1995, Alpine Lake, Colorado

In the backyard of the cabin on Shadow Ridge Road, near Alpine Lake, Colorado, Cynthia luxuriated in the warmth of the sun on her face. A crisp autumn breeze rustled the golden Aspen leaves in the nearby grove, their knobby bark white against the blue sky. Their leaves quaked, shimmering and dancing in the wind.

Cynthia breathed in the heady mountain air. Scented with moist earth, fallen leaves, and chimney smoke, it rendered a clean, peaty aroma. Autumn in Colorado—always her favorite season, but the month of September always difficult.

Filled with so much heartache, the memories of that September so many years ago haunted her. Steering her mind away from it took more effort now, perhaps because her time was drawing close. She'd held on for so long, in the face of so much—but God had fulfilled every promise over her life. Now, her strength was waning, the veil growing thin.

Cynthia yielded to nostalgia, opened the guarded window to her soul, and allowed herself to relive the memories one last time. Closing her eyes, she drifted back to a world away, a time with Isidor. His handsome face as vibrant as the last time she saw him: Friday, September 1, 1967.

It was the day the tanks rumbled through the streets of Athens, the day Lisa was born, and the day she and Isidor kissed for the last time. Her precious Isidor never arrived in New York. Weary, Cynthia sighed. "Jesus warned, 'The thief comes only to steal, and kill, and destroy...'" (NIV)

Cynthia willed the memories into focus. The golden days on Petrádi Beach, the starry nights on Míos, a stack of records playing, and dancing in Isidor's arms. Even the best of memories from 1967 brought bittersweet sadness, for she knew the end of the story.

Her time in Greece inflicted a wound in her heart that never healed, and it birthed the wildest happiness she had ever known, her joy-filled life with Wells and Lisa. They were the miraculous counterbalance that filled the void. Truly Jesus came to give life to the full.

When all was said and done, Cynthia forever held a place-keeper in her heart. A sacred homage to the things that *should have been*. She and Isidor should have been married and grown old together. Gregor and Alexandra should have had long, successful careers. Lisa should have lived a glorious life in Greece, with her loving parents.

Upon return to New York, Cynna, cradling baby Lisa, waited and prayed for Isidor, Alexandra, and Gregor every morning, at Faith Chapel. Her heart leapt with hope at every opening of the tall wooden doors. After six long months, she called the number Tobías gave her.

He confirmed what her heart already knew. Isidor was killed in the gunfire she heard in the house as Tobías drove her and Lisa to safety. Armed soldiers had broken down the front door as she escaped out the back. In an effort to get Alexandra and Gregor out the back, Isidor placed himself between them and the soldiers. He took the bullets meant for them, laying down his life for his beloved sister and her husband.

When Marina and Tobías went to the Andras' home, they found Isidor's body. Despite Isidor's sacrifice, Gregor had been gunned down as well. Barely alive, they hid him in their home and nursed him.

From what Gregor saw, Alexandra was arrested. Tobías eventually received word from underground sources that their son and Alexandra were sent to the Agelástos Island concentration camp. Agelástos held a dark reputation for the brutal torture and execution of political prisoners.

The moment Gregor was strong enough to walk, he spirited away in search of Alexandra. Tobías and Marina never heard from him again.

A world away, life moved forward for Cynna and Lisa. Grieving and alone, Cynna kept her promise to Alexandra, raised Lisa as her own, told no one, and left no trace.

The military occupation in Greece prevailed for eight long, tyrannical years. By the time it was safe to return, Cynthia, Lisa, and Wells were a strong, contented family, and Teddy and Mimi's phone was disconnected.

Pulling herself back to the present, Cynthia said, "Greater love hath no one than this, that they lay down their life for their friends." (KJV) Gregor and Alexandra laid down their lives for their daughter. Isidor laid his life down for Gregor and Alexandra. Isidor said she laid down her life for them, but with the joy of raising Lisa, she did not consider it so. Some days the survivor's guilt was more than she could bear.

Cynthia was unwilling to place herself in the same category as Isidor, Gregor, and Alexandra. She laid down so much less. She had only given up her reputation, a pretentious lifestyle, snobbish parents, and a museum career. In exchange, she received a precious daughter.

Cynthia wept. The loss was as fresh as twenty-eight years ago. As if sensing her mood, the wind shifted and a fresh chill crept deeply into her bones. Picking up her empty coffee cup, she moved inside.

The early morning fire in the wood stove had burned down. The cabin had grown cold, buffeted by the strong winds that rattled the windows. Cynthia shoved a large log onto the glowing embers. It smoldered and took hold, warming the house again. After the trip down memory lane, Cynthia was also ready to stoke old embers of her own. It was time to take care of unfinished business and get her house in order. Her cancer had returned, and she had declined further treatment.

Pulling on an extra sweater, Cynthia climbed the split-log stairs to the third-story attic. Crossing the dark, drafty space, the floor creaked underfoot. At the far wall, she pushed an old trunk aside. Kneeling in the light of the dormer window, she pried up a section of floorboards with a silver-handled letter opener, pulled the time capsule of a shoebox from its hiding place, and set it on the dressing table.

After she stared at her reflection for some time, she decided she was ready at last to take the last step of the long journey. Opening the box, Cynthia took out the Hotel Mákari stationery, laid it on the dressing table, and ran her fingers over the insignia printed at the top. Mákari . . . *I wish for a baby girl.* Gregor got his wish. And in an odd twist of fate, Gregor's wish came true for her and Wells, too. Unable to conceive, they also got Lisa, the precious daughter they wished for. Father-God's hand was in all and through all of their stories.

Cynthia took out the olive wood cross—Isidor's birthday present to her twenty-eight years ago, carved by Luca after his baptism at the Petrádi Beach. Isidor said it was to be a reminder of her summer on Míos, his love for her, and God's steadfast, unfailing love. Cynna assured Isidor she would treasure it always . . . and she had.

Cynthia picked up the purple velvet bag and breathed in the earthy, woody, slightly sweet fragrance of the Frankincense it once held. The aroma as exquisite as when gifted her at the Marinákis' estate on Crete.

Loosening the gold drawstring, Cynthia withdrew the crystal Árgyros Thymíama bottle. Isidor's precious gift, a modern amphoriskos symbolizing a unique work of art that reflected the workmanship of its creator, filled with something greater than itself.

Years ago she filled it with the sand and sea glass from the beach named after her, in place of the incense taken by the soldier at the Athens airport. The Giórgos Hill wine cork from her first date with Isidor replaced the shattered crystal stopper. To Cynthia, the sand, sea glass, and cork were as precious as the Frankincense the bottle once held.

Cynthia pulled the cork free, pouring the contents into a china bowl. Turning on the lamp, she picked up several pieces of sea glass and held them up to the light. Still fascinated by sea glass, she remembered Isidor's explanation. Over the course of as many as fifty years, something beautiful and unique was formed from something broken, cast off, and ravaged by time and circumstance.

Cynthia felt God's presence near. She felt the impression of His voice in her thoughts. Over and over she felt the words . . . heard the words . . . a love letter from God. Picking up a pen, she wrote them on the Hotel Mákari stationery,

Like the surge of the ocean, the roll of the waves,
So is My love for you . . . relentless.
My love is like the sand on the shore,
Multi-faceted and plenty.
You are My sea glass,
Polished by My nature . . . My jewel . . . My love.

Cynthia's tears fell. God had given her a love letter telling her she was His *something broken that became something beautiful*. Like the sea glass, her life and heart had been broken, even cast off.

Now, on the eve of her fiftieth birthday, Father God reminded her that His love was as relentless as the waves of the ocean, and as plentiful as the sand on the shore. Through fifty years of living her life with Him, she was perfected by His nature. *She was His beautiful sea glass, His jewel . . . His love.*

Cynthia's life flashed before her eyes, and she saw how God had been in it all and through it all. He had always known her story from beginning to end. Every moment of her life, He had loved her relentlessly, with steadfast love. Looking back on the whole, she understood how He perfected every broken moment with His love, transforming it into something beautiful.

Yes, she lost Isidor, Alexandra, and Gregor, but He gave her a daughter. Yes, she was orphaned by her parents, and lost her family on Míos, but God had taken their place. Yes, she longed to marry Isidor, but God had sent Wells, a Godly man and loving husband with the strength needed to protect her from the past. A man who loved Lisa as his own. A man who created a new life for her and Lisa, no questions asked.

The first years—heartbroken, grieving, frightened, and always looking over her shoulder—she married for companionship and security. But she honored Wells, and they grew together in the LORD. They became best friends, lovers, and dedicated parents to Lisa. She loved Wells Brenner beyond measure.

She forever kept her promise to Alexandra. She was careful, told no one who Lisa was, and left no trace. After the military occupation was over, she continued to keep the secret for Well's and Lisa's sake. They were a happy family.

Despite their age difference, fate dictated Wells would outlive her. Wells and Lisa would continue as father and daughter. It was not yet time to tell twenty-eight-year-old Lisa the hidden story of her life.

At peace with her choices, Cynthia replaced the floorboards, the space beneath them now empty. She pushed the trunk back into place. She opened the hasp on another trunk and raised the heavy lid. Another time capsule awaited her.

Removing the lid from the long, rectangular dress box, she pushed the tissue paper aside. Folded neatly inside, the beautiful wedding dress from her marriage to Wells. It was a private ceremony in a little chapel, with his sister, Elise Marie, Maid of Honor, holding Lisa in her arms.

So in love with her was Wells, who was also an orphan in his own right, he never questioned why she was a single mother of a two-year-old. He saw her heart for what it was, pure and holy. To ensure her safety from the unnamed demons of her past, Wells moved them from New York to Colorado. By some means, unexplained to her, he reset their family history and obtained birth certificates for them that established an alternate reality, obliterating their past.

Looking back, Cynthia wondered if that had all been necessary. Only God knew. She had faithfully kept her portion of the Covenant.

Cynthia always yearned to tell Lisa of her time in Greece and the immeasurable love of her parents. She wished Lisa knew that every time she looked in the mirror, she was, in fact, beholding an uncanny likeness of her beautiful mother, Alexandra.

Through the years, Cynthia trusted these secrets to God. She had witnessed the Covenant between Gregor, Alexandra, and God when they named their daughter Lisa . . . *My God Is a Vow*. Together they believed the LORD God would faithfully keep His Covenant and reunite them as a family in this life or the life to come. Cynthia believed it too. Once again, it was time for her to do something that *only* she could do for them.

Cynthia pulled her beautiful wedding dress from the box. Holding the dress up to her shoulders, she smiled at her beautiful reflection in the mirror. She hoped that perhaps one day, her three-year-old granddaughter, Cate, would wear it for her wedding. Cynthia neatly folded the dress and placed it back in the box.

Through the years Cynthia often tried, but was never able to throw her Greek treasures away. Now that God had given her His love letter, she understood why. He waited for her to circumnavigate her life, come full circle with her past, present, and future, and behold the exquisite value of the whole. She finally understood that hers was indeed, a life well-lived, a beautiful jewel, perfected by God's love.

Cynthia gathered her Greek treasures and love letter from God, tucked them into the velvet bag, cinched the gold drawstring, and placed them beneath the folds of her wedding dress. Her most meaningful worldly possessions were together in one place at last.

For the second time in her life, Cynthia's two worlds collided. This time it was a blessing. It filled her with peace that could only come from knowing every piece of her heart made it safely home. She prayed that perhaps one day, if it was God's will, her precious treasures would guide Lisa's heart home as well.

As Cynthia placed the top on the dress box, she sang a few bars of "Darling, Dance With Me," the Dorian Onassis song she and Isidor danced to twenty-eight years before. Only this time, it was Father God's voice who sang in her ear, "*. . . give your dreams to me . . . and you will see . . . they'll all come true . . . forever and ever and ever . . .*"

PART THREE

My God Is a Vow
Λίζα

Who guides the destiny of each generation
from the first until now?
I am the one!
I am Yahweh,
the first,
the unchanging one
who will be there in the end!
—Isaiah 41:4 (TPT, *Isaiah: The Vision*)

CHAPTER 56

> Do not fear,
> for I, your Kinsman-Redeemer,
> will rescue you.
> I have called you by name,
> and you are mine.
> —Isaiah 43:1b (TPT, *Isaiah: The Vision*)
> 740–700 BC

Lisa's Story
August 2016, Mios, Greece

To combat the August heat, Lisa chose a sleeveless, white, cotton shift and sandals for the evening at the winery with Lyra and Zenda. Girl Party! She fastened the locket around her neck. It hung perfectly framed by the sweeping circle neckline of her dress. She ran a brush through her full, dark hair, and refreshed her lipstick.

With a pop of her lips, Lisa grabbed her robin egg blue tote and ran out the door. Tonight, the Giórgos Hill wine cork was finally revisiting its place of origin. In lieu of the Fiat, Zenda was driving them in the Sea Jewel Hotel lee-moh-seen. After all, it was a special celebration of their friendship, a last evening together before Lisa flew back to the United States.

Having found no more clues as to why her mother was on the island in 1967, it was time to return home for Cate and Derek's wedding. She had one final act to perform, offering a toast to Dr. Soso Diákos at Giórgos Hill Winery.

Zenda drove them northward along the coast road, the limo climbing above the sea. A lazy sun sagged at the watery horizon, sizzling in a purple-pink haze. Lisa sighed deeply. She missed the grandeur of the Colorado mountains, but now could not imagine a day without an Aegean sunset.

Arriving at the entrance, Zenda hopped out, dangling her keys for valet pick up. Despite the fact there was, in fact, no valet, a young man standing around eagerly took on the challenge that was Zenda, and the generous tip in her hand.

Lisa followed Zenda and Gianna through the gate.

Captivated by the sight of the inner courtyard, Lisa said, "Giórgos Hill is a magnificent venue. I can't believe it's taken me all summer to get back here."

Lyra laughed and said, "Perhaps it was your incessant search for clues that got in the way."

"She's right Lee-zah. You've been running nonstop, and digging in wine cellars."

"Well, it is fitting that I am here to toast Soso at the end of my journey. I would have never come to Míos, if not for him."

Lisa smiled to herself at the sound of his words in her head, "*. . . you've traveled this far looking for answers, so . . . now, if you have enough courage, you do something you've probably never done before. You ask the hard questions . . . color outside the lines . . . you wander out of your comfort zone with reckless abandon . . . you travel a little . . . bit . . . farther! And when you sit on Giórgos Hill and the wine sings a love song to your soul . . . please, drink a toast to me.*"

She had wandered so far out of her comfort zone she couldn't remember what a comfort zone was. And, reckless abandon was her new modus operandi. Looking back, she couldn't recognize her old self.

ELIZABETH TOMME

Thanks to Soso, she had the adventure of a lifetime. The wise professor was right about so many things. He said, *". . . at most, you find out something interesting about your mother of which you had no idea. At worst, you find out nothing, but have a nice vacation on a lovely Greek island."* Lisa considered herself blessed; she had done both.

Lisa learned her mother was indeed in Greece—and never told her. She found the maker of the olive wood cross, the incense, the locket, the Hotel Mákari, the sand, and the sea glass. The only remaining question was, "Why?"

The hostess led them to the far corner of the arbors surrounding a courtyard of intimate outdoor living areas, tables and chairs. Darkness was settling, and a band played Greek music. The ambience was relaxed and casual. Lisa listened to the bouzoúkis and hoped there would be dancing.

Zenda and Lyra came alongside her, guiding her. Zenda put a hand over Lisa's eyes.

"We lead you to table."

"—okay."

When they stopped walking, Zenda removed her hand. A crowd of people yelled out, "Surprise!"

Pleasantly startled, Lisa jumped, squealing with delight, at the surprise party. The whole crowd, everyone from her God-gathered family on Míos, including Agapitos, was there. The only one missing was Nico.

Jack reminded Lisa that he had volunteered to help her research the winery clues. Skender piped up as before, "And, I continued to insist it was a group activity. So, we are all here!"

Peri asked, "How could we let you leave Míos without us give you party?"

Lisa smiled, "Yay! Will there be dancing?"

Peri gave her a look, "How you have party with no dancing?"

The servers delivered glasses and trays of food, and uncorked an assortment of Giórgos Hill wines. There was a party table with one of Sophia's beautifully decorated cakes from Glykó Amýgdalo.

Lisa hugged Sophia. "The cake looks glorious. I can't wait to get my hands on a big, fat corner piece, piled high with flowers. You make the best frosting."

Sophia smiled widely, "Look, it is not farewell cake; it is birthday cake for you. You have birthday soon, yes?"

"September first. How did you know?"

"Little birdie whisper it to me."

The party took off as it always did with this gang. Everyone talking, laughing, and dancing. When a server refilled her glass, Lisa thanked her and asked, "Is the winery this busy every Thursday evening?"

"Eh, more busy tonight." The server pointed to the other side of the courtyard, "We have another birthday party over there."

Lisa looked across the courtyard at the intimate gathering around the table, their faces aglow with candlelight as they raised their glasses in a toast. Contrary to her own boisterous party, it appeared to be rather a somber and sentimental gathering.

The older man at the head of the table happened to look in Lisa's direction as she watched them. In the spirit of the evening, Lisa raised her glass in his direction, smiling and nodding. He stared at her, lost in thought, his glass raised mid-air. The woman next to him spoke, then realized his attention was captivated by something more distant. She followed his gaze and looked in Lisa's direction. She appeared to gasp and put a hand to her mouth.

Lisa's attention was torn away as Demetri called for everyone's attention, proposing a toast to Lisa, her adventure on Míos, and her upcoming birthday. Everyone raised their glasses and cheered.

Lisa wiped away tears, not knowing how she could board a plane and leave this place and these people. Her two-and-a-half months on Míos passed so swiftly. She was not ready to leave. Something yet called to her heart. She knew she must return.

Lisa raised her glass in one hand and the 1967-ish Giórgos Hill wine cork in the other. "I propose a toast. To the man who inspired me to follow my heart and travel halfway around the world to Míos and the Giórgos Hill Winery. To Soso Diákos!"

"*Soso Diákos!*"

Lively bouzoúki music started, and they formed circles and danced. They sang "Never On Sunday," and danced to "Zorba the Greek." At the end of the evening, breathless from dancing and tearful with emotion, Lisa hugged and kissed each one of her God-gathered

ELIZABETH TOMME

family. She thanked them for befriending her and aiding her in her journey.

Only now did she realize just how far she had truly traveled in heart, mind, soul, and body. She promised to return to them. One by one, she bid them farewell, until at last, only the three of them remained.

Lisa looked fondly at Lyra and Zenda. "We're like faith, hope, and love."

Lyra laughed, and Zenda looked curious. "How so?"

"Everyone else has left the party, except the three of us," Lisa explained. "It reminds me of the last verse in I Corinthians 13—these three remain, faith, hope, and love."

Lyra joined hands with them and smiled, "And the greatest of these is love."

"Yes," Lisa agreed, taking one last look at the courtyard of Giórgos Hill Winery, "the greatest of these is love."

Arm-in-arm, they walked toward the entrance. Lisa was beyond reluctant to leave. She was not ready for the night, or her trip to Greece, to end. They stepped from the courtyard into the vaulted great hall of the stone wine cellars. Lisa looked around the cavernous room with its rough wooden beams and enormous racks of wine barrels.

Entirely covering one wall, the glass-doored wine rooms—filled from floor to ceiling with artfully displayed bottles of wine. The opposite wall, a gallery crowded with framed, autographed photos—their celebrity wall. Drawn to it, Lisa walked its entire length. Not recognizing any names or faces, she was sure many of Zenda's hotel guests were pictured there.

Lisa heard Lyra and Zenda talking. She looked across the great hall in their direction. They were deep in conversation with the man and woman from the other birthday party.

As Lisa continued to scan the wall of photos, she came across many in black and white. Intrigued, she peered at the images, the snapshots from decades ago. Her eyes wandered from one photograph to the next, captivated by the images of smiling faces, forever frozen in time—and then they landed with a sudden jolt on one particular photograph. Staring back at her among others was the

GREATER LOVE

joyous face of her mother, and Lisa's look-alike. Her mother was sitting next to the mystery woman from the photo Lyra gave her. The breath caught in her lungs, white noise rose in her ears, and the world stopped turning.

Eyes filling with tears, she touched the photograph. Hearing footsteps approaching, Lisa reluctantly tore her eyes from the photo. Lyra, Zenda, the woman, and the man made their way toward her. They stopped halfway. The woman wiped tears from her eyes. The man walked slowly to her and stopped a few feet away. His eyes searched her face. When he saw the locket at her neck, he put a hand to his heart. Looking as if he'd seen a ghost, his eyes brimmed with tears.

"*Alexandra* . . ." he whispered.

Lisa looked at the photograph, at Cynthia, and Lisa's look-alike. She looked back at the man, searching his face for answers. She prayed he could explain all of Cynthia's secrets to her.

"I . . . am *Lisa*."

He sighed, "Ah . . . My *Mákari* . . . my *Lisa* . . . *My God Is a Vow*." He raised his hands heavenward as he laughed and cried, "My Covenant-keeping God—*thank you*, my God!"

He motioned to his chest, "I am Gregor . . . Gregor Andras . . . *your father*."

Lisa looked into his eyes. Though her mind could not yet understand it, her heart knew it was true.

Evandir Vlochós promised she was named by parents who made a vow with God, and that Míos and God would give her the answers she traveled so far to find.

Gregor opened his arms to her. She stepped into his embrace.

At last, Lisa laid her head against her father's chest. He held her, kissed her head, and wept.

"On the day you were born, I prayed that one day you would understand that *your* God is a Vow who kept His Covenant over your life."

Gregor finally pulled back, taking her face in his hands. "My beautiful daughter Lisa . . . you look just like your mother, Alexandra . . . it takes my breath away."

The woman standing to the side could wait no longer. Rushing up, she opened her arms, "I am Dina Kostas. Your mother, Alexandra, was my best friend, and Cynthia—your mother who raised you and loved you as her own—she was also my best friend."

She hugged and kissed Lisa with joy and tenderness. Dina looked at Gregor, "I am an old woman now; Gregor, is an old man. We were born on Míos, were lifelong friends on Míos. We have loved you and prayed for you these forty-nine years, for God to keep you safe and bring you back home to us. I am thankful we lived to see you. Tonight, we celebrated Alexandra's birthday, just as we did here in 1967 when your father gave your mother that locket."

Lisa put a hand to the locket around her neck. "—the *Mílos Stávros*."

Gregor nodded.

Smiling through her tears, Dina said, "Mílos was my boyfriend, the love of my life."

Gregor asked, "Your mother, Cynthia . . . is she . . . ?"

Lisa blinked back tears. "She passed in 1995. Three months ago I found the Greek treasures in my mother's attic. I believe she meant for me to find them—for them to lead me here."

Gregor said, "Yes, that is like Cynthia, such a strong, courageous, God-filled woman. With love and bravery, she laid down her life for us, for you. We owe her everything."

Gregor took Lisa's hands. "There is much to tell you about the young Cynthia, Alexandra, her brother Isidor, Dina, Mílos, and me . . . in Greece, back in 1967."

Gregor tucked Lisa's hand in the crook of his arm and led her toward the door. "Come . . . come home now. We will get reacquainted, and I will tell you the story of our faithful God who spared your life and kept His Covenant with His children."

Overwhelmed at the thought that Gregor was her father, Lisa was nevertheless eager to hear the story of her life. She already knew God was in all and through all, and she craved the details. She would finally learn *why* Cynthia came to Greece and treasured it all her days.

"Where do you live? Where is . . . *our* home?"

"Near the chorió on the west coast, on a private estate overlooking the sea. Perhaps you have seen the entrance with tall rock walls and wooden gates?"

Lisa's breath caught in her throat. The sight of it had drawn her in. "Yes. I was intrigued every time I passed it."

Gregor smiled at his daughter. "It is called Βίλα Λίζα . . . Villa Lisa."

Looking into her father's eyes, she could not yet comprehend any of this, but needed no explanation to interpret the love and adoration she found there. Lisa remembered the prayer she wrote on the ferry to Míos . . .

My God and Steadfast Companion, I promise to listen for Your voice and follow Your lead. I promise to open my heart to all You have for me, and accept it with courage, strength, tenacity, and thankfulness. I trust You to guide me safely back home.

Lisa held tight to Gregor's arm as they walked through the great hall of Giórgos Hill Winery. God answered her every prayer. She was confident in the days to come He would give her the courage, strength, and tenacity to accept all His answers with a thankful heart.

God had blessed her with *two* loving mothers and fathers, and she longed to embrace it. Trusting God's heart for her on this journey, Lisa asked for a safe journey back home . . . never could she have imagined that would be Greece.

AARONIC BLESSING

The LORD bless you and keep you; the LORD make his face to shine upon you and be gracious to you; the LORD lift up his countenance upon you and give you peace.
—Numbers 6:24-26 (ESV)

PART ONE CHARACTERS

Greek Island of Míos (*Mē-ōhs*)

Cynthia Lee Carter Brenner: Daughter of Frank Lee Carter, Jr., and Joan Starkey Carter, married to Wells Brenner, mother of Lisa Marie Brenner Abbott

Eduard Wells "Wells" Brenner, III: Son of Eduard Alfons Brenner, Jr., and Beatrice "Bea" Marie Wells, grandson of Eduard Alfons Brenner, Sr., and Willa Mae Guthrie Brenner, married to Cynthia Carter, father of Lisa Marie Brenner Abbott

Lisa Marie Brenner Abbott: Daughter of Cynthia Brenner and Wells Brenner, widow of John Abbott, mother of Cate Lynn Abbott

John Abbott: Husband of Lisa Brenner, father of Cate Lynn Abbott

Cate Lynn Abbott: Daughter of Lisa Abbott and John Abbott, fiancée of Derek Dixon

Derek Dixon: Fiancé of Cate Lynn Abbott

Silvie Scott: Owner of The Board Room Coffeehouse, friend and prayer partner of Lisa Abbott

Soso Diákos, PhD (***Sew**-sew Dee-**yah**-kōs*): University Professor, Greek Studies

Gianna Gataki (*Yee-**ah**-nah Guh-**tok**-ee*): Married to Skender Gataki, owner, Aegean Hotel

PART ONE CHARACTERS

Skender Gataki (*Skin-dur Guh-tok-ee*): Married to Gianna, owner, Aegean Hotel

Sophia Adamos (*Suh-fee-yah Ah-thah-mōs*): Married to Hali Adamos, owner, Glykó Amýgdalo Bakery

Hali Adamos (*Khah-lee Ah-thah-mōs*): Married to Sophia, carpenter and builder

Peri Rossi (*Peh-ree Rah-see*): Married to Demetrios "Demetri" Rossi, seamstress and dressmaker, mother of five grown children, grandmother to fourteen grandchildren and two great-grandchildren

Demetrios "Demetri" Rossi (*Dee-me-tree-ōs "Dee-me-tree" Rah-see*): Married to Peri, retired fisherman, father of five grown children, grandfather to fourteen grandchildren and two great-grandchildren

Mia Monterrosa (*Mee-yah Mohn-teh-rhō-sah*): Married to Javier "Javi" Monterrosa, apiculturist, mother of three teenage daughters, homeschooler, research enthusiast, friend and Greek interpreter for Lisa

Javier "Javi" Monterrosa (*Ha-vee-air "Ha-vee" Mohn-teh-rhō-sah*): Married to Mia, is from Spain, carpenter and builder, father of three teenage daughters

Thalia Kyriáku (*Tall-ee-yah Key-rhi-ah-coo*): Divorced, goat farmer, entrepreneur, herb farmer, soap maker, olive oil producer, research enthusiast

Fred "Jack" Jackson: American photographer and artist

Nicholas "Nico" Scala (*Knee-kōh-lahs "Knee-kōh" Skal-uh*): Widower, jewelry maker

Luca Adino, Sr. (*Lou-ka Ah-dee-nō*): Married to Tessa, wood craftsman, father of Luca Adino, Jr., grandfather to Luca Adino, III

Luca Adino, Jr. (*Lou-ka Ah-dee-nō*): Wood craftsman, son of Luca Adino, Sr., father to Luca Adino, III

Luca Adino, III (*Lou-ka Ah-dee-nō*): Wood craftsman, friend of Hali and Sophia Adamos, son of Luca Adino, Jr., grandson of Luca Adino, Sr.

Zenda Roussos (*Zin-duh Rue-zōs*): Hotel owner

Agapitos Stergiou (*Ah-gah-pee-tōs Stair-zhō*): Hotel maintenance

Evandir "Angelos" Vlochós, (*Eh-van-dihr "Ahn-gl-ōz" Vlē-ōh-kōs*): Father of Lyra Vlochos, owner, Mountain Inn

Lyra Vlochós, "Mikrí Mélissa" (Little Bee) (***Lie**-rah "**Mee**-kree **May**-suh" Vlē-ōh-kōs*): Daughter of Evandir Vlochós, manager, Mountain Inn

PART TWO CHARACTERS

Greek Island of Míos (*Mē-ōhs*)

Cynthia "Cynna" Lee Chadwick Brenner: Daughter of Frank Lee Chadwick, Jr., and Joan Starkey Chadwick, intern at the Alexander Archaeological Museum of Athens

Pavlos Ballas, PhD (***Pahv**-lyōz **Bahl**-yaz*): Married to Lena, professor at Athens International University, resides in the Alexander University apartment building, father of Veniamin "Veni"

Lena Ballas (***Lee**-nah **Bahl**-yaz*): Married to Pavlos, resides in the Alexander University, apartment building, homemaker, mother of Veniamin "Veni"

Océane Benoit (***Ooo**-see-ahn **Behn**- wah*): Intern, the Alexander Archaeological Museum of Athens, resides in the Alexander University apartment building, in relationship with Stephanos "Cosmo" Cosmos, A.K.A., Mr. Oh-La-La

Freideriki Kormos (***Free**-duh-rhē-key **Kor**-mōz*): Curator and intern mentor at the Alexander Archaeological Museum of Athens

Isidor Christopoulos, PhD (*Ih-zih-door **Khree**-stoh-pool-**yōs***): Professor of Archaeology at Athens International University, son of Theodoros "Teddy" Christopoulos and Elisavet "Mimi" Christopoulos, brother to Leonidás and Alexandra, brother-in-law to Gregor Andras, love interest of Cynthia Chadwick

PART TWO CHARACTERS

Alexandra Christopoulos Andras (Ah-lēk-**zahn**-drah *Khree-stoh-pool-yōs* **Ann-drahs**): Daughter of Theodoros "Teddy" Christopoulos and Elisavet "Mimi" Christopoulos, younger sister of Isidor and Leonidás Christopoulos, married to Gregor Andras, stage actress

Gregor Andras (Greh-gore ***Ann-drahs***): Married to Alexandra, playwright, Isidor's best friend

Leonidás Christopoulos (Lē-oh-nē-**dahz** *Khree-stoh-pool-yōs*): Son of Theodoros "Teddy" Christopoulos and Elisavet "Mimi" Christopoulos, brother to Isidor and Alexandra, brother-in-law to Gregor Andras

Miki Galanis (*Mih-kēy Gah-lan-ēz*): Owner and Host of the Taverna of Ankistrévo̲, lifelong friend to the Christopoulos family

Bía Nasso (*Bē-yuh **Nah-zō***): Intern, Áthanásiou Archaeological Site, Cynna's roommate at the Áthanásiou Site

Margaret Townsend, PhD: Lead archaeologist, Áthanásiou Site

Evelyn "Evie" Murphy: Paleontologist, Áthanásiou Site

Christopoulos Áthanásiou Site Crew (*Khree-stoh-pool-yōs Ah-thah-nah-sē-you*): Isidor Christopoulos, Pavlos Ballas, Cynna Chadwick, Bía Nasso, Haris Sotiriou, Yiorgos Tsatsos, Ermis Vrettos, Dion Rallis

Michaelídes Marinákis (Mē-kah-lāy-dēz **Mah-rhē-nah-kēz**): Árgyros Thymiama Estate, Sitia, Crete

Theodoros "Teddy" Christopoulos (*Thē-ōh-door-ōs Khree-stoh-pool-yōs*): Married to Elisavet "Mimi," father of Isidor, Leonidás, and Alexandra

Elisavet "Mimi" Christopoulos (*El-ē-sah-vet Khree-stoh-pool-yōs*): Married to Theodoros "Teddy" Christopoulos, mother of Isidor, Leonidás, and Alexandra

Ómi̲ros Christopoulos (*Ōh-mē-rhōs Khree-stoh-pool-yōs*): Married to Ioxánio "Roxie," is Teddy's brother, uncle to Isidor, Leonidás, and Alexandra

Ioxánio "Roxie" Christopoulos (*Ē-ox-ahn-ē-ō "Rock-sē" Khree-stoh-pool-yōs*): Married to Ómi̲ros Christopoulos, is Teddy and Mimi's sister-in-law, aunt to Isidor, Leonidás, and Alexandra

Evandros Vlochós (*Eh-van-drōz Vlē-ōh-kōs*): Married to Kyveli, owner, Mountain Inn, father to Evandir "Angelos," grandfather (Pappous) to Lyra Vlochós

Kyveli Vlochós (*Keh-veh-lee Vlē-ōh-kōs*): Married to Evandros Vlochós, owner, Mountain Inn, mother of Evandir "Angelos," grandmother to Lyra Vlochós

Geórgious "George" Kostas (*Yhorrh-yōs Kōh-stuz*): Married to Barba, owner, Giórgos Hill Winery, father of Dina Kostas

Barba Kostas (*Bahr-bah Kōh-stuz*): Married to Geórgious, owner, Giórgos Hill Winery, mother of Dina

Dina Kostas (*Dee-nah Kōh-stuz*): Daughter of Geórgious and Barba Kostas, heiress to Giórgos Hill Winery, girlfriend of Mílos Stávros

Mílos Stavrós (*Mee-lōs Staa-vrohs*): Athens Jewelry maker, boyfriend of Dina Kostas

Luca Adino, Sr. (*Lou-ka Ah-dee-nō*): Married to Tessa, wood craftsman, father of Luca Adino, Jr., grandfather to Luca Adino, III

Tessa Adino (*Teh-sah Ah-dee-nō*): Married to Luca Adino, Sr., mother of Luca Adino, Jr., grandmother to Luca Adino, III

LISA'S NOTES-TO-SELF

Lisa traveled farther than she ever dreamed possible—taking the adventure of a lifetime in heart, mind, body, soul, and spirit. At the end of the journey, she didn't recognize her old self.

Here's a list of Lisa's Notes-to-Self, a crucial part of her metamorphosis:

- Don't get so busy you forget what's important.
- Let your curiosity get the best of you.
- Wander outside your comfort zone in a positive way with reckless abandon.
- Assume nothing. See the obvious. Ask the hard questions.
- Color outside the lines.
- Buy a ticket.
- Forget boring, risk an adventure.
- Lighten the load. Lose the emotional and physical baggage.
- Ask for God's help.
- Savor meals *al fresco*. Celebrate the flavors and the beauty around you.
- Recalibrate as needed. Life's too short to hurry through meals in front of the television.
- Meet new friends.

- Dedicate your life and business to God. Become a living testimony of God's goodness and boldly inspire others as Sophia did.
- Don't let the enemy win. Don't let yourself or your loved ones go down without a fight.
- Remember, God's not surprised by your life. He's got this. He's got you!
- Immerse yourself in a vibrant culture.
- Chocolate always helps in a crisis. Find a good chocolate shop and buy lots of it.
- Look as glamorous as Thalia in the goat barn the next time you work in the yard. e.g., healthy, glowing, and magnificent.
- Unplug. Turn off the cell phone. Spend meaningful time with God, deepening your relationship.
- Buy real food from local farmers markets.
- Have another thought, a better thought, and welcome the opportunity for change.
- Sleep under the stars.
- Ditch the high-maintenance hairdo and lifestyle.
- Get better at being a tourist when on vacation. Don't take your work with you.
- Swim in the surf and drip dry in the sunshine.
- Lose a few pounds, if needed.
- Be more spontaneous.
- Lose the boring clothes. Get blingy and get glamorous. *Think Zenda!*
- Shred the funeral arrangements and make party arrangements instead.
- Remember life is a song best sung with gusto and a bouzoúki.
- Hire a Greek band on retainer.
- Throw some really great parties and invite people from the highways and byways.
- Party often and party like the Greek.
- Dance to "Zorba the Greek" at least once a week. Dance in a crowd, dance alone—just *dance!*
- Always invite God, Jesus and Holy Spirit to join in your adventures.

STUDY GUIDE

Dear Friends,

I pray that as you read this book and sojourn in Greece with Lisa and Cynthia, you, too, will hear God's voice and experience a deeper relationship with your Heavenly Father. Both Lisa and Cynthia learned the meaning of Greater Love when God inspired them to walk in strength and courage—to wander outside their comfort zones, and travel a little . . . bit . . . farther.

This study guide is filled with questions for consideration and discussion, prayers for meditation, and points to ponder. This guide is suitable for self-reflection or group discussion.

1. If you were Lisa, would you research the unexplained memorabilia found with Cynthia's wedding dress, or would you push it aside to avoid a detour in your busy, pre-planned life? (Chpts 1 and 2)
2. Are you inspired to action by things you cannot explain? How far does your curiosity lead you? Does it become an organized project, or do you fly by the seat of your pants? (Chpt 3)

STUDY GUIDE

3. At the coffee shop, Silvie said to Lisa, "If you tell me what you're working on, I'll know exactly what to pray for." Silvie reminds me of II Corinthians chapter 1, describing God as our comforter, our come-alongside friend in times of trial. (TPT) Do you allow God to come-alongside you in all your endeavors? Don't you love it that Silvie is intentional about *exactly how* to pray for Lisa's endeavor? (Chpt 4)
4. If you found clues pointing in an off-the-wall direction challenging your comfortable view of a friend or loved-one, would you risk learning a new, possibly less ideal reality of them? Could you look at them through Jesus' eyes, could you give them some grace until all was explained, or would you rush toward judgement? (Chpt 5)
5. God gave Cynthia a love letter succinctly capturing her life story and His love for her. Has Father God given you a poem or love letter? In what ways do you hear His voice? (Chpt 5)
6. Father God described Cynthia as His Jewel, His Love. Does He have a special name for you? (Chpt 5)
7. Lisa prayed for God to tell her the story of how Cynthia was polished by His nature. This is a bold, trusting prayer. What bold prayers have you prayed? Was it easy or difficult to receive his answer? Are you still waiting? (Chpt 5)
8. In prayer, Lisa felt God's presence grow near, comforting her wondering soul. He assured her of His love, and that He knew her story from beginning to end and would bring her full circle. What assurances has God given you? Have you considered just how important your story is, and how much every moment of it matters? Do you have any doubt He will bring *your* story full circle? (Chpt 5)
9. Lisa was eager, emotional, and looking for quick answers to Cynthia's treasures, Dr. Diákos said she was playing a short game, when in fact, she must play a long game, look at the big picture and gain perspective. Can you relate to Lisa? How do you focus and gain perspective, especially when your emotions are involved? (Chpt 5)

STUDY GUIDE

10. Filled with resounding doubts, Lisa had to quicken her courage and put her big girl pants on to meet with Dr. Diákos. Owning up to her belief that God spoke the sea glass letter to Cynthia required tremendous faith, but she did not shrink back. Have you been in a similar spot? Did you represent your faith no matter the cost, or do you crave a do-over? (Chpt 5)
11. Obviously there would be no Greater Love story to read if Lisa was not curious enough to explore the clues Cynthia left behind. That aside, if you found Cynthia's clues, would you believe she wished them to be found or remain hidden? (Chpt 5)
12. Are you the adventurous type, or happiest in your comfort zone? Would you ask the hard questions, color outside the lines, buy a ticket and travel a *little . . . bit . . . farther?"* (Chpt 5)
13. Are there times you feel the Great Cloud of Witnesses peering over your shoulder or hear the echo of their lives resounding in your heart? Are you mostly comforted, or are you saddened by these precious moments? (Chpt 6)
14. Uncertain of what was ahead, Lisa journaled a prayer on the ferry to Míos. She recognized God as her steadfast companion, promised to trust Him, and listen for His answers with an open heart. How does such a prayer prepare you to receive the unknown? (Chpt 6)
15. Dragging her wonky suitcase along dockside, Lisa realized she was guilty of also carrying around emotional baggage. Why are we so hesitant to lighten our load of physical and emotional burdens? Why are we so willing to be held back and robbed of our peace of mind? (Chpt 7)
16. A new Giórgos Hill wine cork in hand at her first meal in Míos, Lisa tells Adonis that it alone is all the evidence she needs for a lifetime of belief that God is in all and through all. Would it be enough for you? (Chpt 7)
17. Unsure if there is enough evidence to believe in God, Adonis says, "The joy on your face alone is almost enough evidence to convince me." For the *joy* set before him (giving

STUDY GUIDE

His life to redeem yours) Jesus went to the cross. Is your joy in the ways Jesus works in your life enough evidence to inspire or convince others to explore belief? (Chpt 7)

18. Lisa thanked God for the safe trip to Míos, prayed for Adonis' faith to grow, and asked to be forgiven as she forgave the porters who threw her off the ferry. How do you partner with God as you go through your day? Do you think to forgive others quickly, even for the little things? (Chpt 7)

19. Point to Ponder: Do you ever fear being taken advantage of? Lisa did. At the car rental she faced a dilemma of driving a clunker, losing cash, settling for a scooter, and trusting strangers with her suitcase. In a panic, she prayed for wisdom and was humbly reminded trust was a two-way street and that blessings come in all shapes and sizes. (Chpt 8)

20. On the rooftop at the Aegean Hotel, Lisa raised her arms in awe and praise of God's handiwork in the heavens. What facet of God's amazing creation makes your heart dance in wonder? (Chpt 8)

21. Gianna invites Lisa to a life-changing dinner party. Already in major life flux, Lisa was conflicted with the idea. Then she had another thought, a better thought, "perhaps I should welcome this opportunity for change in my life." Barring unfortunate experiences with marketing schemes, how would you respond to such an invitation? (Chpt 9)

22. Lisa's Note-to-Self: *Food tastes marvelous al fresco!* Life is too short to hurry through every meal in front of the television. I purpose to recalibrate my life, savor more meals al fresco, and celebrate the flavors and the beauty around me. Do you yearn to do the same? (Chpt 9)

23. Gianna introduced Peri, Thalia, Mia and Sophia in the light of their Spiritual Gifts and identities. Would you rather get to know people on the basis of their career and secular identity, or their spiritual beauty? (Chpt 10)

24. Are you part of a God-gathered family? How does your

STUDY GUIDE

relationship with that family compare to your biological family? (Chpt 10)

25. Mia blessed Lisa with the knowledge her name meant, My God Is a Vow. Do you know the meaning of your name? Were you named with purpose? Does it inspire you? (Chpt 10)

26. Lisa believed chocolate always helped in a crisis. What's your crisis remedy go-to? (Chpt 12)

27. Point to Ponder: Luca Adino, Sr., carved a cross for himself in celebration of his baptism. As meaningful as it was, he gave it to a man who asked him for it saying, "Jesus say to give your coat if someone asks for it,' so I give him this cross." (Chpt 13)

28. Intent on glorifying God, and unconcerned about offending others, Sophia painted her life verse, Psalm 104:33–34, on the wall of her bakery. Lisa reflected on the opportunities she squandered, held back, and feared offending others with her faith. She desired to be a living testimony like Sophia. In what ways does this speak to your heart? (Chpt 14)

29. Thalia had six brothers and sisters. Their mother died when they were young. They were very poor—but God always provided for their needs. Consider all the "but God" statements you could make about your own life, and God's provision. (Chpt 14)

30. After spending the day at Thalia's goat farm, Lisa decided that adulting had established a complicated, stressful season in her life. She felt hemmed in, perhaps remorseful. She decided it was time to hit the reset button. What about you? (Chpt 14)

31. Lisa realized God even answered the unspoken desires of her heart. He answered unspoken prayers she lacked the wisdom to ask. Looking back, do you see the times God fulfilled the unspoken dreams of your heart? (Chpt 15)

32. Lisa placed the desire for answers to all her mother's treasures at the foot of the cross. She consecrated her journey to God. What was the last thing you consecrated to God? (Chpt 15)

STUDY GUIDE

33. Point to Ponder: Consider the parental figures in your life. Offer thanks for them, celebrate their lives, their love for you, and the journeys of discovery they inspired in you. If you did not have loving parental figures in your life, I pray you will invite God, Jesus and Holy Spirit to fulfill this role in your life. When you are ready, and in the security of their presence, invite them to heal specific painful memories in your past. (Chpt 15)
34. Nico's blessing over his God-gathered family on Míos: May we grow closer and closer together as family and to our Great Father. May we know His unlimited love and be filled with the Holy Spirit. May we always give Christ a home in our hearts. May we grow in trust and be strong in God's love. In Jesus' Name, Amen. (Chpt 18)
35. Point to Ponder: Nico was known as a man who loved a good party, and gathered people in from the highways and the byways. For Nico, it came naturally to do the things the rest of us only think of doing, but never get around to. So many people are just waiting to be asked. Selfish and untrusting of God, we miss opportunities. The world needs more Nicos. (Chpt 18)
36. The fabulous Zenda entered Lisa's life, and her mind danced at the thought of a surprising new friendship on the horizon. It was certain to be remarkable. Take this opportunity to tell a special friend the marvelous ways they've influenced your life. (Chpt 20)
37. After checking in at the Sea Jewel Hotel Lisa realized, she was not alone in her new surroundings. She felt peaceful. Content. Vibrant of heart and mind. Calm and quiet in her soul. Settled and certain God would supply all her needs. Take a moment, close your eyes and take stock. How do you feel in your soul? (Chpt 20)
38. Carefree, Lisa swam, splashed, and floated in the early morning surf. The water, soothing and reviving. She made an agreement with herself to go for a morning swim every day. Have you honored yourself with any much needed

relaxation? When was the last time you took a vacation or pampered yourself with a spa day? (Chpt 21)

39. Zenda pointed at Lisa lodging a challenge. "This not over unless you quit." Lisa lacked confidence in the moment, but realized Zenda was right. She had not come all that way to quit. She would continue to trust God for answers. Sometimes you must be your own cheerleader, but it's a lot more fun when your friend fills the role. Either way, trust in God and keep going! Who picks you up when you want to quit? (Chpt 23)

40. Lisa was surprised by the celebration of Nico's life in lieu of a funeral. She decided to shred her own funeral arrangements and make party arrangements instead. What do you think of Nico's celebration and Lisa's change of plans? (Chpt 24)

41. When Lisa's family history unraveled, even in her state of shock, she assured Cate, "Everything will be alright. God is with us. He already knows everything about our family, and He's got this." Would you have shared Lisa's trust in God? (Chpt 26)

42. Refusing to trash her parents, Lisa chose trust over betrayal. Recognizing the enemy wanted her to lose faith she declared, "this family's not going down without a fight." Discuss a time you recognized the enemy at work in your family and fought for those you love. (Chpt 26)

43. Lisa prayed, *"Father, You are the first place I should turn when I lose my footing. You always catch me and still my heart."* In her mind's eye, she imagined Jesus rescuing her. She was thankful to be the *one lamb* He sought and carried to safety. In His loving arms, she drifted to sleep. Where is the first place you turn in times of trouble? (Chpt 26)

44. When tortured with troubling thoughts, Lisa intentionally took her thoughts captive, repeating Colossians chapter three: "I will think on things above, where Christ sits at the right hand of God, not on things of this earth." (ESV) What sanctuary verse do you ponder to take your thoughts captive? (Chpt 26)

STUDY GUIDE

45. Gianna asked Lisa, "Is this emergency-meeting-with-the ladies kind-of-big?" Lisa said, "Yes, I need to be with everyone and talk things out." Gianna said, "I'm on it! Lunch tomorrow, at my place for anyone who can make it." Do you have a special friend or circle of sisters you do life with? There's nothing else like it—not a husband, boyfriend, or coworker. To start a forever friends circle, schedule a coffee, brunch, lunch or special time with two to five friends. Get to know each other casually and laugh a lot! Don't be afraid to be real and go deep spiritually, while also respecting other's sensitive wounds. At the end of each time together, schedule the next one and follow-through with it. (Chpt 27)
46. Lisa encouraged herself in the early morning darkness, "It's always darkest before the dawn—don't be afraid to look at things in the light of day . . . keep going." How do you combat those difficult, long, sleepless nights? (Chpt 28)
47. Take a moment to pray Lisa's prayer and thank God for the sisters who do life with you: "Father, thank You for Your goodness, Your grace, Your mercy, Your steadfast love. Thank You for surrounding me with virtuous women. You always provide what I need. I love You and I trust You. In Jesus' Name, Amen. (Chpt 28)
48. Lisa wondered why the Mílos Stávros locket with all of its precious gold, diamonds, and rubies had been given to her. Father God answered, "You are my precious daughter and your price is far above these few small rubies. I have joyfully paid the price. And, I have kept my vow." Lisa (My God Is a Vow) realized God meant he kept her. When did you realize you are God's precious daughter, and he paid the price for you? (Chpt 28)
49. If you were Lisa and Zenda, would you have ventured back to the wine cellar for one last look for clues? (Chpt 29)
50. Lisa found her mother's handwriting in the Hotel Mákari registration book. This brought three revelations: the Hotel Mákari existed, her mother was a guest there, and her mother signed as Cynthia Chadwick, not Cynthia Brenner.

Which of these revelations do you think most surprised Lisa? (Chpt 29)

51. Cynthia revealed her heart to Isidor, "While I am interested in the ancient artifacts, I am only *drawn* to one thing, the True and Living God of the Holy Scriptures. I am not interested in temples built to other gods. The history of the Bible calls to my heart—that is my passion, that's what I truly want to experience in Greece." Consider Cynthia's statement. It honors God's first commandment to have no other gods before him. Spend some time considering the things in your life you exalt above your Heavenly Father. (Chpt 34)

52. Cynthia recognized she was a Child of God, made in His image, for the same purpose as an amphoriskos. She knew she was a precious vessel designed to be filled with something greater than herself—God's presence. As you consider this, ask God for deeper understanding of being created in His image and being filled with His presence. (Chpt 36)

53. Cynthia said, "I am so weak, I'm ashamed of myself. I want to be as courageous, brave, and bold in my faith as Paul." Where did Paul get his strength? Is it possible that we can be as courageous and bold in our faith? (Chpt 38)

54. Isidor was certain Cynthia was brave enough to take a stand for Christ and put her life on the line. Do you wonder if you're brave enough to put your life on the line for your beliefs? (Chpt 38)

55. Before Paul went on trial at the Bema in Corinth, God spoke to him and said, "Don't ever be afraid. Speak the words that I give you and don't be intimidated, because I am with you." Through God's Word, He deposits this same assurance in your heart. Do you feel stronger already? Do you easily forget God's command to not be afraid to speak? (Chpt 38)

56. King Solomon said, "Death and life are in the power of the tongue." Do you take this into account before you speak?

STUDY GUIDE

How often do you speak deadly words over yourself and others? (Chpt 38)

57. Isidor's Prayer of Blessing over Cynna: Our God and Father, Creator and Redeemer, Bless Your child, Cynthia, now called Cynna, Daughter of Strength and Courage. Fill Your amphoriskos, Cynna, with Your presence and create in her a courageous and steadfast heart, as she calls upon You as her Ever-Present Help in times of trouble, as she walks in Your will for her life. In Jesus' Name, Amen (Chpt 38)

58. Cynna was so captivated by the beauty of her first piece of sea glass, she spent every day on the beach looking for more. What unique part of God's creation do you seek out? Do you collect anything that speaks to your heart? (Chpt 42)

59. Teddy recognized Cynna's deep love for her Heavenly Father, and how she honored Him with her life. In what ways do you recognize spiritual depth in others? (Chpt 45)

60. Teddy said people are careless with the word 'love.' Do you agree? (Chpt 45)

61. Point to Ponder: Jesus said we should love one another as deeply as He loved us—the greatest love is love that sacrifices all. (Chpt 45)

62. Cynna asked God for a sign, just a little wink or a nod, a little something extra-special to cling to in the days ahead. A warm breeze stirred. It dried her tears and tickled her skin. A meteor blazed across the sky in a dazzling display. Its sparkling tail glistening in its wake. Have you asked God for a sign? What happened? (Chpt 47)

63. Isidor, his family, and the God-gathered family on Míos lavished Cynna with unconditional love. Through the Christopoulos family, God put a face on His love for her. What is your experience with love? Was it unconditional? Have you experienced God's love through the faces, arms, actions and words of others? Can the way believers demonstrate love affect the way others perceive God's attributes? (Chpt 48)

64. Point to Ponder: Isidor refused to allow Cynna's parents to treat her with any form of disrespect, verbal aggression, or

belittling. God does the same for us. He guards us fiercely from the attacks of the enemy. His desire is that we operate in, and love each other with the fruits of the Spirit. (Chpt 49)

65. Isidor said, "Cynna, strong and courageous. Thank you for choosing me." Cynna responded, "My Darling, I will always choose you. Whatever you ask of me, I will happily do." Choices matter. Through our choices, we honor God and those we chose. It's so easy to exalt something meaningless above them. What keeps you focused on fulfilling your choices and promises? (Chpt 49)

66. A cold fear washed over Cynna. In a heartbeat she realized it was one thing to say you were courageous. To actually face death was the test. Cynna wondered, *How will I react if I'm hauled into the street, arrested, or worse?* Have you experienced this kind of fear or faced death? What would you pray in response to a serious test of your courage? (Chpt 51)

67. Gregor and Alexandra pled with Cynna to take their newborn baby to safety. Was this an act of Greater Love? What decision would you have made if you were Gregor and Alexandra? (Chpt 51)

68. Understanding the consequences of remaining behind in Athens, Cynna urged Alexandra to take her airline ticket and get her baby out of the country. Was this an act of Greater Love? If you were Cynna, how would you have responded to Gregor and Alexandra's request? (Chpt 51)

69. Isidor knelt beside Cynna and asked her to take their niece to safety. Just hours before, Cynna had assured Isidor she had *chosen* him and would happily do anything he asked of her. Consider the choices we make not knowing what the future will hold. If Cynna had foreknowledge, do you believe she would have still made the same choice and promise? (Chpt 51)

70. Point-to-Ponder: Cynna agreed to take the baby to safety, "With God's help." When Isidor renamed Cynna as God's Daughter of Strength and Courage, he prayed she would

call upon God as her Ever-Present Help in times of trouble. Consider how God empowers us in times of trouble. With God-at-work-within-us, and a covering of prayer, God will do more in us than we can ask or think. (Chpt 51)

71. Gregor and Alexandra entered into Covenant with God. "Our Faithful God and Father who keeps *Covenant* with those who love you, we place from this next generation of our family, our baby girl, into Your Merciful Hand. We thank you for your safe care and keeping. We ask you to reunite us again, if not in this life, then in the life to come. As a family, we enter into greater *Covenant* with you in giving our daughter the name *Lisa*, which means, *My God Is a Vow*." Our God is a Covenant-Keeping God. In what ways have you entered into Covenant with God? (Chpt 51)

72. Gregor and Alexandra's Prayer for Baby Lisa: "May you always walk in love as Jesus Christ loved us, and gave his life for us. May you one day understand that your God Is a Vow who kept His Covenant." (Chpt 51)

73. Point to Ponder: In parting, Cynna and Isidor held the olive wood cross between them and said, "Our Lord Jesus Christ is the most important thing we have in common." Relationships flourish with Jesus at the center. Through his Greater Love for us we learn to lay down our lives for others in selfless love that believes all things, hopes all things and endures all things. (Chpt 52)

74. Isidor said to Cynna, "On our first date, I felt certain God brought you to Greece for a unique purpose—I see now that God sent you to Greece, renamed you for strength and courage, and prepared you for such a time as this . . . to lay down your life for others doing something that *only* you can do." What is *your* special purpose is in God's earthly Kingdom? Have you been called upon to do something that *only you* could do? (Chpt 52)

75. In parting Cynna said, "Isidor, you sound as if we'll never see each other again." Isidor replied, "No, My Love, I only wish to leave nothing unsaid. In the days ahead, I never want you to question my love for you, or how you chose to

STUDY GUIDE

spend your life when you said 'yes' to me, 'yes' to my family, and 'yes' to God." As Lisa learned, you never know what a day will hold. Like Isidor, leave nothing unsaid. Say the things you want others to know, gift them with reassurance and certainty of your love for them. Do you regret leaving anything unsaid? (Chpt 52)

76. Tobías said, "If I do not talk much, it is because I am praying for all of us." Cynna said, "I am praying for all of us, too. We can pray together out loud, if you want." Consider the power of agreeing with one another in prayer. We have God's assurance that where two or more are gathered in His name, He is with them. (Chpt 53)

77. Point to Ponder: Soldier's detained Cynna at the airport, ordering her to stand against the wall at gunpoint as they searched her baggage. They slit open the toy lamb, and tossed it aside. Consider the symbolism of Cynna under scrutiny, and the lamb that was sacrificed at the hand of the enemy. Is there a time in our lives we, accused by the enemy, do not stand in the shadow of the cross or Jesus—the lamb who was slain for us? (Chpt 53)

78. Finding the olive wood cross among her things, the soldier eyed Cynna suspiciously. Cynna raised her chin and stuck out her hand. "Please . . ." Shrugging, he tossed the cross aside, "Cheap trinket." The soldier's comment is like a dagger to my heart. What emotions did it evoke in you? (Chpt 53)

79. Cynna held her breath as the soldiers searched her treasures. As precious as these things were to her, they were nothing compared to their lives. If she could only leave with the baby in her arms, it would be enough. At what point or circumstance in your life did you realize your earthly possessions were worthless? Did it change your priorities or the way you live? (Chpt 53)

80. Through her tears, Cynna found the wine cork, wooden cross, stationery, sand and sea glass, the incense bottle, and velvet bag, and shoved her treasures into her purse. At the beginning of the story, could you imagine the significance

STUDY GUIDE

of Cynthia's treasures? Now that you've spent the summer on Míos with her, are they precious to your heart as well? (Chpt 53)

81. After the plane was in the air, Cynna could not explain how they escaped—but God. She nuzzled Lisa, lavishing her sweet head with kisses. The first lullaby she sang to her was, "Jesus loves me, this I know . . ." Reflect on a time in your life you cannot explain your survival, but for God. This can be a physical, emotional, financial or even a relationship event. (Chpt 53)

82. When Cynna's parents met her in New York, her two worlds collided fast and hard. She felt her brain and heart rip apart—it was brutal. Cynna kept her eyes on Jesus and forced herself to focus her thoughts in order to survive. Discuss a time in your life you were torn between two worlds. Did you keep your eyes on Jesus? How did He get you through it? Are you stronger now because of it? (Chpt 54)

83. Keeping her promise and covenant of silence to Gregor, Alexandra, and Isidor, Cynna asked her parents to trust her reasons for coming home with a baby. Have you endured hardship for the sake of keeping a promise? (Chpt 54)

84. With Lisa in her arms, Cynna walked out of the terminal and into her new life. What choice would you have made? (Chpt 54)

85. Scripture to Ponder: Here's what I've learned through it all: Don't give up, don't be impatient; be entwined as one with the LORD. Be brave and courageous, and never lose hope. Yes, keep on waiting—for he will never disappoint you! — Psalm 27:14 (Chpt 55)

86. Cynna's precious Isidor never arrived in New York. Just as Jesus warned, the enemy came to steal, kill, and destroy. Wells and Lisa were the miraculous counterbalance that filled the voids in Cynthia's life. Truly Jesus came to give life to the full. Consider the sorrows and joys of life in light of God's steadfast love and new mercies. He who set the stars

STUDY GUIDE

in motion is He who is mindful of us. In your heart, do you trust him through the bittersweet? (Chpt 55)

87. Gregor and Alexandra laid down their lives for their daughter. Isidor laid his life down for Gregor and Alexandra. Cynthia was unwilling to place herself in the same category, she laid down so much less. Cynna laid her life down figuratively. Do you consider that to be any less of a sacrifice than physically dying to save her friends? (Chpt 55)

88. Ready to take the last step of a long journey, Cynna retrieved her Greek treasures from beneath the attic floorboards. Like Cynna, would you have taken this last step, or left the Greek treasures buried in the attic? (Chpt 55)

89. Thinking of Cynthia and the sea glass, in what ways has God redeemed your broken life and transformed it into something beautiful that is perfected by His nature? (Chpt 55)

90. Through fifty years of living her life with God, Cynthia was perfected by His nature. *She was His beautiful sea glass, His jewel . . . His love.* Her journey took fifty years. How many years has your metamorphosis taken? Are you still a work in progress? Can you look back on your journey with thankfulness for the joys *and* sorrows? (Chpt 55)

91. Point to Ponder: Cynthia realized God's love for her was as plentiful as the grains of sand on the seashore. Think of how many grains of sand are in a mere handful, even that much love from God seems more than we can fathom. (Chpt 55)

92. Cynthia always yearned to tell Lisa of her time in Greece, her parents, and her uncanny likeness to her beautiful mother, Alexandra. Placing her Greek treasures beneath the folds of her wedding dress, her two worlds collided once again—and every piece of her heart had made it safely home. She prayed it would guide Lisa's heart safely home as well. Looking back over your life, do you see how God is in

STUDY GUIDE

all and through all? Do you trust His timing to reveal the special details of your story to you ? (Chpt 55)

93. Lisa missed the grandeur of the Colorado mountains, but now could not imagine a day without an Aegean sunset. Reflect on a place you have visited that captured your heart. Do you feel you left a part of yourself behind? Does it call to you beckoning your return? Do you realize that you are drawn to places of beauty because God created you to resonate with His beauty? (Chpt 56)

94. Thanks to Dr. Diákos, Lisa bought a ticket and traveled farther than she ever dreamed—in heart, mind, body, soul, and spirit. An adventure of a lifetime. Looking back, she couldn't recognize her old self. What is the most transformative adventure you've taken? In what ways did it change you? Was it a lasting change? Would you do it again? (Chpt 56)

95. At Giórgos Hill Winery, Lisa and her God-gathered family formed circles and danced to lively bouzoúki music. Have you experienced the pure joy of dancing and celebrating life with precious friends? (Chpt 56)

96. In the vaulted great hall of the wine cellars, Lisa's eyes scanned the photographs of smiling faces, forever frozen in time—and then they landed with a sudden jolt on one particular photograph. Staring back at her was the joyous face of her mother, and her own look-alike. Describe the emotions you believe Lisa experienced in that moment. (Chpt 56)

97. Gregor's eyes searched her face. Seeing the locket, his eyes brimmed with tears. He sighed, "Ah . . . My *Mákari* . . . my Lisa . . . *My God Is a Vow* . . . I am Gregor . . . Gregor Andras . . . *your father*." He raised his hands heavenward as he laughed and cried, "My Covenant-keeping God—thank you, my God!" For fifty years, Gregor waited in Covenant with God. Upon fulfillment of the Covenant, Gregor raised his hands in praise. Imagine the long, lonely years in between. Do you think Gregor ever gave up hope, or lost faith in God's ability to keep their Covenant? (Chpt 56)

STUDY GUIDE

98. Lisa stepped into her father's embrace. Just imagine feeling your father's arms around you, especially if it has been a while. If not your earthly father—then think of your Heavenly Father and the love for you it represents. Can you even put your emotions into words? (Chpt 56)

99. Lisa said, "I found the Greek treasures in my mother's attic. I believe she meant for me to find them—for them to lead me here." Have you ever followed a trail of heavenly breadcrumbs? Where did it lead? (Chpt 56)

100. Gregor said, "Cynthia was such a strong, courageous, God-filled woman. With love and bravery, she laid down her life for us, for you. We owe her everything." Just think how many lives Cynthia's bravery and choices affected. How different would the story have been if Cynthia had not laid down her life for her friends? (Chpt 56)

101. Gregor took Lisa's hands. "There is much to tell you about the young Cynthia, Alexandra, her brother Isidor, Dina, Mílos, and me . . . in Greece, back in 1967." During her entire adventure on Míos Lisa found the clues proving her mother was there, but she never learned the reason *why*. Imagine her surprise in learning the answers would be told her by her father. (Chpt 56)

102. Lisa asked, "Where do you live? Where is . . . *our* home?" Gregor said, "It is the entrance with tall rock walls and wooden gates, it is called Βίλα Λίζα . . . Villa Lisa." With Gregor's answer Lisa realized she had been drawn home since her arrival on Míos. What makes your heart feel "*at home?*" Have you ever been surprised by feeling at home in a place you've never been before? (Chpt 56)

103. Lisa's prayer that guided her adventure to Greece:

My God and Steadfast Companion, I promise to listen for Your voice and follow Your lead. I promise to open my heart to all You have for me, and accept it with courage, strength, tenacity, and thankfulness. I trust You to guide me safely back home. (Chpt 56)

NOTE TO READERS

I pray that like Lisa, you will stand confident knowing God will give you the courage, strength, and tenacity to accept all His answered prayers with a thankful heart.

Lisa prayed for a safe journey back home. She could've never imagined the answer to that prayer. Sweet friends, I pray God will also lead *your* heart safely back home to wherever you are meant to be.

Blessings and Abundant Joy in Christ,
    Elizabeth Tomme

ACKNOWLEDGMENTS

To my readers, thank you for trusting me with your heart and taking this journey with me, Lisa, Cynthia, and Father God. I hope you will join me yet again for Book Two.

With special thanks, the deepest love, and immeasurable appreciation for everyone who has been a part of my *Greater Love* journey.

To my husband, Curtis—your special brand of encouragement, support, and never-ceasing prayers kindled my dream, *Greater Love*, to become a reality. You quicken my spirit and still my heart.

Nose-kisses to Maximus Braveheart and Maverick "Boo" Mitchell, my feline writing companions. Thanks for sleeping on my desk, spilling my coffee, dumping my notes, CAT scanning my computer, chasing the mouse, walking across my keyboard, and most importantly, taking full responsibility for *all* typos.

To my family and friends, thanks for cheering me on and letting the writer in me come out to play.

To Karen Steinmann, editor extraordinaire and precious sister in Christ. Thank you for embracing *Greater Love* and giving me wings to fly—all to God's glory.

To my Beta Reader Team, P. K. Wedel, Linda Fellows, and Julie Newbold (My Sweet Angel Sister). Your bravery in taking on this project was remarkable. Thank you for your willingness, tenacity, honesty, grace and mercy which was new every morning.

To the Advanced Reader Copy Team, thanks for jumping in with both feet. I couldn't have done this without you and your invaluable feedback.

To P. K. Wedel and Linda Fellows, talented artists. Thanks for your artistic knowledge and insight.

To Catherine Roussou Lenhert, my own beautiful Greek friend. Thank you for the Greek adventure. Worshiping God with you and your God-gathered family on Ios changed my life forever. I found my first sea glass on a beach on Ios. I treasure it always.

To Teresa Browning, my sweet sister in Christ and forever friend. I'm so glad we made that Greek adventure together.

To The Pep Girls, a rare caliber of women whose steadfast love, sisterly advice, and free-flowing fountain of hysterical laughter and Prosecco is the glorious stuff forever friendships are made of. Your encouragement was my rock.

To Wells Brenner, you're a *real character*. Thanks for literally being an integral part of my writing adventure. May your own dreams go far. *Fist bump!*

To Missy Brenner, unflagging encourager, wise counsellor, prayer warrior, and sweet, sweet sister. I love you!

To Matthew McBride, thank you for the music. Your frequent musical moments were the soundtrack for the story in my head and the writing days in my study. If the Hallmark channel ever calls for a movie, I'll expect you in the studio at the keyboard.

To Ewa and Joseph Sederstrom, for sowing into my dream. God indeed gave the increase! I treasure you, your love, and support.

To Lindsay Whalen, Whalen Design & Photography, for your excellence in photography and innovative website design.

To Lauren Burdue, for your imaginative and inspirational graphic design.

To my mentor, Barbara Hartzler Sutton, thank you for your patience and guidance.

To JoAnn Schlabach, talented photographer and friend. Thanks for making time for me in your incredibly busy schedule. You're amazing!

To Rick Newbold, thanks for dousing the flames of my techie fugue on Meltdown Monday.

To my own God-gathered family in special places around the world, you're always in my heart.

Love and Blessings to All!

ABOUT THE AUTHOR

Elizabeth Tomme loves inspiring women to embrace God's friendship and bask in His lavish love. Her writing is filled with endearing characters of faith in courageous roles. With themes of sisterly love, serendipitous adventure, and selfless sacrifice, she immerses readers in God's steadfast love. Elizabeth and husband, Curtis, live in Colorado with their two clever cats and several sassy chickens. Elizabeth's joy in the LORD is boundless; her smile, contagious; her love for others, the forever kind; and her passion for writing, a celebration of God's glory.

Please visit her website, elizabethtomme.com to sign up for her newsletter and join Elizabeth's Forever Friends, receive the latest Covenant Collection Christian Novel information, and other inspirational content.

MORE TO COME . . .

Upcoming in 2025

STEADFAST LOVE
A COVENANT COLLECTION
CHRISTIAN NOVEL
BOOK 2

Milton Keynes UK
Ingram Content Group UK Ltd.
UKHW041328301124
451950UK00006B/68